Leave the Night On

Also by Laura Trentham

THE FALCON FOOTBALL SERIES

Slow and Steady Rush

Caught Up in the Touch

Melting Into You

THE COTTONBLOOM SERIES

Kiss Me That Way

Then He Kissed Me

Till I Kissed You

Candy Cane Christmas (novella)

Light Up the Night (novella)

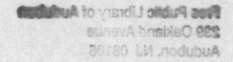

Leave the Night On

LAURA TRENTHAM

St. Martin's Paperbacks

This is a work of fiction. All of the characters, organizations, and events portrayed in this novel are either products of the author's imagination or are used fictitiously.

LEAVE THE NIGHT ON

Copyright © 2017 by Laura Trentham.
Excerpt from *When the Stars Come Out* copyright © 2017 by Laura Trentham.

For information address St. Martin's Press, 175 Fifth Avenue, New York, NY 10010.

ISBN: 978-1-250-13095-2

Our books may be purchased in bulk for promotional, educational, or business use. Please contact your local bookseller or the Macmillan Corporate and Premium Sales Department at 1-800-221-7945, ext. 5442, or by e-mail at MacmillanSpecialMarkets@macmillan.com.

Printed in the United States of America

St. Martin's Paperbacks edition / August 2017

St. Martin's Paperbacks are published by St. Martin's Press, 175 Fifth Avenue, New York, NY 10010.

10 9 8 7 6 5 4 3 2 1

For my mechanic
(Also known as my husband)

Acknowledgments

A big thanks to Steve who made me watch countless hours of car shows on Sunday mornings over the years of our marriage. I can't believe it paid off! He also lent his vast car wisdom to me, including what all the cool cars are. (Except for the Hornet. Not his favorite car, but I loved the look and name.) All that knowledge more than makes up for the weeks he took over our kitchen table to rebuild his car engine.

A special thanks to all the great people at St. Martin's Press. My editor, Eileen Rothschild, is a rock star who makes publishing a joy. From the copyediting to the marketing department, everyone is top-notch and awesome. Another rock star who deserves a high five is my agent, Kevan Lyon, who makes navigating this crazy business a whole lot easier.

A special shout-out goes to Julie Gray Johnson, a member of my reader group who suggested the names for my twin aunts, Hazel and Hyacinth! As soon as I saw the names, I knew they were perfect.

And to all the readers who have fallen in love with Cottonbloom . . . hope you love the Abbott boys as much as I do!

Chapter One

Wyatt Abbott spun a wrench in his hand and whistled appreciatively. He wasn't sure what was prettier, the cherry-red Camaro convertible being inched into Abbott Brothers Garage and Restoration or the woman driving it.

Peeking over the top of her sunglasses, Sutton Mize was sitting tall, moving forward in a series of brake checks, her bottom lip caught between her teeth. Ashy blond hair peeked out of a scarf and called to mind pictures of old school Hollywood actresses, but her red-checked, gingham dress was all Southern sophistication. From being around cars his entire life, he understood what counted was under the hood, but that didn't stop him from admiring a good paint job.

It had been years since he'd come face to face with her. Eighteen to be exact. Judge Mize, her daddy, was a car buff and had been a steady customer of the garage for more years than Wyatt had been alive. Back then, Sutton had been so pretty, he'd alternated between fighting his tied tongue and saying something stupid. Typical, but acutely embarrassing.

Even in as small a town as Cottonbloom, their paths

2

LAURA TRENTHAMLAURA TRENTHAM

hadn't crossed since. Not that unusual considering he was from the Louisiana side of the river, and she was from the Mississippi side. More separated them than just a body of water and a few miles.

She was probably nothing like the girl he remembered, sweet and a little shy but with a spark of spirit that had set him back on his heels.

His older brother, Mack, bumped his shoulder. "She's a beauty, isn't she?"

"She sure is," Wyatt whispered back. Sutton tucked a piece of hair behind her ear, the scarf falling back.

"Tarwater's car could be the key to breaking our restoration plans wide open."

Wyatt should have known Mack was referring to the car and not the woman. Mack was all business, all the time. Wyatt was pretty sure his brother hadn't gotten laid in that calendar year. Not that Wyatt was burning up the sheets around Cottonbloom, but at least he could appreciate a beautiful woman.

"What's Sutton Mize doing with Tarwater's car?" Wyatt asked.

"She wants us to rework the interior—new upholstery, instrument panel, the works. Wants it back to stock if we can manage it. An engagement present." Mack rolled his eyes to meet Wyatt's.

"I hadn't heard the happy news." Shock edged Wyatt's voice. Not that he personally knew Tarwater. Which was a good thing considering Andrew and his father made up Tarwater and Tarwater—lawyers who handled anything from personal injury lawsuits to criminal defense.

The Tarwaters were prominent citizens on the Mississippi side of Cottonbloom and rubbed shoulders with Sutton Mize's family both personally and professionally. A Tarwater-Mize wedding would be the social and political event of the year—hell, maybe even the decade.

Not that he would rate an invite. Wyatt glanced down at his grease-covered coveralls and shifted his feet farther apart. His social circle didn't align with theirs.

"I don't have to remind you how important it is that our work is impeccable." Mack clapped him on the shoulder.

Expenditures to update equipment had weighed heavily on the garage's finances the last three years. But committing to take the business in this new direction after their pop's death—from merely fixing cars to restoring them—had required major investment. Tarwater's car could get them a foothold across the river and even further north into Jackson, Mississippi. The challenge was drawing customers to their backwoods location.

"No pressure or anything." Wyatt laid the sarcasm on thick.

Mack ignored him and scrolled through his phone. "I've got invoices to get out, and Jackson is going to be tied up with the Pontiac. You can pull Willa if you need help."

Willa was the only non-family member who worked at the garage. She'd been working as a mechanic for them going on two years, and Wyatt *still* hadn't figured her out. He enjoyed her dry self-deprecating humor and skill under the hood, but she and Jackson had some Vulcan mind-meld in the garage. Watching them work was like watching a choreographed dance and he was loath to cut in.

"What about Ford?" Wyatt regretted the question before it was out. Saying Ford's name aloud was like Harry Potter speaking of Voldemort.

Ford was the eldest Abbott brother. He'd inherited a twenty-five-percent stake in the garage just like the rest of them. Problem was he didn't equate owning a stake to actually working for it. He was a decent mechanic, but whether he showed up any given day and at what time was anyone's guess. His business degree from LSU set him apart from the family or, more accurately, above them. In

his own deluded little world, Ford was the only one qualified to run Abbott Brothers Garage and Restoration.

"If he drags his ass in, you can have him." The bitterness
emanating from Mack was nothing new, but the last few
months had seen the semi-contained mass spilling over
more and more often into yelling matches between the
two would-be leaders of the garage.

Wyatt's glance crossed with his twin brother Jackson's.
Even from across the garage, Wyatt sensed the same worry
he was feeling about the brewing trouble. What was the
old adage? Never work with children, animals, or family?
Sometimes his two older brothers acted like children and
fought like animals, but they would be blood bound forever. It made for a sticky, tangled mess.

Mack walked off, his shoulders bowed up. Wyatt hoped
Ford stayed away from the shop floor. Maybe he'd headed
to New Orleans or Baton Rouge to schmooze vendors.
That was the one thing Ford excelled at.

The ongoing family troubles had taken years to get
knotted and wouldn't be resolved anytime soon. The sweet
little Camaro, on the other hand, needed his attention now.

"This okay?" Sutton Mize called out, twisting in her
seat to half face him.

He approached and propped a hand on the window frame.
She was taken, and he was a professional, but that didn't
stop his gaze from skating up her long legs to where her skirt
had flipped up to reveal a toned thigh as she mashed the
brake pedal.

"Perfect." He peeled his eyes off her leg before she
could notice.

She threw the car in park. The diamond on her left hand
sparkled under the fluorescent lights of the shop floor.
Damn. Tarwater had definitely "put a ring on it." Sutton
got out and came around the front to join him.

As she walked, she pulled her matching red-checked

scarf to hang around her neck and ran fingers through her hair. The mass of waves tumbled around her shoulders, having lost its battle with the wind—pretty and wild. Her heels tapped on the concrete floor and her skirt swished above her knees. She was Southern femininity and grace.

And he was a grease monkey. A smart and talented grease monkey, who might have been called charming a time or two by the opposite sex, but a grease monkey nonetheless.

"I've been dealing mostly with your brother, Mr. Abbott." She raised her chin in Mack's direction and held out her hand. "I don't know if you remember me, but—"

"Sutton Mize. Of course, I remember you. I'm—"

"Wyatt. One of the twins." She glanced over at Jackson. "Yeah, I remember you too."

Wyatt transferred the wrench to his left hand, wiped his right across the front of his coveralls, and took her hand in a firm shake. "I'm the youngest by a minute, and Jackson never lets me forget it. But that's okay because I'm better looking." He tried on a charming smile, but it felt awkward, like he was twelve again.

"I've heard all sorts of stories about the two of you, Mr. Abbott." Usually that type of assessment was given as half curious, half teasing, but she said it like he might be hiding a communicable disease.

No telling what she'd heard about them. All the Abbott brothers been known to stir up a little trouble in their youth, but time and responsibility had matured them. Mostly.

"Mr. Abbott was our pop. Call me Wyatt. Otherwise everyone's liable to get confused. We have more Abbotts crawling around here than we know what to do with some days."

"I was sorry to hear about your father. He was a nice man. I remember he always had candy in the waiting room." Her smile was wistful and full of sympathy as she pushed her sunglasses to the top of her head.

His stomach swooped like he'd crested a hill going too fast. He stuttered out a rote thanks. Her eyes. He'd forgotten about her eyes, or maybe he hadn't noticed them as a boy. Not blue or green or brown, but a kaleidoscope mixture of all the colors.

Giving himself a mental shake, he slapped on a smile and forced nonchalance. He needed to regain control of himself and the situation. "Now you've got me curious. What have you heard about me and my brothers?"

Although nerves tinged her laugh, a natural throaty quality both relaxed him and cranked up his awareness of her in ways that would have lightning striking him in church. "Nothing bad. Just about the racing. And stuff."

Jackson was the one who raced dirt tracks, even though Wyatt was often pegged as the risk taker. The "stuff" she referred to was probably the occasional hell they used to raise down at the Rivershack Tavern or at bonfires out in the marshes. Since their pop had died, Wyatt had lost his taste for mindless partying.

Interesting the way that rumors carried upriver. He'd assumed his family was beneath the notice of the upper echelon of Cottonbloom, Mississippi—unless they needed a trustworthy mechanic for their precious Beemers.

"Racing is Jackson's favorite pastime. I spend my free time knitting baby blankets and escorting elderly ladies across the street." He waggled his eyebrows.

Her laughter peeled through the garage, and multiple sets of eyes swiveled in their direction, making his coveralls feel like an oven. She clamped her lips together and twisted the engagement ring on her finger.

Childhood crush aside, the ring was a good reminder that she was off-limits. He pointed. "When did you get engaged?"

Her gaze shuttered. "Earlier this spring."

"When's the wedding?"

"Right before Christmas."

He nodded. The early August heat was cut by a breeze snaking through the open bay doors of the garage and the industrial-size fans. "Plenty of time then."

"Is it?" Her face took on a distant quality as if looking straight through the solid cement wall of the garage before she assembled a bright, brittle smile. "Daddy thought it would be nice to have the car done before our engagement party at the end of September. You can have it finished by then, right?"

Time to get down to business. Car business. He ran an assessing glace over the interior of the car. Instrument panel was an ugly, early computerized mod from the nineties. The dark brown leather upholstery was in decent shape but the wrong color. The carpeting would have to go too.

"Shouldn't be a problem as long as I can find parts. Do you want a stock panel or a replica?"

She shrugged. "Stock, I guess? Andrew insists on the best of everything."

"Might take me longer to acquire, but I can make it happen." He turned and propped a hip against the door. "We appreciate your business."

She gave a half shrug. "Don't thank me. My daddy's always loved your garage. He fancies himself a car buff, but ask him to change his oil and he's useless. And your brother Ford talked up the garage to Mr. Tarwater while they were playing golf at the country club. That cinched it."

Bitterness oozed out of old wounds. Wyatt's destiny was to molder away under exhausts and hoods. He couldn't compete with Ford's degree or the connections he was cultivating on golf courses around the south. And Wyatt couldn't blame anyone but himself.

The hammer of the air wrench from the other bay filled the ensuing silence, giving Wyatt a chance to paste a polite façade together. "We have everything we need. You got a ride outta here?"

"My best friend's picking me up at ten." She glanced around.

"It's only half past nine."

"Sorry. I thought the handoff would take longer, but you seem to know what you're doing."

"Hey, we're professionals." He held his hands up and grinned to take any sting out of the statement. Some people understood that restoring a car was a delicate, sometimes frustrating, recreation of the past. Other people thought all they did was change oil and rotate tires.

Her gaze shifted over his shoulder, and he turned to see what had caught her attention. Jackson molded a piece of chrome to replace the rusted one on the Firebird he was restoring. With a focused intensity, he ran his hands over the curve he'd created like an artist admiring his masterpiece.

"It must be satisfying," she said thoughtfully. "Improving things. Fixing them."

"Nothing like taking something that's been damaged or neglected and making it whole and beautiful again."

"Isn't it hard to let them go when you're done?" She transferred her unusual eyes to him.

"Sometimes, but like Tarwater's Camaro, the cars aren't mine. They're only being entrusted into my care for a short while. Once I'm finished, I'll move on to the next project, and it becomes my new favorite. A never-ending cycle."

Her hum was faintly sarcastic. "It has nothing to do with the money?"

"As I'm sure Mack has informed you, my love and

devotion ain't cheap." He put a hand over his heart and winked. "But they are yours. For now."

"From what I've heard, I'm lucky to have your love and devotion even if it is temporary." Her sexy-sweet tease faded as her words hung between them. She shifted and fiddled with her hair. "I mean, the car is lucky. Not me."

The graceful play of her fingers at her neck was hypnotizing. She cleared her throat and took a step to the side. He needed to do something besides stare at her like an ignoramus. He reached inside the car and unlatched the glove compartment. The small space was crammed with papers, a couple drifting to the floorboard.

"You want to help me clean your fiancé's personal effects while you wait? I'll be ripping this whole panel out and the seats too."

Sutton twisted her ring and circled the car to the driver's seat. In Wyatt's opinion, the Camaro was designed with a woman in mind. The engine purred instead of growled. The lines were feminine. The cherry-red paint even matched her nails. Damn, she looked great behind the wheel.

"Are you going to be late for work?" He joined her, taking the passenger seat.

"Yes." She cocked her head to smile at him, her hair falling forward around her neck as she pulled papers from the glove box to her lap. "But, considering I own the place, it'll be okay."

"I didn't realize—" He stopped himself before his foot made it all the way into his mouth and down to his stomach. He'd thought of her only as a socialite. "I thought you were big in that women's group over the river."

"The Junior League? It's a volunteer gig, not a paying one. Honestly, it's hard to find the time these days. My one responsibility this year is organizing centerpieces for the League gala." The fundraiser was the biggest social event

in Cottonbloom and benefitted various charities and pro-
grams on both sides of the river. It got a huge spread in the
Cottonbloom Gazette every year. "My day job takes up
most of my time. My sister and I own Abigail's Boutique
off River Street."

"I can't say I've ever been inside."

"No reason to unless you're buying a present for a
mother or girlfriend . . ." The lilting question in her voice
had him narrowing his eyes. Was she fishing? Before he
could answer, she continued on with a husky laugh that
drew an automatic smile to his face. "Or maybe unless you
like to wear women's clothes."

"I find women's underwear too confining under my coveralls." He kept his face neutral. "I prefer to go *au naturel*."

Her laugh sputtered out, and her gaze brushed down
his body, but faster than a hiccup, she turned her focus to
the steering wheel, her left hand squeaking the leather, the
flash of her ring a reminder of her status.

The flush of color in her cheeks didn't seem to be entirely from embarrassment. Or, more likely, his wishful
imagination was seeing what it wanted and not what was
there. It didn't matter. He didn't matter. He was some Joe
Schmo from over the river that she barely remembered
from when they were kids and would forget again as soon
as she drove off.

The glove box held a few receipts for oil changes and
several from restaurants up in Jackson and down in New
Orleans. Wyatt's eyes widened at the price of some of the
dinners. Andrew Tarwater thought nothing of dropping a
couple hundred of dollars for dinner on a regular basis.

"Dang, you're a lucky girl." Wyatt handed over the stack
of receipts.

"What do you mean?" She took the receipts, the tips of
her perfectly manicured fingers brushing his for an instant.

He pulled his hand into a fist to hide the grease lining

his fingernails. "Fancy restaurants. Tarwater must like to show you off. Not that I blame him."

Her face had lost some of its color, and the receipts wavered in her hand as she shuffled through them one by one. "What in the world?"

Although she seemed to be asking herself the question, he asked, "What's wrong?"

"Nothing. It's probably nothing." She shook a smile back on her face but with a new seriousness. "The glovebox is cleaned out. What else?"

"Check under your seat. Owners always leave stuff behind."

They both leaned over and cast hands under the seat, the position putting their faces close. Her eyes were amazing, and if he was the sort of man who did sappy things, he'd be tempted to write a poem about them. Or a country song.

"Nothing under mine," she whispered, staying curled over her knees.

His fingers brushed fabric. He tugged, but it was hung on something. Changing directions, he pulled harder, and the fabric slipped free with a rending sound. Even before he got a gander at his find, he recognized lace and identified them. He held them up as if putting them on display.

A black, very brief lace thong with a red heart embroidered at the hip. The sexiest scrap of anything he'd ever seen.

He was torn between embarrassment and jealousy. Two emotions that typically didn't plague him. But, for a millisecond, some beast inside of him wailed, imagining Tarwater and Sutton in this car and the various scenarios that might have led her panties to reside under the seat.

"Yours, I assume?" he asked through a clenched, fake smile.

Chapter Two

Sutton stared at the lace concoction. From La Perla's fall collection. Fine Italian lace. Ridiculously expensive for something so small. A special order with the addition of a small embroidered heart to sit at the owner's hipbone. Oh yes, she was acquainted with the underwear but not intimately acquainted. She'd ordered them through Abigail's Boutique, but not for herself. She was too practical.

Wyatt Abbott shook them even closer to her face, obviously expecting her to take them. The thought of touching the lace made her shrink against the driver's door, and she fumbled for the handle, finally finding it and yanking. The door opened and her momentum sent her to the shop floor on her butt.

Her skirt bunched around her thighs, probably high enough for Wyatt Abbott to see her simple cotton pink panties from Victoria's Secret. The fact they weren't white was the wildest she got. She'd even waited for them to go on sale. With a bruised ego and bottom, she scrambled up.

Wyatt hadn't moved. His mouth was parted, still in a slight smile, the panties dangling from his fingers. Instead of the roil of emotions gaining steam inside of her, she concentrated on his hands. They were rough-looking and callused. The nails were short but lined with grease. And they were big. They built things. Fixed things. Put things back together.

A darkness came over his face, clouding his earlier good-humor and giving him an edge of danger she hadn't sensed through his teasing. Instead of getting out of the car from the door, he stood up on the passenger seat, stepped to the driver's seat, and hopped next to her, the black lace of her betrayal dangling in his hand.

"What's the problem?" he asked.

A jackhammering noise from the other bay filled the space so she didn't have to. The crazy thing was that she had sensed something wrong. Something had been wrong pretty much since she and Andrew had gotten engaged.

She'd tried to put it down to nerves or how busy they both were with work. But the truth was she'd been dragging her feet with the wedding preparations. Between the two of them pulling away, the distance had grown until only an echo of what had drawn them together remained.

The hum of a motor and the flash of sunlight on metal drew her attention to the open bay door. Her best friend, Bree Randall, stepped out of her BMW coupe dressed in heels, grey slacks, and a sleeveless silk shell, the pink contrasting beautifully with her dark brown hair and ivory complexion. She was a lawyer for Cottonbloom, Mississippi's city government and had been Sutton's best friend since first grade.

No way could Sutton smile and pretend everything was fine. She grabbed the front of Wyatt's coveralls and looked up at him. The boy she remembered had been too cool and a borderline jerk, teasing her incessantly, almost to the point of tears. The man was still too cool, yet something new lurked behind his ease. She hoped it was akin to kindness.

Bree drew closer. Stuck between a devil she knew and

one she didn't, Sutton took a chance. Her voice was hoarse and begging and she didn't care. "Get me out of here. Please."

Without taking his eyes off her, he called out, "Yo, Jackson. Could you put the lady from the Beemer in the waiting room? Tell her Miss Mize isn't feeling well and stepped out back for some fresh air."

If his brother answered, she didn't hear him. Wyatt put a strong, stabilizing arm around her shoulders and guided her around various pieces of equipment and mechanical parts to a door tucked away at the back of the shop floor. She stepped outside, closed her eyes, and took a deep breath. The freshness of the air counteracted the bile rising in her throat.

Her knees wobbled as the stark reality of the situation and the fallout took shape in her mind. She glanced at the man by her side. What was Wyatt Abbott thinking right now? Probably that she was borderline psychotic.

A huge red barn sat behind the shop, and they passed from sun back into shadows. A body-sized punching bag twirled from a high beam as they passed by. That explained why the arm at her back was so solid. Her heels tapped on the wide-planked floor. The smell of weathered wood was overlaid by something sweeter. Honeysuckle, maybe.

No hay was stored in the Abbott's barn. Two tarp-covered cars, the bottom curves of their tires the only part visible, formed a path to the back where a scratched up leather couch and mini-fridge sat.

"Sorry it's so dusty in here. We like to keep the doors open if the weather's nice because of the views and cross breeze." He took a blue towel from his back pocket and wiped off a section of the couch, leaving yellow streaks of pollen. Getting a little dirty was way down on her list of worries and she plopped down, wrapping her arms around her stomach and leaning over so her forehead nearly touched her knees.

"You want a Coke or tea or something?"

She raised her head enough to see his big hand holding out a bottle. He shifted back and forth in his black work boots, the hem of his coveralls ombréd black to grey with grease.

"It's a little early for whiskey, but I've got that too if you'd rather." He sounded so worried and unsure, she straightened, took the Coke and pressed the cool plastic against her cheeks and neck.

"You must think I've gone batty." She rarely drank alcohol and never whiskey, but for a moment she considered it as a viable option, even though it was still technically breakfast. It was five o'clock somewhere, right?

"I think something really bad happened," he said. "I'm not sure what, but I suspect it has something to do with the restaurant receipts and the underwear."

"Oh God. The receipts." Her mind hadn't even circled back around to those, but everything notched into place like a puzzle whose missing piece turned up stuck on the bottom of a shoe covered with chewed up old gum and bug guts.

His late nights working. Breaking dates at the last minute. His distraction. How long had it been since they'd shared the same bed? Two months? Three? She'd put it down to the natural progression of a committed relationship and the busyness of their lives, assuming things would be better once they were living under the same roof.

"I'm a moron." Tears crawled up her throat and choked off her feeble attempt of a laugh.

She closed her eyes, wishing she could teleport herself back under the covers. The cushion sagged next to her, and she tipped toward him, her shoulder bumping his biceps.

A moment passed before his arm came around her shoulders, and they sank back into the couch together.

She turned her face into the space between his neck and shoulder and took a deep breath, desperately trying to get a handle on her out-of-control emotions. Pain was to be expected, but the flashes of fierce fury took her by surprise.

Easygoing and nice and cheerful were bandied about when people passed compliments her way. At least, she'd always taken them as compliments. Now she wasn't so sure. Maybe all those things were code words for weak and gullible.

Another breath. She concentrated on Wyatt's warmth and scent. So different from the expensive cologne Andrew wore. Wyatt smelled like pine trees and the garage. His dark, almost black, hair tickled her nose. A tear slipped out and she wiped it away with the heel of her hand.

"You want me to go get your friend?" His chest vibrated against her, deep and rich.

Friend? She didn't want to examine the other half of the betrayal. Worse than Andrew cheating on her was who he'd been getting down and dirty with. Her best friend. No. A friend wouldn't sleep with her fiancé behind her back while helping her plan the wedding with an enthusiasm that oftentimes exceed her own.

Sutton ransacked her brain for moments she could point to and say *Aha!* but none came to mind. Bree had been supportive and helpful over the last few months. Lies. How many lies had Sutton accepted as gospel truth? A few more tears escaped along with a ragged breath.

Wyatt made a humming sound that was distinctly uncomfortable, and he pulled away. "Let me—"

She grabbed his coveralls. "No. Don't you get it? That was *her* thong."

He shifted to face her. "Is identifying underwear in a single glance your superpower?"

Despite her life crashing down, a shard of humor sliced through the shock, and her lips twitched. "Expensive underwear. The heart on the panties matches her tattoo. A special order."

"Your fiancé and your best friend?"

Put like that, she felt even dumber. "My life has turned into a cliché."

"It's a cliché because of how often it happens. Nothing for you to be ashamed of. It's them that should feel like chickenshit."

"You don't understand how people like to talk."

"I understand, alright. I just don't care what people say." The defiant edge in his voice spoke of his own pain and sorrows, but right now she only had room for her own. He was quiet for a moment. "You want me to get rid of her?"

Sutton sank back and took a swig of Coke, the burn bringing a different, more welcome, sort of tears to her eyes. "I need to talk to her. Confront her."

"Yeah, but not hurt and crying. You need to prepare. Get mad, then get even."

His advice made her sit up straighter. She'd been raised to smooth feathers, not ruffle them. Her mother had taught her how a smile and pleasant word could diffuse most situations. The lessons had contributed to her business success but hadn't done her personal life any favors. Another whip of red-hot fury flayed her heart.

"She's my ride back over the river." Her voice sounded even and strong, her anger a mast to cling to amid the wreckage.

"I can be your ride."

"But you have work to do."

The look he cast her was full of disbelief. "You're not going through with the restoration, are you?"

The Camaro, the red harbinger of her ruin, had already

slipped her mind. She didn't even like the stupid car. Her daddy and Tarwater senior had hatched this surprise over a round of golf with Ford Abbott after she'd confessed she couldn't think of anything to give Andrew as an engagement present. Only when her daddy had anted up half the money had she agreed. Their "go big or go home" mentality had seemed a ridiculous waste to her.

Dear Lord, her family. What would her daddy say? As a long-standing judge, he was sort of a colleague of Andrew's. She closed her eyes and rocked forward and back on the edge of the couch.

"What if I'm overreacting?" If only this was a bad dream. Yet, did she really want that? An undercurrent that felt vaguely like relief trickled through the anger and humiliation and doubts.

"About which part, your fiancé cheating or who he was cheating with?" Wyatt stuck a hand into his pocket, came out with the thong, and tossed it on her lap.

She leapt up and brushed it off as if she were Miss Muffet and it was a hairy, black, venomous spider. She kicked at it with the toe of her shoe. The red heart mocked her from the black lace. Yet the little girl who'd shared her pimento cheese sandwich with Bree every day during kindergarten wanted to be wrong.

She sank back down to the edge of the couch, feeling like she was shoring up the situation with Scotch tape. "There could be a reasonable explanation. Like she and Andrew went to lunch and for some reason she had them in her purse and they fell out. Maybe I've jumped to the wrong conclusion."

"Maybe." He shrugged. She appreciated the fact he wasn't calling her on her BS excuses even though his face was the definition of skeptical.

"You sure you don't mind giving me a ride?" she asked.

"I'll get rid of your *friend* and take you home. That

should buy you some time to figure things out. Confront her on your terms."

Her initial impressions of Wyatt Abbott were from the viewpoint of a preteen girl. Back then, she'd been self-conscious of her skinny arms and legs and flyaway hair, and whenever she'd come to the garage with her daddy, Wyatt had made it his mission to tease her mercilessly.

What was he like now? On the surface, she'd label him a good old boy. Fun, flirty, simple. Except, his gray eyes were anything but. Not flat like shale, but ready to spark a fire like a flint. Raw emotions provided a sharp awareness. Her memories of him urged her to be cautious with her trust, yet his jaw was set and his shoulders were rolled forward as if ready and willing to go into battle.

"Why?" she finally whispered.

"Why what?"

"Why are you being so nice to me? You hated me as a kid."

"*Hated* you?" He stuffed his hands into his pockets and tipped his head enough to shutter the intensity of his eyes. "I never hated you, in fact . . ." He shook his head.

"In fact what?"

"Not important. Simply put, unlike your fiancé and your friend, I'm not an asshole. If you don't need me—"

"No, I do need you." She stood but misjudged how close he was. They weren't touching, but she could feel his heat and appreciate his strength. "I just . . ."

Wyatt Abbott was handsome, but even more potent than his looks was an intangible confidence and ease with himself. The man probably talked a different woman out of her panties every weekend. Would he cash in on her humiliation for a good story to tell his brothers and drinking buddies? Did it even matter? Whether it was him or someone else, rumors would rush through the town like the river after a storm.

Insecurities pinged between her head and heart, the message clear. *Protect yourself.* But surely, she could at least trust him to get her home. "I would really appreciate a lift home."

He chaffed her arms like a coach might comfort a little kid after a loss. "It'll be okay. You wait here while I handle your friend, okay?"

She nodded, and he strode back toward the garage. Highlighted in a shaft of sunlight, he hesitated at the metal door they'd ducked through and glanced behind him. A zing of warning—or premonition?—skittered down her spine.

Her life had been spun into chaos, yet in that moment, she felt connected to Wyatt in a way that terrified her. Then he disappeared, and she waited to discover if her trust had once again been misplaced.

Chapter Three

Wyatt tried to shake the image of Sutton Mize standing in the barn, her back straight, her tears dried up, her strength of spirit palpable. Despite the fact she'd been dicked over by both her fiancé and her best friend, she would come out the other side shrouded in the same quiet grace. Any other woman of his acquaintance would be either wailing or loading her shotgun.

But not Sutton. No, she had gathered her dignity around her and accepted the small amount of help he was glad to offer. If she'd asked him to drive to the Tarwater and Tarwater law offices and punch Andrew, his only question would have been face or balls.

The garage was busy. Willa was in the pit under the car she had been assigned to work. Jackson was right outside the bay door talking to their Aunt Hazel. She gestured to the twenty-year-old Crown Victoria she shared with her twin sister, Hyacinth. The thing drove like new, mainly because they brought it in at least weekly for a once-over.

Mack had abandoned his invoicing and was examining an old-school Charger that was still up on the bed of a tow truck. A beauty, but a badly damaged one. She might only be good for parts, but Wyatt might be able to fix her.

Already moving on from the loss of the Camaro, he itched to get under the hood.

The garage might have a harder time recovering and moving on, though. Tarwater's Camaro was supposed to provide the jumpstart into Mississippi they needed. Dread circled his stomach at the thought of telling Mack. His brother had broad shoulders, but he was showing signs of strain.

He refocused himself on the task at hand: getting rid of Sutton's ex-bestie without letting the ungentlemanly words lurking at the back of his throat escape. He opened the waiting room door. The woman stopped mid-pace and pivoted to face him.

A cross between impatience and annoyance marred an otherwise pretty face framed by chocolatey brown hair, stick straight and lustrous looking. She popped a hip and drummed her blood-red tipped fingers on crossed arms. The general impression was one of elegance, but the vibe she gave off was animalistic with sexual overtones. A predator. If a man enjoyed his women with claws—metaphorical and otherwise—she was your dream girl.

"Where's Sutton? I've texted her a half dozen times. I have cases up today."

"Wyatt Abbott, mechanic extraordinaire." He forced a smile with as much charm as he could muster to throw her off her game.

She sized him up from head to work boots with a gaze he imagined made lesser men quake. Or confess. When it became clear he wasn't offering up any more information, she made a huffy sound. "Bree Randall, Cottonbloom, Mississippi, city counsel. Where is Sutton?" The last three words came out in a slow, clipped voice as if she assumed his grasp on the English language was tenuous.

"Things are more complicated than we originally

discussed. You can head on, and I'll give Sutton a ride over the river once things are settled."

"She should cut bait and not spend the money. Last I heard Andrew was thinking about selling the Camaro anyway." Over the entitlement in her tone and manner was a confident aura that she was always in the right.

If he wasn't already inclined to dislike her, her attitude cinched it, especially given her fishing analogy and the country accent she hadn't quite been able to shake. His brother Ford carried himself in a similar fashion, and it incited annoyance like a swarm of no-see-ums.

"Restorations generally increase a car's value." The line was a standard sales pitch, but also true. The Abbotts' reputation had been earned through honest dealings.

"I want to see her." She stepped toward the door and waved a hand, shooing him aside.

He planted a shoulder into the jamb and blocked the way. "She's busy."

Shadows passed over her face at his terse answer, but he couldn't discern the cause. Did she suspect that Sutton knew? Did she regret hurting a friend, or was she more worried about getting caught? Whatever the cause, she avoided his eyes while she retrieved her purse and hiked it over her shoulder.

"Fine. Tell Sutton to check her phone." It was a demand, not a request.

Wyatt didn't respond except to step out of the way and toe the door open. He followed close behind, herding her toward her BMW coupe. Her car was all looks with nothing of substance under the hood. BMWs were notoriously high maintenance.

Still chatting with the tow truck operator, Mack sent him a curious look. Wyatt dropped his gaze, wanting to put off adding to Mack's stress for as long as possible.

Bree hesitated at her bumper, fiddling with her key fob. "You sure she doesn't need my help?"

"You've helped enough, don't you think?" This time he didn't bother with a customer service smile.

Bree's eyes flared then narrowed on him. She bit her bottom lip as if questions or more demands hovered, but instead she slid into the BMW without a word, the tinted windows offering camouflage. She spun out of the parking area and onto the two-lane parish road. He stared until she was out of sight.

His aunt Hazel grabbed his sleeve as he stepped back into the shop. Her twin sister, Hyacinth, wouldn't be far away. Wyatt and Jackson were the latest in a long line of Abbott fraternal twins. Every generation had at least one set, sometimes two, and according to family lore, none had ever married. Wyatt and Jackson had found this more amusing than disturbing over the years, joking that they were destined for a set of bunk beds in the old folks' home.

Aunt Hazel's classic beauty was still visible under the sagging skin, wrinkles, and white fluffy hair. But her storybook, kindly grandmother appearance belied the intimidating fire that burned in her soul. Although she was smaller in stature and not as bombastic as her twin, she commanded a room. When she spoke, people listened.

She had more in common, personality-wise, with Jackson, which was maybe the reason Wyatt and his aunt Hazel had always had an undeniable bond. Just like Jackson could see behind his smiles, Hazel had always known when something was troubling him. She wasn't the giver of hugs—that fell to Hyacinth—she was the giver of wisdom, and the person Wyatt had turned to time and again in his youth seeking the guidance of a mother figure.

Hazel shared the same color eyes as her younger brother, his pop. In them, he found the comfort of the familiar, but also the pang of loss. Wyatt leaned down to give her a hug and kissed her cheek, even though she tensed at the demonstration. Her floral perfume shot him back twenty-five years, and he tightened his hold on her for an instant.

"Something wrong with the car?" he asked.

"A funny rattle under the hood. Jackson is taking a look-see."

Since his pop's death, the aunts had brought the car in at least once a week complaining of phantom noises. The brothers knew they were using the car as an excuse to check in on them, and the aunts knew that they knew. But they all continued to play along for reasons that involved pride and stoicism.

"Sounds like Jackson has you covered. I need to ske-daddle." He thumbed over his shoulder and took a step back. "Customer service issue."

Hazel was too perceptive where he was concerned, and he made an escape before her puzzlement manifested into questions he didn't want to answer. Jackson popped up from the side of their aunts' car and stopped him with a wrench held out like the arm at a train crossing.

"Hold up. You haven't kidnapped Sutton Mize, have you?"

"Kidnapped? What kind of man do you think I am?"

"The kind to make googly-eyes at a taken woman. Don't think I didn't notice."

"It's not like that."

"She's engaged to Tarwater."

"She was. Is." The back of his neck crawled and his eyebrow twitched, the omission treading too close to a lie. Normally, confiding in Jackson was a given, but this wasn't his secret to share. Anyway, he didn't know what she planned on doing. She wouldn't be the first woman to forgive a cheater. "I'm running her back to her place. That's all there is to it."

"What about Tarwater's car? You want me to put Willa on it?"

"Naw. Let it sit 'til I get back." He would buy a six-pack on the way home and break the news to his brothers that afternoon. Maybe by then he'd have thought of some way to mitigate the loss.

Jackson's hazel eyes—Abbott eyes, they were called—bored into him with the intensity of a laser-guided missile. "Is everything okay?"

Wyatt heard the undertones. *Are* you *okay?* was what his brother was really asking. "I'm fine, but . . ." He glanced toward the back wall and the barn beyond. "Cover for me, would you? I'll fill you in later."

Jackson turned back to his work without another question, and Wyatt gave him a pat on the shoulder on his way by.

Not sure what he'd find in the barn—women were unpredictable creatures, and Sutton seemed more complicated than most—he shuffled through the door. Between the dust and pollen worked into the grooves of the wood floor and the thrift store couch, any damage she could inflict in a fit of rage might be an improvement.

Instead of a woman who planned to set shit on fire, she appeared serene, standing at the back of the barn, sipping her Coke, and staring toward the woods that spanned all the way to the horizon. The same stance he'd found himself in more often of late.

Memories of summers long gone echoed through the woods. The brothers had taken care of each other while their pop had toiled away building the business. Leaving four boys to their own devices had led to a few broken bones and near-death experiences in the tops of trees or on the river, but they'd survived and even thrived. He missed the simplicity of those days.

"Hey," he said softly.

She spun and he was struck anew at the complexity of her eyes, both in color and feeling. "I feel like I could walk into the woods and come out two hundred years ago."

He understood exactly what she meant. The woods were a magical place where past and present collided and sadness and hope warred. Although the peace he'd once gained from the view had turned to an unexplainable restlessness.

"You'd sorely miss indoor plumbing." His reward was a lightning quick quirk of her lips. He propped a shoulder against the opposite side of the wide barn door. "I often think about my ancestors walking these woods. Same trees, same river."

She made a noise that struck him as polite interest.

"I sent Bree on her way," he said.

His words broke her trance with the woods. Her color heightened and her body tensed. She shifted and leaned her back against the jamb as if needing the physical support. "Was she suspicious?"

"I think so. Wanted to know why you weren't returning her texts."

"I turned off my phone. I can't—" Her voice cracked.

"I get it. Just letting you know that a reckoning is coming sooner rather than later, so you'll have to decide how to play it."

"What play do I have except to face it head-on?"

He picked at the grease under one of his fingernails and looked at her from under his lashes. "You could forgive him. Extract promises it will never happen again. Maybe you'd be happy."

"Puh-lease. I may be gullible, but I have a healthy dose of self-respect." At her declaration, relief calmed the whoosh of his heart. She deserved someone better than Tarwater, but he hadn't been sure she realized it too.

She rubbed her forehead and gave a breathy, ironic

sounding laugh. "You know what's weird? I'm more upset about Bree than Andrew."

"Not weird." But it was surprising.

"Bree has been my best friend since before I can remember. I thought we had each other's backs."

Wyatt didn't have a best friend aside from his family, and he couldn't imagine one of them screwing him over. Except for Ford. Screwing Wyatt over had been Ford's favorite pastime as a kid.

Her eyes were dry, but she looked exhausted and wrung out. He side-stepped to the stairs leading up to the barn loft. "Let me change, and I'll run you over the river."

She straightened and brushed her hands down her skirt, twisting her neck to see up the stairs. "You live here?"

"Jackson and I converted the loft into an apartment of sorts." He gestured impulsively. "Wanna see?"

"I'd love to." A portion of the strain around her eyes and mouth eased. If it made her feel better, he would be happy to provide a distraction.

She preceded him up the stairs and the sway of her hips halted his mental inventory about how messy he'd left the loft that morning.

She opened the door at the top and stepped tentatively over the threshold as if a trap might spring at any moment. A puff of cool air greeted them. A couple of lamps flanked the couch in the living space, but turning them on was unnecessary. Sunshine poured through skylights. His bedroom was in the left corner, Jackson's in the right. His open door showcased an unmade king-sized bed against the far wall.

Two windows were taken up with the air conditioners, but the rest could be opened if the weather was nice. His favorite nights were in the fall when he could stare up at the stars, throw the windows open, and fall asleep to the crescendoing call of the cicadas.

A small kitchen with the bare essentials was along one wall, but neither Wyatt nor Jackson cooked anything more complicated than mac and cheese or canned soup, preferring to head over to the old family house beside the garage to mooch dinner with Mack. But amid the chaos of the garage, the loft was a fortress of solitude.

"This is lovely." She shuffled farther into the room and did a turn that billowed her skirt out from her legs. "Did you renovate it by yourself?"

He followed her as she made a slow circle around the room, her heels tapping hollowly against the dark wood planking. "For the most part. The advantage of being related to half the parish means that I have plenty of people to call on if I need help. Of course, the disadvantage is my dating pool is drastically smaller. Unless I aspire to become a redneck joke."

His weak attempt at humor elicited a small smile, and he mentally tallied it as another victory.

"There are Abbotts all over the parish. Are you kin to all of them?"

"A few I won't claim in public, and a few have jumped the river over to Mississippi, but yes." Tracing his family tree was an avoidance tactic that wouldn't work for long, but he understood her need.

She turned and half-sat on the edge of the window. "What's it like growing up with family all around like that?"

"Annoying." He couldn't go anywhere without running into someone he was related to, however distantly. His youthful indiscretions had been public fodder, but on the plus side, he had a phone full of numbers to call if he needed help. "It can be pretty great too."

"I can imagine it was fun as a kid to always have someone to play with."

The wistfulness in her voice made him want to offer her a hug. Which would be weird, right? He tucked his hands into his pockets.

"You have a sister though. Is she not around Cotton-bloom anymore?"

"How do you remember that?" For the first time since the thong discovery, she turned her complete focus from managing her inward pain and confusion to him. Confessing his childhood crush was a no-go. At his shrug, she continued. "Maggie. A year older, but for some reason, we've never been close. When I was looking to buy the boutique, my dad offered me a loan with the stipulation my sister got a stake and a job. It's been interesting." Her eye roll was so slight, he almost missed it.

"Family businesses are complicated, huh?"

"The absolute best and worst." She'd nailed exactly how Wyatt felt about the garage. "You must run into some of that here. You and your brothers can't always agree."

He hummed at the understatement. If their disagreements got too heated, it wasn't uncommon for them to take it out back and settle things the old-fashioned way. More often than not though, the fights ended in laughter. Basically, the Abbotts were a human resources nightmare.

Some might view their methods as immature and un-professional, but it acted as a release valve to the tension that would otherwise simmer and grow into something far more unmanageable and destructive. The way it had between Ford and Mack.

"I need to change out of my coveralls to run you home." Dirtying the seats of his car was near sacrilege.

"Oh, right." She presented her back and stared out the window. It was a pretty view made even prettier with her framed by it.

He retreated to his bedroom. Changing clothes with

her on the other side of the thin door took on a strange intimacy, even though there was nothing sexual about it.

He stepped out, barefoot and buckling his belt, and met her gaze in the window reflection. Pinpoints of sunlight brightened and intensified her eyes. The intimacy deepened and stretched into an awareness he couldn't quantify, as if her reflection distilled truth rather than distorted it— pain and betrayal, but also a tempered strength.

"Time to face up to reality." She turned, shattering the moment, her voice too high and bright and a blush staining her skin. She didn't wait for an answer, but swished her way down the stairs.

After pulling on boots, he trailed in her wake, not sure how to explain the urge to protect her or the melancholy sadness that echoed in his chest. The girl who he'd crushed on hard had turned into a woman who inspired a tangle of feelings he couldn't ignore.

But the reality was, dropping her off at the curb and waving good-bye would see their paths diverge once more. In fact, this incident, including him, was something she'd probably work hard to forget.

Sutton patted at the inferno raging on her cheeks as she stamped down the steps. Wyatt Abbott unsettled her. Her memories of the boy he'd been didn't line up with the kindness he'd shown her now. Even as she attempted to stay leery about his motives, she could imagine hanging out with him in his cozy loft or on the couch staring out over the woods for the rest of the day, talking about nothing in particular, but laughing a lot.

Out of the baggy coveralls, he was in better shape than she'd imagined. His jeans were well-worn with a fraying split at one knee, and his T-shirt emphasized arms that were familiar with heavy lifting and hard work. She tried her best not to notice or admire. After all she was technically still engaged.

What was wrong with her? Shock. Obviously, she was in shock and was practicing some weird avoidance technique by noticing another man's biceps an hour after discovering her fiancé was a cheater.

The longer the situation marinated in her head though, the clearer it became. She was more upset about Bree than Andrew. Certainly, Andrew deserved blame, but it was Bree's betrayal that prodded her heart with a hot poker, stoking the flash fire of her anger and hurt.

Added to that sickening stew was a feeling of foolishness. Who else knew about Bree and Andrew? In a town as small as Cottonbloom, indiscretions were hard to hide. Even if they had kept things on the down-low and out-of-town as all the restaurant receipts implied, someone knew. Someone always knew.

How long had it been going on? She would check the dates on the receipts she'd stuffed into her purse when she got home, where she'd be free to cry and yell and hit something. Inanimate, of course. She would never go so far as to actually hit someone. Not her style. Her style was to suck it up and move on with a smile. Even if it was fake.

At the bottom of the steps, she stopped one more time in the barn door. If she wasn't so practical, she might believe magic existed in the deep and endless woods stretching over the rise. But the woods did end. Somewhere out there a road or a farm or a strip mall cut them off. Everything eventually ended.

"Thinking about making a run for it?" A humor that had already become associated with him in her mind lilted the question. Yet, it didn't sound rhetorical.

"I'm tempted. Does that make me weak?"

"Makes you normal. Ready?"

She followed him around the side of the barn. A

half-dozen cars in various states of disrepair were lined up in two rows behind an enormous magnolia tree.

He gestured toward them. "Our car graveyard. They're cannibalized for parts, then sent to the salvage yard. We try not to keep more than six or eight back here, otherwise it starts to look like we're running a junkyard."

They bypassed the graveyard to a low-slung, two-door car painted dark blue with a white pinstripe down the side. She ran her finger over the curve of the car's roof. A vented bump in the middle of the hood and round headlights gave an impression the car was a living entity patiently waiting for Wyatt to breathe life into it.

"It's an AMC '71 Hornet." He opened the passenger door and gestured her in.

The interior gave both the impression of age and modernity. For some reason, she pictured him driving a truck—maybe white, definitely big and reliable—not a fast car that held an edge of danger.

He joined her and cranked the engine, the low rumble like the car sighing in pleasure. The supple leather of the seat caressed her hand and not the other way around. It was unexpectedly sensuous.

"You restored it?" she asked, for something to fill the space.

"Yep. Dropped a rebuilt V8 engine under her hood and ripped out the interior down to the frame. He patted the dash. "She was a mess when I found her, but look at her now."

"Gorgeous," she said and meant it. She understood more about dresses than cars, but she could look at a dress on a hanger and see the potential it held for a client. She imagined cars were similar. "Is this your favorite car ever?"

"It's my favorite right now."

"You won't keep it?"

"Nope. I'll sell her soon and find another project car to

fall in love with." The dispassionate tone was surprising considering his prideful, doting manner with the car.

"Will it be hard to sell?"

"People are always looking for classics, and top-of-the-line Hornets like this aren't common. I should turn a tidy profit."

"I meant, aren't you attached, you know, emotionally?"

He shot her a half-amused look. "I don't get emotionally attached to my projects."

Wyatt drove over the steel-girded bridge that separated Cottonbloom, Louisiana, from Cottonbloom, Mississippi, then pumped his brakes before the turn down River Street. "Where am I going? Your shop or your house?"

She should go into Abigail's. The weeks leading up to the Junior League gala were busy and one of the most profitable times of the year for the shop. But her sales skills were currently in hibernation. Maggie could handle a day alone. Wyatt was right, she needed to gird herself. The confrontation was like a storm brewing on the near horizon.

"Home." She gave Wyatt directions.

She sank lower in the seat and pressed her purse against her hollowed-out stomach. The Hornet was barreling toward her new reality. The distraction offered by Wyatt was about to end. No doubt, he was itching to leave the complication of her problems in the rearview mirror.

She switched her phone on. Calls needed to be made. Her phone vibrated and messages popped up on the screen, too fast to read. Texts and calls from Bree and Maggie. Andrew's name listed next to a missed call less than three minutes earlier. He never called during his office hours. Bree must have raised the red flag. Would he come clean or attempt to convince her of his innocence?

Innocent until proven guilty. The old adage whirred through her head. Perhaps she hadn't extracted a confession yet, but she'd certainly amassed enough evidence for a conviction.

Her street was lined with houses from the 1940s and '50s, most of them squat one-story brick homes. Oak trees crossed arms over the street, sunlight sneaking through like ropes of bright light. The sidewalks had buckled in places from the roots, and kids on summer break took full advantage, jumping their bikes over the ledges. It was a happy, vibrant street, but the usual warm, fuzzy feelings didn't materialize through the numbness.

She pointed, and he turned into her driveway. Her house would fit in the front yard of her family home, but its charm compensated for its lack of square footage. The interior had been upgraded by the previous owner, and a meticulously maintained rose garden in the back had sold her on her first viewing.

The announcement three years ago that she'd be moving out of the family home had not been met with congratulations and hugs but tears and pleas to stay on her mother's part. Her father counterbalanced her mother's histrionics with his usual placidness, neither supporting nor condemning her decision. Eventually, her mother's fears of Sutton using her new house as a stepping stone out of Cottonbloom and her sphere of influence had calmed.

He pulled in behind her practical four-door sedan. It looked like the before picture from a joke car ad next to the Hornet. Even at idle, the car's dynamic energy imparted a feeling of impatience, as if the car needed to be exercised like a thoroughbred horse.

"Cute place," he said.

"Not as much personality as your loft, but I love it." The next words came out with a combination of desperation and knee-jerk politeness. "Would you like to come inside for coffee?"

"Another time."

Why did this small rejection resonate so painfully? Pity hid poorly behind the kindness in his eyes, and she dropped her gaze to the slice of sunlight marking a line between them.

Her first taste of being the object of pity and deemed pathetic. Although, she had a feeling she'd been wearing an invisible cloak of patheticness for at least as far back as the receipts went.

Wyatt shifted and drew something from a side compartment. A business card. Of course, this was all business for him. Andrew's car was still taking up a bay in his garage.

Her words stumbled out. "The Camaro . . . I'm not sure—"

"Don't worry about the car right now. We'll figure it out." He flipped the card over and wrote numbers on the back before holding it out between his index and middle fingers. "That's my cell on the back. If you need *anything*, you call me. Okay?"

She took the card, even though she didn't plan on making use of it. As soon as he left, the event that had brought them together in such a strangely intimate way would be hers to deal with alone. Their bond would fade like a friendship formed at summer camp.

Nevertheless, she clutched his card to her chest like a talisman, pasted on a smile, and pushed the Hornet's door open. She hesitated on her slide out, looking over her shoulder at him.

"Thanks for everything. I know we weren't on the best of terms as kids, and dealing with an imploding relationship wasn't on your radar this morning, but you've been great. Really, really great." The words were inadequate, but a simple thanks and a strained smile was all she had to give at the moment.

He returned her smile even as worry pulled at his brow,

a smudge of grease highlighting the crinkle between his eyes. "Call me if you need me. I mean it."

She nodded and closed the door. The Hornet didn't back up until she had her front door unlocked and one foot inside. Once the rumble of his engine had faded, she dropped his card and her purse on a side table in the foyer, grabbed her phone, and kicked off her heels.

She padded down the hall to the kitchen. The silence pressed the walls closer and a feeling of claustrophobia jacked her heart rate higher. She cracked open the window over the sink, but immediately shut it. The riot of color and the scent from the blooming roses, which she typically enjoyed, turned her stomach, too sweet and cloying.

If she called the boutique, Maggie, quiet and intuitive, would guess something bad had happened, so she texted instead, not exactly lying when she said she was sick. Throwing up was a distinct possibility. Next, she texted Bree and asked if they could get together later that night. While she wanted to chicken out and text Andrew as well, she pulled on her big-girl panties—metaphorically cotton and white—and hit his number.

"Sutton. What's going on?" His voice was brisk and lawyerly.

"I'm returning your call." Not the answer he was after, but she didn't plan on making this easy for him.

"Is everything okay?"

"Depends on your definition, I suppose."

After a long silence he sighed, but she couldn't separate impatience from dread. "And by your definition?"

"Not okay." Her words had thickened. She would *not* cry, dangit.

"Are you home?"

She picked at the folds of her skirt and didn't answer, afraid he would hear how upset she was and twist that to his advantage.

"I'll be over as soon as I can clear my schedule." He disconnected.

Anger flared and burned away her tears at his high-handedness. What would happen if she wasn't here when he showed up? His imagined frustration as he beat on her front door and stamped his feet like a toddler made her feel better.

Not that he would show that kind of emotion. He rarely showed any kind of emotion around her, positive or negative. He was calm and collected and blank behind his blue eyes. Passionless.

Not like Wyatt. In their brief time together, she'd seen humor and anger and worry flicker across his face and spark behind his eyes. Who would have thought gray eyes could be so warm? She rubbed her temples to rid herself of the useless thoughts. He wasn't her white knight or protector. He barely qualified as an acquaintance.

Events were in motion. She retreated to her bedroom and changed into black cigarette pants, a kelly-green button down shirt, and flats. The closest outfit she had to a power suit. Her face was pale and her eyes shadowed even though she hadn't lost any sleep over the drama—yet.

Energy crackled as she paced her den. Words flitted through her head. Words she attempted to assemble into coherent accusations. Forty-five minutes later, a knock on her door made her jerk and then freeze. Before her limbs answered the command of her brain, the door squeaked open. Andrew called her name, and footsteps sounded. Not one set, but two. A distinctly feminine voice and a tap of heels echoed in her entry.

While she processed the implications, Andrew and Bree came around the corner and into the den. Andrew was good-looking, with his streaked blond hair and white smile. Maybe a little too white, but he and his father were on billboards and advertisements selling themselves as trustworthy lawyers. He worked out and manscaped regularly. After years of being friends, she'd been flattered and more than a little overwhelmed when he'd pursued her with the same single-mindedness that had brought success in the courtroom.

Why her? The question seemed to take on greater significance now.

Bree slipped in beside him, not touching him but her body language giving the impression of a united front. A united front against her. Tears clawed their up her throat, and she took a deep breath through her nose to keep them at bay.

"I wasn't expecting you until tonight, Bree," Sutton said.

Instead of meeting Sutton's eyes, Bree looked to Andrew, her dark brown hair swishing around her shoulders like a curtain of silk. When they were kids, she'd had frizzy hair, braces, and terrible acne. All that had been fixed with time, expensive salon treatments, and a good orthodontist.

Now Bree was beautiful and sophisticated and gave off a powerful vibe in her power suit and power heels. But to Sutton, Bree would always be the little girl with crooked teeth and bad hair who'd kept her secrets safe. Until now.

"Mother told me the wedding invitations have arrived. We need to nail down who we want to invite. Father wants to add the governor to the list." Andrew strolled to her couch and sat, propping his arm along the back cushion and his ankle on his knee. He was either oblivious to the mounting tension, or his attitude was a courtroom ploy to throw her off guard.

It would have worked if she hadn't caught Bree's eye for a split second. She acted like Sutton might pull a shotgun and take her out at any moment.

Andrew patted the seat next to him, but Sutton wasn't

sure which one of them he was calling over like a favorite dog. She planted her feet and squared her shoulders. "Let's not throw manure around. I assume you know about the surprise I was planning regarding your precious Camaro. While I was emptying the glovebox, I found a stack of restaurant receipts."

"Is that what this is about? You should have called and asked me about them. Those were all business meetings. Potential clients."

"You take clients charged with federal offenses to the nicest restaurants in Jackson? Because *you* need *their* business?"

"Of course not." His smile didn't disappear but his demeanor changed, his tone chiding. "I'm honestly disappointed in you, Sutton."

Even though they were close to the same age, he had a way of making her feel younger and, as a result, insecure. If she hadn't retrieved the last piece of damning evidence from the dusty barn floor and stuck it in her purse, doubts might have swamped her righteous anger.

Instead, her anger swelled until she was royally pissed off. His nerve in the courtroom was legendary, and she was curious how far he'd go to cover up the truth. "How have I disappointed you? Do tell."

The irony didn't make a dent in Andrew's sanctimonious expression. "Trust is the cornerstone for any relationship."

"So when you were working late"—she air-quoted his often-used excuse—"you were wining and dining potential clients?"

"We might get the most press from our criminal cases, but we make the bulk of our money on estate management and wills. Not as glamorous, but definitely lucrative." He gave her the same smile he used for billboards.

"These dinners would be tax write-offs then?"

He made a scoffing sound that was probably supposed to make her feel like an idiot. "Of course."

"Therefore, your father and the firm's accountant would be privy to them."

Andrew's smile faltered, and a sense of satisfaction surged to meet her anger. She had him trapped but wanted to keep him squirming. She pivoted to face Bree. "Sorry I made you wait around this morning for nothing."

"I was worried about you."

Bree was worried alright. Closer to terrified, if Sutton was reading her expression right. Unlike Andrew, Bree hadn't fully mastered the art of lying.

"You called Andrew because you were worried about me?"

Bree answered with a shrug.

"Hang on, I have something for you." Sutton slipped into the dim hallway and took a deep breath. The climax of the confrontation was upon her, and her muscles ached from the tension hammering at her body. She grabbed her purse and stared at the white card on the table with Wyatt's number scribbled on the back. On impulse, she slipped the card into her pocket.

When she stepped back into the den, Andrew was up and whispering to Bree, his expression stony. A smile came to his face as if Sutton's steps into the den pulled marionette's strings. Was his every move orchestrated to manipulate?

"Let's see . . . I know they're in here somewhere." She forced a singsong note into her voice. First, she pulled out the stack of receipts and lay them on the end table. Andrew made a move to take them, but Sutton slapped his hand away. "Don't worry, I'll make sure they make it safely into your father's hands."

"It'd be easier—"

"No!" It was a tone she'd never used with him. Maybe had never used in her life. She'd never needed to.

Andrew pulled his hand back as if she might strike again at any moment.

"Here it is. Yours if I'm not mistaken, Bree?" She sweetened her tone even if it wasn't with real sugar, pulled out the lacy black thong, and displayed it for both Bree and Andrew, the heart front and center.

Bree's eyes widened. Her hand came up to take it before she caught herself and gnawed on her bottom lip, a habit she'd worked hard to break, as a sore would inevitably pop up. Any other time would see Sutton subtly reminding Bree of this fact, but not today. Her instinctive grab for the underwear reinforced Sutton's position.

Andrew lost his full-bore bravado. She imagined this was how he looked during closing arguments of a case he knew he would lose. Did he ever lose? He would today.

"Why would you think those are Bree's?" he asked.

"They're Bree's because I sold them to her. An expensive special order. See the cute little heart? It matches the tattoo on her hip, but I think you know that. Why wasn't your first question where I found them?"

"I don't know." It was not the answer of a high-powered lawyer but a child whose lies had been exposed.

"Because you do know where I found them, right? Under the seat of your Camaro." She tossed the scrap of lace in the air.

Bree caught it and crumpled it in her hand as if she could make it disintegrate. "It's not what you think." Her voice was small and tear-filled, and Sutton had to drown the spark of sympathy that automatically flared.

"Let me take a stab. I think you and Andrew have been gallivanting across two states screwing each other's brains out for last few months. Am I wrong?" She forced a nonchalance she didn't feel into her voice and face, even locating the gumption for a smile.

Bree put her hand on Andrew's forearm, her red nails a pretty contrast to his dark suit. With their coloring a study in contrasts, they looked like handpicked models for the cover of a magazine. "We're in love, Sutton."

Chapter Four

Sutton took a step back, the words like a punch to her chest, making it hard to catch a full breath. "Are you serious?"

Andrew spun away and ran a hand through his hair, ending up at her front window and leaving Bree to do the dirty work. Sutton stared into Bree's dark, almost black, exotic eyes.

Bree nodded and glanced over her shoulder at Andrew's back. "I was working on the Jordan case and in and out of his office. One thing led to another. We challenge one another. We didn't mean for it to happen."

In love. Somehow that hurt worse than the two of them just having torrid sex. "So I don't challenge you, Andrew?"

He turned and half propped himself against the sill, throwing his hands up and letting them fall. "You're nice. And funny. And laid-back. And that was—is—great. But everything was too easy between us. Too . . . boring."

The word reverberated in her head like a gong. "*Boring?*"

He held his hands up. "Bad word choice. But you can't deny there was never any real passion between us. We haven't been together in months, and I'm not sure you even noticed."

"I've been busy. And so have you." As soon as the words were out of her mouth she regretted them. Yep, he'd been busy all right. Doing Bree.

"I'm really sorry." Bree's voice reminded Sutton of the time Bree ate all the cookies on their sleepover. Except this wasn't cookies she'd taken, but Sutton's fiancé.

Sutton jabbed a finger in Andrew's direction. "You waltzed in here talking about wedding invitations and the governor. How long were you planning to keep up the charade? Were you going to marry me and keep things going with Bree?"

Andrew huffed a few unintelligible words and Bree shuffled around to face him. "We were going to tell you soon. Definitely before the invitations went out. Right, Andrew?"

Sutton would have bet her boutique that *soon* would have never come.

Andrew ran his hand through his hair again, the gesture taking on a vain quality now that Sutton's blinders had been smashed to bits. "Breaking things off with Sutton isn't as straightforward as simply walking away from a relationship. Our families are important in Cottonbloom. Her daddy's a judge. I can't afford to make an enemy of him."

Sutton cast a side-eye toward Bree. The implication was clear; Bree's family—a long line of cotton farmers from the north part of the county—weren't important. While they didn't have the kind of connections Sutton's parents had, they were nice, good people. She had loved spending the night at Bree's house and waking up to pancakes and bacon around their small kitchen table.

"I asked and asked but you told me the time wasn't right." Bree pivoted from Andrew to Sutton. "I wanted to tell you right after the first time something happened. I hated keeping secrets from you."

"Please," Andrew said. "You got off on sneaking around. Don't lie."

Sutton wanted to curl up in the corner, stuff her fingers in her ears, and "la-la-la" until she woke up from this nightmare.

Andrew pushed off the sill and crossed to Sutton. When he tried to take her hands, she stuffed them into the pockets of her pants, the fingers of her right hand sliding over the edge of Wyatt's card.

"Give me a chance to make it up to you, baby." He was the definition of sincere and contrite.

Bree's face crumpled, and she took a step back. Shock, anger, disbelief but also heartbreak. Part of Sutton wanted to take Andrew back if only to strike out at Bree, but that part was small compared to the part that wanted to hurt Andrew somehow. Unfortunately, breaking one of his perfect teeth wasn't in her playbook.

"Too late for that." Sutton ran her finger over the embossed lettering of the card like it was Braille. Words poured out of her mouth, bypassing the logical check of her brain. "Anyway, I have my own confession to make. I haven't missed you, because I've been seeing someone else too."

"What? Who?" His indignation was rich, considering his lover stood not three feet from his side.

"Wyatt Abbott."

"From that car garage over the river?"

"That's right."

"He's a mechanic." He imbued the last word with more than a fair amount of disdain.

"Yes, he is. And a darn good one." She didn't know that to be a fact, but Wyatt's confident air gave the impression of expertise. He was probably good at everything.

"How long has it been going on?"

Sutton dug her hole so deep she couldn't see over the edge. "A while now. I suspected you were cheating, so I . . . so I cheated too. With Wyatt."

"Alright, so we've both had some fun. Let's call it cold feet. We can put that aside and focus on making us work."

A sound that might have been a sob came from Bree. She turned and ran out of the room before Sutton could take a step in her direction. The outer door banged shut and quiet fell between her and Andrew.

"God, you are such a jerk. You broke Bree's heart." The fire that burned through her was swallowed under the avalanche of the truth she'd spoken. *You broke Bree's heart.* Not *you broke* my *heart.* A chill slipped over her, the numbing effect slowing her thought processes. Confused. She was confused and needed to get Andrew out of her house.

"Your daddy is going to be upset if we don't work things out. Everything is booked. Everyone knows even if the invitations haven't gone out. Think of the money and face we'll lose if we cancel now." His voice was smooth and persuasive and had charmed her once upon a time.

"You're worried about the money and face we'll lose?"

"Please. You can't tell me you're not thinking the same."

She clung to her weak lies. "I'm with someone else now. Sorry."

He drew up and put his hands on his narrow hips, his expensive suit jacket fanned out behind him. He reminded her of a lizard who puffed up to look more intimating. "You're only saying that because you found out about me and Bree. I'll bet you're making it all up."

Dangit. She averted her eyes even as she realized the move highlighted her lie. Was she any better than Andrew right now? "I'm not lying."

"Right." He drew the word out. "Are you planning to bring him to the gala then?"

A more colorful curse nearly slipped out. The gala was in less than three weeks. Held at the country club, the event was black tie swanky. As she was on the planning committee this year, and Andrew and his family were the sponsors, going together had been a given.

"That sort of thing really isn't his style."

"So that's a no, and it's because you're not actually seeing Wyatt Abbott. Tell the truth."

In true courtroom style, Andrew had somehow flipped the story to make her feel like the guilty one. Sutton shook her head and drew herself up, refusing to be intimidated by him—outwardly anyway. "You should take Bree. Announce to Cottonbloom that there's a new power couple in town."

His eyes grew hooded; a look she once would have pegged as mysterious now struck her as duplicitous. "I'm still planning on taking you. Once you have a chance to sleep on things tonight, I know you'll decide to do what's right."

"Do what's right for who? You?"

"Your father—"

"This has nothing to do with Daddy." As soon as the words were out, a lightbulb went on. It had everything to with him. She strode to the front door and held it open. "Get out."

He followed more sedately, his casualness a veiled threat in and of itself. Not of physical harm but of a battle not yet conceded. "You're overly emotional. I get that. I did something really dumb, but I was scared. I don't love Bree; I love you."

She didn't believe him. Not anymore. Softer now but with no less steel, she said, "Get out."

"I have a feeling you'll come around. Probably best to not do anything rash like tell your parents. You'll feel differently about things tomorrow."

Would her parents be disappointed? No doubt. But while they might be overly controlling and protective, they loved her and would support her no matter what. "We're not living in medieval Europe. You aren't a lordly prince making an alliance through marriage. I thought you actually cared about me."

"I do."

The answer made her burst out in borderline hysterical laughter. She threw her hand up, intending to shoo him away. Sunlight refracted through the diamond on her finger, sending points of light bouncing. The ring felt like a two-ton anchor. She yanked, but it got stuck at her knuckle.

"Are you freaking kidding me?" she muttered as she twisted and pulled at the ring until her knuckle swelled even more. Frustration clawed at her insides, mixing with the pain of betrayal and anger. "Get. Off. My. Porch."

The condescending amusement on his face sent her careening over the edge of what was polite. Words that would have gotten her mouth washed out with soap as a kid flew from the dark, angry pit that was once her heart.

A fair amount of what she interpreted as disgust crossed his face. "No reason to give me back the ring. We'll talk after you've calmed down." He took the steps at a jog and slid into his BMW. He and Bree even had matching cars. They were perfect for each other.

She craved the satisfaction of throwing the ring at his windshield, but it didn't budge. The thought of lopping her entire finger off and mailing it to him ring and all flashed. Talk about medieval. Or was that something a mobster would do? Speaking of mobsters, did she know anyone that could "take care of Andrew?" Maybe not kill him but rough him up a little?

Her clientele was mostly women with too much money on their hands. She pictured the Quilting Bee ladies going after Andrew with canes and knitting needles. Imagining

Andrew getting beaten up by a gang of little old ladies injected some much-needed humor.

But if she had to wear his ring for another minute, she might resort to the finger chopping. What did they do in movies? Butter. Or oil. She retreated to the kitchen.

Standing over the sink, she poured olive oil over her finger and twisted the ring off with ease. After washing up, she held out her hands. The ring weighed a fraction of an ounce, but a weightless freedom took its place.

She stared at the innocuous bit of metal and stone on her counter in a shaft of sunlight, the beauty of the diamond mocking her. The first step to dismantling their farce of an engagement had been taken. What should have been the easiest step hadn't been.

The rest was too intimidating to consider. She checked in with her sister at the boutique with a vague excuse, but skipped breaking the news to her parents. Instead, she retreated to her bed, even though it wasn't even lunch time yet, crawled under the covers, and let the tears flow.

Wyatt circled the body-sized punching bag hanging from the barn rafters, breathing hard, his muscles burning. Imagining Tarwater's face added extra zing to his punches. The intensity and the rhythm of the workout usually offered relief from his chaotic thoughts. Not tonight.

Sutton Mize lurked in the back of his mind no matter how hard he pushed himself. Had she had it out with Tarwater? Had the asshole convinced her to take him back? How weird would it be if he drove by her place to check on her? Stalker weird or nice weird?

He pictured Sutton's eyes turning from teasing to devastated the instant he'd pulled out that scrap of lace. Shuffling around the swinging bag, he landed a series of jabs. He should have known she wasn't the type of woman to get down and dirty in the front seat of a car. She deserved chilled champagne, six-hundred-thread-count sheets, and rose petals. All that romantic crap he rolled his eyes at when it came across his TV or movie screens.

Breaking the news of the lost job to Mack and Jackson had added another level of stress he needed to work out. Jackson had shrugged and moved on, but Mack's current of worry had quickened. Even though Wyatt hadn't been directly responsible, guilt weighed heavily on him. He launched a flurry of punches.

"What'd that bag ever do to you?"

Wyatt startled around, his hands up. Mack leaned in the doorway of the barn, only a few feet away, his feet crossed at the ankles, his arms over his chest, looking like he'd been there awhile.

"It's been a crazy day." Wyatt aimed a couple more punches at where he imagined Tarwater's face would reside before unlacing the sparring gloves.

"You'll need to call Miss Mize about the car."

"I will. She was pretty tore up this morning. I hate to reopen the wound so soon."

"It can sit for now, but by Monday it needs to get gone one way or another."

"I don't suppose pushing it over a cliff would be at all professional."

Mack's lips twitched into the start of a smile. How long it had been since he'd seen his big brother smile? Too long.

Wyatt slapped the gloves against his leg and looked at Mack from the corner of his eye. "Bottom line, how bad does this loss hit us?"

Mack wandered farther into the barn. "Timing could have been better, but we'll survive."

It would be easy to let Mack's deflection stand, but Wyatt forced more questions. "We won't default on any loans, will we?"

"Lord no. Why would you think that?"

Wyatt tossed his hands in the air. "Because you avoid talking to me or Jackson about the finances. A big part of that is my fault for not pushing you, but I know how much we borrowed to upgrade the shop equipment. Jackson and I had to sign the papers too."

Mack half-sat on the back of the couch. "I'd hoped the Camaro might jump start some word-of-mouth business over the river."

Restoring totaled cars and selling them at auction brought in decent money, but if they wanted to grow their name in classic car circles, they needed some big projects from big names.

"I thought Ford had designated himself our ambassador to the north," Wyatt said sarcastically. "Isn't he supposed to be cultivating our name with the elite?"

Mack made a dismissive sound. "He wants to be reimbursed for every fucking golf game and country club lunch. Business expenses, he says. How many projects has he closed in the last year of rubbing shoulders?"

The answer to the rhetorical question was *one*. And it had just fallen through. "Wanna drink?"

Mack waved him off. Since their pop had died, he hadn't had the time or inclination to relax and drink a beer after work. Lately even their dinners together had grown sporadic.

"Things with Ford will work out. They always do," Wyatt said softly, even though he wasn't sure he believed it this time.

Mack rubbed at the dark stubble at his jaw. "Since Pop died, everything feels different. I have no clue what his end game is and no way to control him."

Although Mack wasn't actually the oldest—Ford took those honors—he was the foundation of the family or maybe the sun that the rest of them orbited. He was also the one who shouldered most of the burdens. Not because

Wyatt and Jackson couldn't, it was just the way things had always been, even when they were kids.

"Trying to control Ford will make him do something stupid to spite you. You need to practice subtlety and manipulation."

Mack sucked in a deep breath and let it out with a slight smile. "Not my strong suit."

Wyatt chuffed a laugh. Mack was tough and straightforward and didn't coddle, but he was also steadfast and loyal and had a giant's heart hidden under his gruffness.

Their brotherly bond, which had veered closer to hero worship on Wyatt's end as kids, had been cemented the day Ford had dared Wyatt to climb the huge magnolia tree at the side of the barn. Wyatt hadn't been able to resist the goading. Fucking Ford and his uncanny ability to get under his skin.

In the Abbott family, authorities weren't called to get you out of self-inflicted troubles. You learned real quick to get yourself out, preferably in one piece. An hour later, he'd made it down with only bruises and scratches, his face streaked with tears. Urging him on, Mack had waited at the bottom to catch him in a hug.

"You want me to cozy up to Ford? See if he'll drop some clues about his plans?" While Wyatt didn't like their brother any more than Mack did, he had something Mack lacked—the ability to snap on a mask of easygoing good humor.

"I hate to ask you to do that." Mack glanced at him from under his lashes.

"I'd be happy to. Anything you need, bro, anytime."

Mack nodded and scraped his boot along the wood floor, his eyes downcast. Something else was bothering him.

"You sure you don't want a beer? Or we could hit the Tavern like old times?" Wyatt asked.

"Nah. I've got some paperwork to finish." He thumbed over his shoulder.

"How about we go fishing this weekend then?"

"I need to evaluate the Charger that came in this morning. Not sure if it's salvageable. Might have to move it to the graveyard." With that, Mack retreated. The garage was his life, his reason for being. Nothing else mattered—except for family.

Worries circled like buzzards after a kill. Troubles were stalking close but Wyatt couldn't see them clearly enough to form a plan of attack or shore up his defenses.

By the time he'd showered and pulled on jeans and a black Abbott Brothers Garage T-shirt, the temperature had downshifted into pleasant territory. Jackson was at the track. Wyatt could head there or to the Tavern on his own, but a vague restlessness needled him like a bug that wouldn't land long enough for him to slap dead. Tonight, he'd chalk it up to Ford and Mack and the garage.

As he was grabbing a beer from the fridge, his ringtone sounded. A Mississippi number popped up on the screen. "Hello?"

"Hi. Hello. It's Sutton Mize." The raw emotion in her wavering voice squashed his leap of satisfaction at her simple greeting. "I hope you don't mind me calling you this late."

"It's not late by my reckoning. How are you doing?" He winced. The polite question usually merited a slingshot, "fine, thanks" answer.

"I'm . . ." She drew the word out.

"Forget I asked that. I'm an idiot. Or so my brothers like to inform me on a daily basis. What can I do to make things better?" He tensed, hoping she didn't blow off the offer as a platitude.

"Actually, I was wondering—" She blew out a sharp breath. "Can we talk? Face to face, I mean."

"I can swing by your place right now." How much of

an eager beaver had he sounded like? He forced a more measured tone. "Or whatever."

"That would be great. I live on—"

"I know where you live. I dropped you off this morning, remember?"

"Of course you did." Her laugh was brittle, but at least it wasn't tears. "It seems like a lifetime ago."

"You need anything?"

"I don't suppose you have a DeLorean tricked out as a time machine under one of those tarps in your barn?" A dry humor laced her voice and the rigid set of his back relaxed. Making jokes was a good sign. Or a sign she was close to a nervous breakdown.

"Afraid not."

"A dump truck of chocolate to bury my troubles under?"

"I might be able to scrounge something up."

"I'll see you soon, then?"

"You can count on me."

She disconnected, and he stared at the phone, his restlessness appeased for the moment. He had a mission and headed to the Hornet with a spring in his step, refusing to examine his change in mood. The car's body curved like a femme fatale, and he skimmed a hand over the smooth metal of the hood on his way to the driver's side.

The garage sat well outside of town on a two-lane parish road that didn't see much traffic. Bad for business, but good for the soul. Clouds wisped across the sky, haloing the almost full moon and casting an eerie light. The hum of cicadas and the call of night birds filled the heart of summer, and lightning bugs flashed in the trees along the side of the road.

He took a deep breath, the loamy air tinged with salt and wood smoke. It was a perfect night for a bonfire and a little trouble. He slid into the seat of his car and ran his fingertips over the leather stitching of the steering wheel.

He cranked the engine and closed his eyes, enjoying the sound, but also listening intently for any knocks or skips. He heard none. Good thing, since he'd added her to the list of cars to take to next month's auction. He'd invest the profit into another project. He'd driven the Hornet a good six months, which was a long time for him. Time to move on. He enjoyed the car, but he wasn't in love.

He flipped on the headlights, popped the clutch, and coasted onto the road. Crossing the river took him into Mississippi. The dividing line of their town and fortunes.

Sixty-plus years earlier, Cottonbloom had been one town. With the opening of the college, the Mississippi side had attracted the doctors and lawyers and professionals, while the crawfish industry and manufacturing ruled the Louisiana side, bringing good blue-collar jobs to the parish.

The economic and social rift grew after WWII, and then sometime in the fifties, the town broke over fishing rights on the river. While there was no push to reunite the towns of Cottonbloom—state loyalties had been bred into the new generations—the divisiveness that marked the last sixty years had eased since the inception of the shared yearly Labor Day festival.

That didn't mean the sides weren't still competitive. The high school football rivalry meant nothing in terms of state titles, and everything in terms of pride. Cottonbloom Park, sitting on the Louisiana side, had been revamped, and a baseball league had restarted and become a major social outlet for both sides.

The divide hadn't affected Wyatt growing up. He'd been happy in Louisiana, in his family, in the garage. His life was complete and whole and happy. Except for the recent troubles with Ford. And that vague restlessness he'd been touched by of late.

He made a pit stop at Glenda's Diner. She had the best pies and cobblers on either side of the river, and he got two slices of lemon meringue to go. He parked in front of Sutton's house, grabbed the carton, and headed to her front door, his stomach flopping like a bullfrog trying to escape a gig. Why was he nervous? This was nothing approaching a date, it was a mission of lemon meringue mercy.

She opened the door before he made it to the front porch steps. Her hair was back in a ponytail, and she was bare-foot and in tight black pants that hugged her curves, her toe nails a glittery, bright purple. The playfulness of the choice surprised him.

Her eyes were red-rimmed and slightly swollen, but she smiled, and although it was strained, her eyes had an echo of the sparkle he'd noted that morning before the shit hit the fan.

"Thanks for coming." She gestured, her movements jerky as if she too were nervous, and led him into a den with bookcases and a wall-mounted TV. The ceilings were low, but instead of feeling closed-in, the room felt cozy.

"I brought two slices of Glenda's famous lemon meringue. Are you game?" He held them out.

She pressed one hand against her stomach and took the carton with the other. "I don't think I've eaten since break-fast. Pie sounds perfect. I'll brew some decaf."

Once she'd disappeared into the kitchen, he moved toward the bookcases. His heel knocked against something, shifting it. A bolt of gauzy dark blue fabric slipped off a stack tucked to the side of the bookcase, unrolling on its fall. He picked it up and did his best to rewrap the slippery fabric, making a mess of it. Hidden partially behind a chair several more bolts were propped against the wall. The fabric stacked on the floor consisted of delicate looking laces and more gauze.

She turned the corner and stopped short. "What are you doing?" Her voice pitched high.

"Sorry. Knocked it over. What's all the fabric for?" He waved a finger over the cache.

She didn't return his smile, marching over to clutch the bolt to her chest as if he'd threatened to drop a baby over a balcony. "It's for nothing."

"It's obviously for *something*."

"A stupid hobby is all." Her half-shouldered shrug and the way she said it made him think she was repeating some-one else. Maybe her parents. Maybe Tarwater.

"I doubt that. Knowing you, it's something very profes-sional and pretty awesome." He might not have gone to college, but he could add two and two. She sold clothes, so why wouldn't she make them too? "Do you design stuff for your shop?"

She shifted the bolt back against the wall into the shad-ows and chewed her lip, her gaze darting toward him. Running her hand over the fabric in a caress, she said, "Not to sell. I'm not good enough."

"Who says?"

"I do. I'm not trained or anything, I taught myself. Trial and error."

"That's how I learned to take an engine apart and put it back together. Nothing wrong with the method." He looked around. "You do your sewing here or at the shop?"

"Here. I turned a spare bedroom into a work area."

"Will you show me?"

"Why would you want to see it?" Suspicion slowed her words.

Why did he want to see it? Maybe because he wanted to know what she was passionate about. What she cared about.

"Curiosity?" When she continued to examine him as if he'd asked to see her medical records, he added in a sing-song voice, "I brought you pie."

"Okay, fine." She led him halfway down the narrow

hallway and stopped with her hand on a doorknob. "You're not allowed to laugh."

The moment had taken on an importance that outweighed a simple show and tell, and he wondered if Tarwater had dismissed her design aspirations. He put a hand over his heart. "I would never."

He held his breath while she took a deep one. Finally, she pushed the door open and flipped the light on. A mechanical marvel of a sewing machine sat under the window. A worktable with a ruled edge was covered in fabrics, and white paper cut in different sized panels were scattered around. In the midst of the chaos, a black dress hung on a headless torso.

The only experience he had with women's clothing was removing it, but even he could tell the dress would be at home in a magazine spread. "You made this?"

"Designed it from scratch." Through the uncertainty and nerves was pride. He recognized the same spark when he finished an engine rebuild.

"I'd bet you'd have women beating down the door at Abigail's for it."

"I couldn't display this next to a Vera Wang. Who would buy it?"

He had no clue what a Vera Wang was so couldn't argue the point. "You'll never know unless you take a chance. You could hang it with the other fancy dresses and see if it sells on its own merit."

She fingered the edge of the sleeve that hung limply on the form. "Just hang it up and see if it catches anyone's eye?"

"What else are you going to do with it? Stick it in the back of your closet? Seems a shame."

He could see the seed sprout even though she didn't respond. She nudged her head toward the door. "Coffee should be perked."

She led him into a kitchen that had been refurbished but retained a quaint, fifties style charm. Black-and-white subway tile supplied the backsplash over dark grey granite countertops. A window over the farmhouse-style sink was framed by blue and white checked curtains.

Their talk turned small and innocuous. They both agreed Rufus's had the best barbeque, but the best pizza was the place just off the river on the Mississippi side.

She moved the slices of pie from the carton onto small white plates in front of bar stools at the high counter next to napkins and forks and poured them both coffee in delicate-looking cups with matching saucers. The contrast with the loft's galley-style kitchen, which was stocked with the finest paper plates and plastic silverware, was telling.

They sat side-by-side and ate the first few bites in silence. About halfway through her piece, she wiped her mouth, cleared her throat, and fiddled with her fork, an air of expectation making him shift toward her.

"I asked you over because"—she took a breath and said on the exhale—"we need to talk."

Even though they weren't involved beyond sharing a handful of childhood memories, one terrible morning, and a piece of pie, the dreaded words ricocheted around his stomach, demolishing his appetite. He put his napkin and fork back by his plate. "Okay."

"I've done something ill-advised." She slipped off the seat and paced on the other side of the counter. "No, I should call a turnip a turnip. I've done something dumb."

"Is this about Tarwater's Camaro?"

"No, but it does have to do with Andrew and Bree." She rubbed her forehead. "You were right that Bree suspected something was up. They both showed up not long after you dropped me off."

"That was bold."

"Yeah, that's what I thought too. Honestly, I got mad. Really mad." She sounded embarrassed about a perfectly normal reaction considering the circumstances.

"Good for you. Did you break something over Tarwater's head?"

No hint of amusement broke through her solemn expression. "I wanted to hurt them—him—and I sort-of, kind-of involved you. I'm so incredibly sorry." The last spurt out on what might have been a sob, but her eyes were dry and huge and her hands covered her mouth. Horror. She was horrified.

Had she killed them and needed help disposing their bodies? He tried a weak laugh. "Am I supposed to be dueling Tarwater at dawn or something?"

"Nothing so chivalrous. I told Andrew and Bree that you and I were involved. Romantically." Her voice dropped to a whisper. "Sexually."

"Well, now." It wasn't often something shocked him. The state left him at a loss for a casual quip.

"I don't think Andrew believed me, but I guess Bree did. Or wants to anyway. I got a couple of calls this evening from *friends*"—she imbued the word with sarcasm—"asking about you and me in a very roundabout way, and I realized things had already spun out of control. I didn't want you to hear from someone else. Please, don't hate me."

She was back to covering her mouth. This time her eyes shimmered with tears, but not because her fiancé had cheated on her with her best friend. No, she was upset and worried about how the rumor might affect him.

"You think a little talk about the two of us together would make me mad?"

"I don't even know if you have a girlfriend. She might—"

"I don't have a girlfriend." He picked up his fork and took another bite of pie, his appetite fully restored. In fact, he felt downright jolly all of a sudden. "I don't mind you using me as a shield, if that's the kind of help you need."

"But I told them we'd been involved for a while."

He shrugged and took another bite, her worry over his reaction tipping him to the edge of laughter, although he was careful to hide it. "How does Glenda get her crust to taste so good, do you think?"

Her lips moved, but no sound came out. Finally, she said, "A heap of Crisco and some lemon zest, I would guess."

He hummed, scraping up the crumbs. "I might take up baking if I can charm the recipe out of her. What are my chances, do you think?"

"Wyatt." Her firm tone had him looking up. "Do you understand what I've done? I've told a lie that now involves you, and if everyone isn't already talking about us, they will be tomorrow."

"You make it sound like this is the worst thing you've ever done." He made a scoffing sound.

Her eyes flared wider, her lips pinched, and she gave a tiny shake of her head.

"Good Lord. This is the worst thing you've ever done, isn't it?" A smile defeated his best efforts to keep his amusement at bay.

She took up pacing again, her thrumming angry-tinged energy hypnotic. "Bree stood there and told me they were in love. *In love.* It was humiliating and embarrassing, and I was so mad. Your card was in my pocket, and I just . . . gah!" She stuck her tongue out and made a gagging sound.

Now he did laugh. "For a minute there, I thought you'd killed them and needed help dumping their bodies out in the swamps."

"You thought I had murdered them in a fit of jealousy?" Her laugh was throaty and unexpectedly sexy. "You underestimate my pathetic niceness."

Her self-depreciating summation gave him pause, but before he could delve further, the doorbell chimed followed by a quick rap on the front door. Sutton froze, her laughter silenced, her smile pulling into a grimace.

"You expecting company?" He slid off the barstool and brushed his hands together.

She shook her head.

"Let's really give them something to talk about, shall we?" Wyatt waggled his eyebrows and stepped toward the door. She caught his wrist as he reached the foyer. Although he could easily pull out of her grasp, he paused and she grabbed onto both his arms.

"It could be my mother. Or father. Or even Andrew."

A shadow was visible through the window, the street light giving it monster-like proportions. Wyatt bristled with aggression. Even though his knuckles were sore from his earlier round with the punching bag, he wouldn't mind teaching Tarwater a lesson in basic human decency in the most primal way.

"One can hope," he said darkly. "My car's parked in your driveway. Won't be hard to connect the dots from it to me, but I'll slip out the back if you want."

Her hands tightened on his arms, the foyer too dim to make out her expression, but her voice was strong. "No, I want you to stay."

He went for the doorknob, wrapped a steadying arm around her waist, pasted on the smile that had charmed more than one woman home with him, and opened the door.

Bree Randall stood on the other side, wearing the same clothes from that morning, but looking unkempt. Her blouse was untucked, her mascara had smudged around her eyes, and her hair looked like she'd driven over with her head stuck out of the window.

Sutton tensed. He squeezed her waist, and she took the signal, letting her weight fall into him.

Bree's astonishment was projected clearly by her darting eyes. "You weren't lying?"

Chapter Five

Sutton's senses went into overdrive. The feel of Wyatt's soft cotton shirt under her fingertips and the hard planes of his chest under that. His scent of clean laundry and the pine she'd noted earlier in his loft. Was it an aftershave or cologne, or had he absorbed the magic of the pine trees around the barn?

His hair was a smidge too long to be classified as neat, and he hadn't shaved in a couple of days. With his black T-shirt half-tucked, his broken-in jeans, and scuffed boots, he skated on the edge of sloppy but somehow managed to fall into the category of sexily rumpled. So different from Andrew, who kept himself well-groomed. Metrosexual, she'd once joked. Only once, because he'd taken offense at the term.

Wyatt was a few inches taller than she was, but not so tall as to cause a crick in her neck. She stared at his profile and the way his dark hair curled a little at the ends. He was saying something. Like a radio dialing into a station, his words registered out of the static of her brain. ". . . lying. What kind of person poaches her best friend's fiancé?"

"It's not like she's all good and innocent like she wants

everyone to believe, considering . . ." Bree waved her hand around. Her dismissive huff was more defensive than insulting, but her next words fell between them like flint to dynamite. "I sure never expected her to hook up over the river with someone like you, though."

"What's that supposed to mean?" Sutton turned and put herself between Wyatt and Bree, her back to his front. Tension wound Wyatt's muscles tight with static energy, ready to explode.

Bree's gaze met hers, and Sutton could see the arrow being drawn. "You've always acted like you're better than the rest of us. Holier than thou. You"—Bree flicked her gaze over Sutton's shoulder to touch Wyatt before it returned with another arrow notched—"are not his type. He'll get bored with you soon enough. Like Andrew did."

Her words landed like a physical blow. "Have you always hated me?"

Bree's face changed, and she deflated, her body curling in on itself. One of her red-tipped nails, the formerly perfect manicure chipped, found its way between her teeth. "I don't hate you. I didn't mean any of that. Not really. I came here to talk."

"Fine." Sutton gave a sharp nod. Bree stepped forward but Sutton put her hand on the doorjamb, blocking any path inside. "Say your piece out here."

Wyatt hadn't moved, a solid wall that gave her strength. She reached behind her, finding his hand, and he laced their fingers. The strangeness of the situation wasn't lost on Sutton, but she didn't have to time to examine the implications.

"Alone?" Bree's voice was small and thin and contained none of the confidence she had honed over the years.

Maybe Sutton was weak or just plain dumb as she'd told Wyatt, but she loosened her hand from his and turned to catch his eye. "Go on. I'll be okay."

Wyatt gave her waist an answering squeeze. The gesture from a man she'd not particularly liked when they were young, yet who had her back—literally—lent everything an unreal cast. Add to the fact the girl she'd known all her life was spouting hate toward her, and the universe's fundamental laws seemed topsy-turvy.

Wyatt retreated into the house. Waiting until he was out of sight, Sutton stepped out onto the porch and leaned against the metal railing.

Bree nudged her chin toward the door. "Andrew thinks you lied about him."

"Is that what you came over to talk about?"

Bree smoothed her hair, but it was a lost cause without a straightening iron. "It wasn't planned, you know. Andrew and me. It just happened."

Sutton's hum was dry and ironic, but she wanted to believe Bree. Wanted to believe it was a crime of passion.

"I dropped some files off late, and we ordered a pizza and talked about the case and then about the engagement and other stuff. We have a lot in common. He made me laugh and feel." Bree tilted her face to the sky and shook her head, but not before Sutton noticed her brimming tears, "important and smart and desirable. It didn't start as sex. That's what I wanted you to know."

A branch from a burning bush curved over the porch rail. She needed to trim it. The mundane thought filtered through the clamor of painful realizations. It was a thousand times worse to know their affair hadn't started with simple sex. Bree and Andrew had discussed her and found her lacking. She fingered the fiery red leaves, plucking them off one by one. They hit the white porch flooring like drops of blood.

But another fact emerged from the stew of betrayal and humiliation. Losing Andrew would require a Band-Aid; losing Bree would require a heart transplant. Would all her memories of Bree be tainted? Besides her family, Bree was the one constant in her life. Now that constant was gone, and the equation had to be rebalanced.

After denuding the branch as far as she could reach, Sutton crossed her arms and stared at the trail of blood-colored leaves. "What do you want from me? My blessing? Fine. You have it. Ride off into the sunset with your Prince Charming."

"Oh God." The anguish in Bree's voice drew Sutton's gaze up. Bree was fisting her hair and rocking slightly on her feet. "He ended it with me tonight. Told me he's going to win you back."

"But I thought the two of you were *in love*?" Her words hit their target, and the petty, humiliated part of her celebrated with jazz hands and high kicks.

"He still loves me," Bree said with a conviction not reflected in her body language. A tear slipped down Bree's cheek, and she sniffled.

"Is this your way of apologizing? Because this is seriously the worst apology ever."

"I'm sorry. I really am." Bree wiped her cheek with the palm of her hand like a little kid. "I want you to promise not to take him back."

Any bloom of sympathy wilted under a bleak sadness. When had their friendship taken a detour? Nothing Andrew could do would persuade her to take him back, but she didn't say that aloud.

Bree chewed on her bottom lip, worrying a red place that was sure to get bigger. "You'll forgive me, right? You always do."

Sutton didn't merit a heartfelt show of anything from Bree. God, she really was a pushover. Too easy-going. Well, no more. Things were going change starting now. "Are you out of your ever-loving mind? This isn't like the time you ripped my 'N Sync T-shirt in fifth grade.

Don't text me. Don't call me. Don't stop by. I don't want to see you."

"For how long?"

"I don't know. Maybe forever." While she wished the sentiment could come to pass, practically speaking, they would run across each other. Cottonbloom was hardly a metropolis. At the very least, unless one of them skipped it, they would all be at the gala ignoring whispers and dodging awkward conversations.

"I know you don't mean that. Listen, I'll call you tomorrow, okay?" Bree backed down the steps holding Sutton's gaze.

"Whatever," Sutton said under her breath. The role of forgiving nice girl who never rocked the boat would have to go to her understudy tonight. Not only was she going to rock the boat, she planned to blow the mother-flipping thing to smithereens.

As Bree's taillights disappeared, Wyatt stepped out. "Nice."

She bristled. The innocuous word took on shades of a four-letter epitaph. "You think I was too nice? You think I should have shoved her down the porch steps? Were you hoping to see a girl fight?"

He didn't smile but humor seemed to emanate from him like a natural scent. "I'm not condoning assault and battery in any form. I meant nice job of not caving."

Sutton let her balled-up hands fall from her hips to the rail behind her. He was right; for once, she hadn't caved. "I've always been the peacemaker. The compromiser. Now I see what that really means."

"And what's that?"

"It means I'm weak. And stupid."

"That's not true," he said gently but with a firmness that eased her self-castigation.

"Maybe not stupid, but way too fu-u-u"—she stumbled

over the word she really wanted to say and threw her hands in the air—"frigging nice. See, I can't even make myself say the f-word."

His lips twitched once, but then his eyes narrowed and pinned her with an unexpected intensity. "I'm curious, and you don't have to answer if you don't want to, or haven't decided, but will you take him back?"

"Not if hell freezes over. Not if it snows in Mississippi in July. Not even if a wizard gifted him a heart."

"So that's a hard pass?"

Somehow she found her lips curling into a smile to match his. "Hard as the diamond I'm going to throw in his face."

Headlights flashed as a dark car turned onto her street. She squinted her eyes. "Nuts. It's Andrew."

Wyatt didn't even glance over his shoulder. "You want to rub it in his face?"

"Rub what?"

"We're supposed to be seeing each other, right?" He stepped forward, wrapped an arm around her waist, and hauled her up against his body. "Kiss me."

"Wh-what?" She lay her hands flat on his chest, thinking she should push him away, but not actually doing it.

"You want to gig Tarwater? Kiss me."

She dropped her gaze from his hypnotic eyes to his expressive lips. Neither smiling nor frowning, but parted, the invitation clear. She dabbed her tongue on her bottom lip.

A kiss right here, right now would be on the edge of wild and reckless. Hadn't she lamented the fact she was too nice and normal and . . . beige. Yep, that's what she was. Or even worse, maybe taupe.

Wyatt was all color. His energy, his laughter, his impetuousness. She craved color in her life. In an attempt to muffle her inner monologue, she relaxed against him and ran her hands up his chest to link around his neck, his hair tickling her fingers.

She was attracted to him. She'd recognized the pull that morning even as she'd denied and squashed the urge. Now she gave herself over to the feeling, fisting her hands in the soft strands and fitting her body close.

A flare of amusement had his lips quirking, but she didn't sense he was laughing at her expense. A car door slammed, but Sutton couldn't tear her gaze away from his face. His eyes were gray, but in the shadows they appeared as black as the night sky, deep and limitless.

Without letting sensibility overrule her burst of recklessness, she popped up on her toes and mashed her lips to his, cursing her lack of finesse. Before embarrassment seized hold, he took control, easing the pressure enough so he could take her bottom lip between his teeth and run his tongue along it. She gasped, her nerve endings firing like she'd stuck her finger in a socket.

Everything turned vague and fuzzy except for Wyatt himself. She became hyper-aware of everything about him. The ends of his hair curled around her fingers. His chest was hard and his arms even harder. He dominated her, but instead of trepidation, a warmth spread from her stomach outward. Car tires squealed but registered in a different dimension.

One of Wyatt's hands smoothed down her back and cupped her bottom. She arched into his touch and snaked a leg around his calf. All the while, his lips and tongue worked an alchemy that incited both lassitude and desperation. She could remain in the sphere they'd created together for the rest of the night.

Wyatt lifted his head. A mewl of protest came from something inside of her he'd awakened, and she coasted her lips along the stubble of his cheek, searching for his mouth. Searching for more. She found what she sought and pressed closer to him, dropping her hands from his hair to run along his shoulders and back.

With a rumble that made the place between her legs quake, he dropped both hands to her bottom and maneuvered her around until her back was against the brick side of her house, his weight pressing into her from shoulders to hips. She could feel him, all of him, against her. He wanted her. This wasn't a pity kiss. Or at least not *just* a pity kiss. She wasn't so taupey beige boring that she couldn't arouse him.

A honking car alarm a few houses down burst the spell. His hands jerked and fell away from her butt. He put a few inches between their torsos, although his hips still pressed into hers. She squirmed against him, her body not ready to cede control to the growing part of her that was more than slightly aghast at their public display.

He studied her, his eyes unreadable in the dark, his usual good humor not present. Her jangling nerves sent words tripping out of her mouth. "I think he saw us."

"Doubt he could have missed that." Still, he didn't release her.

She was thankful for the bulk of the house at her back. Her knees were as wobbly as if they'd been shot with Novocain. "We put on a good show, huh?"

"Was that what it was then? A show for your ex?" He took a step back but kept her caged in by his arms on the side of the house.

A glance to her left showed his right forearm, dotted with dark hair, and muscled. The urge to lean into it and run her lips along the length was strong. He raised an eyebrow as if expecting an answer to his question. She'd hoped it was rhetorical.

"Wasn't it? Something for him to think about?" Although they were a repeat of his words from earlier, undercurrents of anger wavered from him. The people pleaser inside of her reared, and the two words popped out before she even had a chance to consider why. "I'm sorry."

"For what? Are you sorry we kissed?"

Her thoughts scattered as she tried to get a read on him, but his expression remained a mystery. Ironic considering how jokey and transparent he normally seemed. Was there more to him than the annoying kid she remembered or the laid-back party boy people talked about?

She tried to locate an innocuous reply, but only the truth resided in the mish-mash of desires in her heart. "No, I'm not sorry we kissed. Are you?"

Her voice sounded raw with a wealth of uncertainty from her recent rejection. What could Wyatt say? He *was* sorry. Sorry he'd opened the Pandora's Box that was Sutton Mize. Their blazing, unexpected kiss had unleashed something he wasn't sure could be contained. He wanted her. Badly. And, based on her response, she wanted him too.

Yet she was in a terrible place. Betrayed by both her fiancé and her best friend. How long did it take to recover from something like that? Days? Months? Years? Fate had dropped him into her life at the worst possible time—or best, depending on your outlook. She was ripe for a rebound.

Even through all the crap that had been dumped on her over the course of a day, her spirit shined through like the first rays of sun after a storm. Which was why he refused be *that* guy. The one who made her forget for a little while only to leave her more broken in the morning.

"You want to come back inside?" The invitation was muddied by the confusion in her voice.

He backed away until the back of his thighs hit the porch rail, and he grabbed hold of the rough metal to keep from grabbing her. "I'm working tomorrow. Got to get up early."

A few years ago, he might have talked himself into staying and justifying his actions by saying they were both con-
senting adults. But he'd changed and couldn't pinpoint
when. Even before his pop had died, the parties, the drinking, the supposedly good times had worn him down. Friends
of his that he'd once pitied, after they'd gotten married
and tied down, incited a sharp pang in his chest when he
saw them out and about. His pop might have smiled and
told him he was growing up. Finally.

It was a damn shame too, because he would have loved
to discover all the places Sutton's blushes flared and wake
to her tousled hair and sleepy eyes. Eyes that would turn
mortified by morning. She would end up hating herself and
even worse, hating him. He couldn't bear the thought of
taking advantage of her vulnerability. She deserved better
than Tarwater and better than a one-night rebound.

He shuffled toward the porch stairs. "I'll be around. You
call or text if something changes or you need to talk or
whatever. I'm serious."

She stepped forward as he stepped back. "Could I ask
a favor?"

He planted his feet even as his body leaned toward her,
dreading and anticipating her request. If she asked him
outright to take her to bed, he wasn't sure his gentlemanly
impulses would withstand the direct assault. "Shoot."

"I've made a mess of things. Until I figure out how to
handle it, could you not deny anything is going on? I know
it's a lot to ask."

Disappointment and relief mixed like a science experi-
ment gone bad. "Sure. We don't get many gossips at the
garage, believe it or not. Except for my aunts." He wouldn't
be surprised to see his aunts Hyacinth and Hazel first
thing, and outright lying to them was not an option.

"I set myself up for the humiliation of two public re-
jections in less than twenty-four hours. I mean, who does

that?" A dry self-deprecating humor bubbled up. Maybe it was her coping mechanism or maybe her natural optimism, but either way, her attitude made him want to kiss her again.

One kiss he could recover from. Eventually, he'd forget about the way she felt in his arms—soft and needy and pliant—and move on. Two kisses might be his tipping point.

"Bye, Sutton." He continued a backward shuffle toward his car.

She stood framed by the light of her door. Raising her ring-less left hand, she gave him a little wave and disappeared. He banged his forehead against the steering wheel a couple of times before heading over the river and to his empty bed. Doing the right thing was the worst.

Chapter Six

Wyatt heard his aunt Hyacinth before he caught sight of her. She was gregarious and funny and well-liked. No doubt, Hazel was somewhere, taking everything in with her silences that said more than any lecture. The sisters were a little too much like him and Jackson for comfort.

Hyacinth rounded the corner in an Adidas tracksuit, still spry at sixty-something. Neither of his aunts encouraged birthday celebrations, so it was difficult to nail down their exact age. Probably something to do with the way they were raised, the oldest of six and raised marsh-mud poor. His pop had been the youngest, but ironically, the aunts were the last of the siblings left on this side of the graveyard.

Wyatt hauled himself out of the pit to give her a hug, taking care not to smear her with grease or dent the helmet of nut-brown hair she had done once a week at the beauty salon. With a broad face, prominent nose, and too-wide mouth, she'd never qualified as a great beauty like Hazel, yet something about her was distinctly appealing, and she'd turned down a number of marriage proposals.

He'd asked her once if she regretted not saying 'yes,'

and she'd smiled and told him marriage wasn't her destiny. The twin curse struck again.

"You having trouble with the Crown Vic again?" he asked.

"Do I have to wait until I have car trouble to see my favorite nephew?"

He was immune to her buttering-up smile. The brothers took turns holding the favored spot depending on what she was after. "Of course you don't."

The aunts had answered the call of duty after his mother had left but Wyatt had never felt like a burden. He counted himself lucky to be part of a family that took care of its own. Not everyone could say the same.

His mind drifted to Sutton. She had seemed so alone. Lonely. Had he done more damage walking away like he did? His thoughts took a turn. That kiss . . . it had been—

"Wyatt." His aunt snapped so close to his face, her hand was blurry.

"What?" He refocused on her.

She propped her hand on her hip, her gaze pointed and one corner of her mouth drawn back. "I said, people are whispering about you."

At least Sutton had given him a fair heads up. His reputation was tarnished enough not to show any additional mudslinging. "Don't tell me some silly rumors brought you down to the shop."

"Silly? I heard you broke old Judge Mize's daughter and that Tarwater boy up? True or not?"

Sutton needed time to do damage control, but evasion was easier said than done when faced with his aunt. He turned to the car and applied the socket wrench to an already-tightened bolt. "You know how it is."

"Not so much. Why don't you enlighten me, young man?"

Lord help him. "Young man" was one step away from the use of his full name. He didn't see any way out of this but to tell at least the partial truth. Not without drawing her wrath down on his head which meant no casseroles or cobblers dropped off for weeks. And peaches were at their peak. Jackson and Mack would put his balls in a vise.

He scratched his twitching eyebrow. It was his tell, and she knew it. "It's complicated."

"Wyatt Jedidiah Abbott."

And . . . there it was. He winced as if the words held some physical power over him.

She continued. "You bear the name of a great man. A general in the Confederate army. Try to live up to it."

Pointing out that his ancestor was on the wrong side of moral history and was spoken about less than kindly by the darker-skinned branches of their family tree wouldn't help his cobbler cause. "The gossip is exaggerated. It's true that Sutton and Tarwater have ended their engagement, but I played no part in it. I assure you, I haven't brought disgrace to our family name."

"Are you acting a gentleman?"

"I have acted totally and completely a gentleman." The scorching kiss aside, by walking away last night, he could claim the title with nary an eyebrow twitch.

The tension in his aunt's face eased, the crinkles smoothing, even as her color remained high. "How in the world did your paths cross?"

"That cherry-red Camaro in the parking lot."

"It would be over a car. When's the last time I saw you at church, young man?"

At least she hadn't invoked his full name again. "Easter?"

"There are all sorts of nice girls at the First Baptist I could introduce you to."

"Sutton is a nice girl." The words popped out with a

defensiveness he hadn't had the chance to mask. His aunt's gaze sharpened like a set of ginsu knives hawked on her favorite channel—the Home Shopping Network.

"I see." Curiosity and speculation dripped from the two words. She didn't question him further yet didn't break their stare either.

The sweat prickling his neck had nothing to do with the heat. Even as familiar as he was with her methods of obtaining confessions, he broke. "I know it's a lot to ask, but please don't stoke the fires more."

"It's all my Bible study will want to discuss."

"Isn't there some Bible verse about the sinful nature of gossip you can throw out?"

His aunt's eyes took on the light of a religious zealot. *"Keep your tongue from Evil, And your lips from speaking deceit."* Hyacinth could spout scripture from one side of her mouth while tippling moonshine with the other.

Wyatt put his arm around her shoulder for a quick squeeze. "Sounds perfect. Where's Aunt Hazel?"

"Giving Ford the what-for. Although I doubt it will do any good. It's like talking to a termite-riddled tree stump."

"I didn't realize he was back." Wyatt was torn between dread and glee. There would be hell to pay once Ford found out about the loss of the Camaro job, but watching his diminutive Aunt Hazel lay into Ford was something not to be missed. He waggled his eyebrows. "Let's go see how he's faring."

"So unchristianlike," she muttered, but followed close on his heels, potential lightning-strike be damned.

He shuffled up next to Jackson as their aunt Hazel said, "Ford Jubal Abbott, have you forgot your raising?"

Suppressing a snicker, he elbowed Jackson who didn't look over but the corner of his mouth twitched enough to flash his dimple. Hazel had a temper that was difficult to rouse but once awakened was legendary.

Ford stood over her with his hands fisted in the front pockets of his khakis. "What raising? All Pop cared about was the garage."

Mack stepped forward. "That's not true and you know it. Pop worked hard to keep us clothed and fed. He turned this place into a business that we could all be proud of."

Ford's muttered obscenity had Hyacinth performing a faux pearl clutch. Any residual humor leaked out of the situation like oil from a blown gasket.

"You'd best apologize. Then get your butt under a hood and earn your keep." Mack jabbed a finger toward Ford. No one doubted or questioned Mack's authority on the shop floor. Except for Ford.

"I inherited a quarter of this place just like you. I got my degree and came back to help build the restoration side of the business. Don't you think I want it to succeed? Except you don't trust me, do you?"

Mack's silence was answer enough. Not that Wyatt blamed Mack, because Ford wasn't exactly a model employee, but he was their brother. And, damn, his feelings looked genuinely hurt.

While Wyatt didn't particularly want to play Ford's champion, he found himself stepping forward anyway. "We appreciate what you're doing, bro." He ignored Mack's side-eye and clapped Ford on the shoulder. "Did you make any headway in Mobile?"

"I didn't get anything signed, but—"

Mack's harrumph squirted lighter fluid on the combustible situation.

"What if I sold my share to a stranger? What would you do then?" Ford and Mack squared off like two alphas.

Wyatt sucked in a breath between his teeth. That kind of talk was traitorous. Instead of threatening to string him up by his toenails, Mack remained calm. Too calm. "This is a family business and it's going to stay that way."

"Is it? I've got someone lined up that's willing to pay me more than my share's worth. I'd be a fool not to take it."

Wyatt's stomach fell away as the ramifications swirled.

"Ford, you can't mean that." Hazel reached for his hand, but Mack beat her, grabbing Ford's shirt and hauling him within reach of his other fist. Hyacinth pulled Hazel to the periphery of what was turning ugly.

Mack's control had snapped like a rubber band stretched too thin. "Who is it?" When Ford didn't answer, Mack shook him, and said, "I should—"

A clatter sounded from the bay door and everyone turned. Sutton Mize was bent at the waist, righting a portable jack.

"Hi." She waved a hand that was painted with a line of black grease. She was in a blue-and-white polka-dot dress and heeled sandals.

A shock of pleasure blew hot in his chest but morphed into worry. She was avoiding his gaze like he had cooties. Had she gotten back together with Tarwater?

Mack gave Ford a slight warning shove on his release. "Miss Mize, you must be here for the car. Let me get the keys."

"The car?" Her confusion in turn confused Mack.

"Your fiancé, I mean, Tarwater's Camaro," Mack said. "That's why you're here, right?"

"Oh, *that* car." As if surprised it was still there, she glanced over her shoulder where the chrome bumper of Andrew's car was visible under a protective cover in the parking lot. Clearing her throat, she finally met Wyatt's eyes. "Actually, that's not why I'm here. Sorry I interrupted your . . . discussion, but I was hoping to borrow Wyatt for a minute."

Wyatt took a step toward her, already determined to give her whatever help she needed.

* * *

The logical plan Sutton had hatched at midnight after spending hours tossing and turning in her bed qualified as delusional and borderline crazy in the face of so many stares.

No one had even noticed her drive up or step inside. The tension in the garage was palpable. If she hadn't knocked over some metal arm-looking thing on her shuffle backwards, then she might have made an escape to live another day instead of dying of embarrassment. The glance she shot toward Wyatt sealed her fate. She flushed as if he'd telepathically triggered the memory of their kiss.

"I've got some calls to make." Mack cleared his throat and retreated, his gaze pinging between her and Wyatt.

Ford's smile seemed genuine. "Sutton. A pleasure to see you. I hope these boys are treating you and that pretty little Camaro well. Andrew's going to love his surprise."

Her face heated. Ford must not have heard about her and Andrew. Or her and Wyatt for that matter. That only made things worse in a way. She wasn't sure she could stomach repeating the news over and over.

"Nice to see you too, Ford." She flapped the neck of her dress to counteract her heated anxiety.

Jackson had slid under a car, leaving only his legs in view, but a woman in baggy coveralls and a ball cap pulled low kept one eye on the unfolding drama. Two older ladies who looked nothing alike yet seemed to go together like salt and pepper shakers were also not-so-subtly eavesdropping.

"Sorry I wasn't here yesterday to get things settled, but I've been down in Mobile drumming up business. Andrew's a lucky man snagging a woman willing to overhaul his Camaro." Ford shifted and waved his hand toward the parking lot. "Willa, why don't you move it into a bay?"

Willa didn't move or speak, reminding Sutton of a trapped animal. This was likely to be the first of many awkward moments, as the news filtered through town. She held up her left hand and wiggled her bare fingers as if presenting exhibit A in a trial. "Andrew and I are not together anymore."

"Not together?" His voice was incredulous, and she braced herself for probing personal questions, but instead he asked, "What about the Camaro? Are you cancelling the contract? You can't do that."

"I . . . I . . ." She had signed something but hadn't read the fine print. Was she obligated to pay a penalty? After all the trouble she'd put Wyatt through, she should pay something. She already owed him more than she could repay. Again, she questioned her sanity in coming.

"Come on, we can talk out back." Wyatt ignored Ford, and his warm smile helped order her jumbled thoughts. When he held out his hand, she grabbed hold as if it were as natural as the birds singing at dawn or the lightning bugs coming out at dusk in the summer.

"Sorry." She sent Ford a tight smile and wondered what he was thinking about her.

Actually, the exchange was a perfect example of her issues. She cared too much about what people thought. Always had. Had she been born that way or conditioned by parents who made decisions with consideration of their place in Cottonbloom society? The age-old question of nature or nurture.

Wyatt traced the same path to the barn they had taken the previous morning. This time, though, she was more determined than devastated.

"You want something to drink?" He moved to the small fridge that hummed in the corner.

"Iced tea if you've got it."

He returned with two red Solo cups filled with ice and tea. She took a sip, buying time to figure out how to present her plan, but he beat her to the punch.

"Not sure how much you heard or inferred, but please ignore the family drama."

"Sorry I interrupted. I was trying to ease back out before I hit that thing with the arms." She rubbed at the grease on her palm with a finger, smearing it.

"Let's get you cleaned up before you ruin that pretty dress." He pulled a disposable wipe out of a canister and took her hand in his.

The cloth was cool and damp against her skin and smelled faintly of lemons. He wiped long after all traces of black were gone, his thumb glancing over her fluttering pulse point before letting go. Her hand hung suspended in the air before she came to her senses and pulled it to her side.

"That thing was a car jack, by the way." At her shrug, he asked, "Haven't you ever had to change a flat tire?"

"It's only happened twice, and I called Aaron's Garage."

He clutched at his chest. "Darlin', that hurts. Aaron is barely qualified to operate a car jack."

Her lips twitched despite her mounting nerves. "He's perfectly nice and capable."

"Not as capable as me." The intonation in his voice made her think of things other than simple mechanics, and she swallowed past a sudden lump.

She stuttered out a few words that made no sense together and ended up nodding and taking another sip of tea.

"Next time you have a flat, you call me." He leaned against the back of the couch and crossed his feet at the ankles, a repose of casual confidence. "Or better yet, I'll teach you how to do it yourself."

"That sounds fun." Silence fell between them. The kind that made heat rush up her neck and into her face. "Listen, about what Ford said, do I owe you something for pulling out of the deal?"

"Naw." He dropped his gaze and stomped on a raised nail in the flooring.

She did owe them, but he was too nice to make her cough up the money. "Be honest, Wyatt, is this going to leave the garage in a fix? Financially, I mean?"

"The money was decent, but we hoped the Camaro would bring us more high-end restorations from your side of the river. Don't worry about it, we'll find another foothold."

She shuffled to the open barn doors and gazed over the woods, her mind spinning. His admission had given her the leverage to work her plan into reality.

With her father's reelection campaign in full swing and the gala approaching, her social calendar was exploding. Instead of being the object of condemnation, poor, spurned Andrew would garner sympathy, and Sutton would be forced to wear her Scarlett Letter.

If she showed up alone, people would assume either she'd had a one-night stand with Wyatt and gotten caught by Andrew, or she'd made the entire thing up. Which she had. The practical part of her insisted on taking the high road. Let the drama play out with a faked serenity. Except the petty, humiliated part of her wanted the opposite.

"You're probably wondering why I'm here," she said.

"You don't need a reason to stop by the garage." He bit at his lower lip. "By the way, my aunt Hyacinth's Bible study down at the First Baptist is hot on the trail. I managed to put her off with a partial truth, but I couldn't outright lie."

The gossip about her and Wyatt had legs like a Louisiana jackrabbit. While she was surprised how quickly word spread to this side of the river, the fact he couldn't lie to his aunt poked both her guilt and relief into life. "I feel terrible about putting you in this position. I'll bet you rue the day I walked in your garage."

"*Rue the day.*" He repeated the phrase with a dark, dramatic flair, then chuckled. "That sounds unnecessarily dire. Anyway, technically, you drove into my garage."

She wished she possessed the confidence he had in his little finger. Instead, her courage frayed. Through the pounding of her heart and a tight throat, she said, "I want to make a deal."

"Does this have something to do with Tarwater? Has he been harassing you?"

"I've seen neither hide nor hair of him." Agitation prodded her into a pace, and she held her cup so tightly that the plastic caved in and made a crinkly noise.

She set it down and forced her hands still. "It's actually more like a business arrangement."

A wariness tempered his sympathy. "Go on."

She debated the merits of running back to her car, heading home, and burying her head under the covers for the foreseeable future. Instead, she launched into the little speech she'd practiced in the shower. "I know that we didn't get along as kids, but it seems like—"

"Hold up." He raised his hand. "Why do you keep saying that?"

Veering off script this early scrambled her already exhausted brain. "Because it's true. You picked on me constantly and wouldn't leave me alone. You threw a snake on me. An honest-to-God snake."

"It was a baby garter snake. Not more than six inches long. And I didn't throw it exactly. It wiggled out of my hands." His wide-eyed innocence was ruined by a mischievous half smile. "I thought girls loved baby animals."

"Yeah, fuzzy ones. Cute ones. Not slimy poisonous ones."

"Garter snakes aren't venomous. Or slimy, for that matter. Now if it'd been a salamander—"

"It was not cool." She pressed her temples. "Did you

interpret my scream as one of delight? And how about the time you followed me into woods and scared me so bad, I fell into the river? My dress got ruined."

"To be fair, my plan was to make you laugh. I had no idea you were that clumsy. But I jumped in after you. I wouldn't have let anything bad happen to you. That's why I followed you. To keep you safe." Although he retained a slight smile, his eyes had grown darker and stormier.

She wasn't sure how to marry their differing memories of the same events. "Whatever. That's all in the past. It's the here and now that concerns me. Look, I need to be able to hold my head up in this town."

"You haven't done anything wrong."

"In reality, no, but instead of Andrew being the bad guy, people are assuming that he broke up with me because of something you and I did."

"So?"

"*So*? Everyone thinks it's *my* soul needs praying for on Sunday morning and not his, dangit."

"Someone actually said that?" His lips twitched, and in a few years maybe she would see the humor in the situation. Today was not that day.

"Not outright, but I'm surprised lightning hasn't destroyed half of Cottonbloom with all the faked piety that was shoved at me this morning." The unusual amount of foot traffic in the shop from Junior League members and churchgoers had set off alarms. All of them had attempted to work the conversation around to her and Andrew and Wyatt. Especially Wyatt. "Your reputation doesn't help matters."

His twitching lips fell into a frown. "What reputation?"

"People say you know how to have a good time and tend to—" *Sleep around* wasn't exactly accurate, but he'd left a string of broken-hearted women in his wake. "Not commit to one woman for very long."

If she had to quantify his expression, it looked like hurt

feelings. "You should know better than anyone not to believe everything you hear."

"Of course I don't believe it." From the look on his face, her denial registered as weak at best. And, to be honest, she was counting on his casual attitude when it came to dating. Or fake dating.

He crossed his arms over his chest. "What exactly do you want from me?"

She had offended him. The Sutton of a day ago would apologize, tuck tail, and retreat. But she wanted to be someone different. Someone bolder. "What if I asked Daddy to talk up the garage amongst his friends at the country club and drum up projects that would get you attention to make up for the Camaro?"

"That'd be great, but since you're posing this as a business arrangement, I assume you require something in return." For the first time with her, he was guarded and distant and slightly intimidating.

She took a deep breath. What's the worst that could happen? She'd already been humiliated and everyone was talking about her already. If he laughed, she would walk out with her head high and avoid him the rest of her life. "I want you to take me out. Not real dates. Fake ones."

He blinked. At least, he hadn't laughed. Yet.

She continued before he could flat turn her down. "I need to buy some time for the rumors to settle down. The gala is our busiest time of year besides prom. Part of why women come to Abigail's is because they trust me. If I lose their good opinion, they could easily take their business to Jackson or Baton Rouge."

"I feel real bad for you, I do. But—"

"And, my father's up for reelection." Her next argument came out with more desperation. "I can't stomach going to fundraisers or dinner parties alone when Andrew will be there, maybe with Bree. I just can't."

"Sutton . . ." He shook his head and she had to look away from the pity she saw in his eyes.

"This is all my fault for wanting to get revenge or whatever." She ran a hand through her hair. "And I dragged you in as an innocent party."

"Innocent might be overstepping a tad." His chuckle brought her eyes up to his. "The kiss on your front porch was my idea."

Her mouth dried at the mention, and she dabbed her lips with her tongue, the memory potent enough to rule her dreams the night before. His gaze dropped to her mouth. If she was being a hundred percent truthful, a small part of her hoped for another soul-scorching kiss. Just for show.

"This would be a short-lived agreement," she said.

"For how long?"

Her mind whirled. She hadn't expected to get this far. "The League gala is in less than three weeks. We could go together and that would be it. Our last date."

"Fake date."

"Exactly." She wasn't sure what to make of the sarcasm in his voice. "The gala would be a great opportunity for you to meet potential clients for the garage."

A whistle sounded, and Wyatt pushed off the couch. "That's my cue. Come on and I'll walk you to your car."

He hadn't given an answer, but her gumption level was nearing empty. Eyes tracked their walk back through the garage and out into the parking lot. Wyatt didn't pay them any mind. Why couldn't she do that?

He stopped and kicked a rock. It skidded all the way to the side of the road. "All right."

"All right, what?"

"I'll fake date you in return for some good word of mouth for the garage on your side of the river. Although I'm not sure what you expect. Country club dinners? Golf outings?"

"Nothing so formal. You know, dinner, drinks and stuff."

He propped a hip against the trunk of her car. "It's the *stuff* I'm getting hung up on. How physical do you want to get?"

Very. The word popped through the filter of her brain. Luckily, she didn't actually say it aloud. "People need to believe that we're actually dating."

"You're saying you want plenty of PDA?"

Yes, her body screamed. Her voice cracked, her mouth as dry as the Mojave Desert. "Nothing crazy. Hand holding and maybe the occasional kiss." At his raised eyebrows, she rushed to explain. "We've already kissed, right? What's a few more times?"

How pathetic had she sounded? Lord help her, even the thought of kissing him again had left her needing a fan and smelling salts.

His dancing eyes calmed and narrowed slightly. "I don't want to take advantage of you. You're feeling vulnerable and hurt and I don't want to add to that."

Behind his concern lurked another message, one that resurrected her pride. "You think a couple of your kisses will make me forget I was cheated on and fall for you or something? A little full of yourself, aren't you? I mean, the gall to think I would faint at your grease-covered boots over one little kiss and—"

"You've made your point." Instead of getting mad or defensive, he grabbed her hand and tugged her closer. "But you can't deny you enjoyed that kiss on a purely physical level."

Her wounded pride commanded her to jerk out of his hold, but her hand rebelled and curled around his thumb, her finger tracing a callus. "Yeah, well, you enjoyed yourself too, mister."

"Why do you assume that?"

Lightheadedness came over her, and the possibility of fainting at his grease-covered boots became a real possibility. Unable to stop herself, she glanced down to the bottom of the zipper on his coveralls. "Because I thought I could feel it. You, I mean."

She followed the track of his zipper up with her gaze to meet his eyes. A flush stained his cheeks.

She continued. "I'm not looking for a rebound. Whatever we do is purely for the sake of our agreement."

"How about I meet you at Abigail's after work on Friday? We can grab a pizza and hash out the details while being seen together."

Her relief was a physical thing, untying the knots in her stomach. "Good plan. Fridays at the pizza place are busy."

He took a step toward her, and she had to tilt her head back to maintain eye contact.

A spark of tease returned to his face, quirking the corners of his mouth. "Is everyone loitering in the open bay watching us?"

She shifted to see over his shoulder. "Ford and Mack and two older ladies are."

"Those are my aunts, Hyacinth and Hazel. Twins, just like me and Jackson."

"The ones with the gossipy Bible study?"

"Exactly. Should we start convincing people right now with some practice PDA? I can guarantee word will circulate through the ladies' church groups on both sides of the river."

"A kiss?"

"Isn't that what you want?" He looped an arm around her waist.

Her life had careened off the rails, but as a return to the straight and narrow seemed unlikely, maybe she should stop thinking so much and go for it. She didn't know what to do with her hands, settling them first on his lower arms then his chest. Nothing felt natural. He took one of her hands and linked their fingers.

"What should I do?" she whispered.

"Whatever you want to do." Was the challenge in his eyes real or a reflection of the battle raging inside of her?

Be bold. The dictate came like twin arrows from her brain. She obeyed, pitching closer and touching her lips to his. His soft hum encouraged her to wiggle closer and drape her arm on his shoulder.

Like the night before, everything outside the two of them fell away. The heat of the morning sun couldn't compete with the heat they generated. Her dreams hadn't done him justice.

His mouth parted and as if dancing, his head shifted one way and hers the other. She touched her tongue to his. The knot of desire that had remained tangled since the night before grew in her lower belly.

A recklessness came over her, so foreign and powerful she couldn't control it. She wound her hand in the hair at the back of his head and forced him even closer. All the while his tongue and teeth were doing delicious things to her mouth. His hard body made her want to wrap her legs around him and beg him for more. Maybe a no-strings-attached rebound was *exactly* what she needed.

Her hand in his stopped her. Their fingers had remained tight around each other and grounded her in something that wasn't purely physical. It was honeyed and gooey and a little bit scary.

She pulled away first. His lips followed, skimming over her jaw to nip her earlobe. Somewhere she located the good sense to let go of his hair and push against his chest. Her elbow turned to rubber when he trailed his lips down her neck to suck gently.

"Sweet Jesus," she said in a breathy moan.

"I want to hear you say my name like that someday."

His voice was gravelly, his breath against the hot place on her neck inciting shivers.

But another kind of shiver went down her spine. A warning. She twisted out of his arms and dropped his hand. Already she missed their hold on each other. "That's not . . . we're not . . ."

He blinked as if the same blinding fog that afflicted her during their kiss had enveloped him as well. "No, of course not. Just practicing in case someone was to overhear us."

"Yeah, good idea." She peeked over his shoulder again at the crowd of his family witnessing their kiss. At least Wyatt's back had provided a certain amount of privacy.

Under the desire and embarrassment, a confidence that had been absent so long she barely recognized the feeling coursed through her.

He had agreed to her harebrained scheme, and they were going to see each other again in a few days. Cool. She should play this cool. She had a feeling the smile on her face was anything but. It felt more like a kid-on-Christmas-morning grin.

"I'll see you Friday after work?" she asked.

"It's a date," he said with a smile.

Chapter Seven

Friday came and went so slowly, Wyatt was convinced the shop clock needed new batteries. But the sun in the sky didn't lie, and the workday stretched to forever. He tried to squash his eagerness to see Sutton, but it welled up through the alarms his logic issued.

"Any word on Tarwater's car?" Jackson asked as they cleaned up the pit and sorted tools back in the box.

"Not yet. I'm surprised he hasn't stormed out here to pick it up himself. I'll ask Sutton tonight."

"What are y'all going to get up to?" Although Jackson's tone veered casual, Wyatt knew better. His brother was attempting, in his stoic way, to impart a message.

"Grabbing a pizza over the river. What's on your mind?"

"Nothing." They continued with their work, the clang of the tools into drawers filling the expectant silence. Wyatt waited his twin out. Jackson closed the drawer and turned back to face Wyatt.

Wyatt was the anomaly looks-wise amongst the brothers with his almost-black hair and gray eyes. Jackson had inherited the Abbott brown hair and hazel eyes, but he'd gotten something from their mother too. A streak of wildness ran deep beneath his calm, quiet exterior. People thought Wyatt was a risk taker, but watching Jackson dominate a dirt track wasn't for the faint of heart.

Still, he could be counted on to keep his cool under the stress of family drama and gave good advice—whether you wanted to hear it or not. The problem was Wyatt had a feeling Jackson's advice would be in direct opposition to what Wyatt wanted.

"Sutton Mize was engaged as of earlier this week," Jackson said.

"Yep, but she's not anymore."

"I heard the jabber about why, and I saw the tail end of that kiss you shared in our parking lot. But I also know you weren't seeing her before she brought Tarwater's car in, so what gives?" Jackson planted his feet and crossed his arms over his chest.

Lying to his twin wasn't only inadvisable, it was impossible. They had a way of seeing past each other's bullshit that was sometimes welcome, sometimes annoying. "Short story is that Tarwater is a dick and was cheating on Sutton with her best friend. She broke off the engagement and to save face insinuated that she and I had been a thing for a while."

"You and she are going to keep up the charade to make Tarwater feel bad?"

"Something like that." Wyatt turned away and picked up the dirty, blue, shop towels.

Jackson grabbed Wyatt's arm and forced him around. "You like her."

"Everyone likes her. She's nice."

"I mean, you *like* like her. You have since we were kids—I've not forgotten how you walked around with cow eyes around her—and that kiss out front wasn't pretend. You two nearly melted the asphalt."

Jackson's twin powers had veered sharply annoying. "I maybe, sort of like her. What's wrong with that? She's single; I'm single."

"She's been single for less than a week. She's using you."

"I'm using her too. In return for me squiring her around, she's going to get her judge daddy to talk up the garage at the country club. Send some more projects our way to make up for the Camaro."

"That kiss was all a selfless act for the garage?" Jackson's sarcasm was not appreciated.

Wyatt had to look away from his brother's gaze which prompted a muttered curse from Jackson.

"Do not fall for this woman, Wyatt. Whether she means to or not, she's going to rip your heart into little pieces and feed it to the gators before she goes back to her old life."

"We're not getting serious. In fact, we agreed that after I take her to the gala, it's over."

Jackson didn't look pleased with the news. He looked worried. "As long as you don't delude yourself into thinking it's anything more than that. She'll be back with Tarwater or someone like him by Christmas."

Because the thought had already burrowed into his chest, Wyatt's reaction was knee-jerk and defensive. "Someone like him?"

"You know, sophisticated. Worldly. Rich. Well-connected. Well-groomed."

"Fuck you," Wyatt shot back, but there was little heat to it. Jackson was right. "I've been told I clean up real nice."

Jackson's smile revealed his dimples. A rare sight since their pop had died last year. "Doesn't count if it's from a female relative over the age of sixty."

"Sutton and I are putting on a show until the gala. That's when it ends. No need to worry yourself over me." They finished tidying the pit and took up posts on opposite sides of the open bay door. The sun trekked toward the horizon and threw orange and purple across the sky like a finger painting by a three-year-old.

"You ever think about the family curse?" Wyatt finally asked.

"What curse?"

"The one about Abbott twins never getting married."

"I'd call it more a blessing than a curse. And I don't even want to know why you're worried about it all of a sudden." Jackson sent an eye roll in his direction and headed toward the office where Mack worked on spreadsheets.

Thankful for the privacy, Wyatt headed to the loft to clean up, taking time to scrub the grease from under his nails. Jackson's warnings reverberated in his head. He might not be invited to the governor's mansion anytime soon, but Hyacinth and Hazel had taken it upon themselves to domesticate them after a fashion. He knew enough not to fart in public or eat with his fingers. He could even manage a credible two-step on a dance floor. He was plenty sophisticated enough for either side of Cottonbloom, dammit.

Wyatt might not be rich like Tarwater, but the garage provided a good living. And as their reputation grew in classic car restoration circles, they might even pull business from bigger cities like New Orleans or Jackson, Mississippi. Unless things nosedived into the swamps.

It didn't matter. Jackson was right about one thing. Whatever he and Sutton were doing was temporary. The milk in his fridge had a longer expiration date than their fake relationship.

Instead of grabbing the first available clean shirt, he flipped through his closet and waffled between two different plaid button-downs, finally settling on the green-and-blue because Aunt Hyacinth had told him once it brought out his eyes.

Although he hadn't invoked it in a while, temporary and fun would be his mantra until it stuck. He would enjoy the PDA and her company and that's all. It shouldn't be an issue considering he was a certified expert in temporary and fun.

Wyatt grabbed the keys for the Hornet. The growly engine rattled the restlessness and worry out of his bones. He rolled down the windows and enjoyed the gloaming through the pine trees that lined the two-lane road into town. The scent was earthy and familiar and comforting.

The last streaks of the sun were fading when he crossed the steel-girded bridge and turned onto Mississippi's River Street. In a fit of pique or spite or maybe idiocy, the road that paralleled it on the Louisiana side was also called River Street, making giving directions and mail delivery a crapshoot.

He parked down the street in an isolated spot to avoid the possibility of a flung-open truck door marring the Hornet's paint job. Several couples and families were out enjoying the common area by the river. Children played tag, their squeals and laughter carrying over the soft background of the flowing river.

He hesitated at the corner. Abigail's Boutique was the first business on the street that ran perpendicular to River Street. He was a few minutes early. A shadow moved in the store.

He approached the door and rubbed his hands down the front of his jeans. A line of headless mannequins displayed a variety of clothes from a simple sundress to a floor-length beaded gown. A crimp in his stomach so unfamiliar that it could only be nerves made him hesitate. He resisted the urge to lurk outside and forced himself inside the shop.

The first thing that hit him was the attractive feminine scent. The next was an unfamiliar woman looking at him like he was there to rob the store.

"Uh, hi." He held up both hands where she could see them, waving one, and tried on his most charming, non-threatening smile. She continued to stare.

"I believe this is the one you're referring to, Ms. Eckert."

Sutton's voice drifted from behind a curtained room at the back of the store a second before she emerged. Her flower printed skirt rippled as she brushed by the curtains, her torso obscured by voluminous fabric that reminded him of a giant peach.

"Wyatt." Surprise lilted her voice high and for a moment, he panicked.

Did he have the day wrong? Or had she not really wanted to get together? Maybe she regretted their deal and hoped he'd crawl back into the greasy pit from whence he'd come. Or even worse, maybe she and Tarwater were back together. A lot could happen in three days.

"Do you mind if I finish up with Ms. Eckert? Come on back and I'll find you somewhere to sit." She hung what turned out to be a peach-colored dress with a very full skirt in a dressing room. "Actually, we could use a man's opinion, if you're up for it."

"I'll give it a shot." The relief that chased his panic away made his voice veer way more enthusiastic than he'd ever felt about ladies' clothing—unless it was on his bedroom floor.

He weaved his way through the racks of clothes to where a counter flanked in weird tree-like structures draped in jewelry and scarves faced two dressing rooms.

"And what's your name, young man?" Ms. Eckert offered a hand, which he shook. She was thin to the point of bony, her hair scraped into a low, short ponytail of black and silver, emphasizing her best feature, a long, graceful neck.

"Wyatt Abbott. Nice to make your acquaintance, ma'am."

"Abbott, Abbott . . . Any kin to Howie Abbott?"

"Yes, ma'am. A second cousin. My brothers and I own Abbott Brothers Garage and Restoration over the river."

"How nice." The woman turned back to Sutton, and without the woman's assessing gaze, he relaxed and shuffled to the counter, propping a hip against the side.

Sutton got the woman set up in a dressing room and joined him. "Sorry about this. She came in five minutes ago needing a dress for the gala." Her voice was so low, he leaned closer to hear.

"I don't mind, but I'm not sure how much help I'll be. I don't know anything about"—he waved his hand and knocked the necklace covered tree with his elbow, catching it in time to avoid dumping everything on the floor but bumping into her—"this sort of thing."

She caught his forearm on a slight laugh. Her eyes were tired and a little sad. Before he had a chance to think beyond the need to make her feel better, he tucked her hair behind her ear. "How are you doing?"

"I haven't been sleeping great, but I'm okay." Although she seemed reluctant to admit it, he was glad they were beyond a polite, "fine, thanks."

"Has Tarwater come back around?"

"No and I've ignored his calls and texts. Unfortunately, I can't drop off the face of the earth entirely. I'm on the gala planning committee, and besides prom and Christmas, the gala is our most lucrative time of the year." She glanced to the side. "But I've been looking forward to tonight."

Had she been eager to see him or be seen *with* him? He didn't know and tried not to care. Before he could respond, Ms. Eckert emerged from the dressing room. "What do you think?" Sutton took a breath, but the woman held up a hand. "I want the young man's opinion."

He tensed while the woman's gaze travelled the length of his body down to his black boots, not in a sexual way but rather like she was sizing him like a female praying mantis before she devoured her mate.

He ran his hands down the legs of his jeans again. He would rather rebuild a blown transmission than have to tell the woman the truth. It was too low cut, too voluminous, too adolescent. Basically, too everything for her.

He glanced over at Sutton. Her eyes danced with laughter, even though she kept it confined to one corner of her mouth.

He swallowed. "I think you look real pretty, but . . ."

Ms. Eckert put her hands on her hips and cocked her head. "But?"

"It seems to me that a black dress would be more suited to a woman of your obvious elegance." A *ding, ding, ding* went off in his head. He pushed off the counter and headed to a promising-looking rack of floor length dresses.

"What are you doing?" Sutton asked with a hint of panic that told him if they had been playing a game of hide-and-seek he was getting warm.

"Looking for the perfect dress." He panicked a little himself when he wasn't sure if he would recognize her design amidst the masses, but he needn't have worried. He flipped a pink dress to the side and there it was, its quality obvious. He pulled Sutton's dress out and glanced from it to Ms. Eckert. She looked about the same size as the headless torso in Sutton's workroom.

Sutton grabbed a sleeve of the dress and tugged. "Not this one."

He dropped his voice. "Let her try it on. If she hates it then no one need be the wiser."

They engaged in a staring contest. She blinked first and let go of the dress with a huff. "Fine."

Wyatt presented the dress to Ms. Eckert with a dramatic flourish. She ran a hand over the lace at the top before taking the hanger. "It's lovely."

The minutes that passed seemed long. Sutton kept her distance and fidgeted with the rack of dresses between pacing. Finally, Ms. Eckert emerged, performed a twirl that swung the skirt around her knees, and faced the floor-length mirror. "It's almost perfect. I'll need someone to take up the bust and shorten the sleeves a tad. I didn't see a label or price, though, dear. How much is it?"

Sutton's mouth opened and closed, but no words or numbers emerged.

Ms. Eckert spun this way and that looking at herself in the mirror, a self-satisfied smile not doing much to soften the sharp planes of her face. "This dress will make anything Mrs. Carson shows up in look like rags."

Wyatt took the tag off the nearest dress. The name Vera Wang was printed above a price that almost made him choke. Instead, he rattled off the number and waited for a response.

"Excellent. Ring me up while I change, would you, dear?" Ms. Eckert didn't bat an eye and retreated to the dressing room.

He stood to the side while Sutton bagged the dress and completed the transaction. Ms. Eckert handed over a credit card without a change of expression. She turned to grace Wyatt with another of her mantis-devouring gazes, but directed her question toward Sutton. "Who is accompanying you to the gala, dear?"

Sutton's gaze pinged to him and back to the register. "Mr. Abbott is."

"Isn't that interesting." It was a statement that didn't require an answer. Sutton handed over the dress, and this time Ms. Eckert smiled at him. "I very much look forward to seeing you, young man."

"Likewise, ma'am."

Sutton followed Ms. Eckert to the door and flipped the sign to CLOSED. Not sure how she was going to take his meddling, he braced his hands on the counter and leaned back.

She waved out the window then turned, hands on hips. "I can't believe you did that."

"Can't believe it in a good way or bad way?"

"Both, I guess. You made Ms. Eckert pay the same for my dress as a Vera. That's crazy." Her tone veered toward shock as she approached him.

"Crazy good or crazy bad?"

Now that she was closer, he could see the spark in her eye was due more to excitement than anger. In fact, her multihued eyes danced, any hint of sadness stomped out. The thought he'd had anything to do with her happiness made him feel like he'd been dropped into a vat of warm, furry puppies.

"She didn't even argue. Just pulled her credit card out. All because of you." The way she looked at him added more adorable puppies.

"You're the one who designed it. Sewed it up and stuff. All I did was find the dress on the rack. I wasn't even sure it would be there."

She moved behind the counter, and he turned to watch her close up the register. Her movements spoke of routine, yet she did it with grace. Like she did everything. "I sold a dress. What should I do now?"

"Sew up another and sell it too."

"You make it sound so easy."

"Doesn't have to be hard." He gestured toward the door. "Didn't her reaction give you any confidence?"

She shut the drawer to the register and stared at him for a moment. "Let me put this in the safe and grab my purse."

After she disappeared through the curtains with a zippered bank bag, he wandered to the nearest rack of clothes and lifted the price tag. "Holy hell, I'm in the wrong business."

"Sticker shock?" Her voice had him whirling around.

"I could buy a top of the line socket wrench that would last twenty-five years for how much this costs." He waved the silky arm of the shirt around. "Seems to me you could have charged even more for that dress."

Sutton adjusted the hangers so they were equally spaced out and led him toward the front door. "What women will spend and do to look good borders on insanity."

"Honestly, I'm not sure the average male even cares."

They stepped out into the night. Darkness had crept closer, and the common area had cleared out, most of the vehicles gone. The sound of the river was amplified between the buildings of the street.

"You're cute if you think women are buying clothes to impress a man." She threw a teasing smile over her shoulder before turning back to lock the front door of the shop. "Women dress to impress other women."

He fell into step next to her and linked his hands behind his back. "Is the lingerie you sell to impress other women too?"

Her pace picked up as if his words had spurred her forward. He mouthed a curse and wanted to kick his own tail. He caught her arm and forced her to face him. "I'm sorry. I wasn't thinking."

"You're right, the lingerie is to impress men." The concrete of her expression cracked into something that resembled a smile, but her eyes no longer danced.

"Do you wear all that lacy stuff?" The question shot out of his mouth in a need to fill the silence.

A slight tease eased into her smile. She slipped out of his grip and continued on, saying over her shoulder, "Wouldn't you like to know?"

Hell yes, he wanted to know. More than he wanted to know the secrets of the universe. He caught up with her in time to open the pizza restaurant's door and gesture her through. She led the way to a booth, and he slid in across from her. The few people in the restaurant didn't seem to be paying them any attention.

A teenaged waitress approached and exchanged pleasantries with Sutton. The girl was sullen but polite and plopped waters and two menus down.

"Thanks, Amy." Once the girl retreated Sutton laced her fingers over the menu and stared at him intently, but a lightness was back in her attitude. "The moment of truth. What do you like on your pizza?"

He leaned over to match her stance, putting their faces only a few inches apart. "As much of everything that can fit."

"Me too. Tony's specialty is my favorite."

"The only pizza worth ordering."

She gave a little cheer. "Andrew never let me order anything but a veggie pizza." Her gaze skated off to the side. "I'm sorry."

"What are you sorry for now?" He wanted to force her eyes back on him, but didn't.

"I shouldn't bring him up when I'm with you."

Although he didn't particularly want to discuss Tarwater's pizza habits—or any of his habits for that matter—Wyatt wasn't her new boyfriend. He simply had to keep himself from becoming too attached to her smiles and dancing eyes. *Temporary and fun.*

"No worries. How'd your parents take the news?" he asked.

"With minimal wailing and gnashing of teeth actually." The waitress returned and they put in their order. Without him having to prompt her for more information, Sutton picked up their conversation. "Mother's wringing her hands raw about what everyone is saying but she's mad as a wet hen about Andrew. Daddy ruffled his morning paper and grunted and then went out to shoot birds."

"What'd you tell them?"

"As little as possible for the moment. They know Andrew was messing around on the side, but I didn't tell them it was Bree. And if they've heard any rumors about us, neither one of them has mentioned it." She touched the blank space where her engagement ring used to be as if fiddling with it was a hard habit to break.

"I'm glad they're supporting you."

"Underneath all the social posturing and formality, my parents are great. Maggie is too."

A silence that had a tinge of first date awkwardness fell between them. He searched for a new subject. "Who did you name the shop after? Is Abigail your mother's name?"

"No, we inherited the name when we bought it. It's a tragic story actually. Abigail was considered the catch of the county back in the fifties—runner up to Miss Mississippi in fact. The governor's son was courting her, and everyone thought they would marry, but she ran off with a man from over the river and was never seen again. Her parents renamed the store as a plea to return or a memorial. No one knows for sure."

Her story niggled a memory. "She never returned?"

She dropped her voice to a whisper. "Some people say the man murdered her and that's really why the town split."

He chuffed. "She wasn't murdered."

"You sound like you know her."

"If it's the same one, then your Abigail married an Abbott."

"Get out." She playfully shoved his arm, and her fingers dropped to play with the rolled up cuff of his shirt. Her voice turned dreamy. "Abigail Abbott. Do you know what happened to her?"

He didn't move, afraid he'd scare her off. "Her parents disowned her. Renaming the shop was their way of thumbing their noses at her. She and her husband moved a couple of parishes over and raised a passel of kids. They came to a family reunion when I was a teenager. If she's still alive, she'd be pushing ninety now."

"Were they happy? Did she have regrets?" Her hand tightened on his forearm.

"Does anyone make it through life without regrets?"

Chapter Eight

Sutton couldn't tear her eyes away from Wyatt's. The longer she stared, the more colors she could see. Gold and even green ringed his iris. She felt like she was standing on the high dive and looking down into the water with a combination of nerves and excitement.

She'd never been nervous around Andrew. They'd known each other since they were young, so things had felt natural and comfortable. Too comfortable. She hadn't fallen in love with him; she'd fallen into a relationship with him.

Wyatt was different. Her stomach and heart played dodgeball in her chest, the feeling not in the least bit comfortable. Yet at the same time, she wanted to scoot closer and prayed for an oven malfunction so their pizza would take all night getting to their table.

"Here ya go." Amy materialized out of nowhere and slid the pizza on the table. Sutton pulled her hand away when Wyatt broke eye contact to smile and thank the girl.

Amy's braces flashed before her lips pressed closed around the metal as if she forgot it wasn't cool to exhibit any form of happiness at her age. She backed away and tucked her frizzy blond hair behind an ear, disappearing into the kitchen.

"How do you do that?"

"Do what?" he asked around his first bite of pizza while fanning his mouth, looking genuinely perplexed at her question.

The man had no idea he mounted a charm offensive every time he smiled or opened his mouth. "First you win over Ms. Eckert, and then you make a girl, who is painfully aware of her braces and every other perceived fault as only a hormonal teenager can be, smile and blush."

He glanced toward the other side of the restaurant where Amy was delivering waters to another table. She glanced toward them before quickstepping back through the swinging kitchen door.

"I didn't mean to," he said defensively.

"Don't worry, you weren't being creepy. You were being sweet." Sutton propped her elbow on the table and her chin in her hand, toying with the pizza on her plate. "Girls like Amy desperately want to hide yet at the same time long for someone to actually see them."

"Seems a little counterintuitive. You weren't anything like that as I recall." He took another big bite and was almost at the crust.

"Are you kidding me? I was painfully shy and skinny and a late bloomer. I had no boobs to speak of until I was almost out of high school." That was only a slight exaggeration. "I didn't get asked out on a single date. Not even to prom."

He dropped another slice onto his plate and sat back. "I don't believe you. You were the prettiest girl I'd ever seen."

She stared at him, nonplussed. He looked sincere. "Are you teasing me? Because I have photographic evidence to the contrary."

He shrugged and took a bite of pizza, chewing and swallowing while he continued their staring contest. "Not teasing. I remember everything about you back then."

"You didn't hate me." The realization was like a lightning strike.

". . . course I didn't. Why else would I have been picking on you?"

"Why else indeed?" she murmured.

"Those Mississippi boys must have been blind idiots."

She'd long ago left teenage insecurities behind, but his statement bolstered her present-day battered self-confidence with a bolt of happiness. It was so acute, she smiled automatically. "Maybe they were, but it was okay. I had Bree."

Her smile dropped. For an instant, she'd forgotten about the painful Bree-sized aneurism on her heart. They had been partners in crime and had laid out on her driveway and dreamed as big as the stars they stared at.

"Have you talked to her?" he asked gently.

"Nope. She called and texted, but I've ignored her." She took a bite of pizza but more for appearances' sake than real hunger.

"You think you'll ever be able to forgive her?" Wyatt finished his second piece.

"Even if I can, it won't ever be the same, you know?" She picked off a pepperoni and popped it into her mouth. "Have you ever been betrayed like that by a friend?"

"A friend? No." He hesitated with his pizza halfway to his mouth and then put it back down. "But a brother? Sort of."

"Not Jackson?"

"God, no. Jackson has my back no matter what. Mack too. It was Ford." Resentment was stamped on his face and colored his voice.

She leaned forward, instinctively wanting to give comfort. "Did he cheat with your girlfriend?"

"Something way worse." His voice dipped into grief. "He bought a car that was meant for me."

His answer took her by surprise, and she cleared her throat to try to rid herself of her inappropriate giggles. "I'm sorry."

"It probably sounds ridiculous to you, but that car was going to be my first. I was sixteen and had worked since I was twelve, saving and scrimping money. I pored over the used car ads in the *Cottonbloom Gazette* every week for two years, waiting and watching for the perfect car. I'd know her when I saw her."

He pulled his wallet out and unfurled a creased newspaper cutout with a grainy color picture and the title "With some TLC, she could be your Beauty! 1970 Hemi Barracuda." The car was red with powerful lines. The hood was up, showcasing the engine. A couple of the panels looked damaged, but otherwise, it really was a beauty.

Her spike of humor was gone as quickly as it came. Even if she couldn't understand the attachment, his hurt was as real as hers. After all, he had carried the evidence for over a decade.

He continued. "The June twenty-ninth edition. I made the mistake of announcing my find at the dinner table. I was so proud and happy and planned to go see the man after school the next day. Ford beat me to the punch and drove up in the car that afternoon waving the title." He shook his head, the distance in his eyes spanning the years.

"What happened?"

"He was so damn smug. I jumped him. Jackson said I was crazed. Ford was bigger than me then and managed to get away before I could do any permanent damage." He took a bite of pizza and most of the angst drained out of him. "Unfortunately."

"After all that, he didn't offer to sell you the car? Or give it to you?"

He made a scoffing sound. "He offered to sell her at a huge mark-up, the asshole. He's always tried for the easy

money. What really chaffed my hide though was the way
he pimped the poor girl out. Redneck all the way with huge
wheels and fenders and a Confederate flag paint job."

"What happened to her?" Somehow in her head the car
deserved a feminine pronoun, representing all women who
were powerless and taken advantage of by men.

"He wrapped her around a water oak out on some back
parish road six months later. Totaled her. It was almost a
blessing." He didn't believe it. She could tell from the way
his mouth tightened and he looked away.

"You were biding your time until he lost interest and
you could swoop in to save her, weren't you?"

His shrug was reminiscent of a teenage boy trying not
to care. "I sound like a total weirdo, don't I?'

He sounded like a man who got attached. "Have you
ever forgiven him?"

A smile quirked his mouth. "This is where I should be a
good example and say, yes, of course, we hugged it out and
I forgave him. The truth is when it comes to Ford, I keep
one eye on my back."

"He owns part of the garage, right? That's what you
were arguing about when I butted in the other morning."

"Each of us has an equal stake."

"Who makes the big decisions? Or do you vote?" She
raised her brows.

"How's it work between you and your sister?"

"I'm in charge. Even though she's a year older, she
doesn't want to make the decisions. I wouldn't say we're
besties, but we get along."

"You're lucky then." He shook his head, his attention
focused on the task of tearing his crust into small pieces.

She waited, but when it didn't appear he planned to
elaborate, her curiosity got the better of her. "I get the impression Mack is your unofficial leader. Would you rather
it be you?"

His head shot up, amusement tempering the earlier melancholy about his lost car. "Good Lord, no. Invoices and taxes make me break out in hives. I'm all about the cars. Ford and Mack have been in a power struggle since Pop died."

"Based on your trust issues, I assume you back Mack."

"Anyone with a lick of sense would back Mack. He lives and breathes the garage. Ford is . . ." Wyatt looked to the floor as if searching for a word on the old, dingy tile. "Unreliable is a nice way to put it. Pop could rein in his delusions of grandeur, but now he's gone."

The hollowness in his voice and lack of expression told her how much he missed his father. The thought of hers gone made her stomach flop over. She touched the back of his hand. "I don't know what I'd do if I lost Daddy."

"Loss is part of life. Doesn't make it hurt any less though." He captured her hand when she went to pull it back.

She struggled to find a coherent thought with his thumb rubbing circles on the back of her hand. Searching for a way to cut through the swelling intensity, she landed on a superficial subject. "You and Jackson look so different. I wouldn't have guessed you were twins."

His thumb stilled, his hand tightening around hers. "Jackson is a cookie-cutter Abbott. I used to be jealous. I take after my mom so I'm told. Or maybe I really am adopted like Ford kept telling me when we were kids."

Real pain hid behind his joke. She tried to keep herself from asking the obvious. Deep, meaningful conversations shouldn't be part of her plan, but she was too far down the road to turn back now. "What happened to your mom?"

"Ran off. Four boys in five years plus a husband who was more interested in cars than her would probably drive any woman to run. Pop got rid of all her pictures afterward, never talked about her, and I was too young to remember what she looked like."

His thumb resumed its caress. Each pass sensitized her nerve endings until it was almost painful. Yet she didn't want him to stop.

"That's terrible." She wasn't sure what was more terrible, his mother leaving or his father's callousness in not allowing his sons to remember her. "Have you tried to find her now that you're grown?"

"Why would I? She didn't care enough to stay." Behind the defiant words, his tone vibrated with uncertainty.

"People change. Maybe she regrets leaving, but can't find her way back after all this time without some help."

"Maybe she doesn't want to be found."

"Maybe she doesn't." A few beats of silence passed. "Do you miss her?"

"Don't really know what to miss, if that makes any sense. Jackson and I were barely out of diapers when she left. The aunts kept us fed and made sure we occasionally bathed and combed our hair." His voice was distant. "I think Ford was affected the most. I remember he used to get really mad."

"Did you boys ever go to counselling?"

"Like laid out on a couch talking about our feelings? You're cute." His smile was slow and sexy and crinkled his eyes. How could he veer so quickly from heartache to easy-going humor? "We worked out our issues under the hood of a car as soon as we could hold a wrench."

Their gazes met and melded, until nothing else existed except for him and the weird connection that had bloomed in the middle of a crappy situation. Maybe it made for good fertilizer.

"Are y'all ready for your check?" Amy's voice cut them apart, her attention fixed on Wyatt, who took the trembling ticket from between her fingers. She stood there with a smile that cracked around her braces.

Wyatt dug out his wallet and handed over a twenty-dollar bill. "Keep the change."

"Thank you so much." Amy backed away.

Wyatt seemed unfazed or more likely oblivious. "You ready?"

Sutton wasn't ready for the evening to end. Reluctance had her inching slowly out of the booth. Once outside, they strolled back toward Abigail's. Stars winked from the sky, the moon cast in yellow.

The giant oaks that had stood sentinel for hundreds of years had been felled by a tornado that had hit Cottonbloom three years earlier. New trees had taken their place, but it would be a hundred years before they grew into behemoths that blocked the night sky.

Would Cottonbloom still be the same quaint town then? Would Abigail's still exist? Her sense of melancholy was edged with impatience. One thing was certain, she wouldn't be here in a hundred years, so she needed to make the ones she had count.

"We didn't even talk about our arrangement," he said. "Did you have some ideas?"

Her steps slowed. Honestly, she hadn't been thinking about their agreement or Andrew or Bree or anything beyond him. Did that mean she was moving on or burying her head? "Daddy's big election year pig picking is tomorrow afternoon."

"Are you inviting me?"

"I sure don't relish showing up alone, and it'd be a good place to meet some potential clients for you. A win-win." She glanced at him for a reaction, trying not to be too obvious. Even though she wasn't asking him on a real date, the wait was nerve-racking.

"Yeah." He drew the word out. "I could do that."

As she was filling him in on the time and what to wear, two cars turned onto River Street, their headlights blinding her like camera flashes. They parked, and the sudden plunge into darkness made her blink. The sound of male voices carried across the street. The group of three or four men were making their way toward Antonio's.

Her eyes readjusted to the darkness. Mike Derouen, an associate lawyer in Andrew's firm, was among them. The other men registered with various levels of recognition. All of them were in Andrew's work or social circle.

Mike raised his hand in greeting. She returned the gesture, thankful he didn't trek across the street for a visit. He'd probably heard the news.

"You know those guys?"

"Colleagues of Andrew."

"Well, then . . ." He took a step toward her and his big body blocked out the street light. She instinctively took a step back and another until her butt hit rough bricks, still warm from the hot afternoon sun. He bracketed her with his arms by her shoulders. The slight edge of danger emanating from him was a serious turn-on.

She leaned into him and took a deep breath of spicy, yummy man. Their faces were close and her lips were already tingling in anticipation, yet her prudish brain balked. They were in public against a brick wall. "What are you doing?"

"Fulfilling my end of our bargain." He thumbed over his shoulder toward the group of men who were almost to the pizza place. "You want us to be seen, right?"

Her aroused buzz was replaced by the little voice in her head telling her how dumb and naïve she was. All for show. She needed to remember that. Two kisses that rocked her world and shredded her good sense did not make whatever they were doing any more real. In fact, knowing he was kissing her in return for business induced a tawdry, icky feeling.

She put her hands on his chest, her intention to push him away stalled at the feel of his thumping heart and warmth. "I'm not sure I can do this after all."

"Do what?"

"The fake PDA thing. It's not my style."

"You think I make it a habit to fake date women?"

"That's not what I meant, but . . ." She didn't want to hurt his feelings again.

"Tell me exactly what you've heard about me, Sutton."

His voice was rumbly and almost hypnotic, but she couldn't decide if he was mad as hell or amused. Conjuring up a lie was beyond her, so she went with the unvarnished truth.

"I heard you're good with your . . . wrench." Her glance down was as instinctive as her retreat had been. She held her breath in the ensuing stillness.

"Out of all the tools available, you didn't pick screwdriver?" He bobbed in to lay a kiss on the tip of her nose. "You're so dang cute."

He pushed off the wall and walked down the sidewalk, his hands in his pockets, whistling something unintelligible. The sense of danger was replaced by a sweet affection.

Wyatt wasn't sure why his good mood had been restored so quickly in the face of her rejection. She could deny it all she wanted with her words, but she'd wanted that kiss as much as he had. Her body couldn't lie. The flush that made her perfume scent the air between them. Her lean closer and the drowsy, sexy drop of her lashes.

He wouldn't be taking her to his bed at the end of the night, but he didn't care. Which meant he needed to back down and reexamine what the hell his intentions were. While he was at it, he would try to figure out why he'd gone on and on like a loser about his dream car and his absentee mom.

She ran-walked in front of him, forcing him to stop or plow her down. "We need to hash this out before tomorrow."

"Okay. Our PDA won't consist of lip-to-lip contact. Does that make you feel better?"

"I guess."

He was gratified her agreement emerged disgruntled. "We'll smile and laugh and hold hands tomorrow. Perfect boyfriend material, right here." He gestured down his body.

Instead of garnering a laugh which was his intent, she remained serious. "What are you going to tell your drinking buddies about me?"

"Nothing because it's none of their business. Don't you trust me?"

"Not really. My best friend lied to me. My fiancé cheated on me." Her shrug was accompanied by a huff. "You and I barely know each other."

She'd been burned. Telling her he was trustworthy wasn't enough. He'd have to prove it to her, but that wouldn't happen tonight. "Don't forget I'm getting something out of this deal too. You're going to get your bigshot daddy to talk up the garage, right?"

"But you have to know that I can't guarantee anyone will end up hiring you."

Jackson was right. Wyatt had liked her when she was a girl, and now that she was a woman, he liked her even more. Their deal offered him a way into her life he otherwise wouldn't have. He was smart enough not to blow the opportunity.

"I'm willing to take that risk."

Her laugh was self-deprecating. "I'm sorry. With everything that went down and our spotty history, I wasn't sure if you were playing me or not. It's not you I don't trust as much as myself. Not sure I ever will again."

"All you need is time and a little TLC." His gaze caught on his car, all alone at the end of the street. A before and after shot popped into his head. "My Hornet was all rusty and sad-looking when I found her. Begging for someone, anyone to uncover what was underneath."

"Are you comparing me to a rusted-out junk car?" Her tone was more offended than amused. She popped a hip and raised her chin. "I'm not some charitable case and you aren't my fairy godmother."

"Hey, that's not what I meant." Their conversation had hit a patch of black ice and was spinning out of control.

"What *did* you mean?"

He stammered out a few unintelligible words. She walked away, and he followed.

"Am I basically your pet project?" She whirled on him, only inches separating them.

The conclusion she'd drawn made her sound like she was broken, which was far from the truth. "Not at all. But Tarwater and Bree left you beat up."

"You think you can fix me?" The night cast her face in mystery.

She didn't need fixing in his eyes. She wasn't broken, only a little battered and bruised. What she needed was time to heal and lick her wounds without someone trying to take advantage of her. Like him.

The honorable thing to do would be to end things now. The rumors would die fast enough, and some other Mississippi man, probably acquainted with her family through the country club, would start to circle, moving in to take what Wyatt selfishly wanted for himself.

"How about this? I'll play your boyfriend in front of all your Mississippi friends and family. You'll help me drum up some business for the garage. And along the way, I'll teach you how to have fun again. Smile. Laugh. Shake the rust off." He tensed, wondering if he'd made things even worse.

She stared into his eyes for longer than was comfortable, and he wasn't sure what she'd found, but when she finally spoke her voice had softened with a sense of thoughtfulness. "I might have misplaced my laugh."

"I'll help you find it. Let's aim to actually have some fun at your daddy's pig picking tomorrow."

A ghost of a smile that reminded him of the wispy clouds against the light of the moon crossed her face. "Not sure fun goes with a reelection party. Especially since it will be our first big outing. We should aim lower."

"How low?"

"Survival will be a win."

His laughter echoed off the brick storefronts. They were in front of Abigail's.

She scuffed the toe of her shoe against a crack in the concrete. "I'm parked around back. You'll pick me up around three tomorrow?"

He nodded, and she disappeared into her shop. No lights came on. He backed away and made his way toward the Hornet, waiting until he saw her pull out of the narrow alleyway and onto the main road.

His mind whirred on the way back to the garage. He parked in the lot and was halfway around the side, headed to the barn, when a familiar voice stopped him.

"Come and sit a spell, would you?"

He hadn't noticed Aunt Hazel on the porch swing of their old family house. Mack had shared it with their pop, and like calling dibs, he'd remained after Pop's death.

"Where's Mack and Aunt Hyacinth?" He climbed the steps and joined her on the swing, the chains squawking with the extra weight.

"Trying to kill each other at gin rummy."

Cards was a favorite pastime of the Abbotts. Their many greats-grandfather had won land in Cottonbloom Parish in a poker game. Verdict was still out whether he'd cheated or not.

The night gathered around them like a fuzzy blanket. The rhythm of the swing lulled him, and his discussion with Sutton scrolled. Curiosity about his mom had been niggling him since his pop had died, and Sutton's gentle probing had revived his questions.

"Will you tell me about my mom?" At first, he thought the request would be met with the same reaction he'd gotten from his pop the one time he'd found the courage to ask. Silence followed by storming off.

"You remind me of her." His aunt's voice didn't reflect the fear that reared in him at the comparison. The fear that he was too much like his mama had lived inside of him ever since he had realized he didn't look like his brothers.

"That's a terrible thing to say."

"No, it's not." She huffed. "You boys—Hobart especially—demonized her after she left."

"Deserted us is more like." The sentiment came out like propaganda he'd been fed his whole life.

"Maybe, but Hobart fell in love with her for a reason. Your mother knew how to have fun."

His heart thumped in his ears, his aunt's assessment hitting too close to the mark with him. "Doesn't sound much like a compliment to me."

Hazel's voice had drifted years into the past, and she ignored his observation. "Problem was she didn't know how to weather life when things weren't fun. Having all you boys so close together couldn't have been easy. A set of twins to boot. And let's face facts, your daddy loved that garage above all else."

"You're blaming Pop?" Defensiveness bristled through him like a wild animal being poked.

Hazel patted his knee, but he jerked it away. "Life is complicated. People even more so. Your daddy was a good man, but he wasn't without his faults. None of us is."

What if, along with his hair and eye color, he'd inherited his mama's ways? He'd never had a serious girlfriend. He still lived much like a teenager, eating canned ravioli and boxed mac and cheese. "I wouldn't run off."

"No one is afeared you will." Hazel shifted and laced her fingers together on her lap. "Except for you it seems."

Even in the dark, he could feel her eyes boring deep for the truth, and she would find it. She always did. As a kid he'd wondered if she was a swamp witch, but when he'd asked, she laughed and laughed. Although she'd never actually denied it to his recollection.

"I've been feeling restless of late," he finally admitted. "Maybe it's the infighting with Ford. I don't know."

"Ugly business that." An ominous humming sound came from her throat. "How old are you?"

The change in direction threw him, "Twenty-nine. Why?"

"Almost thirty. Maybe you don't want to run away but settle down."

His aunt's words uncovered something he'd buried deep. "Not possible. What about the curse?"

"Wyatt Jedidiah Abbott, do not tell me you've bought into that poppycock."

He winced at his name. "But the string of unmarried Abbott twins is legendary."

"All by choice, if you ask me." The righteousness in her voice faded. "Don't use flawed family history as an excuse to never fall in love."

Snapshots of Sutton scrolled through his mind. Her head tossed back in a laugh, the beauty of her eyes, her hand on his arm offering comfort. He groaned and leaned his head against the metal chain.

Not her. He could not fall for Sutton Mize. A woman

who was barely out of a serious relationship and way out of his league. A woman who was using him to save face and for a good time. Did the universe have that big a streak of irony? Or was it truly a curse?

Before Hazel could get out her scalpel and probe deeper, he brushed a kiss on her soft cheek and stood. "I'm bushed."

He was halfway down the steps when she said, "I know where your mom is. Come see me when you're ready to find her."

His body locked up, and his head grew swimmy. Two deep breaths unlocked his muscles, and he walked away with his body and mind weighted with too many worries. Before he stepped foot in the barn, his twin alarm sounded.

Everything was dark, the back door open to the moonlight. Jackson was sprawled on the couch, a beer bottle dangling from his hand. Wyatt grabbed two more from the fridge, uncapped them, and joined his brother to stare out at the seemingly endless expanse of trees lit by the moon.

"How'd things go?" Jackson set down his empty bottle and took the proffered beer.

"Good. Fine." The two words were too simple to convey the tangle of his feelings.

"Seeing her again?"

"Tomorrow. I'm taking her to a pig picking at her parents' house."

Jackson grunted and took a swig.

Wyatt scraped at the label on his bottle. "You ever wonder where our mom is? What she's doing? If she's okay?"

"You mean the woman who's never tried to get in touch even though she damn well knows we're still here?" The force of the bitterness in Jackson's words took Wyatt aback.

Wyatt had missed their mama in an abstract way, not a way that gouged him hollow, but Jackson's loss seemed more immediate and personal. "I'm taking that for a no?"

"Don't need her. Don't need anybody." Jackson took a

long pull of his beer and knuckle-punched Wyatt in the arm. "Anyway, I'll always have you, right?"

Wyatt cast a side-eye toward his twin. Jackson tipped up the bottle and killed the rest of the beer. While it was true neither one of them would be truly alone as long as they were both alive, it didn't feel like enough for Wyatt. Not anymore.

He had two choices, either end his arrangement with Sutton after the pig picking or ride out the two weeks, try not to do something stupid like fall for her, and then start looking for something serious. He had to consider that their agreement might bring business into the garage and ease the tension that had taken up residence like an un-welcome squatter. He could surely survive two weeks with Sutton Mize.

Jackson got up and stretched, jostling three empty beer bottles at his feet. The clatter sent a nesting bird flying from one of the bushes. It wasn't like Jackson to drown his troubles. He usually met them head-on.

"What's going on with you?" Wyatt asked.

"Worried about Ford and Mack and the garage. Same as you, I'd guess. I'm heading up."

"Are you sure that's all it is?"

"Yep." Jackson was an expert at hiding his emotions behind a legendary stoicism, but Wyatt knew better. His twin had an unshakable loyalty to those he loved that was humbling. His emotions cut deep, and he hadn't been the same since their pop had died.

Wyatt didn't press him further, shifting to watch him shuffle toward the corner stairs to the loft. The receding clomp of boots left Wyatt alone with his chaotic thoughts.

Chapter Nine

Sutton ran a brush through her hair and touched up her lipstick in the hallway mirror, keeping an eye on the front door. The sound of a throaty car engine drew her to the window.

Wyatt pulled into her driveway. Before he even had a chance to get out, she was locking her door and smoothing the folds of a sundress she'd designed. White eyelet overlaid a simple matching sheath dress underneath. She'd changed three times, knowing everyone's eyes would be on her.

Even though no one was there to note his boyfriend-like behavior, he came around the car to open the door for her. She slipped by close enough for her skirt to brush against him and to smell the hint of his piney cologne.

"You look real pretty."

"Thanks. So do you." She gave herself a mental slap upside the head. "I mean handsome. You look handsome."

His laughter was good-natured, and instead of flushing with embarrassment, she returned his smile. He did look handsome in flat-front khakis and a light blue golf shirt. Not fancy, yet a drastic change from the work coveralls and the broken-in jeans she'd seen him in.

When she made a move to slip into the seat, he stopped her with a hand around her wrist. "That dress . . ."

"It's one of mine. Is it not good enough? Should I change?" She fiddled with the folds.

"No." The word came out forcefully before his tone normalized. "It reminds me of the dress you had on the day you fell in the river."

Her nosediving confidence stabilized. "You remember?"

"I told you I remembered everything from when we were young." His eyes were hooded, not giving anything away, but his voice had roughened.

"That was my favorite dress, and my dunk in the river ruined it. This was my vision of a grownup version."

"I was a big jerk back then, but you have to know that I just wanted you to notice me." He let go of her wrist, and she slid into the seat, a little stunned at his declaration. He shut her door and made his way around.

The drive to her parents' house was less than ten minutes, but a fit of uncomfortable nerves had her searching for something to say. "The mayor's going to be there. Our state representative too."

"Good to know. I'll try to avoid scratching my balls before I shake hands." Although his voice was light, an edge had her turning in the seat.

She sighed, kicking herself for saying the wrong thing—again. "I'm sorry. I'm really nervous. Everyone's going to be looking at us, wondering what's true and what's not. How are we going to pull this off?"

"You care too much what everyone thinks." He shot a look from the road to her and back again. "All this stuff you're worrying about isn't important in the big scheme of things."

Maybe he was right, but her life had been confined to the narrow path of everyone's expectations. Breaking loose was like trying to escape a heavily guarded chain gang.

All she knew right now was that she was glad to be going into the party on his arm and not alone. If that made her a selfish coward, then so be it.

Cars were already parked on both sides of the street on the approach to her parents' house. Wyatt slowed, looking to both sides.

"You can go up to the front. Daddy saved a spot for me," she said.

He pulled into the circular driveway and drove to the front of the house, pulling next to an SUV. "The judge does know I'm coming, right?"

She hummed and pulled the door handle, but only had one foot out when he drew out her name with a warning. "Sutton? Tell me your parents know I'm coming."

"I mentioned that I might bring someone." She had a feeling she would regret not giving her parents fair warning of the identity of her date. A "don't ask, don't tell" mandate about her personal life had been enacted.

"What about our agreement?"

If hurt that she had no right to welled up. He didn't actually care about her. They weren't even friends. He was here with her for one reason and one reason only—his family's garage. "I'll pull Daddy aside for a chat."

He nodded, seemingly satisfied, and got out. She bypassed the double oak doors of the house and led him through a wrought iron gated arch with yellow jasmine flowers dripping from all sides.

In the twenty years her father had been an elected judge, his yearly pig pickings had become legend. What had started as a potluck for his first election campaign had turned into a fancier affair. This year's was bigger and better with the election fast approaching.

Pit masters tended to two pigs in the ground at the back of the property, the smell mouthwatering, and caterers circulated with finger foods and drinks. A portable bar was set up on the patio, and chairs and tables were set up to overlook the wildflower-covered field down to the river. It made for a pretty picture.

She stepped from the cover of the jasmine into a shaft of sunlight that had her squinting. Was the initial ebb then increased buzz of conversation her imagination, or was everyone talking about her? Her ears burned.

Wyatt's hand was strong around her waist as he leaned in to whisper, "How about a little alcoholic fortification?"

"Yes, please."

He slid his hand to her lower back and led her toward the bar. Her mother held court under one of the giant, standing umbrellas that kept the guests from melting.

"What's your poison?" he asked.

"White wine spritzer."

"Coming right up."

After he'd excused himself, her mother broke free from the couple who had commanded her attention and trekked in her direction. Sutton considered making a run for it, but her mother was there before she could decide which direction offered the best chance of escape.

"Hello, dear." Her mother leaned in to glance her cheek against Sutton's and give her an air kiss.

"Nice turnout."

"Not bad." Her mother surveyed the crowd with a critical eye before returning her attention to Sutton. "Fair warning: your situation is the talk of the party. How are you holding up?"

The sudden switch from hostess to mother brought tears to Sutton's eyes. Yes, her mother could be controlling and overly protective, but only because she loved her. "I'm doing okay. Is Bree here?"

"She wisely sent her regrets yesterday." Her mother's voice was tart.

"What about Andrew?"

"Still coming last I heard. The man is either truly regretful and wants to make nice or oblivious." Her mother did not suffer fools kindly, and it was obvious in her tone what she considered Andrew.

Wyatt returned and handed Sutton her wine spritzer, keeping what looked like a Jack and Coke. She took a too-big sip, the fizz burning her nose, and coughed.

Wyatt patted her back. After she regained her composure, he slid his hand down and curled it around her waist. Her mother's expression sharpened.

"Mother, this is Wyatt Abbott."

"Mrs. Mize. Nice to make your acquaintance. You have a lovely backyard." He held out a hand and took her mother's. For a moment, Sutton thought he was going to brush a kiss over the back like some old-school Southern beau, but he only held it for a moment before letting go. Wyatt didn't seem the least bit intimidated by her mother, who was formidable in attitude if not size.

"We're partial to the view." Her mother gazed toward the river before snapping her focus to Wyatt. "You and your brothers own a garage over the river?"

"Yes, ma'am. Your husband has been a loyal patron for as far back as I can remember. We still do mechanical repairs, but our business is moving toward the restoration of classic cars. That's our real passion."

When it looked like her mother was going to launch into a game of Twenty Questions, her daddy's voice boomed across the open space, calling for her mother. She excused herself and Sutton looked heavenward in silent thanks. "Don't ask, don't tell" apparently didn't mean that her mother didn't know exactly what was going on.

"You handled my mother perfectly. Very polite and charming." She shuffled toward a wall of evergreens for both shade and cover.

"You sound surprised." He was smiling, but a wrinkle

appeared between his brows as he took a sip and surveyed the crowd. "I might be a Louisiana swamp rat, but my aunts made sure I learned how to speak to my elders."

She shifted toward him and put her hand in the middle of his chest, waiting to speak until he looked at her. "You've been nothing but a gentleman. More so than any of my actual boyfriends."

"Even Tarwater?"

"Especially him."

"How do you mean?" His eyes turned flinty, and he seemed to bow up like a wild animal ready to defend itself. Or her.

She couldn't seem to tear her eyes away from his or remove her hand. No one had ever looked at her like this, and considering their arrangement, she didn't know what to make of it. His heart beat against her palm, a solid, comforting rhythm that eased the beat of her own into slower and calmer waters.

"He wasn't abusive or anything. But he never loved me. I was a means to an end. The end being taking my father's judgeship when he retires." Her horse wasn't any higher. She'd let the relationship happen to her because it had made everyone else happy. The events were as much her fault.

"If that lump of humanity didn't appreciate you, then his loss." He wrapped his hand around her nape, his thumb brushing the sensitive skin behind her ear.

She wanted to believe him. Or at least wanted to believe that he thought she was special in some small way. Because despite her bias against him from when they were kids and her current situation, she was struck by the fact he was more than a little special himself, and he deserved to hear it.

"I think—"

"Wyatt Abbott, you old dog, didn't expect to see you here," a deep male voice came from behind her.

Wyatt dropped his hand, and she turned.

Sawyer Fournette, the husband of Regan Fournette, Cottonbloom, Mississippi's state representative, approached with an easy grin and his hand out for a friendly shake and shoulder bump with Wyatt.

"How do you two know each other?" she asked, unable to keep an answering smile off her face.

"I was a couple of years behind Sawyer in school," Wyatt said.

"Of course, I'd forgotten . . ." She let her thought stay unsaid.

"That we're both swamp rats?" Sawyer's grin took any bite out of the nickname some Mississippi residents used for their brethren on the other side of the river.

"How do you like living over here?" Wyatt asked.

"I've been assimilated."

"You mean brainwashed? I heard you played for a Mississippi team last baseball season." Wyatt's tease spoke of a long-standing, comfortable friendship.

Sawyer made a scoffing noise. "Cade about hung me upside down over a gator's nest for defecting, but it made Regan happy." He glanced over his shoulder to where his wife chatted with a group of older ladies. Regan was casually sophisticated in a dress Sutton had sold her that spring and her customary heels, her strawberry blond hair twisted up.

Sawyer continued. "You and your brothers should team up with Cade. You boys would decimate all comers."

"The garage takes up too much of our time and energy."

Sawyer rolled his eyes in Sutton's direction and thumbed toward Wyatt. "I tried to get our boy here to play for the high school baseball team. Three guesses what his excuse was—no time because of the family garage. Those Abbotts have oil running through their veins."

While they chatted about their respective siblings and caught up on gossip about their extended families, Sutton studied Wyatt. He was built like an athlete, although she might have picked football as his sport.

Regan sent a friendly wave in Sutton's direction and called for her husband. "Sawyer, I want you to meet someone."

"She's lucky I like shaking hands and kissing babies." Sawyer's gaze bounced between them. "Hope I'll be seeing you at more stuff up here, Wyatt. Good to have some Louisiana friends to commiserate with at these political shindigs."

"You make our parties sound boring." Sutton's faked outrage was ruined by a smile she couldn't stop.

"You said it, not me." Sawyer backed away, wagging his finger in their direction with a wink. "You need to take her out to a bonfire, Wyatt. Show her some real fun."

"Good idea. See ya, bro."

Sawyer turned and quickstepped to his wife, throwing an arm around her shoulders and hauling her in for a kiss on the temple. Their connection was obvious even from twenty paces. Her heart ached a little.

"Would you?" She transferred her attention back to Wyatt.

"Would I what?"

"Take me to a bonfire."

His eyebrows rose along with one corner of his mouth. "If you want to go."

Pre-dumped Sutton never would have seriously considered going. "You promised me fun, right? I've heard about them."

He laughed softly. "It will never live up to what you've heard. Just like me."

"What do you mean?"

"You've heard things about me, right? My guess is most of it's either not true or greatly exaggerated."

"So you're not the greatest lover either side of Cotton-bloom has seen in a half-century?" The flirt in her voice bubbled up unexpectedly.

His look of surprise was followed by booming laughter, and she couldn't help but join him. Their agreement didn't feel very businesslike. It was tinged with a burgeoning friendship, flirtation, and more than a slight attraction—at least on her part.

"Okay, you got me. That one's true," he said between guffaws.

"What's so funny? I love a good joke." Her daddy, Judge Mize, or simply the Judge, as he was known around most of Cottonbloom, hauled her to his side in a slightly sweaty hug.

He wasn't physically imposing, but carried himself with the bluster of a bigger man and had a voice that could instill fear in lawyers and criminals alike. Her daddy liked to joke they were one and the same. With a full head of blond-silvery hair and the tanned faced of an outdoorsman, he reminded her of an aged lion, still prideful and strong and attempting to retain control of his territory, which included her.

She suppressed another spate of giggles and deflected. "Great turnout."

"All the important players showed up." He cast a glance over his shoulder before turning his assessing eyes on them. "Good to see you, Wyatt."

Her father held out a hand. Wyatt took it, and her father seemed satisfied with the firmness of his grip. Her daddy counted himself an excellent judge of character, although after he gave Andrew his stamp of approval, his abilities must be called into question.

"Nice to see you somewhere beside the garage, sir. How's the Escalade running?"

"Excellent. Not a bit of trouble with it." Sutton's daddy pursed his lips. "I've played golf with your brother Ford a few times now. I invited him this afternoon as a matter of fact."

"Did you now?" Wyatt's voice lowered and turned dry. "Can't wait to see him."

"Yes, indeed." He wiped a white handkerchief over his forehead. "Sorry the deal with Tarwater's car fell through. I could tell Ford was mighty disappointed."

"No worries." Wyatt glanced in her direction. "But if you know of anyone else looking to get their car restored, please send them in our direction."

A half hour of flirting and having fun with Wyatt, and she had flubbed her end of the bargain. Forgotten, is more like it. "Yes, Daddy, could you point them in the Abbotts' direction?"

"Sure, sure. Your father was a good mechanic and even better man. I know he'd be proud of you boys." Her daddy clapped Wyatt on the shoulder, but his attention had shifted to something or someone else. "If you two will excuse me."

A silence she interpreted as uncomfortable settled between them. "I'm sorry."

"For what now?"

"I should have said something first. I'll do better, I promise."

He cocked his head and looked her over. She wasn't sure what he saw, his expression giving nothing away. He shook his head and finished his drink, the ice tinkling. "You'd be happier if you worried less about making everyone else happy."

His assessment was so unexpected and on-point, her knee-jerk response was automatic. "I'm happy."

"That's what you tell everyone—even yourself."

She took a sip, but the wine had a hard time making it down her tightened throat. She'd lost her fiancé. And best friend. Deep down, she was lonely. And scared of taking chances.

"I love Abigail's," she said unable to mask the defensiveness in her voice.

"I sense a 'but' in there." His perceptiveness stripped away the polite façade she usually maintained. Things she'd not told her sister or her parents or Andrew slipped out.

"I really wanted to get a fashion degree from Savannah College of Art and Design. Instead, I went to Cottonbloom College, majored in business, and lived at home. When my parents offered me the money to buy Abigail's, I couldn't turn it down." She chuffed and shook her head. "That's a lie. I wasn't brave enough to break free. But, my parents love me."

"I can see that they do." His voice was understanding and soothing. "Believe me, we're more similar than you can imagine."

With an unexpected clarity, she recognized the truth behind his smiles. "Are you lonely too, Wyatt?"

His eyes flared wider, but he didn't break their connection, the ebb and flow of feelings between them intense and difficult to define.

"Maybe." His mouth may have uttered the equivocation, but his eyes said, "Yes."

"But you have your brothers."

"Lots of love there. But since Pop died, we've drifted apart. If I walked away tomorrow, Mack and Jackson would take up the slack and keep working. They wouldn't miss me."

"That's not true." A desperation tinged her denial.

If Wyatt disappeared tomorrow, she had no idea how his brothers would feel, but *she* would miss him. Terribly. It made no sense, but her life had stopped making sense the moment he'd pulled Bree's panties from under Andrew's seat.

She stumbled back onto a semi-logical path of thought. "You're a natural salesman, you know. You put people at ease. You're trustworthy. You should go around to car shows and drum up business for the garage."

"Can't. That's Ford's self-designated area of expertise. As he likes to remind us whenever he can, he's the one with a marketing degree. The only one of us who went to college." The bitter flavor in his voice was shocking when compared to his usual tone.

"Degree or not, people like you. Anyway, drumming up business doesn't seem to be Ford's top priority."

"What do you mean?"

"Golf at the country club several afternoons a week. He's on everyone's guest list these days." She gestured around them. "This lifestyle can be appealing to some people."

Wyatt ran a hand over his jaw and caught what sounded like a string of four-letter words into his palm.

"What's wrong?" she asked.

"Maybe nothing. Maybe a nuclear warhead about to hit the garage." He leaned so close, she could make out the start of his five o'clock shadow that her fingertips itched to explore.

"Can I trust you?"

The question jarred her out of the runaway train of her inappropriate thoughts. "Of course you can."

"Has Ford put out any feelers to sell his part of the garage?"

The argument she'd interrupted days ago fell into place. "Surely, he can't do that?"

"Nothing in the will forbids it. Pop assumed all of us loved the garage as much as he did, but Ford was never happy working there. Not sure why Pop couldn't see that."

She glanced toward her parents, standing side-by-side and entertaining their constituency. They'd had the best intentions when they'd convinced her to stay in Cotton-bloom and later pushed her at Andrew. "Families are complicated."

"Understatement of the millennium." Worry drew his eyes into a squint and tightened his mouth.

She put her hand on the curve of his shoulder and shifted to stand in front of him so he would have to look at her. "I haven't heard anything, but I'll ask around."

"That'd be great. I'd really appreciate it."

"The least I can do considering . . ." She waved her hand around.

"Considering what?" His confusion seemed genuine.

"Don't pretend this isn't boring. You'd probably rather be anywhere else." She rolled her eyes.

"Hey." He waited until she met his gaze through her lashes. "Doesn't matter where we are, spending time with you is no hardship. If things had been different, I would have asked you out for real in a heartbeat."

Her world tipped and realigned itself along a new axis.

His confession hung between them. Yes, she was the sweetest, sexiest thing he had ever crossed paths with, but telling her wasn't something he should do. Not with their arrangement and her recent heartbreak coloring everything—and not in a happy rainbow kind of way. She would assume he was manipulating her for his own gain just as Tarwater had done.

As if summoned from Wyatt's damning thoughts, Tarwater stepped through the jasmine bower in seersucker pants with a grin that rivaled a catalog model's. For once though, Wyatt was thankful for the interruption. He put his arm around her shoulders and hauled her tight against him. He had a part to play, after all.

"Tarwater has arrived. Alone."

"Mother told me Bree sent her regrets."

Wyatt hummed. "Maybe she has a heart after all. Unlike your ex. Who—don't look—is headed this way."

The guests in their general vicinity all seemed to strain toward the three of them.

Wyatt's cheeks were growing sore from his fake smiling. He debated on extending a hand, but if Tarwater rejected it, he didn't want to escalate the flames of gossip. He settled on a polite, "Afternoon, Tarwater."

"I'm surprised to see you, Andrew." Sutton's voice was cold and calm. Wyatt wanted to give her a high five, but confined his response to a smirk in Tarwater's direction.

"Only natural I should be invited. I'm one of the Judge's biggest supporters." Tarwater fiddled with the rolled-up cuffs of his loose white linen shirt. "Although lately I've been wondering if the county needs some new blood in the judicial branch."

The silence that settled after his announcement was on par with the countdown to a bomb exploding.

"Is that a threat?" Although anger heated her words, a smile remained on Sutton's face. "You'd never beat Daddy."

"Your little indiscretion has garnered me countywide sympathy." Amusement sharpened his features in a feral, unattractive way. "Still time for me to get on the ballot."

"*My* indiscretion. That's rich." She huffed a laugh.

Tarwater looked like a tomcat ready to pounce. "Are you ready to admit that you and Abbott here made the whole thing up?"

She slipped an arm around Wyatt's waist and notched herself even closer into his side. "We didn't make anything up."

Wyatt heard the slight waver in her voice. Maybe that was her tell, like his twitching eyebrow. He laid a kiss on top of her head. "Sorry, Tarwater. We're together. And happy. Where's Bree?"

Tarwater made a *pfft* noise and walked off as if they weren't worth his time.

"Could he actually give your dad a run for the judge-ship?" Wyatt asked, keeping his gaze on the back of his enemy's blond head.

"I don't know," she said with a vague worry that in turn worried him. "He's young and successful and handsome."

"You forgot fake and dishonest." Tarwater stood with a group of men who together looked like an ad for some preppy clothes catalog. The kind of catalog Wyatt ripped apart and used to soak up oil stains. "And he's not *that* good looking."

"You sound jealous." Her voice was singsongy, and the spot she poked underneath his ribs had him squirming away with laughter. "Oh my stars, you're ticklish. I never would have guessed a big, sexy dude like you would be ticklish."

Her words punched away his laughter, and he grabbed both her wrists to stop her jabs. "You think I'm sexy?"

She pinched her lips together before she muttered, "Maybe." But her eyes said, "Yes."

He wanted to lean down and kiss her. Not to prove something to Tarwater or Cottonbloom, but because he wanted to—desperately.

A hand fell on his shoulder and dug into muscle. He let go of Sutton and whirled. Ford stood there with murder in his eye. Or at least the promise of a good beating.

"What are you doing here?" Ford didn't bother to mask his exasperation and annoyance. He'd fit right in with Tarwater and his ilk in light-colored dress pants, a pink button down, and a blue-checked bow tie.

Wyatt forced a smile. "That's no way to greet your baby brother."

"Haven't you done enough by losing the Camaro? I'm here to clean up your mess."

"It wasn't my fault." The denial sprung out before he could stop it. Ford had worked his way under Wyatt's skin like a rash when they were kids, and he had never found a cure.

"Whatever." Ford pulled his mouth into something resembling a smile. "Hello, Sutton. Where's the Judge?"

She stepped between them, facing Ford with her hands on her hips. "Around. And busy."

Wyatt almost smiled at the shooing tone of her voice. Was she trying to protect him?

"Can I talk to you? Alone." Ford bored his stare over Sutton's head and into him.

"Sure. Give me a sec." Wyatt waited until Ford stepped out of earshot, let out a breath, and tilted toward Sutton. "You gonna be okay if I leave you here?"

She grabbed his hand. "Are *you* going be okay?"

His heart warmed like it had been wrapped in an electric blanket. He leaned in to brush his lips against her cheek, unable to find the words to answer her.

Ford had a drink in hand by the time Wyatt joined him. Ford nudged his head, and Wyatt followed him out into the field of flowers.

"I like your clip-on bow tie. Real suave." Wyatt kept his voice teasing. No reason to get Ford more riled up than he already was. "The Camaro wasn't my fault, you know."

Some of the fight went out of Ford. "I know. I heard what happened. It's frustrating, you know?"

"Mack said the garage could weather the loss."

Ford kicked at the ground, uprooting a flower. "It's all about the garage surviving."

His bitter sarcasm wasn't anything new, but Wyatt studied him with fresh eyes. He looked like hell. Dark smudged under his bloodshot eyes, and new lines bracketed his mouth. He'd always been leaner than the rest of them, but now he bordered on downright skinny. Was it stress or something else?

Wyatt squeezed Ford's shoulder. "Are you okay, bro?"

Ford killed his drink in one go. "I'm fine."

"You don't look fine. You look like shit."

"At least I have nice clothes. That the best you could come up with?" Ford waved a finger over Wyatt's khakis and plain golf shirt.

As insults went, it was lame. Ford wasn't even trying, which planted more worry. "I could help you."

"Don't need your help." Ford's shoulders squared. "Give me a week, and I'll bag an even bigger project for the garage. What will Mack have to say then?"

"Probably 'good job.' Unless I'm mistaken, bringing in business is kind of your job, right?" Wyatt kept his voice light. He wouldn't win any confidences if Ford was on the defensive.

Ford ignored him and tipped his glass back, but only ice remained.

Wyatt continued. "Listen, what you said the other day about selling out . . . You didn't mean that, did you?"

"Nah. Just trying to get a rise out of Mack." Ford didn't meet his eyes, making it difficult to get a read on truth or lie.

Someone Wyatt didn't recognize greeted Ford like a long-lost frat brother. Wyatt slipped away, his talk with Ford doing nothing to alleviate the foreboding feeling following the family like smog.

He scanned the crowd for Sutton and spotted her in conversation with an older lady. Sutton's smile was warm and genuine. As if she sensed him watching her, she glanced up before he could play things cool.

Her smile didn't fall but changed into something more complicated. Something that tangled the slipknot holding them together. He shook off the feeling when her father called for everyone's attention.

His stump speech was followed by food and lots of it. Wyatt stayed by Sutton's side, but he was little more than a curiosity to the stream of people he was introduced to. By the time dusk was on them, his head hurt from the sun and constant smiling. He retreated to the field and rotated his jaw.

He startled when Sutton slipped her hand in his elbow. "When I was a kid, I would hide in the flowers, pretend I couldn't hear Mother calling, and tell myself stories about the things I saw in the clouds. But if I was feeling really brave, I would go all the way to the river and look for skipping stones."

Lightning bugs blinked amongst the wildflowers. It was hard to believe the same river had unknowingly connected them. "Jackson and I used to do that too. We'd fish or catch frogs or swim."

"You had a built-in best friend." A hint of wistfulness had him shifting to see her. The orange glow of the sun glinted off her blond hair and made her eyes sparkle.

"The very best. You had a sister."

"We're closer now, but her nose was always in a book. She didn't need a friend. I was alone a lot except when I was with—" Pain that looked almost physical in nature flashed over her face. The thought of losing Jackson made Wyatt's stomach crimp.

"You miss Bree," he said.

"Crazy, right?" She picked a small purple flower on a long stem and plucked the petals off. "I've actually picked up my phone to call her before I remember."

"Hey." When she didn't look up at him, he stopped the flower carnage with one hand and took her chin in his other, forcing her to look at him. "You can call me anytime, day or night."

"Are you my friend?"

Friend didn't seem the right label. He wasn't sure what they were becoming. The beauty of her eyes put him into a trance-like state. A woman called Sutton's name and shook him free of whatever spell had been cast. She appeared just as dazed and glanced toward the river. If she suggested they run through the field and to the river, he'd grab her hand and go.

"Mother asked if I would stay and help clean up," she said finally. "You don't have to wait around."

The disappointment was sharp and unexpected. "I guess that's my cue to skedaddle."

"Thanks for coming with me."

"Sure." If this had been a real date, he would have kissed her. But he had agreed he wouldn't do that again. He waited for her to suggest another event or date. She didn't. "I'll be seeing you around?"

When all she did was nod and watch him back away, he stuffed his hands into his pockets and turned, passing under the arbor and toward the cold comfort of his car.

Chapter Ten

Sutton crossed her legs and wiggled her foot. Her phone's blank screen mocked. It was Wednesday, and they hadn't made another date at the pig picking. She'd held her breath at the end hoping for . . . something. Not a kiss but at least an invitation somewhere. Or had he been waiting for her to suggest something? Her limited experience didn't extend to whatever it was they were doing.

The past four days had been interminable without even the hope she'd see him again. That morning a plan that had been percolating since the pig picking manifested itself into action. While Wyatt had been in conversation with Ford, she had chatted with Mrs. Alfred Knowles, a widow of twenty-odd years who still went by her husband's name.

The small talk had consisted mostly of gardening, roses in particular, but when Sutton mentioned who her date was, Mrs. Knowles confessed to having her husband's old car sitting in her garage. A 1982 LeBaron convertible that hadn't been driven in over a decade. While the car might not be the classic that Wyatt and his brothers sought, how many other car widows were roaming around Cotton-bloom?

He *had* invited her to call or text him anytime, and this

was as good an excuse as any. Her fingers trembled slightly when she picked up her phone to text him.

Can you take off early and meet me at Abigail's?

She stared at her screen. What if he'd decided she wasn't worth the trouble and never texted back? What felt like an hour ticked away. She should have contacted him before now or not at all. She banged her head against the glass countertop a couple of times. Her phone pinged, and she made a grab for it.

Give me 30 to clean up.

According to her phone, a mere two minutes had passed since she'd sent her text. The self-doubt-induced time warp left her feeling queasy.

She checked her appearance in one of the floor-to-ceiling mirrors. Flared blue and white checked skirt, simple, button-up white blouse, and embellished flip-flops. Nothing she'd designed, but cute. She fluffed her hair and paced the floor, checking the street every few seconds.

Her sister put the paperback she was reading face down on her lap and propped her chin on her fist. "What's with the ants in your pants?"

"I'm waiting for someone." She side-eyed her sister. Maggie watched her with her dark, permanently curious eyes. If they were closer, Sutton might confess nerves and uncertainty.

She forced herself still when his car made the turn onto River Street, which meant her pent-up nervous energy was trapped. Her internal organs danced a jig. When he entered, she locked eyes with him, and everything inside of her settled down like a cat finding its favorite spot in the sun.

She smiled, but he didn't smile back. Not immediately. His gaze raked her from head to toe with such intensity, her toes curled. For a long moment, she was content to have him in her eyesight.

"Are you in need of my stellar fashion advice?" The corner of his mouth quirked as he weaved his way through the racks.

Her smile widened if that was possible, and she closed the distance between them, no longer content to just see him. She allowed her hand to brush lightly against his arm below the black sleeve of his T-shirt.

"Hey, Mags, you mind if I take Wyatt down to the Quilting Bee?" Sutton asked.

"No problem. Slow afternoon anyway." Her sister sounded close to laughter, but Sutton didn't look away from Wyatt, her gaze hungry after so many days apart.

He opened the boutique's door and gestured her through. "Are we going to join a quilting circle?"

"Not exactly. I had the spark of an idea at the pig picking, and I'm thinking the Quilting Bee is the best place to put out some feelers."

"You going to fill me in or let it be a surprise?"

She stopped under the shady overhang on the sidewalk. "Two words: Car. Widows."

He took a deep breath and on the exhale said, "What?"

"Widows whose husbands passed away and left cars behind. Cars that the wife might not be interested in maintaining. Mrs. Knowles has an '82 LeBaron sitting in her garage gathering dust."

"That's one of the ugliest cars known to man and a dime a dozen." He crossed his arms over his chest, emphasizing his biceps.

She had the urge to trace the bulge of muscle with a fingertip, but tucked her hands between her and the brick wall instead. "But how many neglected cars are sitting in garages around Cottonbloom? Surely one or two will be worth your talents."

He considered her before a slow smile spread across his face, crinkling his eyes. "You may be on to something.

When we go to trade shows, we target men for the most part. But realistically how many widows are wandering Cottonbloom?"

"I don't know, but this is the place to start." She nodded toward the door. "Are you game?"

"I'm up for anything you suggest, darlin'."

His suggestive drawl hit her blood stream like a sugar rush. Was he talking cars or something else entirely? He'd invaded her dreams every night since that first "give 'em something to talk about" kiss on her front porch.

"Let's start here and see what happens, shall we?" With him, her flirty tone came naturally, and he responded by propping a hand on the bricks by her head and leaning in. The gleam in his eye made her feel less like a pity project or an agreement and more like a woman.

Two ladies stepped out of the Quilting Bee and cast them curious looks. Even though being seen was the point of their alliance, this moment didn't feel like it was for the benefit of stoking the rumors. It felt private and personal.

Or was it simply the product of her overactive imagination? Her nerve dissolved under the summer sun and threat of an audience. She straightened and slipped out of the cage he'd drawn around her with his body.

"I'll introduce you around. If none of the ladies here have cars stashed away, maybe they know of someone who does." She led the way inside the Quilting Bee before he could question her weirdness.

Ms. Effie held her arms out but bypassed Sutton for Wyatt. "Wyatt Abbott. I was telling Hyacinth last Sunday that I hadn't seen you at church in a coon's age." Ms. Effie gave him a hug and stepped back, still patting both his arms. "I was getting ready to invent some car problem so I could check up on you boys."

"We're same old, same old. And you don't have to make anything up. We always have coffee brewed, and I'll make myself available to share a cup anytime." Wyatt's charm was easy and natural and genuine.

With a hold on Wyatt's wrist, Ms. Effie leaned toward Sutton as if imparting a secret. "I used to be sweet on their daddy, but his mistress was that dadgum garage. When not even my cupcakes won his heart, I gave up. But I kept a soft spot for these boys. I'm glad to see you two keeping time."

Heat flushed through Sutton despite the churning air conditioner. "Yes, well . . ." she cleared her throat and cast a pleading look toward Wyatt which he answered with only a quirk of his lips.

"Now, what can I do you for?" Ms. Effie asked. "Interested in a quilt?"

"Actually, we're here because I had an idea to help the Abbotts' garage," she said.

"Do tell, but come over here and do it while I straighten the fabric remnants."

They followed her to the far corner where quilting squares of all different patterns and shades were stacked in cubbies. She joined Ms. Effie in refolding stacks that had been riffled through by customers.

Wyatt pulled up a chair and gestured with two fingers. "Give me some."

While the three of them folded, Sutton explained, encouraged by Ms. Effie's hums. "I don't suppose you have an interesting car tucked away somewhere?" Sutton finally asked.

Ms. Effie gave an unladylike snort. "The only thing my no-good husband left worth keeping was my son, but I might know some ladies who would fit the bill. I certainly don't mind spreading the word."

Sutton clutched a piece of fabric to her chest, wanting to jump up and down and hug someone, preferably Wyatt. "Thank you so much."

She and Wyatt stayed to finish the job, and Sutton wasn't

surprised at all to see him lean down to give the old lady
a kiss on the cheek. "There's a coffee cup waiting on you
at the garage, you hear?"

"I'll be by soon to let you know how I get on." Ms. Effie
waved them off. "You two run along and have fun."

Once they were back on the sidewalk, Sutton's excitement boiled over. She did an impromptu clog she'd learned
during her years in dance. "Why aren't you more excited?
This could be huge."

"You're more than enough excited for us both." His
laugh was good-natured, but his next words deflated her
balloon of excitement. "If Tarwater taught me anything,
it's not to count my cars until they pull into the garage, and
sometimes not even then."

"I'm sorry." She couldn't help but feel responsible for
the predicament she'd left him and his brothers to handle.

He grabbed her hand and maneuvered her into a narrow cutout between brick storefronts, affording them a
modicum of privacy. "Hold up. You have nothing to apologize for."

"But, if I had—"

"Gone ahead and married that lying sack?"

She gave a little laugh. "Not much of an option, huh?"

He reached out and fingered a piece of her hair. She
froze, not even daring to take a breath. "What are you doing
this evening?" he asked.

"N-nothing." Her date with a pair of sweat pants and
her latest design project could wait.

"Do you want to get a little wild?"

Her rise to the challenge in his voice was becoming
easier. "What'd you have in mind?"

"There's a bonfire tonight."

"Are we invited?"

Laughter burst from him, and he was so close, she could
feel the vibrations.

"What's so funny?" Even though she had a feeling he was laughing at her, she found herself smiling.

"I'm picturing one of the boys getting formal invitations printed up on flowery stationary. As long as you have a couple of bucks for the keg, then you're welcome."

"Even though I'm not a swamp—" She cut herself off before the derogatory nickname made it completely out.

"Don't worry, I'm sure there will be some other 'Sips out there slumming it." His tone remained good-natured.

"In that case, I'd love to go." She smoothed her skirt. "Should I change?"

His gaze skimmed down her body, leaving a path of awareness in its wake. "You look perfect. Let's grab some food before we head out."

While they waited for the sun to go down, they shared a pizza before loading into his Hornet. Two-lane country roads led them into a part of the parish she'd never explored. Her jitters grew with every mile and escalated when he turned off pavement and onto the dirt lane. Rains had gouged twin tire tracks, leaving them muddy. The back wheels of the car spun in a particularly deep rut.

"Are we stuck?" She clutched the dashboard with both hands.

"Not for long." He backed up to gain traction and took a different tack, slipping and sliding and rocking through the ruts. "I probably should have stopped off at the garage for a work truck though."

"Because we're not going to make it?"

"Because cleaning up the undercarriage of this car is going to take hours." He shot a smile in her direction and patted her knee. "Even if we did get stuck, we'd get a tow out or a ride home. No worries."

His hand remained on her knee, his fingers curling to brush the sensitive underside. Now she was nervous for entirely different reasons. Confusion ran roughshod through her thoughts. No one was there to bear witness to his touch.

The steering wheel jerked, and he grabbed it with both hands, keeping them moving forward toward the tree line. They left the rain-soaked field behind for higher pine-needle-strewn ground. His headlights glinted off metal and chrome through the trees. He broke through the narrow copse and parked next to a black truck.

With the engine off, whoops and hollers drifted from the crowd gathered around the bonfire. Jeans and shorts with tank tops or tees were all she saw.

"You ready?" He had his door open and one foot out.

She opened up the visor and checked herself in the vanity mirror. "I'm going to kill you."

"What? You look fine."

"I look fine if I was headed to a church potluck." The cut of the white blouse and length of the skirt were too prim.

Surely she could manipulate her clothes into something that said "party" and not "bible study." She rolled the waistband of her skirt, taking a couple of inches off the length. Next, she popped the top button of her blouse. She thrust her shoulders back and turned to him. "Is that better?"

The cleavage she'd exposed would be considered tame by any normal man's judgement. Obviously, his judgment was impaired, because the curves inspired a litany of gibberish he barely managed to contain to a grunt.

"Ohmigod, you're right. I still look like a Mary-Sue." With one hand, she popped another button open and shimmied until her chest was exposed to her bra line. "Better?"

"Better." If his voice sounded like it had been beaten against river rocks, she didn't comment on it.

She pushed the door open. He fumbled with his door handle while trying to coax blood flow from his little brain back to his big one. By the time he emerged, she was waiting and linked her arm through his.

"To make this look real I should laugh at all your dumb jokes, right?"

His gaze snagged on lacy edge of her bra, but with brain functions restored, he raised his eyes to safer regions. "You should laugh if you feel like laughing, and what do you mean by dumb jokes? I'm hilarious."

"One of your exes tell you that?" In the flickering flames of the bonfire, her eyes twinkled and sparked all different colors.

"The gauntlet has been thrown. My mission tonight will be to get you to laugh so hard beer comes out of your nose."

She made an *eww* sound and gave him a playful hip bump. The mingling groups of people around them were blurs in his periphery.

Someone grabbed his upper arm. "Dude, did you not hear me calling?"

He turned and met the smiling eyes of Jace Abbott, five years his junior and a cousin, once or twice removed. "Hey, man."

"It's been forever since you've graced us with your presence." Jace's smile was lopsided and had charmed more than one country girl into the bed of his truck to watch the stars come out. It was also aimed at Sutton.

Wyatt slipped his arm around her shoulders and narrowed his eyes at Jace while making brief introductions. They exchanged pleasantries and small talk, until something his cousin said made Sutton laugh a little too heartily.

Wyatt beat back the green-tinted splinters that worked themselves into his psyche. Sutton Mize was not his. She was only pretending to be his no matter how convincing her smile and lean into him was.

Wyatt led her toward the keg at the far edge of the crowd. Because he hadn't been around as much lately and was with Sutton, friends and family stopped him to chat and get introduced.

Once he reached the keg, he stuffed a twenty into a red solo cup sitting on a stool and filled two cups from the spout. He handed one to Sutton and drank half his down in one go.

Delmar Fournette, an old swamp rat with bowed legs and a talent on the mandolin, clapped Wyatt on the shoulder on his way to the stool. He perched on the edge and tuned his instrument.

Delmar was one of those men whose age was indeterminate, but the impression was one of vast experience yet a feeling he'd be around forever. Wyatt remembered him stopping by the shop to visit with his pop in the evenings, sometimes with his mandolin. The plaintive notes would echo against the concrete of the bays and give a brief, melancholy life to the inanimate nuts and bolts.

"How're you doing, old man?" Wyatt asked.

"Fair to middling. Can't complain." He strummed a few chords. "Miss your father."

The chords settled into a Cajun-flavored song that had been his pop's favorite, and Wyatt's whispered "Me too" was lost in the music.

More and more lately, he sought a missing part of himself that had nothing to do with drinking a few beers and exchanging laughs. That good-old-boy persona felt like a shirt he'd outgrown. The disquiet had besieged him even before his pop's death, but the magnitude of that earthquake had forever changed the landscape. The achingly familiar music sent aftershocks through him.

Sutton's expression was serious, equal amounts of worry and curiosity on display.

"You want to walk down to the river?" he asked.

She would be well within rights to mount a protest. A retreat wasn't what he'd offered or what she'd signed up for. She'd come for a party. An experience. If she insisted on returning to mix with the crowd, he would paste on a smile and show her a good time.

"Sure. Let's go." She slid her hand into his. "There isn't a chance we could run across an alligator, is there?"

"Probably not with all this noise." He thumbed over his shoulder as they strolled toward the dark, silent tree line.

"*Probably* not? Don't tease me about this, Wyatt. My mother terrified me with stories of little Mississippi girls wandering off and getting dragged all the way across state lines by gators." Echoes of childish fear pitched her voice high.

"Sounds to me like your mother spoon-fed you some tall tales. She didn't want you near the river or Louisiana, if I had to guess." He didn't add that while not yet common, as more people built along the coast shrinking their habitat, gators had been spotted along the river on both sides of Cottonbloom.

Her hand relaxed in his. "You're right. Mother has always veered protective. Maggie never had an urge to explore or push boundaries. She stayed in her room and read for hours and hours. When I came along, the only thing that seemed to work was instilling the fear of God, gators . . . everything, I suppose."

"You don't seem scared now." He helped her over a rotting log. The trees closed in around them, blocking the moon and muting the light from the bonfire.

"Then I'm hiding it better than I think. Accepting Andrew's proposal was the coward's way out."

"What do you mean?" Fallen pine needles muffled their footsteps, and the darkness lent an intimacy he equated with a Catholic's confessional.

"Marrying Andrew was the path of least resistance. My

life's trajectory was sending me hurtling toward that final destination, and I was too weak to jump off."

"You're free now."

"Not because of some great leap of bravery on my part. I've let life happen to me. Do you know what I mean?" Her sigh was like a shush of wind through the leaves.

He thought about the college scholarship he'd given up to stay in the safety of the garage with his family. "I know exactly what you mean."

The sound of the river grew louder, muffling the shouts and laughter behind them and widening the feeling of solitude. They reached the bank, and he guided her to sit on a mossy spot at the edge of the bank under a river birch. Wispy fog rose from the river, an earthy smell mingling with the smoke from the bonfire.

"If you could go back, would you go to that design school in Savannah?" he asked.

When she answered, her voice was soft as if she didn't want to wake the world around them. "Actually, my big dream was to move to New York and make a name for myself."

"You don't want that anymore?"

"I won't lie, I thought about packing a bag and taking off after the Camaro fiasco, but not to follow my dream— to escape my nightmare." She played with the collar of her shirt, her fingers long and graceful and smooth, so unlike his dinged, work roughened hands. "The other night when Ms. Eckert loved my dress and bought it, I realized what I want."

"Tell me."

"I want to start my own label, but not in New York, here in Cottonbloom. I'll start small—a few pieces in Abigail's and see where it goes. At least I can say I tried."

"I predict you won't be able to keep up with demand." He had full confidence in her abilities.

She leaned her head against his shoulder and whispered, "Thanks."

Her fingers brushed his, and she didn't seem bothered by the calluses and nicks. The sweetness of the moment was reflected in a whippoorwill's song high up in the trees. Night sounds and the river muted the need for conversation.

"What about you?" she asked. "What's your dream?"

"I'm living my dream." He said it so confidently, he almost believed it himself, but his eyebrow twitched, and he pulled his hand away from hers to rub at the offending line of jumpy nerves. Before she could probe deeper, he stood. "Didn't I promise you fun and games?"

Chapter Eleven

His answer was superficial, but Sutton didn't press him. Fun was good. Fun was what she needed, not the seriousness of her confessions in the dark.

Yet she didn't move.

All black and whites angles in the shadows, he was strength and passion and so far out of her realm of experience that she was afraid.

But fear was double-edged. Her mother had taught her daughters that chances were not to be taken, because they inevitability led to failure. Yet fear and excitement were kissing cousins. The kind of fear Wyatt incited made her want to follow him anywhere.

She pushed up from the soft moss, and they picked their way through the underbrush, the light of the fire a beacon through the trees. If he wanted to have fun, then she would keep things light from here on out. "So there's Ford and Mack . . . why didn't your daddy give you and Jackson vehicle names too?"

"Actually, Barrett-Jackson is a big auction house for cars.

"Why are you Wyatt and not Barrett, then?"

"Story is that my mom put her foot down. Apparently,

I have her eyes, and she wanted to name me." Although his voice didn't reflect any angst, she sensed his mother was a cut that had never healed.

Her hand found his like a magnet finding its mate, and she knitted their fingers together. Music drifted through the trees. Not the haunting melodies from Delmar Fournette's mandolin, but country music from the speakers of someone's truck.

"You know how to two-step?" Wyatt asked.

"No, but I learned how to waltz and foxtrot during cotillion, a lot of good that does me."

Wyatt tugged her into a faster walk. "I'll teach you.

"No way. Not in front of everyone. I'll look like an idiot." She pulled at his arm, but inertia was on his side.

"That's your fear talking. Come on and take a chance on me."

Even though he was talking about something as simple as a dance, the moment felt like a tipping point. Fearful or brave? Which did she choose?

She quit fighting and let him lead her into the circle of light. A handful of couples danced, but a majority of the partiers hung around the edges talking and watching. Before her feet could mount a rebellion and retreat, Wyatt spun her around and put a firm hand on her upper back, holding her other hand in a typical dance hold.

"The two-step is simple. Four steps, two quick, two slow. I step forward on my left, and you step back on your right. Okay?"

She made an affirmative sounding hum and tried to assimilate what he was saying, but heat streaked across her back where his hand branded her. All the eyes fixed on them didn't help her concentration.

He counted them off, and she made it two steps before screwing up. She bit the inside of her cheek. "I can't do it."

"You're acting like this is worse than a firing squad. What are you thinking about?"

"Amoebas."

He gave a slight shake of his head before bursting out in chesty laughter that sent vibrations through his hold to her. "Dare I ask why?"

"I feel like we're being examined like reproducing amoebas through a microscope."

"If I recall my high school biology, amoebas are asexual. I'm not. Forget about everyone else and look at me."

She focused on his face. The flickering fire set gold sparking in his gray eyes, and since he'd invited her to, she let her gaze linger on all his features, but especially his mouth. His lips were mouthing "quick-quick-slow-slow," and she dabbed her bottom lip with her tongue, remembering what they'd felt like against hers.

"You're dancing." His sweet, sexy lips turned up in a smile.

She glanced down and stumbled once, but he righted her easily and got her back in rhythm. She returned her gaze to his mouth. The two-step was fun, but his body was too far away. Could she request a slow dance? A song where he'd be forced to pull her close, her temple against his cheek, her lips against his throat, his long, hard body flush with hers.

The song switched to something slow and sultry, and Sutton almost broke out into the Hallelujah Chorus. Wyatt didn't miss a beat. He skimmed his hand down to her lower back and pressed her against him. She slid both her hands around his shoulders and let her lips brush his skin.

Heaven. She was in heaven in his arms. Melodrama had never been her thing, and passion had always been an abstract concept. Until now. Until him.

Yet, it wasn't real.

She could almost pretend his arms tightened around her out of possessiveness or need, but she knew better. How could she mourn the loss of something that didn't exist? Something that had never been in her grasp and never would be?

But what if she asked him to make it real? For only a night if that's all he wanted. She could be that girl, couldn't she? The kind that could appreciate the physical without getting her emotions wrapped up in a simple act. Granted, it would be a new part for her, but she longed to be someone new, someone different.

The music ended mid song and groans went up around the crowd. She and Wyatt peeled apart, her lips coasting across his cheek and glancing across the corner of his mouth. She couldn't look him in the eye, afraid of the truths he might discover.

She'd never be *that* girl. She hadn't had the proper training. How would she move on if he lived up to even half her fantasies? The future would consist of her sister and a multitude of stray cats for company.

A man called his name, yet he didn't take his hands from her body.

"Someone needs you," she croaked through her dry, narrowed throat. *I need you*, she wanted to say but didn't.

"Stay here. I'll be back in a jiffy." His voice sounded as raw as she felt inside.

She stepped back into the shadows and chafed her arms, cool without the heat of his body and her desires to warm her.

"You and Wyatt, huh?" A feminine voice had her spinning around. The woman sitting on the tailgate of a truck was attractive in a way that matched the sexy, throaty quality of her voice. This woman had never attended a cotillion. Church either, if Sutton had to guess.

"Yeah. Me and Wyatt." Sutton didn't move, not sure what she was dealing with.

The people she'd met, men and women alike, had been curious about her and Wyatt, but they'd also seemed surprised. If she and Wyatt hadn't met over a thong in his garage, she wouldn't have stood a chance with him, no matter what he'd said.

"I'm Candace." She held out a hand.

Sutton stepped closer and took the polite offering. Candace's rough hand seemed older than her body and face. "Sutton. Nice to meet you."

"You're a 'Sip, aren't you?" No malice sharpened the woman's words, and a smile flashed before she took a swig of beer.

"What gave me away? The Sunday school clothes?" Sutton gave a little laugh.

"Never seen you out here, is all. And you have a way about you. Come on and sit a spell. The boys will have Wyatt looking under all their hoods before long."

Sutton slid onto the truck gate, the fabric of her skirt catching on a patch of rust. "Have you known Wyatt a long time?"

"Since we were kids." Candace leaned back, her gaze narrowing on Sutton. "Can I give you some advice?"

Sutton sensed whatever wisdom Candace was getting ready to lay at her feet would chase away any lingering hope.

Candace didn't wait for an answer. "Wyatt is a great guy. Amazing in fact, but for the sake of all that's holy, do not let yourself fall in love with the man."

Sutton wanted to look away from the woman, but couldn't.

"I see the way you look at him," Candace said.

"I'm not in love with him." She would swear it with one hand on a stack of Bibles and one on her heart.

She wasn't capable of anything as complicated as love. Yes, her insides tumbled like an out of kilter washing machine around him. And, okay, she thought about him way too much. Basically during all her waking and sleeping hours. But none of that had anything to do with love.

Silence fell and the woman continued to hold Sutton's gaze long after it became uncomfortable.

"Were you in love with him?" Sutton asked.

"Of course, I was." Candace's ready agreement knocked the breath out of Sutton, and as a result her next words came out more aggressively than she intended.

"Are you still?"

Candace's smile made Sutton feel childish. The woman flashed a thin gold band on her left hand and shifted to look toward the crowd of men. "I've been happily married going on seven years. Had a child, lost a child. Lived a lifetime while Wyatt's been treading water, moving from one woman to the next."

"We're having fun. That's all this is." Sutton's voice was less than convincing, and the snort of laughter insinuated Candace obviously wasn't anywhere near convinced.

"Wyatt loves his project cars more than his women. All those Abbott boys do. It's either in their blood or their raising or both." She touched the back of Sutton's hand with callused fingertips, and Sutton sensed nothing but kindness. "Have your fun but have a care with your heart."

Candace hopped off the tailgate and strolled off without a backward glance. Where darkness overtook the firelight, she put her arms around a wiry man not much taller than herself, and they disappeared into the night.

Sutton stayed planted on the tailgate. Everything Candace had said rang true. Hadn't Wyatt insinuated that she was basically his project? Once she was deemed drivable again, he would lose interest, his attachment temporary. Yet he kept a decade-old advertisement for a car in his wallet like he was pining for an unrequited lover. The pieces didn't fit.

A rough-looking man with a full, dark beard and barrel-like physique encased in overalls shook her out of her reverie. "Are you coming home with me?"

Shock left her speechless and scooting down the tailgate.

"In your dreams, you dirty old coot." Wyatt came around the other side of the truck, his voice teasing. "She's coming home with me."

"You'd better get her out of my truck then, because I'm ready to head."

She hopped down and smoothed down her skirt. The man raised the tailgate and winked at her, emanating good cheer.

The crowd was breaking up and the fire dying. Wyatt exchanged good-byes and handshakes or shoulder slaps as they weaved through the crowd to his car. Once cocooned inside, he cranked the engine and turned to her.

"What'd you think? Did it live up to your expectations?"

"It was fun. A lot tamer than I expected though."

He laughed and got them headed through the ruts back to the main road. "Told you so. Any craziness is confined to the occasional fight or to one of the young, stupid boys showing off to impress a woman."

He steered the car through the section that had spun their wheels without an issue. She bit the inside of her lip and stared at his hand maneuvering the gearshift. The backlight of the instrument panel lit a long scratch on the back that she'd felt earlier. The urge to kiss it and make it all better had her leaning toward the door, Candace's advice reverberating around her head.

"What now?" he asked. The car bumped through the last potholes and onto the smooth pavement of the parish road.

"I'd better head home. I have to work at the boutique tomorrow."

"We should do something tomorrow night." His voice took on a rumble that reminded her of his car.

"We should?" A flare shot off in her chest.

"Good night to be seen and keep those rumors afloat."

She brightened her voice to keep the disappointment from showing. Fun, fun, fun. That's what she was having. "Okay, where should we go?"

"What's your usual hangout?"

"My couch with a movie and junk food."

His laugh cracked in the small space as if she'd made a joke. Sadly, she'd been dead serious.

"Do you play pool?" he asked.

"Tried a couple of times in college, but I was terrible."

"I'll teach you. It's easy once you understand it's all about the angles."

He pulled up beside her car, still parked on River Street close to the boutique. Leaving the car idling, he opened his door and came around the front to open hers and offer a hand out of the low bucket seat.

She slipped her hand in his. Standing put them close together. He had her blocked between his body and the car. He tilted his face toward hers. Their lips were inches apart, their breath mingling. He was going to kiss her. Fireworks detonated in her stomach, this time of the colorful Roman candle variety.

He patted her shoulder, took a step back and cleared his throat. "Alrighty then, I'll pick you up at your place tomorrow night."

Incapable of coherent words, she nodded and forced her feet to move. Only when she was driving away did his car turn toward the bridge that would carry him over the river.

Why was she doing this again? Revenge. It had all

started from some petty need to hurt Andrew and Bree. And to save face in the town with her father's reelection. Selfish reasons. The situation was spinning out of her control. While it wasn't love, she couldn't deny a knotted, tangle of feelings existed for him. Was karma turning to take a bite?

Chapter Twelve

Dusk was falling by the time he picked her up for their "date." She'd picked out a tight black scoop-necked T-shirt in a thin silky-textured fabric from the boutique and paired it with tight ankle-length jeans and red heels. So far out of the realm of her demure skirts and dresses, the outfit felt like a costume.

The costume of a badass biker chick. She decided to embrace the look.

Wyatt's eyes had widened and skimmed down her body. His stuttering, "You look good . . . great . . . I mean, amazing," had her throwing her shoulders back and working the heels with confidence.

Until she nearly twisted her ankle on a crack in the pavement.

In the car, she studied his profile, completely beyond her abilities to interpret. He rolled his window halfway down, and she gave up, closing her eyes. The evening air swirled around the cabin, whipping through her hair when they hit the parish road. The smell was distinctly Cotton-bloom, river and salt, earthy and elemental.

The Hornet's engine downshifted, and gravel crunched under the wheels. She opened her eyes and tension trickled down her spine. It was early yet but the lot of the River-shack Tavern was more than half full. This time she hauled herself out before he could round the bumper to help her.

"Are you nervous?" he asked.

"A little."

He shrugged. "New place, new people. Only natural."

She hummed in agreement even though that's not what was making her nervous. It was him. The way he smelled fresh like dryer sheets. A scent she'd never thought was sexy but somehow on him, it was unbearably so. And the way he held her elbow as she navigated the gravel lot in her heels. And the way his faded jeans molded his thighs.

The man at the door greeted Wyatt like an old friend, clasping his hand, bumping shoulders, and engaging in a brief discussion about sticky pistons. Throughout the ex-change, the man's gaze kept wandering from Wyatt to her in a way that raised her awareness and hackles.

"Later, Butch." Was she imagining Wyatt's cooler than normal tone? She glanced over her shoulder at the man.

"Come on back out and see me if you get bored, sweet-heart." The man perched himself back on the edge of the stool and winked.

She whipped her head back around and leaned closer to Wyatt. "Was he coming on to me?"

"He's obviously desperate." His dismissive tone dented her badass biker-chick persona.

A wall of noise hit her on her first step into the tavern. Unintelligible music overlaid with the buzz of conversa-tion and laughter and the click of pool balls. A haze of smoke ringed the lights, but the smell was faint, and she noticed only a handful of people with cigarettes. She took a step toward the pool tables, but Wyatt steered her in the opposite direction.

"How about a drink first?" He led her to a long, dark-stained bar and raised two fingers to get the attention of the lone bartender.

Unlike at the bonfire, she fit right in with the rest of the women, most of whom were in shorts or jeans.

"What's up, Clint?" Wyatt extended a hand for a quick shake.

"Wyatt, my man. You want to start a tab?" From a distance and with his long beard, she'd thought him older, but he appeared to be close to her age.

Clint's smile was friendly, but not in a creepy way like the bouncer's had been. She returned his smile, folded her arms over the bar, and relaxed.

"Yep. This is Sutton, by the way." Wyatt tilted his head toward her, and the bartender mimicked her stance on the other side of the bar, his arms folded, a smile crinkling his dark eyes.

"Nice to meet you, Sutton. What's your poison?"

Besides indulging in an occasional glass of wine, she'd never been much of a drinker and had missed out on the requisite college parties by living at home. She studied the rows of bottles over his shoulder, but didn't see a single bottle of wine. She racked her brain for a drink that wouldn't make her sound totally dorky.

"A Jack and Coke, please." It was the drink Wyatt had ordered at the pig picking. She knew she liked Coke, at least.

"Coming right up. You want your usual, Wyatt?"

Wyatt raised his chin in answer and shifted to prop his elbow on the bar, facing her. Clint slid a long-necked Coors Light in front of Wyatt and poured a healthy amount of whiskey in a tumbler, topping it with a squirt of Coke.

"Cheers." Wyatt clicked the neck of his beer against her glass.

She took a small sip and ran her tongue over her upper

lip. Alcohol mixed pleasantly with the familiar bite of Coke, and she smiled around the rim. She could drink Coke mixed with whiskey all night long.

A few sips in and warmth bloomed from her stomach through her body, driving out any lingering nerves. She wouldn't think about anything but the superficial. She was out with an attractive man at her side. It was all about casual fun.

"So, you come here often?" she asked and promptly burst into giggles. "That was not a cheesy pickup line. I meant, you seem to know everyone."

His smile went all the way to his eyes. "I either went to school with them or church or worked on their cars. I'm sure it's like that over on your side too."

For some people it was, but it had never been like that for her. Her web of connections was skimpy and involved the women who frequented the boutique or ladies in the Junior League. She took a bigger sip to avoid answering.

"You ready to try pool?" he asked.

She drained the rest. "I think I want another."

He didn't say anything, only lifted two fingers and Clint was there with a fresh drink. She followed Wyatt across the bar to the pool tables. The buzzy feeling in her body was pleasant, and the glances tossed in her direction only bolstered her confidence.

The only free table was in the back corner. She set her drink on a high table and fumbled her way onto a stool to watch Wyatt corral all the balls into a triangle. He leaned over the table, and her gaze went to his butt. Lordy, he had a really nice butt. Not that she was a butt connoisseur, but she was pretty sure his would make a "best of" list.

He turned around. Now her eyes were on his crotch and the formerly pleasant heat ignited into a wildfire. Feigning casualness, she forced herself to look to the side while taking another sip.

"You want to break?" he asked.

"Break what?"

He laughed. "And here I was thinking you had an evil plan to hustle me. Come here and I'll show you."

The drinks had left her joints lubricated. Behind his obvious amusement was a hint of something darker. Something that buzzed through her like the whiskey.

"I racked the balls into a triangle. You hit the white ball with the blue end of the stick to break them apart." He handed her the pool stick and set a white ball over a red mark on the green felt. "Lean over and let me help you get lined up."

She leaned over and put her palms flat on the felt. His body curled behind hers, their thighs touching. She canted farther down, barely stopping herself from wiggling back against him.

"Grab the stick with both hands." His voice was close to her ear and she arched up. The part of her brain still functioning properly took up the pool stick. He positioned her hands and fingers. "Take a smooth, confident stroke."

Her brain combusted. Who knew pool could be so sexy? Somehow under his guidance, she moved the stick enough to hit the white ball into the triangle of balls at the end of the table.

She turned her face, her nose an inch away from nuzzling into his cheek. "So that's how you break balls."

His balls might not be broken, but they were definitely in a state of upheaval. The attraction between them had tipped from simmering to explosive and he could only assume the whiskey was to blame. Apparently, Sutton Mize was a lightweight.

He glanced over at her. A mistake. Her gaze was on his mouth, and the way her teeth and tongue were worrying her lips made him feel like a rabbit being stalked by a fox.

He threw himself backward and grabbed his beer from the table.

She took up her drink and shook it, making the ice tinkle. "I'm going to get another drink. You ready for another?"

"Naw, I'm good." He'd worked on enough wrecked cars from drunk drivers that he limited himself to one drink when he was out and driving.

Where in the stew had that walk come from? Her hips swung, her legs long and sexy in her tight jeans and high heels. Male heads turned as she headed to the bar.

"What's going on, *Boug*?" The man's voice came from behind him, but the lilt and Cajun slang identified him like a photograph. His distant cousin Landrum Abbott, from a branch of the family tree that was populated by offspring between an Abbott and a free black woman before the Civil War. It had been a not-so-secret scandal.

"When did you sneak in?" Wyatt turned, and they hugged.

All the same age, Wyatt, Jackson, and Landrum had all come up through school together. While Wyatt and Jackson's obsession was cars, Landrum's was football, and he'd earned a scholarship to LSU. Instead of entering the family crawfish business when he'd graduated, he opened a car dealership in Baton Rouge, cashing in on his fame.

"Didn't sneak. You were otherwise occupied." Laughter danced in Landrum's hazel Abbott eyes. "I thought for sure Daddy was fibbing."

This thing with Sutton was growing more complicated by the hour. His family hadn't shown interest in his love life for years and now all of a sudden, everyone was all up in his business. Alarms had been echoing for a while now, but he could no longer ignore the blaring.

Last night at the bonfire had seemed more like a real date than anything he could remember. And tonight . . . when she'd stepped out of her house in that shirt and those heels, he'd been unable to come up with a suitable compliment. Not to mention the way she'd bent over the pool table brought to mind the dirty dreams he'd welcomed every night since he'd met her. They'd become a clear and present danger to his sanity.

Wyatt debated the merits of trying to throw Landrum off the scent, but he knew Wyatt almost as well as Jackson did. "We're hanging out. That's all."

"If you're just hanging out, you won't mind the Harrison brothers making a move on her." Landrum pointed the neck of his beer toward the bar and shook his head. "Those boys are too competitive for their own good."

Wyatt whirled and sure enough, the Harrison brothers had flanked Sutton. They were nice and decent-looking and charming in an aw-shucks, good-old-boy way that drew women like bees to pollen. The three of them had partied together more than a few times, and Wyatt considered them friends. The Harrisons were harmless.

Sutton had another Jack and Coke in her hand, and a smile on her face. She was meeting new people and having fun. Exactly what he'd promised.

Except the whys and wherefores had grown fuzzy and indistinct. She didn't belong to those boys, she belonged to *him*. Check that—she didn't belong to anyone. Indecision when it came to women was like wandering a foreign land. He'd always held the upper hand because he made sure not to care too much.

Clint set three shot glasses on the bar. Sutton took one, clinked glasses with both brothers, and tossed it back, tapping the bar with her fist and laughing. One Harrison gestured toward Clint with two fingers for a refill.

Aw, hell no.

Not taking his eyes off her, Wyatt handed the pool stick to Landrum and stalked toward the trio. She killed the second shot and gave each brother a high five, turning her back to the bar and propping her elbows on top. The stance pulled the fabric of her T-shirt taut across her breasts.

He wasn't the only one who'd noticed the expansive view. Both Harrisons were sightseeing. Wyatt's hands twitched, ready to remove the brothers' heads in a fashion that involved blood and broken vertebrae.

Her gaze snagged on him, blazing a path from his head to feet and back again. As soon as he was in arm's length, she grabbed him and pulled him close enough to be granted the same view the Harrisons had enjoyed. He had a hard time being any more gentlemanly than they had been.

"I made some new friends." Her smile held the simple joy of a kid finding a friend on the playground the first day of school. "Jimmie and Jason. This is Wyatt."

"We're acquainted." Wyatt gave both brothers a look that he hoped read as "back the fuck off before I break your faces."

"Sorry, dude." Jimmie's lips twitched, but he hit Jason's arm with the back of his hand. "Let's scoot, bro. Nice to meet you, Sutton. See you around, Wyatt."

Wyatt grunted and transferred his attention to Sutton now that the immediate threat had receded. She resumed her position against the bar, and with any other woman he might suspect the showcase was on purpose. But her glassy eyes and soft mouth had him suspecting she needed the support. He propped his hands on either side of her.

"You're playing a game without knowing the rules, sweetheart." He kept his voice low.

"What do you mean?"

"I've seen how those boys work."

"Oh really? What do they do for a living? We didn't get that far in the conversation." Her voice was vague and her gaze was locked on his, but her hands walked up his chest, playing in the fabric of his shirt. She glided her fingertips down his flanks and across his ribs. His body, already on heightened alert, sent blood rushing south. Was she even aware of what she was doing or the effect her touch had on him?

"I meant they were working *you*. Flirting. Looking to get you home with one—or both—of them."

"Flirting?" Her bemusement drove his ire off the cliff.

"Why do you think they were buying you drinks and staring down your shirt?" His gaze dipped deliberately, attempting to incite some embarrassment on her part.

Instead, she drew her hands into fists around his shirt and tilted her face, exposing the line of her neck. "You bought me drinks and are staring down my shirt. Are you trying to get me home?"

Caution tempered the hot poker of lust beating at him. What was happening? Was this real or for the benefit of the milling crowd? He glanced to either side of them. No one seemed to be paying them any attention in the crowded bar, and Sutton was laser-focused on him.

Even if it was real attraction, he wasn't like the Harrison brothers. He didn't use alcohol to manipulate a woman home with him. Didn't need to.

"Have you ever been drunk before?" he asked.

She shook her head. "Uh-uh. I lived at home during college, and I was a good girl."

"Good girls can get drunk, you know."

"Not according to Mother. And heaven help me if I went home with a guy from a bar." Her eyes were wide, and her bottom lip was caught between her teeth.

The woman was entirely too concerned with what everyone else thought. What would happen if the natural sexiness lurking behind the puritanical philosophy her mother had hammered into her was unleashed on the male species?

"Lightning wouldn't strike you down." He ran his hands

down her arms and leaned closer to whisper in her ear. "Good girls can have sex too. And enjoy it."

More of her weight seemed to be pulling at his shirt as if she were hanging on for dear life. He'd never had a problem with self-control, but somewhere on the walk from the pool table to rescue Sutton, it had gotten waylaid. What would happen if he stepped up and took her home? Would she wake with regrets? Would he?

He pulled away from her, untangling her hands from his shirt. "Your shot." At her look of confusion, he added, "We have a pool game to finish."

"Right. Yes. Balls and sticks and breaking things." She led the way back to the table, looking more wobbly in her heels than she had earlier.

Landrum had taken up the stool, his grin conveying exactly what he thought of the unfolding scene.

"Landrum, this is Sutton." Wyatt killed the last of his beer, grimacing at the lukewarm, pissy taste. Everything seemed to have soured.

While Landrum and Sutton shook hands and exchanged pleasantries, he took a shot, sinking two balls.

"So Sutton, what are your intentions with my boy here?" Landrum asked as Wyatt came up behind her. Wyatt gave him a dirty look, but Landrum ignored him, his eyes twinkling with mischief.

"Wyatt is teaching me to have fun." Sutton propped her elbow on the table and cupped her chin.

"I'd say you picked the right man for the job," Landrum said.

"I think so. He's funny and laid back and stuff." Her standard assessment of his character had Wyatt shaking his head and ready to interrupt, when she leaned closer to Landrum and tapped her chest. "But, you know, he's got depths. Really deep depths."

"Does he now?" Landrum darted a meaningful look over her shoulder to Wyatt.

"Your shot, Sutton," Wyatt said.

"Excellent." She slid off the stool, took the stick from his hand, and sashayed to the table. She rocked her feet shoulder-width apart and bent at the waist. His gaze trailed down her legs to her heels, the denim molding to her curves. She tossed her hair and looked over her shoulder. "Which ball am I trying to hit again?"

"Hit the white one into one of the stripey balls."

She nodded and turned back to the table, taking a stab at the cue ball but whiffing it. She straightened with a muttered, "Well I never."

Landrum whistled under his breath and slapped Wyatt's back, his wink saying more than Wyatt wanted to hear. "I like her. I can't wait to hear how all this works out."

All this could end only one way. With him and Sutton resuming their lives on opposite sides of the river. Whatever they shared would soon be memories. Whether those memories would be tainted with bitterness or nostalgia or forgotten entirely remained to be seen.

"Don't you have somewhere else to be?" Wyatt asked Landrum.

"Not really." Landrum took another pull off his beer before meeting Wyatt's narrowed eyes. "Oh wait, actually I do need to go over there." He gestured vaguely toward the bar, got up, and took Sutton's hand in his. "I hope I'll be seeing lots more of you."

"That would be lovely." Her smile was warm and genuine.

Once Landrum had gone, Wyatt gestured toward the table. "Try again."

She draped herself back over the felt, her bottom shimmying as she set her feet. If he didn't know her better, he would guess she was toying with him. Or torturing him, more like.

He positioned himself behind her but maintained a buffer between their bodies. "Look at the cue ball."

The sweet scent of her hair was at odds with the smoky bar. "The white one, right?"

He hummed an agreement. "It's all about angles and trigonometry. You remember that from school?"

She invaded the neutral zone and notched her bottom into his pelvis as she took her stroke. The cue ball bounced against the side of the table and missed hitting anything else.

Foolish thoughts like spinning her around and lifting her on top of the pool table circled his addled mind. *That* would give both sides of Cottonbloom fodder for the rest of the year. He put a few feet between them.

"I missed." She shot him a fake pout. She seemed to have a hard time focusing on him and her face was flushed.

"It's time to go home."

"No, it isn't. I'm having fun."

"Tomorrow morning is going to come quick and hard." His last words echoed in his brain, the definition of a Freudian slip.

Her eyes had flared wider, the kaleidoscope of colors brimming with energy and light. "That's what she said."

Her response, so totally unexpected and cheeky, set him laughing harder than he had in a long time. Her husky laughter entwined with his.

"Aren't you working tomorrow?" he asked.

"Screw work. I wanna have more fun." The hands she slipped to his waist stole all moisture from his mouth. Were the confusing signals for the benefit of the crowd? Was he supposed to play along?

"Well, I have to work, and there's nothing worse than hearing a metal grinder the morning after a late night."

"I'm surprised you're being so sensible and *bo-ring*."

He didn't rise to take her bait. "You'll thank me in the morning."

"Will I?" Something in her eyes shifted and smoldered and he thought he might burn alive, but her easy-going smile doused the flames. "Fine then, let's go."

She led the way to the door. They got separated by three people heading to the pool table they'd given up, which afforded Wyatt a clear view of Butch openly admiring her ass.

"Eyes on your own paper, Butch," he murmured on his way by.

"No crime in looking, now is there?"

For the second time that night, Wyatt considered the merits of rearranging a friend's face.

Sutton put her arms out and tilted her head back, stumbling into him. "Isn't it a beautiful night?"

The moon shined through a few wispy clouds, the stars only slightly dampened by the parking lot lights. It was beautiful, but not as beautiful as she was. And that was the problem.

He opened the door to the Hornet and she slipped in, sending him a smile that crimped his insides. His crush on her when they'd been kids had been epic. He'd never imagined getting a shot with her as an adult, yet already he sensed them barreling toward an ending.

He got them on the road. She rolled her window down and closed her eyes, the wind tossing her hair around. His gaze went back and forth between her and the road. The bridge over the river seemed to symbolize the differences they would never be able to reconcile.

When he was beginning to wonder if she'd dozed off, she leaned over the console.

"Can I ask you a question? Something serious?"

"Alright," he said cautiously.

"Do you find me doable?"

His hand jerked on the steering wheel and sent the car skidding on the shoulder before he righted it. "Do I *what*?"

"Find me doable? Because that no-necked bouncer and those two brothers did."

He choked on a gulp of air. What was happening? Had he crossed the river into the Twilight Zone instead of into Mississippi?

Her voice was as bland and conversational as if discussing commodity cotton prices. "Because I find *you* doable. Very, very, very, *very* doable."

Her string of "verys" slurred together. She was drunk, which meant her thinking was impaired. Or . . . he glanced at her. Maybe, just maybe, the whiskey had stripped away her social niceties like turpentine to peeling paint, and she was being honest.

She snaked her free hand to the back of his head, threaded through his hair, and tugged. Lightning zigzagged through his body, striking somewhere between his legs, and for the first time in years, he ground his gears on his next shift.

"You have a fine ass, Wyatt Abbott."

"I do?" The words coming out of her mouth stymied his thought process.

The smile that turned her lips wasn't anything he'd seen before from her. It was a dangerous smile. A smile that revealed the sensuality she kept locked away. He would sell his soul for the key.

"All this stuff with Andrew and Bree and you has made me realize something." She made a disgusted sound, let go of his hair, and slumped back in the seat. "I'm beige."

"And that's bad because . . . ?"

"Beige is blah and boring and nice."

"Nice is not a bad thing. People like nice."

"Tonight is the craziest I've ever gotten, and that's just plain sad. I'm sick of being a goody-two-shoes."

"You're not a goody-two-shoes."

She turned back to him, her eyes flashing in the passing streetlights. "I want more."

"Okay, we can hit another bar one night this—"

"No." Her confidence seemed to dim, and she chewed on her thumbnail as if in deep thought. Finally, she balled both her hands on her lap and said, "I don't want to fake date you anymore."

Her words rushed over him like tsunami, tumbling his insides. One minute she was calling him doable and declaring his ass was fine, the next telling him she didn't want to see him again. He'd gone into this knowing it was temporary. Just not this temporary. He'd been counting on having until the gala to prepare himself for the final act. But this was good. It would be a relief not to have to pretend with his family, with her, or himself.

Except, her announcement made him feel like grabbing a six-pack on the way home and drinking himself into oblivion.

"Whatever," he muttered, turning onto her street and giving the car some gas so he could get the night over with as soon as possible.

She grabbed his forearm, her thumb making circles on the underside. "I know I insisted on no lip-to-lip contact, but I haven't been able to stop thinking about kissing you. When I'm working with little old ladies at the boutique, having dinner with my parents, trying to go to sleep." She gave a feminine little snort that was the definition of cute. "*Especially* when I'm trying to go to sleep."

He pulled into her driveway and hit the brakes so hard he locked his seatbelt. How was he expected to operate heavy machinery in this state? He put the car in park and shifted to face her. "You think about me in bed?"

"Yes." She drew the word out with a hiss. "In bed. Out of bed. My fantasies are plentiful and varied."

"But you said you don't want to go out anymore."

"No, I said I don't want to fake date you. I want to real date you. Or at least, real hook up with you. I don't want to flirt and dance and have fun out in public and not follow through."

It was like someone had plugged in twinkling Christmas lights inside of him, and he was the kid standing in silent awe. Speechless and overcome.

In the silence, horror snuck into her wide eyes. "Ohmigod, you don't want to. That's fine. Not a problem. Forget I ever said anything. We can go back to the way things were and—"

He put a finger over her lips to quiet the outpouring of words. "I never said I didn't want to. Give me a second to process all of this."

"Thank goodness." Her lips moved against his finger, and he dropped his hand before he did something foolish like trace his fingers over her lips. "I want you to show me . . . things." She made a Vanna White–like gesture.

Her words applied spurs to his heart, sending it into a gallop.

She continued. "To be clear, I'm not looking for a relationship. That's why this is so perfect, because I know you don't want a relationship either."

The twinkling Christmas lights shorted out. "How do you know I want?"

Her brow crinkled. "You never get serious, right? You're constantly on the hunt for a good time. Well, me too."

He couldn't even argue the point since it was true. Or had been. Problem was what used to qualify as a good time only managed to make him feel weary.

"Do you ever think about kissing me just to kiss me and not because people are watching?" she asked softly.

"Maybe." His shrug reflected more hurt feelings than anger.

This sort of proposition should have sent him into cartwheels. Instead he was acting like some needy asshole who required a helping of cuddles with his sex. That had never been what he was about. He was about exactly what she was offering him. No feelings to get hurt or heart to break. No strings, good-time sex.

"Never mind." She grappled the door handle. The brash confidence the alcohol had imparted seemed to be wearing off like a witch's potion.

The woman had been put through the wringer by her best friend and her fiancé. Despite her wishes otherwise, she *was* nice. And sweet. And cute. And unbearably sexy in a way she didn't even understand. Not yet anyway.

No way could he let this opportunity to be with her in whatever way possible slip through his fingers. While the ramifications went on repeat in his head, she slipped out of the car and headed to her door.

He rolled down his window and shimmied half-way out to see her over the top. "Hey, Sutton!"

She turned with only a slight wobble, jutted a hip, and set her hand on it. "What?"

"For the record, I find you extremely doable."

"You do?" The hopeful, vulnerable lilt to her voice almost had him climbing out to sweep her into his arms and straight to bed, but he didn't want her to wake later with alcohol-fueled regrets.

"I do. Go sleep it off. We'll talk about your doableness tomorrow." He waited until she disappeared before backing up.

With one last glance at her house, he drove off, knowing

he would be dreaming about her and hoping she'd be dreaming about him. Whatever they were doing was like two tectonic plates shifting. He smiled in the face of impending disaster.

Chapter Thirteen

Sutton woke to harsh sunlight, a spinning room, and a mouth that felt stuffed with cotton bolls. She blinked up at the ceiling, willing her stomach to calm down. A banging and her sister's voice calling her name came from the vicinity of the front door.

"I'm coming." The words croaked out and she cleared her throat. She tossed off her covers and shuffled toward the door. Whiskey was the devil's drink.

Sutton cracked the door open, squinting against the sun. "What's up?"

"*What's up*?" Maggie stuck her foot in the opening and forced Sutton to back up a step to make room. "What's up is that it's 8:30 and—" Her sister sniffed. "You smell like smoke and look like you slept in your clothes. *You* tell *me* what's up?"

Her sister looked ready to cast down a biblical judgment from on high. Sutton needed time to come up with an excuse. "Would you get some coffee brewing while I shower and change? Then, I'll tell you everything."

The smile she used to cover the lie felt weak, and she backed out of the room before Maggie could expose the mile-wide fault lines. Telling her sister everything wasn't an option, but lying didn't settle well either. A half-truth then. When had she become so adept at dodging the truth? The hot water soothed the throb in her head to a dull ache. Hot coffee and painkillers should do the rest.

Memories of the night surfaced. Not that she'd forgotten. She hadn't been *that* drunk, just tipsy enough to throw herself at Wyatt and suggest a no-strings-attached fling. Did that qualify as courageous or stupid? She supposed it depended on what happened next.

She scrubbed her hair clean, but nothing could scrub away her embarrassment. It was well deserved. She'd called him *doable,* for goodness' sake. Like sticking a hand under her bed and searching blindly, she reached for whatever else was hiding under the familiar feeling.

The one emotion she didn't find was shame. Instead, an edge of excitement mixed with a thrumming arousal lingered like her hangover. Wyatt made her feel beautiful and sexy and want things. And what she wanted more than anything was him.

More of his laughing eyes and slow-build smile that made her insides play musical chairs. The way he opened doors and guided her with a hand on her back. His body, hard and hot and sexy, and his hands, big and rough and capable.

She rushed through her morning routine, pinning her damp hair into a twist and slipping on a sundress and sandals. Blessedly, her sister only side-eyed her as she poured a steaming cup of coffee and washed down two pain relievers with the first sip.

Maggie enjoyed organizing the pretty clothes, but wanted none of the responsibility of balancing the books or paying off loans or worrying about inventory at the shop. She was reliable, but secretive, oftentimes distracted, and protective about her free time. Although she was still young and pretty in a buttoned-up kind of way, she didn't date.

That Sutton was aware of anyway. They had never been the sort of sisters who shared secrets. Especially secrets of the boy variety.

"I went out last night," Sutton said.

Her Ms. Obvious statement was met with an eye roll. "With Wyatt Abbott, I assume?"

She couldn't get a read on Maggie's mood or attitude. Defensiveness snuck into Sutton's voice. "He taught me to play pool over the river at the Rivershack Tavern. It was fun."

"What about Andrew?"

"What about him? I'm moving on."

"Rebounding, you mean." Maggie chuffed and narrowed her eyes over the rim of her mug. "This breakup is temporary."

"No it's not."

"A combination of cold feet and the fact you haven't dated much?" The way Maggie said it made Sutton think she was repeating something she'd heard.

"Is that what Daddy said?"

"Andrew came by last night for a drink. He wants you back."

"That's rich. More like he wants to make nice with Daddy so he won't get all his cases thrown out. As if Daddy would be so petty and unprofessional." Sutton made a disgusted sound and drank more coffee before she said something she would regret.

Something on her sister's face, part speculative and part angry gave her pause. Maggie had always been quiet around Andrew, and Sutton had suspected a wide streak of jealousy. Like poking at a tender spot, Sutton said, "Andrew is a jerk, you know."

"I know." The unexpected strength behind those two words, as if Maggie was ready to go to battle for her, not against her. Maggie set her coffee mug down on the table and hugged Sutton. "I'm happy you finally figured it out."

In the Mize family, love—for their country, for God, for each other—was something that was understood and not normally demonstrated with hugs or words. Emotions were kept inside like a genie in a bottle. Which made her sister's show of sympathy and support mean even more. Sutton tightened her hold around Maggie's back and laid her forehead on her shoulder, tears springing to her eyes.

"I never trusted him." Maggie's voice vibrated between them.

Sutton startled back. "Why didn't you say anything?"

"You seemed infatuated, and Mother and Daddy were happy." Her shrug was knowing, and Sutton wondered what else her sister had seen and understood from her position on the sidelines.

"Have you heard anything else?"

"Like all the stuff about you and Wyatt running around? Which I didn't completely buy . . . until this morning."

Sutton swallowed, her mouth dry. "Has the talk been bad?"

Another shrug from Maggie, this time accompanied by a glance away. "Some people have said some not very nice stuff, but who cares?"

As much as Sutton tried not to care, she did. A little. But mostly she felt like someone who'd narrowly escaped a car accident. The minute she'd accepted Andrew's proposal what had once only chafed had turned slowly suffocating. With Wyatt, she could breathe again, and the air was unexpectedly sweet.

"I'm sorry if I've made things difficult for everyone."

Maggie waved her off. "Don't worry about me. I tune it all out. How about you? Are you going to be okay?"

She didn't know what Wyatt's answer to her proposition

would be, but his parting words had given her hope. Whatever happened at least she was taking chances and going after what she wanted for the first time in her life. "I'm going to be better than okay."

Maggie nodded, her eyes singularly focused on Sutton. The experience unsettled her, and made Sutton realize the two of them co-existed all their years together, but hadn't interacted on more than a superficial level. Until now.

"Now then, I heard another rumor. Did you sell Ms. Eckert one of your dresses?" Maggie asked.

Sutton bobbled her mug, dripping coffee on her skirt. "Where did you hear that?"

"She was telling all the ladies during the Wednesday night potluck at church about the fabulous dress you designed. Several asked if you had anything else on the racks, and I had no idea what to tell them."

Maggie should play poker, because her expression was guarded and unreadable. Was she mad or hurt or both by the omission? "Wyatt talked me into putting one out to see what would happen, and then one thing led to another and Ms. Eckert ended up loving it."

"I've been wondering if you'd ever find the gumption to display something. How much did you charge her?"

Sutton rattled off the exorbitant number that Wyatt had taken off a real designer's price tag. Maggie's jaw dropped. "Do you have anything else ready to sell?"

"Are you serious?"

"These women are willing to pay for a one-of-a-kind gown. Let's see what you have."

Sutton checked the clock. "We're going to be late opening up."

"I doubt there's going to be an evening gown emergency at nine in morning in Cottonbloom." Maggie's laugh cracked like a slap against Sutton's still aching head, but her sister's reaction galvanized her courage and prodded her into action.

Together they sifted through the clothes Sutton had finished and picked out several pieces to display in the boutique, including two gowns. The slight dissonance that was the soundtrack of their relationship had righted itself into a harmony that was as pleasant as it was unexpected.

They opened the boutique by ten, and as she straightened the racks of lingerie in the back, her thoughts drifted to Wyatt and his crooked smile and teasing jokes. When she tucked the peach dress onto the sale rack, she thought about the way he'd charmed Ms. Eckert and Amy and pretty much everyone he crossed paths with, including her. She conjured images of him bent over her teaching her to play pool, the corner of his mouth twitching as if he knew exactly how badly she wanted to cross a line and kiss him.

He made her want the naughty things that she'd spent a lifetime suppressing because she'd been taught achieving the label of "good girl" was valued. But by whom? Certainly not Andrew or Bree.

Wyatt was helping her understand it was natural and more than okay to explore her desires. She wanted him to be her guide into a brave new world. The burning question was whether or not he wanted the job.

The bell over the door tinkled, and a shot of adrenaline popped her off the stool. Dread replaced excitement.

Andrew stepped through the racks toward her. Maggie's gaze followed his progress then shot to meet hers, but a customer had her cornered. Sutton gave a slight shake of her head. Backup would not be required, but it was nice to know her sister looked ready to throw down.

"Are you holding my car hostage?" The smile on Andrew's face was in direct contrast to the hard edge of— was that disgust?—in his voice. The combination grew a sour feeling in her stomach that had nothing to do with her hangover.

"You're welcome to pick it up from the garage at your leisure." She put the glass display case between them. "In fact, I'm sure Wyatt would appreciate you getting it out of their parking lot."

"As a matter of fact, I went by this morning with Father and there was no sign of my car. No one was around but Ford, who told me he had no idea where it was."

"Maybe someone stole it. Honestly, I couldn't care less." She was getting good at sprinkling artificial sweetener on her smile.

"You'll care when I sue those small-town hick mechanics for everything they own." From anyone else, the threat would be as hollow as the Grand Canyon. "Unless . . ." he drew the word out.

Manipulation was his game, then. More dangerous than spite or revenge and less easily evaded. "Spit it out. I have work to do."

"The gala."

"What about it?"

"I'm the emcee and you are on the planning committee. It makes sense we would attend together." The logic he infused in his illogical conclusion was part of the reason he was a successful trial attorney.

Nerves had kicked in, dampening her palms and leaving imprints on the glass top. She clasped her hands behind her back. Show no weakness.

"I already have a date. Take Bree." The surprise and flash of irritation on his face had her performing an internal fist pump. "By the way, I don't appreciate you trying to manipulate me."

"I wasn't." He chuffed a laugh, but it seemed directed at himself. "Okay, maybe I was. A hazard of the job, I suppose. The truth is I want to mend things with you."

"I don't—"

"I know." He held up his hands as if surrendering. "But we were friends once, weren't we?"

Had they been? She'd known him through school and church and family connections for as long as she could remember. But they hadn't been friends—not really. Wyatt knew more of her dreams and desires in two short weeks than Andrew had guessed over a lifetime.

"Actually, I don't think we were."

His mouth opened and closed, but nothing came out.

The bell on the front door chimed in the silence as if signaling the end of round one. Outlined by the morning sun, Wyatt stood for a moment in the doorway. In contrast to Andrew's orderly suited appearance, he was chaos incarnate in his ripped jeans and half-tucked red T-shirt, his hair too long and stubble shading his jaw.

Women on both sides of the river would have stampeded over her in a heartbeat to be the recipient of the smile he aimed at her. It was startling to compare the openness of Wyatt's smile to the calculation in Andrew's.

"Hey, babe," he said softly, his eyes darting to Andrew. He was only playing his part, her head chided, yet the endearment lit a dozen sparklers in her chest.

"I wasn't expecting to see you this morning."

"Brought you some coffee." He held up a to-go cup with a Glenda's Diner logo across the front. "Thought you might be feeling the effects of last night."

Andrew pointedly ignored Wyatt. "This can't seriously be a thing."

Wyatt made a funny face over Andrew's shoulder which made her answer emerge on a spate of giggles. "I'm not a liar like you." The words wiped the smile off her face.

She *was* a liar. Did that make her as bad as Andrew?

Wyatt ambled over, slipped his arm around her shoulders, and pressed a kiss on her temple. "Morning, Tarwater."

"Where's my car, Abbott?"

"Jackson and I dropped it off safe and sound at your place this morning. If you ever decide to restore it, I'd be happy to pass along the estimate we put together."

Andrew stepped closer and poked a finger in Wyatt's chest. He tensed against her, but a smile remained on his face, and he didn't move to retaliate or threaten Andrew. "You can stick that estimate where the sun don't shine. I'll never bring another car to your shop, and I'll spread the word so none of my friends do either."

He transferred his cold fury to her. "Don't come crying to me when this swamp rat dumps you back in the mud, darlin'."

Comebacks weren't her strong suit, and before she could formulate one that wasn't a variation of "get the hell out," Andrew did an about-face and strode out the door.

Maggie tiptoed closer with clothes hung over her arm and pointed to the dressing room. Her customer was hot on her heels taking in her and Wyatt with the wide-eyed stare of a rubbernecker. More fuel for the fire.

She grabbed Wyatt's hand and led him through the swinging door to the storeroom and office in the back of the shop. The carpet dead-ended into gray cement floor. Only in the back did the high-end feel of the shop fade into the utilitarian. She shut the door of her office. "I am so—"

"Stop." He took her shoulders and gave her a little shake. "Stop apologizing. I wouldn't have inserted myself into your business if I wasn't willing to take a little heat."

"As I recall, I'm the one who begged you to jump in the fire with me. And his threats . . ." She rubbed her forehead, not sure if the pounding going on behind her temples was a return of her hangover or a result of the confrontation.

"I doubt he can hurt the garage."

The fact he'd used a qualifier didn't set well with her.

Doubts meant uncertainty and uncertainty meant her lies might hurt innocent people after all. "What can I do?"

"Tell me if all that last night was you being drunk or if you really meant it?"

The question sent her careening around a hairpin curve. Why had her lips gone numb? Was that post-whiskey related? "Which part?"

"The part about how awesome my ass is." A teasing smile that could only be described as naughty crinkled his eyes.

Could a person actually die from acute embarrassment? Her heart tripped over itself on its way to a heart attack. "True. All true. I wish I could blame it on the alcohol."

His smile lost a little of its brightness. "Why is that?"

"Because it would make being around you easier." She might as well open the junk drawer of her feelings. "I'm attracted to you. Like, 'it's all I think about' attracted to you. "

Her words seemed to cast a spell on him. He was frozen with a half-smile on his face.

"Like I said, I'm not ready to have any sort of relationship, but I can't help the way I feel. That doesn't mean we—you—have to do anything about it. In fact, wipe your memories clean of all this doable talk. We can go out a couple more times before the gala. Or not or—"

"Hush it, woman." His hands were still on her shoulders and he squeezed hard enough to get her to look up at him. What she saw both scared and excited her. The heat level in his eyes registered at inferno. "What if I don't want to forget?"

Instead of enduring the uncertainty in silence as she might have done once, she asked, "What does that mean exactly?"

"It means I'm not good at relationships either, so if you want to mess around, I can oblige you." He didn't say it in

an Al Green *Let's Get It On* voice and the difference in
his melancholy tone and the sentiment rattled her.

"How could I say no to such a romantic offer?" She
chuffed and took a step back.

He slid one hand from her shoulder to her nape, gently
massaging. "Bad choice of words. This is what I know. I
ache every hour of the day for you." He tangled his fingers in her hair and held fast, the tug sending go signals
to her body. "I wanted you that very first night when we
kissed on your porch, but I didn't want to take advantage
of you. We both have to go into this with wide-open eyes.
That way no one gets hurt."

He backed her up against her desk, and she was grateful both for the support and the fact there was nowhere
to retreat. She was in uncharted territory. If the response of
her body was any indicator, she liked the way he talked to
her. A lot. In fact, he'd broken the gauge she used to measure sexy.

There was so much she wanted to say, but the same old
fears and constraints tied her tongue. Is that the way she
wanted to live the rest of her life? She wanted to jump but
didn't want to see the fall, and closed her eyes. "I want you
too, Wyatt. So bad."

"Tell me." His lips tickled her ear and sent shivers racing down her neck and tightening her nipples. He wedged
a knee between hers, and she wrapped her leg high on his
thigh as if they were performing the steps of a practiced
dance.

"I want you to touch me—" A vibration against her
thigh made her gasp. Shouldn't that sort of sensation be
taking place about six inches to the right? It vibrated again.

Wyatt pulled out his phone and dropped his forehead
to her shoulder, a guttural sound of frustration coming
from his throat. "Jackson is probably outside honking."

If the fire alarm sounded, she wasn't sure if her legs

would have supported her out the building. "You'd better go then."

He took a step back and pointed at her. "Tonight. I'll be here at closing time."

He backed out of her office, and after raking his clothes-stripping gaze up and down her body, disappeared. The bell over the door chimed faintly, and she stumbled around to the other side of her desk and collapsed in the chair.

Tonight. The culmination of days and nights of fantasies was going to come to a head tonight. *Come to a head.* Laughter, one part euphoric, three parts nerves, stuttered out at her slip. She reviewed everything he'd said. No one, certainly not Andrew, had ever said such things to her.

Something niggled though, and it was only that afternoon that it registered. He'd said he wasn't *good* at relationships, not that he didn't *want* one.

Chapter Fourteen

"So, tonight?" Sutton closed out the register, and Wyatt followed her through to her office.

She squatted in front of a safe and zippered the money into a bank bag. Her skirt billowed on the floor, making for a pretty picture. As she closed the safe door, she smiled up at him, her eyes alight with something he couldn't define.

But, by God, he hoped he'd put that light in her eyes. Warning flares shot off. He was treading into dangerous territory. Jackson had warned him. Yet Wyatt couldn't stop. He wanted her any way he could get her. If that was only for a little while, then he needed to make his time count.

The only problem was he was exhausted. Exhausted from a long week of work and worry. A similar strain had showed around Jackson's eyes that evening as they'd cleaned and put away their tools. The situation with Ford had the feel of an unexploded bomb. Wyatt's only hope was that it was a dud, and things would settle down soon.

She rose, her smile morphing into thoughtfulness. "You're tired."

He let go of his mask. "Exhausted. You must think I'm all talk and no action."

She turned away to straighten papers on the desk. "I don't want whatever this is to feel like an obligation. I'm not a charity case."

Aw, hell. The hurt in her voice was like a foot-long paper-cut on his heart. "You're not an obligation or a chore, believe me. What do you normally do on a Friday night?"

Why had he asked that? She and Andrew had probably had a standing date. He moved to her side, crossed his arms, and leaned back against the desk so he could evaluate her reaction.

"You're going to think I'm pathetic. And boring." Her voice didn't betray her, but he knew she was sensitive about being both.

"Boring gets a bad rap. So does the color beige." He winked, sparking amusement in her eyes, and his tension ticked down a notch. "Anyway, after the day I've had, boring sounds perfect."

"What happened?" She turned, her focus switching from inward to him in a blink. Her breast brushed his biceps, and it clenched instinctively.

"The usual family problems."

"So it's okay for you to know intimate details about the implosion of my engagement, but you won't share your family problems?"

He bit his bottom lip and noticed her gaze drop to the movement. The awareness that simmered between them flared. "I'll tell you everything, but we have to do whatever you normally do on a Friday night."

When she looked back up at him, her eyes were dancing. "Remember what I said about my standing date with my couch and junk food? I wasn't joking. Let's head to my place."

He followed her home and parked on the street. By the time she'd gathered her things from the car, he was waiting on her porch. Once inside, instead of dumping everything on the floor which was her instinct, she stashed her purse in a closet and disappeared down a hall, her voice fading with her retreat. "Make yourself comfortable."

He tucked his hands into the front pockets of his jeans and bypassed what appeared to be an even taller stack of fabrics than last time to peruse the built-in bookcases. Mystery and true crime books were interspersed with romances and fantasy paperbacks. All in alphabetical order like a library. He enjoyed reading too, although mostly car magazines or service manuals.

"I love to read." Her voice had him turning around. "But sewing has taken over my free time."

She had changed out of her high-end work clothes into a tank top that hugged her curves and cotton boxer-style shorts. Her hair was loose around her shoulders, and her face was make-up free, but her cheeks were pink from the scrubbing and her eyes were just as big and bright without mascara.

She looked natural and fresh and like someone who'd be happy hanging out in a garage or renovated barn or hiking through the woods hunting for peace. Wyatt's stomach took a swan dive. He opened his mouth, but no words formed in his addled brain.

Her shoulders scrunched toward her ears, and she rubbed her arm. "This is how I like to hang out. Take it or leave it."

The combination of lilting uncertainty and defiance had him taking a step toward her and then another. "Trust me, I'll take it."

The innuendo in his voice couldn't penetrate her innate shyness, yet her chin rose to keep their gazes locked. "You're making fun of me."

He rubbed a piece of hair that had been teasing her cheek between his fingers, the softness startling. "You look real pretty in your dresses and heels, but I like you a little messy and wild. Makes me feel like I'm home."

Her eyes flared. Damn, had he revealed too much? Her smile banished his worries. He didn't care how far the fall or how messy the impact when she smiled at him like that.

"Take your boots off and get comfy." While he did her biding, she cued up a screen with a list of movies. "See if anything catches your eye while I make us some popcorn."

He took the remote and relaxed back into the couch. Noises from the kitchen distracted him—the familiar sound of popcorn but also her sing-humming to herself, off-key enough to make the tune unrecognizable. Every new facet she revealed fascinated him.

She was the polished trendsetter of Cottonbloom, Mississippi, talented designer, successful business owner, and daughter of a prominent judge. But she was also a woman who blushed easily, couldn't carry a tune, and liked to hang out at home on Friday nights. He was still smiling when she walked in with a bowl of popcorn and shaking a bag of candy.

"Are you ready to get super wild? Because it's about to get crazy up in this joint." She ripped the candy bag open with her teeth, poured the candy over the popcorn, and then tossed the empty bag over her shoulder. She hesitated, her eyes shifting to the side.

"You really want to put that bag in the trash, don't you?"

Rolling her eyes and with a self-deprecating laugh, she handed him the bowl, grabbed the bag, and disappeared into the kitchen, coming back empty-handed. "Sorry, but I like having a tidy, well-organized place."

He took a handful of candy-infused popcorn. "Again with the apologies. You think Abigail's would be half as successful if you weren't incredibly organized"

"Probably not."

She settled into the crook of his arm as if it were completely natural. And, it was, wasn't it? They were taking things from fake to real. Except they had hadn't discussed the looming expiration date. Fun, they were having fun. If he told himself enough, maybe he'd believe that's all it was.

"You'd better eat that before the chocolate melts in your hand." She tapped his wrist.

The salty-sweetness hit his mouth like an explosion of goodness, and he reached for more, grunting his approval.

She took a daintier portion and flipped through movie choices with the remote. "I assume your family drama revolves around Ford."

"Have you had the chance to ask around about him looking for a buyer?" He tensed as if waiting for a kill shot.

"Daddy hasn't heard anything, and he knows everyone."

Wyatt laid his head back on the couch and stared at the ceiling. That was good. Ford's threats could very well be all bluster. "It's been like walking on egg shells at the garage all week. Ford and Mack get on like gators in a bath tub. Always have."

"Can't they find a way to compromise?"

"Problem is they don't agree on anything. Not how to run the garage or build the business. Ford wants to schmooze customers, promise things we may not be able to deliver. Mack takes a hard, honest line that sometimes turns people off when they're used to salesmanship."

"Sounds like you need 90% Mack and 10% Ford."

"More like 0.001% Ford," he said with a chuckle that died as his brain limped around his family's problems slower than normal. "Ford never had an interest in the garage. Not even as a kid when it was like our Hot Wheels toys come to life. But Pop couldn't let him find his own way. Couldn't understand why Ford of all of us—the oldest, the one he doted on—didn't care."

"Did your father play favorites?" She played with his hair, her fingers hypnotic and sending him further down into the vortex of memories.

"Not consciously." The need to defend his pop stemmed from guilt at a deep-seated resentment he'd never been able to exterminate. "Don't think badly of him. He was a good man. Honest. Honorable, if such a thing exists anymore."

"Oh, I'd say it does." A smile lightened her words, and he lifted his head to see her. The warmth in her eyes was a favorite blanket, a teddy bear, and fresh-from-the-oven chocolate-chip cookies all wrapped up together. Her smile faded into thoughtfulness. "My father is good man too, but that doesn't mean he's infallible. He's still human."

Even more than his brothers, she would understand. The words he forced out were roughed with emotion. "I love cars. I love the garage."

"I'm sensing a 'but.' " She raised her eyebrows in a knowing mimic of his words to her.

He could still feel the excitement and happiness in his heart when the force of his pop's pride had rained down on him after he'd rebuilt his first transmission. He'd long ago come to terms with his decision, and what had felt like a sacrifice when he was eighteen seemed more like fate now. Yet, questions of 'what if' surfaced when the flotsam of daily life grew thin. No one, not even Jackson, knew what he'd given up to work in the garage.

"I gave up a full ride at LSU to work in the garage."

"Did your dad make you stay?"

"Of course not." He shifted closer, the different colors of her eyes blurring. "I never told him. Never told anyone. Only the guidance counselor at school knew I had applied. Jackson had already decided to stay and maybe part of me was afraid to go off on my own. I don't know."

"You? Afraid?"

He tucked her hair behind her ear. If she knew how

scared he was of her, would she laugh? "You might be surprised. Anyway, staying made my family happy, and I don't regret it."

Another stroke of her hand in his hair set weights on his eyelids.

"What would you have majored in?" she asked.

"Mechanical engineering."

"You probably wouldn't have learned anything you don't already know." Another stroke had him blinking to keep his eyes open. "How did your father die?"

A queasy feeling came over him. Yet with her next to him, words that usually stayed bottled up came rushing out like opening a shaken can of Coke. "Heart attack on the shop floor. One minute he was torqueing a bolt and humming the Beatles, the next he'd collapsed."

"When did it happen?"

"Almost a year ago." The dread had been building day after day for the last week, setting everyone on edge, although no one had discussed it. Maybe after they got through the anniversary of his death, things would normalize.

"I'm so sorry." She brushed her lips against his forehead and into the hair at his temple.

"Jackson and I gave him CPR. Doctors said there was nothing we could have done." He didn't even attempt to sound together and strong.

Instead of offering platitudes like the preacher and undertaker and ninety-nine percent of the funeral goers had, she wrapped her arms around his shoulders and swayed them ever so slightly. He wasn't sure how long he stayed wrapped in her arms, but when she finally loosened her hold, he felt lighter than he had since his pop had died.

"You still want to watch a movie?" she asked.

"Sure. Put on whatever you had queued up next."

"It's a period drama."

"Start it." Truth was he favored action movies, but all he wanted was for her to keep doing whatever she was doing while he rested his eyes. Just for a minute.

Wyatt startled awake, his heart loud in his ears, disoriented in time and space. His dreams had spun him into his childhood, and he half-expected to find himself in the top bunk he'd fought Jackson for when they were five, cozy and safe under his Spiderman covers.

But he wasn't. That time in his life could never be recreated. His pop was gone, and he was a grown man with big problems. A hollowness in his chest expanded, making itself known. His senses began a catalogue. He was cozy under a different blanket, and the soft body pressed into him beat back the yawning bleakness.

The curtain of her blond hair spread across his shoulder and the curve of a cheekbone was highlighted in a sliver of light from the windows.

Sutton. Something deep within him whispered her name. A plea. He didn't think he'd spoken aloud, but she responded by arching her back in a cat-like stretch.

They were laying on her couch, and the TV was off. Birds trilled outside, warming up for their morning songs. The sun wasn't up but the promise of light chased away the inky darkness. A time in between dreams and reality.

He shifted to put his back against the cushions, brushing her hair away from her face and both wishing for more light and hoping the sun never rose. After amending their agreement, he didn't have to deny himself any longer.

He gave way to his desires and let his mouth drift to hers. Her lips were the perfect combination of salty and sweet. A soft moan and squirm to get closer signaled her wakefulness.

If their first kiss was about revenge and their second

about sealing their bargain, this kiss belonged to just the two of them. Gentle, yet devastating, the kiss made him want to stay in limbo with her forever.

He took her mouth in a series of gentle nips and forays, not wanting to push her too far, too fast. But she wasn't playing by the same rules, her hands spearing into his hair and tugging him closer.

Her throaty, breathless sigh made his typical morning erection even more painful. Was she even aware the sexy little noises she was making drove him insane? He pulled back. Her eyes were closed but she'd pulled her bottom lip between her teeth, letting it go slowly, as if she was aware he was watching and wanted to tease him.

She ran her hand down his chest to his arm, the pull she exerted light but commanding, and hooked her leg over his. Her nipples poked at the thin fabric of her tank top. Through it all, her eyes remained closed. He didn't want to be a faceless fantasy.

"Look at me." His voice was roughed with sleep and more emotion than he wanted to claim.

Her eyes fluttered open, the shadows cloaking them both a blessing and curse. As much as he attempted to keep his thoughts hidden, he longed for all her secrets.

"Wyatt, please." Her voice was husky and wanting.

His name on her lips offered satisfaction. If he could only have her for a little while, he not only wanted to leave her with memories she'd never forget, but make sure she understood how desirable and powerful she truly was.

He kissed the delicate skin at her neck and skimmed his hand over the curve of her bottom. "Please, what? Stop?"

"God, no!" Her response was so quick and vehement, he squeezed her butt and sent her wiggling closer. "I want you to touch me."

"I am touching you."

While her body might be speaking to his loud and clear, he needed her to be comfortable enough with him to ask for what she wanted.

"Come on, baby, you told me you had fantasies. Tell me what you want."

"I want more of your hands on me." She rotated her hips. "With less clothes in the way. And in a different spot."

He bit the inside of his mouth to keep from laughing. She was still skittish, but so sweet. The heat coming off her body had increased tenfold, but it seemed less an embarrassed flush and more of an aroused one. How far down did her blush go? He pushed her to her back and came over her on one elbow, tracing his index finger along the skin above her tank top.

"Like this?" he asked.

"Lower."

He inched his finger toward her nipple, smiling at the sexy impatience of her little mewls and wiggles. Circling the tight bud, he continued the torture.

"Turnaround is a bitch, Wyatt Abbott." Her softly whispered threat contained more than a hint of tease and humor.

Not so skittish after all. He hummed and whispered, "I look forward to it."

He leaned to kiss her smiling lips at the same time his fingers found her nipple. She bucked up, her tongue tangling with his and her hand clutching his arm in a grip that stung in pleasure-pain. He continued to play with her nipples over the fabric of her tank top.

"I need more." Her legs moved against his, her pelvis circling against the thigh he had wedged in between.

He moved his hand down and under her tank top to stroke the soft bare skin of her belly. "This good?"

She spread her legs farther apart. Her eyes remained

open, but were heavy-lidded. "About a half foot lower would be a helluva lot better."

She had claimed the title of goody-goody and called herself beige, but she was dead wrong. Naturally sensuous, she burned red-hot in his arms, but tempered with a sense of humor that would make hard times easier and good times better.

In that moment, Tarwater crowned himself the biggest idiot in the state of Mississippi—and that was saying something. But what Tarwater couldn't appreciate, Wyatt could. And would, for as long as possible.

He smiled and dropped a kiss on her lips. Someday soon, he take his time and explore, but for now, time was of the essence. He raced against the reality of the morning.

He slipped his hand between her legs and pressed over the cotton of her shorts. She grabbed his neck and arched to press herself against his hand. Blowing out a slow breath, he tugged her shorts and underwear down, and she wiggled to kick them off. Lightly, he ran his fingertips up her inner thigh, goosebumps breaking out over her skin in his wake. Reaching his destination, he found her wet and swollen.

She threw her arm over her eyes against the light suffusing the room. He played in her folds, teasing her before heading where she needed him the most. He forced himself to pay attention to her face as he varied his touch to determine what she enjoyed the most. He settled into a rhythm that quickened her breathing and had her hips moving in counterpoint.

"You're so fucking sexy."

She tensed against him and shook her head. He stopped, and she grabbed his wrist. "Wyatt, please."

"Look at me." He repeated his command, desperate to keep her from hiding from him.

Her eyes fluttered open, and she tilted her face toward

his. It was bright enough now for him to see the uncertainty in her eyes. While she might not be inexperienced, she was an innocent when it came to understanding her desires and power. He could fix that. He took her hand and moved it to the front of his pants.

"You're so . . . so . . ." She swallowed.

"Hard? Because of you."

"I was going to say 'big' but 'hard' works too." Her breathlessness made him smile. As did the fact she didn't snatch her hand away when he slipped his between her legs once more. She stroked him over his pants, not firm enough to get him off, but he didn't plan on complaining.

He leaned in to kiss her neck. "Did you touch yourself when you were fantasizing about me?"

He barely heard her whispered, "Yes."

Unable to help himself, he slipped a finger inside of her. With a cry, she orgasmed, squeezing his erection so hard he saw stars. She rode out her pleasure on his finger, and he bit and sucked at her neck in an attempt to maintain control.

Once she'd calmed, he raised up on his elbow. Her hair was tumbled over his arm and around her flushed face. Her legs were still spread wide, and he stroked her gently with his fingers, loving her silky feel. Her hard little nipples against the thin cotton were too tempting, and he leaned in to nip at the closest with his teeth.

"What do you want?" The tentativeness in her question felt born out of her need to please. What he wanted wasn't important right now. He needed to leave before the call of her body to his became too loud to deny.

"I want you to think about this and what *you* want next." He moved on top of her.

For a moment, he didn't think his body would obey his brain's directives to keep moving. She felt perfect underneath him, and he could be inside of her in a matter of seconds. Sending an apology to his erection, he found the willpower to rise.

She popped up to her elbows. "We can't be done."

"Don't worry, we're just getting started."

"But you're leaving. I don't want you to go." She scrambled up and struggled to put on her shorts, getting both legs in the same hole on the first try. He would have laughed if he wasn't feeling just as discombobulated, his hands trembling on his kindergartenish attempt to lace his boots.

"I promised Mack and Jackson I would be there today." Although he hadn't actually promised in so many words, today of all days, he belonged at their sides. As an excuse, it was fire- and waterproof.

"Later, then?" Looking satisfied if slightly pissed off, she followed him to the door.

Would Jackson or Wyatt need him tonight? Or maybe he would need them. It seemed appropriate for them to be together. "I'll text you and let you know about tonight."

He leaned in to capture her reddened lips in a kiss and noticed the hickey on the side of her neck. Should he warn her? He smiled against her mouth. Part of her aim was still to convince the town she and Wyatt were an item. What better way than an adolescent mark of possession?

"Are you working today?" he asked.

"For a few hours."

Anticipation was the strongest aphrodisiac and might help him get through the day. "You know all those fantasies you mentioned? How about making a top ten list for us to work through."

He walked away before the hot look she gave him incinerated his pants.

Chapter Fifteen

Sutton pushed the door to the boutique open. A deep voice from the rear of the store stopped her in her tracks and set her nerves jangling. Her daddy never dropped by to see how his investment was panning out. In fact, he often offered to turn the loan into an outright gift, but she insisted on transferring installments into his account the first business day of every month.

Not that her father would mean to manipulate her to his own ends, but he would do it "for her own good." She'd heard that phrase from both her parents often enough to choke on it.

"Here she is." With an ironic tilt to her lips, Maggie slipped by Sutton and whispered, "He pumped me like an empty soap dispenser for the dirt on Andrew and you and Wyatt Abbott."

"What'd you say?" Whatever else had come from her humiliating break with Andrew and Bree, Sutton was getting to know a side of her sister she'd never seen and she liked it.

"Not enough to satisfy him, so watch out."

Maggie escaped and left Sutton to paste on a smile and

launch her first deflection. "Are you looking for something to give Mother for your anniversary?"

His face blanked for a moment. "Is it September already?"

Her father never forgot a golf game but was hopeless when it came to birthdays and his anniversary. She put the jewelry counter between them. "Almost. A repeat of last year will get you sent to the couch, and you know your back can't handle that. How about a pendant or an antique broach?"

He waved his hand. "Fine. I trust your taste. Pick something and wrap it up for me."

She was tempted to choose something gaudy and outrageous. As she was unlocking the sliding door in the back, he tilted her face to the side with a finger on her chin.

"What's that on your neck?"

She checked herself in the oval portrait mirror and slapped a hand over the obvious red mark marring her otherwise pale skin with a gasp. Her first hickey at nearly thirty years old. She was going to do very bad things to Wyatt for this. Very bad things that she hoped they both enjoyed.

"I think it's . . . poison ivy."

"Really?" Her father's skepticism was well-deserved but no way was she going to tell him the truth.

"Must have touched some and scratched myself while I was pruning the roses." She grabbed a scarf off the display, knotted it around her neck, then laid a lovely cameo broach on the counter. "Now, how about this one?"

Her father ignored the jewelry to turn his judge-and-jury gaze on her. "Andrew came by the other night."

"Maggie told me. I know you and Andrew have to maintain a professional relationship, and you golf with him and his daddy, but I would appreciate if you'd refrain from discussing me."

Her father sighed and shot a glance toward Maggie, who was doing her best to ignore them while still bending her ear in their direction. "I don't want to see you throw away a good thing is all. He's contrite if that makes any difference."

"Why are you defending him? You want me to be with someone who respects me and treats me well, right?"

"Of course I do." Red stained her father's ruddy cheeks.

Good. He should be ashamed of himself. "That is not Andrew."

"Does Wyatt Abbott treat you well?" He gestured toward her neck and the place Wyatt had branded with his lips felt like it was on fire. "I thought he was squiring you about town as a friend. Is it something more than that?"

How to answer that? Considering what had transpired on her couch that morning, she hoped to goodness it was something more. "Wyatt is a good guy. Honest. Funny." *And panty-meltingly sexy*, she added in her head.

"He's not . . . our kind, Sutton." He held up a hand to cut off her gasp. "I don't mean that unkindly. I respected his father. But he wouldn't be comfortable hobnobbing with your friends from the Junior League, and you wouldn't be comfortable out in the boonies with his friends."

"He wasn't an embarrassment at the pig picking, and if you must know, he took me to a bonfire out in the country, and it was fun." She cursed the defensiveness that snuck into her voice. Her father was right; she hadn't been wholly comfortable. And while Wyatt had looked good in khakis and a golf shirt, imagining him in a tuxedo at the gala was like putting a top hat on a gator.

"I don't mind recommending him as a mechanic, but be careful he's not using you for your connections." The warning in his tone was clear.

Anger from some deep, dark place she'd ignored for years oozed out. "Andrew is the one who was using me for my connections, Daddy, and if you can't see that, then you need glasses."

"The Tarwaters have been family friends for decades."

"Did you and Andrew discuss the election for your position?"

"He assured me I have his support."

"I would ask a few questions at the county courthouse and make sure he hasn't filed papers to run against you."

"He wouldn't." The surety in her father's voice was unshakable. And maybe he was right.

Any residual anger receded, and she closed the door on it. "Who are you playing golf with this afternoon?"

Once he was on the subject of golf, he was hard to stop, and she ushered him out the door, still discussing his handicap. She hadn't even made it back to the counter to recover when the bell tinkled, and Bree swept over the threshold, pushing sunglasses to the top of her head.

Her dress was cute, her hair pin-straight, but as she drew closer, the dark circles under her eyes and general air of strain made her look worn and tired. "I thought the Judge would never leave. Did you tell your parents everything?"

"How else was I supposed to explain breaking things off with Andrew?"

"They hate me. I was at church, and your mother refused to even say hi to my mom." Bree ran a hand over a pretty midnight blue dress on the nearest mannequin.

"I'm sorry." And she truly was. Bree's parents were nice people and didn't deserve to be ostracized, especially at the place that preached forgiveness. "I'll talk to Mother, but she never met a grudge she didn't invite in for a good long visit."

Bree flashed a smile, but it was brief and settled into an even deeper sadness. Guilt niggled at Sutton like a splinter left to rot, but she kept her mouth clamped shut.

"I've been doing a lot of thinking," Bree said. "I'm sorry for what I did, but also the way I acted afterward. I was a real bitch."

"No arguments here." The anger that had burned so hot toward Bree was getting harder and harder to stoke.

"I've always been jealous of you."

Nothing Bree could have said would have shocked Sutton more. "Of me?"

"The way you grew up. All that money. And you're so natural and nice, people gravitate toward you. People don't like me. They're afraid of me, I think."

"*I* liked you."

"I know, and I screwed that up forever, didn't I?"

Sutton couldn't locate an answer. A week ago, she would have yelled "hell yes," but time had blurred the black-and-whiteness of the situation.

Bree covered her face with both hands and continued. "When Andrew started coming on to me, for the first time ever, someone thought I was better than you. Then I really did fall in love. I'm the worst person on the face of the planet."

A badass. Sutton was a badass and didn't want to be the beige girl that people walked all over. But, faced with a weeping Bree, her heart splayed open and the truth spilling out like her life's blood, Sutton couldn't not offer help.

She pulled her former best friend in for a hug and patted her back. "Yeah, falling in love is way worse than that little Korean dude threatening to annihilate the world. Or those Chinese hackers that stole state secrets. I should get Daddy to throw you behind bars for life."

A laugh sputtered through Bree's sobs. "How can you joke about this? I ruined your life."

Her life didn't feel ruined. The opposite in fact. She felt alive and excited and optimistic. She was coming out of the closet—literally—with her clothing designs, and Wyatt . . .

The man had set up camp in her thoughts. Strike that, he was building a fortress.

"Did you ruin it?" Sutton grabbed a box of tissues from behind the counter and nudged Bree's shoulder with it. "Because I'm not the one crying my eyes out and looking like I haven't slept in days."

Bree took several and blew her nose. "You look good."

"You're welcome to Andrew, you know. If you and he can make it work, then go for it." She wouldn't dance at their wedding, but nothing but indifference surged thinking of them together. On the other hand, she might dance if it was the two-step with Wyatt.

More tears welled in Bree's eyes. "He hasn't given up on you. He loves you."

Sutton had to remind herself they were talking about Andrew and not Wyatt. "He never loved me. He wanted to be the Judge's son-in-law, not my husband." She paused for a moment. "Do you think that maybe a small part of you wants to be a prominent lawyer's wife and not Andrew's wife?"

"All I know for sure is that I wish I'd never hurt you."

She wasn't ready to give Bree the absolution she so obviously craved, but for the first time, Sutton could see a time in the future when she would. "I know, but you did."

A breath shuddered out of Bree, but she contained any more tears. "Are you this happy because of Wyatt Abbott?"

The question struck her like a slap. Not the kind given in anger but the ones you gave people who had fainted. Sutton blinked at Bree. Was she *happy*? She definitely wasn't unhappy. Any woman who had been cheated on and dumped by her fiancé *should* be unhappy. Was there something wrong with her that she wasn't?

Ignoring her philosophical crisis, she touched the spot on her neck where Wyatt had left his mark. In the most basic of ways, he'd made her very, very happy this morning. "Yes, Wyatt makes me happy."

"I'm glad. Is it getting serious?" Bree asked, her eyes lighting with a shrewdness Sutton associated with her job as town counsel. Was Bree interested as a friend or ferreting out details she could use against Sutton later?

Forgiveness and trust weren't one and the same. Would she ever blindly trust a friend or lover again? "I need to get back to work. Inventory." She worried how easily the lie rolled out.

Bree rubbed her arm, hunched her shoulders, and took shuffling steps backward. Shades of the uncertain girl with frizzy hair and acne Sutton had known so long ago had her hand coming up, but she stopped herself before the gap between them was bridged and turned her back to Bree.

The tinkling bell on her exit signaled a transition. Whether it was a death or rebirth, Sutton wasn't able to tease out. Her life had become irrevocably complicated over the last weeks. Wyatt was the one golden thread to grab hold of through the mess.

What he offered was pure physical pleasure plus a sprinkling of hope and laughter. The fact they got along and could talk and make each other laugh didn't mean anything. It was fundamentally about the simple act of sex.

She toyed with the scarf around her neck. Problem was the morning interlude had marked her deeper than a hickey on her neck. Echoes of pleasure from that morning mixed with the self-doubt circling her head.

"You hear all that, Mags?" Sutton asked.

"Your life has been more exciting than any of my books." Her sister popped out from behind a mannequin she was fitting with one of Sutton's gowns. "I'm putting this in the window, and I guarantee it will bring people in."

Sutton couldn't watch. She imagined it was like watching your child go up onstage and perform. A combination of hope and worry and terror.

She retreated to her office and stared at her phone. Crazy colorful sex. That was the goal, right? He'd told her to get a list of fantasies ready. Except it wasn't the feel of him, thick and hard in her hand, that held her focus, but the depth of sadness in his eyes. He had been hurting last night.

Thinking about U. There. A simple yet open-ended text. Minutes passed. He was probably in the middle of some complex mechanical thing under a car. Or maybe he regretted everything. She paced.

Thinking about U2. And this morning. But have to cancel tonight. Sorry.

Her stomach swooped, and her hands grew clammy. *Is it work?*

Not work, but I'd be terrible company. Talk to you tomorrow though. Promise.

K.

She tapped her phone against her chin. He wasn't blowing her off. Whatever was making him bad company involved his father's death. Whether it had been a day or a year, Wyatt's grief was still raw.

As crazy as her parents drove her, losing either one of them would be devastating. Wyatt had now lost both his parents, one through abandonment and one through death. Her chest tightened in reflected pain. Even with him over the river and miles away, she wanted to soothe him somehow.

What did one do for a death in the family? In Cottonbloom, grief was counseled with casseroles. So what if his father had died a year ago? Wyatt was still grieving him. She would whip something up and drop it by the shop. No strings attached. Just like their relationship.

* * *

Mack squeezed Wyatt's shoulder on the way out the door. It was the only acknowledgement of the one-year anniversary of their pop's death. Sadness and melancholy had spread over the garage like an oil spill.

The fact Mack was retreating to the house before Wyatt had packed up said more than words. Jackson had already disappeared. Probably heading for the racetrack. He seemed to work out most of his problems going round and round as fast as possible.

Yet . . . Wyatt had needed his brothers. He wanted to sit around and trade stories about their pop, but none of them were good at talking about the important stuff. Him included, he supposed.

He picked up his phone and stared at the texts between him and Sutton. He had been honest. That didn't mean he didn't want her. He did—badly—but he wouldn't be able to hide the intensity of his need under a flirty, superficial smile. Not tonight.

Still, his thumbs hovered over the keypad. The comfort of her company and her body called, but that's not what they were doing. His already aching heart squeezed painfully.

He turned off the lights in the shop and stood there for a long moment. The quiet was disconcerting and lonely as hell, the shadows pressing at him. He backed out the door and took deep breaths of the humid air. It wasn't even five. The night stretched to forever.

He stripped off his shirt, strapped on gloves, and let the punching bag bear the brunt of his grief. His arms burned and sweat trickled down his back. It was only when his lungs ceased to pull in enough oxygen that he stopped and hung on the bag, swaying like they were dance partners. He rested his forehead against the canvas and closed his eyes.

"Are you finished or was that round one?" Sutton's voice came from behind him.

He turned, praying his lack of oxygen hadn't turned him hallucinatory. She leaned against the doorway of the barn, a bottle of wine in one hand and a covered dish in the other. She was in a tight white V-neck T-shirt, a striped skirt, and flip-flops with big pink flowers between her toes. The smile on her face was hopeful and sweet and a little sheepish.

He wanted to chalk his weak knees up to his workout, but he had a bad feeling she was the cause. His insides buzzed like a streetlight at dusk.

He didn't want to be alone.

He wasn't like his brothers, who shut down and turned inward when troubles came to call. His pop's death had been devastating for all three of them, but Mack and Jackson had remained stoic, and needing comfort signaled a sign of weakness in his family.

Every nerve ending screamed at him to take her into his arms, but he resisted. Barely. "I'm calling it a draw. Whatcha you got there?" He hoped he didn't sound as pathetic and needy as he felt and gestured with his chin toward her hands.

"Casseroles heal all hurts." She held up the bottle of wine and examined the label. "And if that doesn't work, alcohol should do it. I can drop this off and go, but"—she shifted on her feet and bit her bottom lip—"I had a feeling you might need company."

"What gave me away?"

She took a step forward and his feet shuffled to meet her halfway. He took the wine bottle, and she put her free hand in the middle of his chest. His heart felt like it was trying to break free of its confines to experience her touch.

"I couldn't stop thinking about everything you told me last night. I had a feeling you might need a friend." She shrugged a shoulder but didn't drop her hand. "Is that crazy?"

"I happen to relate to crazy. It runs in my family." He wrapped his fingers around her wrist and glanced his thumb across the soft back of her hand. She leaned even closer to him. So close he could feel the residual heat coming off the dish propped on her hip.

"Your family is not crazy." Her voice was breathless and vaguely distracted sounding.

"Have you heard about the curse?"

"What curse?" Her hand twitched on his chest, her fingernails scraping against his skin erotically.

"There's a long history of twins in my family. My aunts Hyacinth and Hazel are the previous generation's set. Jackson and I are the most recent."

"Guess that means one of you boys will have twins."

"No set of twins have ever gone on to get married. A bunch of Abbott old maids and bachelors." He tensed although he wasn't sure what he was waiting for.

She was silent for a moment, a crinkle appearing between her eyes even as she smiled. "You don't really believe that will happen to you, do you?"

What had been a funny family story had turned into an ominous one. After the last two weeks, he was very much worried that would happen to him. Admitting that would cement his crazy status. Her gaze dipped to where their hands entwined over his heart before rising to meet his.

A long moment passed in which all they did was stare into each other's eyes. The bond between them was strengthening by the second. He recognized the danger, uncuffed her wrist, and stepped away.

"Looks like there's plenty to share. You wanna come up?" His voice sounded strange.

She followed him toward the loft stairs. "I don't know

if you classify as crazy, but I'd say you've inherited more than a touch of wildness."

"I'm afraid you're going to be mighty disappointed." He halted midway up the stairs and turned.

She took one more step, putting them so close he could kiss her. She tilted her face up to his, her tongue dabbing along her bottom lip. His breathing accelerated as if he'd gone another round with the body bag.

"No way are you going to disappoint me." Sutton's laugh was throaty and sexy.

Her eyes were hypnotizing and his stomach swooped. Clearing his throat, he continued up into his loft. Without her eyes on him, he found his footing, but he could feel her presence like a caress.

Once inside, he backed away as if she were an explosive. "I need to hop in the shower."

"Take your time." She veered toward the kitchen area. "I'll pop the casserole into the oven to heat back up and open the wine. Daddy made me promise to let it breathe."

Out of sheer cowardice, he stayed in the shower long after he'd scrubbed himself clean. He rubbed the steam off the mirror, seeing a fuzzy reflection of himself. She was returning the favor and here on a mission of mercy.

He glanced around and cursed. His habit was to streak around naked, and he'd been so intent on escaping her, he hadn't brought any clothes in with him. He wrapped a towel around his waist and poked his head out the door. The smell of the casserole made his mouth water, and the bottle of wine was in the middle of his small table uncorked.

Had she left? He took a step out of the bathroom, and she straightened from a long shadow at the window, holding a water glass filled with red wine. Water dripped from his hair and down his chest and back, and his grip on the towel at his waist tightened.

They stared, and the longer they stared the more electric the air grew between them. Wyatt had never experienced the kind of gravitational pull she exerted with any other woman. Whatever storm brewed behind Sutton's eyes had nothing to do with casual fun.

He held his ground this time, but the challenge he'd sensed in her faded into a smile he recognized. It was the one that made her eyes crinkle and settled a warmth that helped burn away his worries of the future.

"You get dressed, and I'll set the table." She had kicked off her flip-flops and her skirt swished around her thighs as she headed to the kitchen area.

He left the door cracked and grabbed a pair of broken-in jeans and a T-shirt. Watching her putter around the kitchen through the narrow opening, he pulled his clothes on. She was on tiptoes reaching for something on the top shelf. The homey sight settled a knot in his belly and an ache in his chest. Whatever affliction he was suffering was more complicated than simple lust. It felt closer to longing.

He wasn't sure where the night was headed, but he made his bed just in case they got up close and personal with it. He covered the stew of frustration and anticipation with a smile and joined her. A quick peek inside his oven revealed a bubbling, cheese-topped casserole.

"Five minutes to go. Time enough for a glass. Daddy has good taste; the wine is delicious." She got down another water glass and poured him some.

"I'll bet the Judge would be horrified if he knew we weren't using proper glasses."

Her laughter was slight yet held a tease. "He'd probably disown me."

He sat down, the table only big enough for two. It had been handed down from an Abbott relation when he and Jackson had been furnishing the loft. Most of the hand-me-downs they'd replaced with nicer things over the years, but the table was so seldom used, they hadn't bothered. He and Jackson usually ate on paper plates in front of the TV. Two mismatched dinner plates were flanked by silverware. Sutton was probably used to eating off china.

He took a sip of the wine. He was more of a beer connoisseur, but even his inexperienced palette sat up and took notice. It was good. She joined him and the silence that followed wasn't the comfortable kind.

They weren't friends or lovers or even dating by the strict definition. But potential for all three brewed between them.

"Did you want to talk about it?" she asked softly. "Your father, I mean?"

The way she said it made him think she already knew, so what was there to say? But then her hand snuck across the neutral zone of the table and covered his. He shifted his hand so their palms slid over each other, his rough and callused from his work in the garage, hers soft and feminine.

"Pop died a year ago today."

Her fingers knit between his, and she squeezed. "I'm sorry. I wish you'd told me last night."

He shrugged.

"Where are your brothers? Why aren't you all together?"

"Jackson's racing. Mack is probably sitting in the dark with a beer. Ford was a no-show today."

"Would you rather be alone?" She shifted as if she was pushing up, and he tightened his hold on her.

"No." He half-closed his eyes and took a too-big sip of the wine. "I cancelled earlier because this isn't what you signed up for."

"What do you mean?"

"You know what I mean," he said softly, forcing himself

to look her in the eyes. He could say more, but it would be the opposite of fun and flirty and superficial.

"I'm not going anywhere." She didn't flinch.

He dropped his gaze to the purple depths of his glass. "Pop's ghost hung over the shop all day, but we kept our heads down and worked."

"Did you and Jackson talk about it?"

"Jackson is a lot like Mack. He doesn't need to talk. Doesn't need people. I'm not sure he even needs me."

"That's not true."

Wyatt made a scoffing sound and took another sip.

"Tell me more about your dad." Her gaze was on the play of their fingers.

"He was . . ." He sighed. "Everyone's friend. Lovable. Always laughing. He was the glue that held the family together."

"Just like you, then."

He was ready to protest, but her smile silenced him, her eyes trying to strip away his already shaky defenses. He killed the rest of the wine and set his glass down with a thump. "I like to have fun. That's why you propositioned me, right? Nothing special about that."

"Oh, Wyatt." The slight exasperation in her voice was tempered by humor and something else he couldn't put his finger on. She disentangled their hands and rose to stand in front of him. He shifted to accommodate her between his knees, and she lay her hands on his shoulders.

She leaned in, and he took a sharp breath, thinking—hoping?—her destination was his mouth, but instead she veered to whisper in his ear. "You are the most lovable, amazing man I've ever met."

When she lifted her hands from his shoulders, she took a weight he'd been carrying around so long he didn't realize it until it was gone. Her words circled his head. She thought

he was amazing? And, *lovable*? What did that even mean?
Stuffed animals were lovable. Dogs were lovable.

He shifted to watch her take out the casserole with a
singed pair of oven mitts. The domesticity of the scene
made him reel—off-balance and unsure and searching
blindly for his next move.

He was the one supposed to be teaching her how to
loosen up and tap into her wild side. Instead, here she was,
soothing his demons and tempering his grief.

She spooned portions onto their plates, hers with a modest helping and his plate piled high with an Italian looking mishmash of meat and noodles, and added two pieces
of buttery looking bread tucked to the side. His first bite
registered as a religious experience. With his second, he
was sure Sutton qualified for sainthood.

"You like it?" she asked.

His grunt was caveman-like.

She took a bite around a smile. They made small talk
for the rest of the meal, mostly about the travails of owning businesses in a small town. The conversation waned
as they split the rest of the wine.

The night was at a crossroads. He swirled the wine and
watched it lick the edge. Without looking up at her, he said,
"I want you to stay with me tonight."

"Are you sure?" Her voice was tentative. She was
doing her best to be wild and reckless, but she *was* nice
and sweet and everything he'd ever dreamed of finding in
a woman.

"So sure that it's scary."

A hint of sadness colored her smile, a forewarning
of what was to come. She didn't speak, only stood and
held out a hand. He blew out a slow breath and rose to
meet her.

"You left me in a bad state this morning. Why'd you do
that?" The change from serious to teasing in her tone was

abrupt and wasn't the real Sutton. It was someone she thought she should be for him.

He should play along and be the guy she'd recruited for her endeavor, make her tell him all her fantasies, but he couldn't. Not today. "I didn't want to take advantage of you. Needed to make sure you really want me."

Her face softened. Weaving their fingers, she molded herself against him and wrapped her other arm around him in a hug that was close to a stranglehold. Except everything about her was soft and feminine.

He nosed into the hair at her temple. Already her scent was summoning memories of kissing her and teaching her to play pool and dancing around the bonfire.

"I do want you," she whispered.

He felt as much as heard her words. It was enough. It would have to be enough. He swept her into a cradle hold, and the noise she made was half-shocked cry, half laugh.

"What are you doing?"

"Sweeping you off your feet?" He smiled, but the sentiment took a skimming hit at his heart, leaving a painful crease. If he'd been a rabbit or squirrel, he'd advise putting the creature out of its misery.

He dropped her across his bed and came over her on his elbows, brushing her hair back from her face. Diffused light from the setting sun filtered in from the skylight and windows, broken up by fast-moving, dark, storm clouds. It made sense the weather would mimic the complicated nature of their relationship.

He needed to keep this simple. Except her eyes pulled him in like a hypnotist, and his heart spun out of control. She cupped his cheeks and lifted her head to reach his lips. The moment they met, his existence narrowed to that moment. Nothing else mattered.

He took control, pressing her into the mattress and taking the kiss to the next level, touching his tongue to hers.

Her slight gasp spurred him to take the kiss deeper. He lifted off her enough to work her T-shirt up and over her head, tossing it over his shoulder.

He leaned down to nip at the soft, white skin above the white lace of her bra. Her nipple received the same treatment. She grabbed his shoulders and tried to pull him back on top of her, but he resisted. As much as he wanted to bury himself in the comfort she offered, tonight had to be about her, and if he kept his hips pressed between her legs, his resolution to be unselfish would get voted down by more primal instincts.

He stood up, his gaze trailing over her body. "Take off your skirt."

She shimmied off the skirt and kicked it to the side, a touch of shyness giving her movements an endearing awkwardness. He peeled off his shirt, and it landed on top of hers on the floor. One of her hands came up to cover her chest while her legs cut against each other. A natural seductiveness lurked under the trappings of what she'd learned was proper, and he would be the man to set it free.

He might not be her first lover, but he'd be the one she remembered forever, dammit. His good intentions were dented when she propped up on an elbow and ran her fingertips over the prominent erection next to his zipper. She tugged at his belt, and he grabbed her wrist.

"Not yet. First you." He was dimly aware he spoke like a man whose native language wasn't English.

He squatted down, hooked his hands behind her knees, and pulled her to the edge of the bed. Her gasping yelp turned into a breathy moan when he ran his tongue along the center of the impractical scrap of lace she called underwear. He hooked them to the side and did what he'd been thinking about since forever.

His emotions were raw from grief over his father, worry over the garage, and frustration over her. Being between her legs and hearing his name on her lips soothed the rough edges of his spirit even as his body clamored for more. She was already hot for him, but he wanted her wild.

When her hands speared into his hair and drew into fists, pulling at his scalp, he glanced up to find her watching him. His tongue stilled. The moment was more intimate than any they'd shared, the barriers between them demolished.

Sutton had assumed sex with Wyatt would be fun and light and satisfying, similar to their interlude on her couch. This felt more like life and death. Like she might die if she didn't get him inside of her.

"Please, I need . . ." Was that her voice?

"Tell me. You have to tell me."

She again propped herself up on a shaky elbow and reached between his legs. If anything, his erection had grown bigger and harder. "You. Inside of me."

He didn't say anything, but reached around her to unhook her bra and draw it off. She'd purposefully worn sexier-than-normal underwear, half hopeful, half scared they'd end up exactly where they were—in his bed.

Yet the urge to cover herself like a prudish heroine from a Victorian novel was undeniable. That wasn't the kind of heroine she wanted to be. She wanted to take charge and be bold, but couldn't quite put a stamp of ownership on her sexuality. She half covered her breasts with an arm.

He leaned over her and dropped a simple kiss on her lips. "You're beautiful and sexy and perfect."

Truth smoldered in his eyes. Courage. He gave her courage. She put her hands on his bare flanks, the skin hot and smooth, the muscles taut. Her reward was a smile. In a quick move, he lowered his head and took one of her nipples in his mouth.

Her eyes might have rolled back in her head for a second.

The mind-blowing pleasure was short-lived. He stood, unbuckled his belt, and pushed his pants down and off with a feline grace.

His erection bobbed at eye level, and her courage went on hiatus. She scooched back on the bed, but before she escaped his reach, he grabbed her panties and yanked them down.

He crawled to join her in the middle of the king-size bed and came over her. This was it. Tensing, she closed her eyes, spread her legs, and waited. Nothing happened. She opened one eye to find him looking at her, his head tilted.

"What are you thinking right now?" His voice held all sorts of questions.

"I'm ready for you to . . . do it."

"Why is your face all scrunched up like you're preparing for a flu shot?"

Oh God, she was blowing it. And not in the sexy sense of the word. She attempted to smooth her expression. "After this morning, I figured you'd want to, you know, get yours. I'm ready."

"You're not nearly ready." He rolled them so she straddled him and pushed her to sitting. The position startled her into indecision. What did he expect her to do?

He circled his hips and ground his erection against her. She undulated involuntarily. It felt so amazing, she did it again. And again. Her head fell back, and she stifled a moan. His hands spasmed on her thighs, and she stopped, worried she did something wrong.

"Don't stop, babe," he said gruffly.

"I don't know what to do."

Instead of making her feel foolish, his slow smile made her confidence bloom. "Do what feels good. And don't worry, we're both going to end up with a smile on our faces."

The flash of self-consciousness at her position—naked

and dimly backlit by the lights from the kitchen area and
the setting sun—was seared away by the intensity of his
gaze. She continued to grind along his length until she
wasn't only ready, she bordered on frantic.

He slid his hands from her thighs, up and over her hips
to circle her ribcage. The calluses along his palms rasped
pleasurably along her nerve-endings, and his thumbs
brushed the underside of her breasts. Her nipples peaked,
and she arched into his touch.

"More, please." The words emerged from her strangled
throat on a shallow breath.

As if he'd been waiting for her cue, he maneuvered
her as if she weighed nothing to pull her nipple into his
mouth. He reached for a condom and rolled it on, brushing the most sensitive part of her with his knuckles. She
couldn't wait a second longer.

She shifted back, and his erection pushed inside of her
an inch. They moaned in tandem, the hum vibrating from
her nipple to between her legs, and he moved his hands to
her hips. She was thankful, because any sort of physical
coordination was beyond her.

Slowly, his grip firm, but not biting, he guided her until
he was buried deep. He felt perfect inside of her.

"Are you good?" The breathlessness in his voice was
gratifying.

"So, so good." She peppered his face with kisses until
her lips met his, and he assumed control. Even though she
was the one on top, he possessed her. Any vague worry
over her easy surrender disappeared with his first thrust.

The rhythm he set was slow, each glide deep. The chase
to orgasm was on, and her body responded by picking
up the pace, no longer needing his hands for guidance. He
pushed her to sitting, interrupting her rhythm, but the position moved him even deeper. She braced herself on his
chest, his muscles tensed.

"Go on, take what you need," he said in a guttural voice she barely recognized as his.

The concept was foreign. She'd never been given freedom in bed. Sex had been an orchestrated, textbook affair. But Wyatt had turned everything she thought about herself on its head. The freedom was intoxicating, and she rose and fell on him, not worried about whether or not he was enjoying it or how she looked doing it.

She moved her fingers to where they were joined, and he whispered encouragement. Her orgasm swept over her, turning her movements clumsy, but his hands were there to steady her and keep the rhythm intact.

His thrusts became harder, lifting her up, until he too succumbed, his body bowing inward. As soon as he turned lax underneath her, she collapsed to his chest, her face buried in his neck. Their breathing slowed together.

She wasn't sure how long they lay there. Minutes, hours, a lifetime. Her thoughts were scattered and varied, but the one that jumped out was a silent call of thanks to Andrew. Without his betrayal, she would have never had this experience with Wyatt.

The question that jabbed at her was whether their explosive passion was like two chemical elements that were inert until combined or whether it was all Wyatt. Was sex always like this for him? Did it matter?

It shouldn't, but it did. Still, she wasn't naïve enough to ask him if she were special. The dissection of truth and lie would take her out of the moment, and the moment was very good. That's all the new and improved Sutton wanted to concentrate on.

He shifted her to his side and rolled over to dispose of the condom. Too relaxed to cover herself, she ran her fingertips over the muscles of his back. He gathered her in his arms and tucked her against him.

With their legs tangled in the sheets and Wyatt tracing

masterpieces on her back, Sutton felt like she was floating as close to heaven as she could get without actually dying. Although that orgasm . . . she might have seen God. She had definitely called His name with more emotion than she'd ever used in church.

A premature darkness had snuffed out the dying light. Lightning flashed, followed seconds later by rumbling thunder. The storm was still miles away, but getting closer. She was thankful for the excuse to stay a little longer.

"Storms terrified me when I was little. I used to crawl in bed with Mack." His voice was faraway and dreamy.

"Not Ford even then?" She explored his body in a way she'd never been comfortable doing with Andrew. One of his hands was tucked behind his head, and the bulge of his biceps inspired awe.

"Ford was the reason I was so scared. Told me stories about how a hurricane blew through and drowned half the parish. It's why I took the top bunk and made Jackson sleep under me. How's that for brotherly love?"

She laughed softly. "I don't remember stories of a flood like that."

"That's because he lied to scare me. Of course, I had put a salamander in his bed earlier that week. Too bad I was too dumb to connect the two incidents."

She chuffed a laugh and nuzzled at his neck. "Not dumb. Young and innocent. Did Mack tease you too?"

"Naw. He's an old soul as Aunt Hazel would say. Always been too serious. Not sure he knows how to have fun."

"What about Jackson? Does he know how to have fun?"

"A different kind than most people are used to. He loves to race. Not sure what he's chasing out on the track or if he'll ever catch it."

His heart beat under her ear, a soothing tempo that urged hers to match. "My father and Bree came to see me today."

"Busy day. What did they want?"

"Apparently, Andrew isn't giving up on getting back together. Bree told me she was jealous of me, and that's part of the reason she took up with Andrew. She apologized, and it felt real this time."

"Did you accept?"

"I didn't *not* accept." She explored the thick dusting of dark hair on his chest and followed the line down his belly to the sheet. His torso was solid and thick, with muscles earned through hard work and not in a gym.

He grabbed her hand, his body rumbling with laughter. "Is this the turn-around you threatened me with this morning?"

She tilted her head back to see his face. His eyes were closed, his smile sultry. If he wasn't bothered by the temporary nature of their relationship—maybe hook-up was more accurate—then she'd try not to be either. People did this sort of thing all the time.

"You can forgive her that easily?" he asked.

"We're not friends, but not enemies either. I don't know what she is or what she'll be to me in the future." She slipped her hand under the sheet to his hip and explored the curve of his buttock. "Daddy's worried you're using me."

"Did you tell him that *you're* the one using *me*?"

Her heart stuttered, no longer synchronized with his, and she propped up on her elbow. "I'm not using you."

He smiled an unfamiliar smile—smaller and sadder—and pushed her tangled hair over her shoulder, his hand staying to caress the skin. "You don't need to lie to me."

She couldn't hold his gaze and sank back down to his chest, but her utter contentment had been invaded by worry and more than a little anger.

"I'm not surprised Tarwater wants you back," he said as she tried to get her whirling thoughts under control.

Finally, she said, "It's all political. Andrew is gunning for Daddy's judgeship."

"You're selling yourself short. Maybe he didn't realize what he'd had until it was gone."

She harrumphed. "Please."

In a blink, he'd rolled on top of her, any hint of lassitude gone. "You're amazing in bed and out. Any man with a functioning brain cell would want you."

Irritation colored the still simmering arousal. "You're using me too. You only agreed to date me to get business for the garage, right? Sex is an unexpected perk."

He bared his teeth and pushed her hands above her head. She didn't understand the roil of emotions on his face, but the brush of his erection between her legs incinerated her questions, except for one. "You want to do it again?"

He transferred her wrists to one hand and reached for a condom as his answer. She spread her legs wider, her need, now that it had been uncaged, had grown exponentially. He pushed inside of her and dropped his mouth to hers. Brutal and taking, his mouth tried to impart a lesson she was in no mood to learn. She nipped at his bottom lip.

He was angry, and so was she, yet she still trusted him to bring her pleasure and not pain. As his thrusts turned as hard as his kiss, her hips rose to meet his, and she shattered around him. This time it wasn't the Almighty she called for but Wyatt, over and over, urging him to join her.

When he did, his hands loosened on her wrists and weaved with hers, his body still grinding into her, prolonging her orgasm and bringing tears to her eyes for reasons she couldn't pinpoint but which were more than purely physical. She turned her face to the side and squeezed her eyes shut like a dam against the tidal wave of emotion.

As the wind and lightning and thunder grew more violent outside, whatever storm had raged between them abated. He brushed his lips against her temple and pulled back.

"Tell me I didn't hurt you."

"You didn't." Her voice came out shaky, and she tucked her chin against her shoulder to stem the wobble.

"Why are you crying, then?" He unwound their hands and forced her to face him.

"I don't know." It was such a girly thing to say, but it was true. He hadn't hurt her physically, yet something inside of her ached just the same. Another tear tracked from the corner of her eye and into her hair.

The last week had taught her the need to protect herself, and she was loathe to expose a weakness to anyone, especially a man who had no allegiance to her. After they were over and done, what would he say about her to his friends at the Tavern or to his brothers?

"What are you going to tell people after the gala . . . after we're over?"

"I don't want to think about us being over when we're just getting started." His gray eyes swallowed her in warmth and kindness and melancholy, the stew of emotions mimicking the ache inside of her. "But if you're asking whether or not I kiss and tell, the answer is no. Whatever happens between us, stays between us."

His answer didn't sooth her, and with a shock she realized why. She didn't care what anyone else thought or said about her. Only what Wyatt thought of her mattered. This moment had nothing to do with Andrew or Bree or her father or even Cottonbloom. It was for them.

Her instincts urged caution. Overanalyzing the situation while he was still between her legs, his chest rubbing her breasts, was foolhardy. She curled her legs around his thighs and brought him closer.

"Even I can't go three rounds without a break, darlin'." Would she ever tire of his laughter? Husky and sexy and rough. He squeezed her hands and rubbed his cheek against hers. "You sure you're okay?"

The affectionate gesture made her heart tingle as fiercely as the sex had made her body tingle. "Better than okay. That was more intense than I expected is all."

Worry lingered in the pull of his lips, but he didn't pursue the line of questioning. Instead, he rolled off of her with a sigh. Thunder rumbled in the distance, the storm settling into a steady rain against the windows.

She pulled the sheet up to cover her breasts and sat up, unsure of what was expected. "Should I . . . ?"

"Stay? Yep. Grab a T-shirt from the top drawer if you want, but naked is even better. You shouldn't be out driving in this mess anyway."

Her car had excellent windshield wipers, but she wanted to stay, so why fight it? She'd never slept naked before, not by herself or with anyone else. It seemed a decadent and very non-beige thing to do.

After cleaning up in the bathroom, she bypassed his drawer and slipped back in bed to cuddle up against him. Worries about what would happen in the morning wormed into her head. Her parents would expect her at church in the morning, so she'd have to leave before then. Between the rain and the warmth of his body, sleep claimed her before she could make a plan of escape.

Chapter Sixteen

Wyatt opened his eyes to morning light streaking over the sky. The storm had blown itself out sometime during the night, leaving the world freshly washed. It felt like a new beginning.

Pins and needles shot through the arm that was pillowing her head, but he tried not to move and wake her. How well had she been sleeping since everything had gone down with Tarwater and Bree? Not well judging by how quickly and deeply she'd fallen asleep last night. Or maybe he'd worn her out. She'd certainly done a number on him.

He flexed his arm and grimaced. She stirred, her eyes fluttering open. Again, the complexity and depth of her eyes made his breath crimp. Every single time. Her hair was a mess around her head where he'd run his hands through it. Her lips were soft and full in the vulnerable state between sleep and wakefulness. She was the prettiest thing he'd ever seen.

Their conversation from the night before loomed like an approaching waterfall he'd be forced over in a rotting barrel. He cursed the gala and briefly wondered if he could sabotage it. Using broken logic like a tree falling in a forest, if the gala never took place, this thing between him and Sutton wouldn't ever have to end.

He was being naïve and fanciful. Gala or not, Sutton would eventually come to the conclusion that he fit like a square peg in her round little world. But right here, right now, she smiled at him like they stood a chance at forever.

"Morning, sunshine." He leaned in to kiss her forehead before working his abused arm out from under her head.

"Morning." Her sleepy smile morphed into panic. "Morning? What time is it?"

He lifted his head enough to glance at his bedside clock. "Almost eight."

A shriek accompanied her launch out of the bed. If he hadn't been so startled, he would have thoroughly enjoyed watching her shimmy back into her clothes. "Late for another date?"

"Yeah, with God. Church starts at eight thirty."

"Why not skip? I doubt He keeps score."

"Actually, it's not God I'm worried about. It's Mother. And Daddy for that matter. He likes to campaign with a united family front." She dropped to her knees to look under his bed and came up with her underwear. "Why don't you come with me?"

"Excuse me?"

She sat on the edge of the bed and pulled them on, giving him a last glimpse of her bare bottom and thighs. "Come with me. I can introduce you around. Might drum up some business."

He hesitated. He wanted to go with her but not to be seen by the gossips or drum up business for the garage. He wanted to go for no other reason than to be able to sit beside her and hold her hand.

"Okay," he said slowly as he tossed the sheets aside. "What should I wear?"

Her smile was bright and uncomplicated. "Khakis and a golf shirt or button down is fine. I'm going to have to wear this. We'll be late getting a seat as it is."

They shared the small bathroom. She twisted her hair up and stuck a clip in it. He handed her a toothbrush still in its packaging.

Her gaze met his in the mirror. "Do you keep a stash of new toothbrushes for your one-night stands?"

He stopped mid brush. If he had to put a finger on her attitude, he would put it squarely between hurt and pissed. He spit out the foam in his mouth. "Jackson and I tend to buy things in bulk because we hate to shop. Anyway, we aren't a one-night stand."

"No?"

He rinsed his mouth and shook his head. "Between now and the gala, I'm going to wear you out, woman. Now brush your teeth so I can give you a proper good morning kiss."

She ripped the packaging off so fast he had to stifle laughter. While she finished freshening up, he dressed in the same pair of khakis he wore to the pig picking and a button down.

"You look great." Shyness tinged her smile, which was quite a switch from the wild woman who'd ridden him into oblivion the night before.

He grabbed her hips and fit them together. "So do you."

His mouth swooped to take hers, but she only allowed a quick peck before bobbing her face to the side and slapping him on the butt. "No time to mess around, stud. We've got a back pew to hold down."

He let her go, her playfulness as much a surprise as her invitation to church was, and followed her down the stairs. They met Jackson coming through the back door of the barn, his sparring gloves on and his shirt off. Wyatt was relieved to see him in one piece.

"How was the track?" Wyatt asked.

"Fast and loud."

"Did you win?"

Jackson's eyebrows rose and a rare smile flashed. ". . . course, I did."

"You sleep better afterward?"

"A few bad dreams brought on by Mack's crappy couch." Jackson raised his eyebrows, and Wyatt sent him silent thanks for not interrupting his night with Sutton. He was so out of practice, he hadn't even given his brother a heads up.

Jackson's gaze flicked to Sutton and back. "Where are you two headed?"

"Church in Mississippi." Jackson's mouth unhinged, and Wyatt held up his hands. "Don't lecture me right now. We're late."

Jackson gave a slight shake of his head and turned his back to them to concentrate on driving his fist through the bag. Wyatt guided Sutton toward his car, a hand on her lower back.

"What is he going to lecture you about?"

"We can take my car. You want to drive?" His avoidance tactic worked if her gasp was any indication.

"You'll let me drive the Hornet?"

"Sure, why not?"

"Because your car is worth five times as much as mine."

"I'm counting on you not to run it into anything." He tossed her the keys, and she scampered to the driver's side to slip behind the wheel.

The engine growled, and she turned to him with a kid-in-the-candy-shop smile. "The first and only time I got to drive Andrew's Camaro was the day I brought it into the shop, and I kept it to under twenty-five miles per hour."

She worked the gearshift and clutch and got them rolling forward with only a small jerk. Once on the road, she hit the gas but maintained control. He never worried the car was getting the upper hand and relaxed back into the seat to watch her.

Her excitement reminded him of his first time behind the wheel of a real car, one with a V8 engine and rear-wheel drive. The experience had turned his love of cars into an obsession. He'd been ten, barely able to see over the wheel and reach the clutch.

His gaze drifted down. Her sun kissed legs worked the pedals, and he drifted back to the night before. He forced himself to watch the road to stave off his body's natural reaction. Church, they were headed to church.

She pulled into the packed parking lot, maneuvering the car down a long row of trucks and cars to a spot at the end. A few other latecomers trickled through the side doors with them.

Organ music swelled over the murmur of conversations. After exchanging a wave with her mother up front, she took his hand and tugged him toward the back. They settled onto the cushioned pew. He wasn't much for the hymns or preaching, but the light through the stained glass windows that lined the sanctuary filled him with something resembling peace.

Long ago Sunday mornings squirming between Aunt Hazel and Hyacinth bubbled up. Memories he'd thought lost. Aunt Hazel would pull candy out of her pocketbook to keep him still. Not the cheap peppermints his dad kept around, but the good stuff—chocolates and caramels and taffy.

Something had stuck from those times because the hymns were familiar, and he could recite the prayers word for word. He draped his arm over the back of the pew, and Sutton shifted into the crook of his body. He laid his hand, palm up on his thigh, and without any prompting, she slipped her hand inside.

As if an angel sent him a message from on high, one thought exploded in his head. He couldn't let Sutton slip out of his life after the gala. His senses sharpened and turned inward, the preacher's voice a murmur of white noise. He had to keep hold of her . . . forever.

Yes, the timing was crappy. She didn't want to get serious, but he could bide his time. You didn't go into restoring cars without a motherlode of patience. Rebuilding an engine took weeks of delicate work. Even once he was done, he wouldn't know if he'd been successful until that first crank. It was the scariest, most exhilarating part of his job.

Could he wait until her heart was healed and ready for love again?

A bombastic song from the organist and the rustle of people standing brought him back to reality. Sutton's attention was taken by an elderly man who'd come in late and sat on their left. Wyatt looked around, feeling like a freshwater fish dumped in the ocean.

Ford stood at the end of their pew, smiling and shaking the hands of the people shuffling out as if he were the preacher. Checking to see that Sutton was still occupied, Wyatt joined the line of people until only he and Ford remained.

"What are you doing here?" Ford's teeth were clenched in a smile.

"What are *you* doing here?"

"I asked you first." His rising ire cut away his smile.

Wyatt shrugged and tried to keep a smile off his face. The game they played was childish but satisfying. "I came with Sutton. Aunt Hyacinth know you've jumped the river?"

"Aren't you taking this plan to drum up new business a little far? Someone's going to get hurt."

"I have no clue what you're talking about." A protectiveness rose and drowned out any humor from the situation.

"Andrew's told me his theories and none of them involve the two of you actually dating."

"Are you and Tarwater besties now or something? I'd watch your back with that one," Wyatt said.

"I don't think he's the one I need to worry about stabbing me in the back."

"What's that supposed to mean?"

"Please, you know exactly—" Ford put on a sunny smile like flipping a switch. "Hi, Sutton."

Sutton looped her arm through Wyatt's. "Hi, Ford. Nice to see you."

"Actually, I needed to chat with your father. Do you know where he disappeared to?" Ford asked, any hint of his animosity toward Wyatt vanished.

"Looks like he's already made a beeline for the parking lot."

Ford shifted so Sutton couldn't see his face, but Wyatt could. His expression took on the feral toothiness of a predator ready to attack. "I'll be talking to you later, *little* bro."

Wyatt resisted the urge to flip his middle finger in response. Anyway, the dig was weak. Ford might be the oldest, but Wyatt had two inches on him and working in the garage had made him tougher and stronger. All Ford's Mississippi socializing and golf afternoons were taking a toll.

"Does my brother make regular appearances on Sunday?" Wyatt leaned in to whisper his question to Sutton, keeping his eyes on the back of Ford's head.

"Every Sunday for the past few months."

Was Ford forging connections to help the garage or was he inserting himself into the social strata he'd pined for from afar? He sure as shit wasn't coming because he'd found religion. Before Ford was out of sight, a group of women surrounded them, their voices blending into a high-pitched chatter that reminded him of a murder of crows.

Although they seemed to be directing their outpouring of words toward Sutton, their gazes examined him as if trying to determine his species. Sutton performed introductions and their names—Emily and Chloe and Olivia—were as trendy as their clothes and blowouts and their beauty pageant smiles. They were virtually indistinguishable.

Sutton, on the other hand, looked delightfully unkempt. She was make-up free, and her hair mussed. She looked like she'd rolled out of bed after spending the night out doing very naughty things. Which as a matter of fact, she had.

She leaned over to whisper in his ear. "Quit that."

"What?" He attempted a look of innocence; but was pretty sure it came off like a kid who'd been caught with his hand in the cookie jar.

"Quit stripping me naked in your head."

"I wasn't doing anything of the sort." He dropped his faked outrage for an insinuating rumble. "But now I am."

"Wyatt." The playful slap she gave him was accompanied by a flush of color, but not one of embarrassment. No, it was all arousal. What would she do if he tossed her over his shoulder and headed back to his bed? What would the upper crust of Cottonbloom, Mississippi, think?

She slipped her hand into his and squeezed. More than anything, the gesture turned him from an outsider into someone who belonged. Belonged at her side.

One of the crows gained his attention. "Will we be seeing more of you on Sundays, Mr. Abbott?"

Not sure how to answer that question, he sidestepped it. "Call me Wyatt. I'd hate to be confused with my brothers. I suppose you ladies are acquainted with Ford?"

"Ford is an absolute sweetheart, isn't he?" The other women nodded and murmured their agreement. Wyatt pasted his lips shut and hummed to keep from speaking his mind.

Sutton tugged him backward down the pew and toward the back door. "I'll see y'all at the League meeting on Tuesday. Wyatt and I need to scoot."

The sunshine was blinding, but the storm had ushered in a cool front that dropped the humidity and turned the temperature pleasant. Escape was in sight when an older, distinguished looking lady flagged Sutton down.

"Mrs. Carson probably wants to talk about the centerpieces for the gala. Can you give me a minute?"

"I'll wait at the car." He took a few steps backward. She bent down to put her head close to the older lady.

He turned, stuffed his hands into his pockets, and ambled toward the Hornet, his gaze on the faded yellow lines of the parking lot.

"Glad I caught you alone." Ford's low voice came from the shade of a white flowering crepe myrtle on a landscaped bank.

Instead of laying into Ford with his suspicions, Wyatt tried a different tack. "You know what yesterday was, don't you?"

A shadow of reflected grief passed over Ford's face. "Yeah. Didn't see any reason to show up someplace I'm not welcome."

"You're our brother; you're always welcome, but a promise not to sell out to some third party would relieve the tension around the shop."

At Ford's long silence, Wyatt thought he might have gotten through to his older brother. Ford stepped closer, and Wyatt braced for a hug.

"You need to head back over the river, keep doing what you're good at, and let me handle cultivating connections that will turn into projects." Ford's tone was dismissive.

Resentment that Wyatt had stuffed away for years

sprang out like a trick snake from a can, and he shoved Ford's shoulder. "You want me to stay in the pit, elbows deep in grease. That about right? You have no fucking idea what I'm good at. I could have gone to college like you. You're not some special snowflake."

Ford adjusted his sport coat. "Threatening me like we're on the school playground only proves my point. You're not the kind of man we need to take Abbott Brothers Garage and Restoration to the next level. And neither is Mack."

Shoved somewhere deep inside him was the fear that Ford was exactly right. "And you are with your fake smile and fake manners?"

Ford glanced over Wyatt's shoulder and stalked off.

Sutton touched Wyatt's arm, and he startled.

"Everything okay?" she asked.

"Not really, but nothing I can do about it right now." Or at all, he feared. Ford had deftly sidestepped any promise of not selling out. Was that by design? He shook off the confrontation.

The sky was blue, the sun was out, and Sutton was at his side—for now. He wasn't one to let opportunities vanish through indecision.

"How about we grab some of Rufus's barbeque and head back to my place for a picnic in the woods?"

"Only if we can stop by my house long enough for me to shower and change."

"Sounds like a plan." He slipped behind the wheel. The growl and vibration of the engine helped stamp out the residual anger and worry from his confrontation with Ford.

Her house was a less than five-minute drive from the church. She stowed her purse and shoes. "Do you want to brew some coffee while I get ready? Everything is in the cabinet above the pot," she said before disappearing down the short hall and closing the door.

His faint hope she'd invite him into the shower to

keep her company died a quick death. That was okay, though; he'd have all day and hopefully all night with her. He busied himself with the coffee maker, the aroma filling the room.

As he was pouring himself a cup, the doorbell rang, followed immediately by a brisk rapping. No use in pretending no one was here considering his car was out front. He tiptoed toward the door and peered down the hall. Hearing nothing, he continued on toward the shadowy figure he could see on the other side of the door.

A bad feeling simmered in his belly, but he forced a smile and opened the door. Sutton's mother stood frozen with her hand raised for another knock. When it became clear she wasn't going to say anything, he stepped aside and gestured her in. "Good morning, Mrs. Mize. Coffee just finished perking. Want a cup?"

"Where's Sutton?" She pushed her sunglasses on top of her head and brushed by him, heading straight to the kitchen.

"Shower." He didn't miss the pointed gaze she aimed in his direction, but chose not to acknowledge it.

A faded version of Sutton, Mrs. Mize had straighter blond hair cut into a chin-length bob. She cut a trim figure in her rose-colored Sunday suit. Fine lines etched her eyes and mouth, but he could tell she fought the encroachment with every weapon available. Only her neck and hands betrayed the creep of years.

It was the color of her eyes that marked the biggest difference with Sutton. Mrs. Mize's were a light, clear blue, not the complex swirl of her daughter's. If eyes were the window into the soul, he wondered what the difference meant.

She poured herself a coffee, obviously familiar with where everything was stored in Sutton's kitchen. With both hands wrapped around a mug, she turned back to him. Her intense scrutiny amped up his nerves, and he fought the urge to look away or squirm.

"You were at church today," she said.

"Sutton invited me. It was a very nice service." If the woman asked him any specifics about the sermon, he was screwed. His mind had been wholly occupied with Sutton.

Mrs. Mize put her mug on the counter, slowly and carefully, as if gathering her thoughts. "Can we talk honestly, Mr. Abbott?"

"I'd prefer that to pussyfooting around."

A smile flashed so quickly, he blinked, sure he'd imagined it when confronted once again by her funereal face. "My daughter recently ended a very serious relationship."

"I'm quite aware. I was there as a witness."

She hummed. "Is what Sutton told us true?"

"If you're talking about pulling another woman's panties from under the seat of Tarwater's car, then yes. Sutton wouldn't lie to you." Or would she? He had no idea what she'd told her parents about him or them.

"In that case, good riddance. I need to make sure my husband no longer includes Andrew in his foursomes for golf. He'd like to pretend it never happened, but some things can't be forgiven. Sutton is too good for Andrew." The steel in her voice indicated that while the judge might rule the courtroom, his wife ruled everything else.

"I agree on all counts."

Mrs. Mize picked her coffee back up and took a sip, her eyebrows rising. "She's too good for you too. You have the reputation as an excellent mechanic and quite the ladies' man."

"Don't believe everything you hear. Except about my skills under the hood of the car. That's all true." When her expression didn't change at his thin attempt at humor, he rubbed his nape and shifted on his feet. Looks like he was having his coffee with a side of honesty. "Your daughter is amazing and funny and beautiful and I . . . like her. A lot. Last thing I want is to hurt her."

What he didn't add was that he was at high risk for getting demolished by her. Totaled, in fact.

She harrumphed, the corner of her mouth drawn back. Between the caffeine and waiting for her verdict, his heart thumped so hard it was a wonder she couldn't see it. She must have taken lessons passing down judgment from her husband.

"That coffee smells divine." Sutton came around the corner with a white fluffy towel wrapped her body, showcasing her long legs. "Mom!"

"You sat so far away that I didn't have a chance to chat with you and your young man after the service."

"I guess you two have had a chance to talk now?" Sutton pulled the towel tighter around her body and shot him a panicked look.

"We have. Maggie and I were going out for lunch since your daddy will have his butt planted in front of the TV all afternoon with a bag of Cheetos. But it seems you have plans and I'm going to get out of your hair." She deposited her mug in the sink and nodded at Wyatt. "Nice to see you again, young man."

She stopped to give Sutton a kiss on the cheek and whisper something in her ear that had her glancing in Wyatt's direction. "Toodleloo, kids," she called out on her way out the door.

"How awkward was that?" Sutton asked.

"On a scale from one to ten? At least an eleven."

"I knew I should have gotten dressed, but I thought—" She covered her mouth.

"You can still think. We can think." He grabbed the long edge of towel, leaned against the counter, and pulled her between his legs. "I'm always in the mood to think."

"No way can I think after walking in and seeing my mother in the middle of my kitchen. Did she embarrass you?"

"She was feeling out my intentions. It was actually really sweet."

"What did you tell her?"

He wasn't quite ready to quit pussyfooting around with her. "Promised not to hurt you."

She slapped his shoulder. "Why'd you do that? She might come after you with my granddaddy's old shotgun after we part ways."

"Explain to me again why we're doing this?" He wasn't sure what he was asking, but he was getting more confused by the day.

She backed away, clutching the edges of the towel together. "You were okay with this last week." The defensive edge to her voice bisected his chest and left his heart exposed.

Life could change in a week. Life could change in a day, an hour, a single moment in time. His pop's sudden death had taught him that. The problem was his life had changed because of her, but her pivotal moment had been when he'd pulled those panties from under the seat. It had nothing to do with him. He had merely been a bystander.

The question now was what to do about it. Was he a quitter or a fighter? He had twenty years of evidence to support the fact he never backed down from a challenge. It had gotten him stuck up trees and beat up on the playground, and he wasn't ready to give up on her.

"I'm still okay with it." He tugged her close and brushed his lips across hers. "Go get dressed. I promised you a picnic."

Chapter Seventeen

Sutton pulled on shorts, a T-shirt, and tennis shoes. Checking herself in the mirror, she slapped some color into her cheeks before pulling her hair up in a ponytail. Wyatt's line of questioning made everything go topsy-turvy in her head.

Things had gotten messy, and thoughts of the gala grew an ever-expanding pit of dread in her stomach. He was her rebound. Better to end it before she did something stupid like fall for him. She smiled at herself in the mirror until it looked natural. Fake it until you make it.

Wyatt stood at the sink, his back to her, as he washed the coffee mugs. The man was a sex god who cleaned up after himself. How had someone not snapped him up and put a ring on it?

His ex-girlfriend Candace's words traipsed through Sutton's head. He was a drifter in spirit if not actuality, going from one woman to the next. She was only a pit stop. Or even worse, a project.

"I'm ready," she said softly.

He dried his hands on a dishtowel and turned with a smile on his face. But deeper emotions hid behind his eyes and gave her pause. Her heart stumbled with the sense of vertigo.

"I called Rufus and put an order in. Should be ready by the time we get there." He led the way to the door, and she locked up behind them.

When they were in his car, she said, "I didn't think he took calls on Sunday mornings. It's usually packed."

"I'm special." His wink lightened the mood and restored her sense of equilibrium. "Rufus is an old family friend. Plus, the shop orders so many lunch plates we basically keep him in business."

He left Sutton waiting in the car while he picked up the barbeque, and they were back on the road in five minutes. They filled the time with talk about current events and shared simple things like their favorite movies and TV shows, finding more common ground than she expected.

He stopped off at his loft to grab a quilt and flung it over his shoulder, leading the way out the back of the barn and into the woods. The magic that resided in the woods reached out and pulled her closer.

They crossed from sun to dappled shadows at the tree line. Birds trilled and the wind rustled the leaves. Trailing behind Wyatt, she looked around. It was a typical, normal wood, and the sense of magic dissipated, leaving her with an edge of sadness.

She shook off the feeling and smiled at Wyatt when he turned for her to catch up. "Where are we headed?"

"River's not far."

"No gators?"

"Probably not." His smile was sly and teasing.

"You heard anything from Ms. Effie?"

"A couple of ladies have called for estimates."

She gasped and slapped his arm. "That's awesome. So at least two new projects?"

"Not exactly. Mack will give them an estimate of the work and what the car might bring at auction. He's honest to the core. Sometimes dumping money into a car doesn't make financial sense if they want to turn a profit. Restoration ain't cheap."

"I didn't realize how difficult it was to woo a client."

"Kind of like wooing a woman."

"Har-har." A root tripped her up, and she grabbed his arm, not letting go once she'd regained her balance. The muscle felt nice under her hand, and he was officially hers for now. The sound of water flowing became louder, and his pace picked up.

"Guess what Mags did," she said.

"Apply to clown school."

Her laughter spurted out and echoed back. "She convinced me to sell some of my work at Abigail's. She even put one of my gowns on a mannequin to display in the window."

"That's great. How'd it feel?"

"I was afraid to look. But she thinks it will attract customers." Her sister's confidence in her clothes still had the power to bring stinging tears to her eyes. Maybe Sutton would find the courage to go through the front door on Monday morning.

"I have no doubt you'll be a success." Wyatt laid a kiss on her temple and gave her a soft smile. "There's my favorite tree."

Where the earth fell away to the river, a hulking evergreen stood sentinel. Branches curved to the ground giving it a teepee-like feel. The needles were sharp and piney-smelling. Sutton let go of Wyatt's arm and hunched to see under the branches, but they were thick.

"Come around here." Wyatt held back a limb and she ducked under.

Braches as thick as her leg pinwheeled from a huge

trunk—the only opening was a lookout over the river that had been trimmed. The ground was covered in brown fronds. Wyatt spread out the quilt and gestured for her to sit.

"This is the perfect hide-out."

"That's what we thought too when we were kids."

She lay down on the quilt and stared up into the spokes of the tree. It was mostly bare inside where the sun didn't penetrate, leaving a surprisingly amount of room. "Have you ever camped out here?"

"A few times, mostly Jackson and I snuck out here to shirk our work and fish. First time either of us got drunk was out here." He joined her, shoulder to shoulder.

A few minutes passed with the two of them just being.

"You regret last night?" he asked softly.

"No." The word came out more forcefully than she intended, but at least it was the truth. She was tired of the last two weeks of deception. She turned her head to look at him. "Last night was . . . something else, right?" She'd wanted to say "special" but wasn't sure it would qualify as such for him.

He rolled to his side and gave her a kiss that tasted of coffee and pine. "It was amazing. You were amazing."

She didn't care if he was giving her line, it was exactly what she needed to hear. He trailed his hand up her leg, the rasp unbearably arousing, her nerve endings singing. His fingers slipped under the edge of her shorts and her butt canted toward him instinctively.

She grabbed his shirt in both hands and pulled him closer, wanting him over her. A repeat of last night.

He resisted. "We can't."

"I don't care if someone sees us."

"We'd be safe enough from prying eyes, but I don't have a condom."

"I don't care." The desperation of her voice took them

both by surprise, and she crash-landed in reality. Heat suffused her face, words caught in her throat.

"I don't want a quickie out here in the woods, worrying about roots and fire ants. I want to spread you out on my bed and spend all night loving you."

His words sent a different sort of heat streaking through her body. She let go of his shirt and linked her fingers around his neck. Their lips met again, but this time the urgency was overridden by a sweetness that had her heart squirming.

She wasn't sure how long they kissed, their hands exploring each other's bodies over their clothes. Was this what it felt like to be a lovesick teenager?

He lifted his head and blew out a long breath. "Our food's probably cold."

"I don't care." This time she laughed as she said it.

"That's treading close to sacrilege. And on a Sunday too." He tsked and sat up.

She didn't protest, turning her face into the quilt. It was from his bed and retained a hint of his scent and . . . something sexier. Maybe the imprint of their night together. Later. They would have a later. The thought muffled the timer ticking down.

They shared the cooled food, trading stories about their childhoods. Or mostly Wyatt told tall tales about running wild through the woods. Funny stories but with an overtone of melancholy that spoke to her stronger than words, considering the solitude of her own childhood.

Her phone chimed a text. She glanced at the screen. Her father inviting her to Sunday dinner. Although his choice of words veered toward insistent. She turned her phone over. Reality wasn't welcome.

They spent another hour wading in the river shallows and skipping rocks. She wiggled her toes in the mud. Her makeup was probably long gone, her hair was a windblown mess, her clothes streaked with dirt, yet she didn't care. Wyatt had climbed onto the bank and was cleaning up their picnic. Mundane chores that he performed with an economical grace.

Gray shimmered through the clear water, drawing her eye, and she reached for the object. It was the half shell of a river oyster, the inside smooth and pearled, the gray complicated by a multitude of colors. She closed her hand around the roughed edges and held on tight.

"Are you ready?"

What would he say if she said no? If she begged him to stay under the evergreen all night wrapped in the quilt. Instead, the part of her that didn't believe in magic smiled and nodded.

On their walk back, Sutton slipped her hand into his. People held hands all the time, but the simple gesture gave him hope that whatever was growing between them didn't have to die after the gala. He would build a careful case as to why they could work, but he could start by showing her. Another fiery roll in his sheets would make a strong point.

Raised voices echoing from the barn blew his plan to smithereens. Even if he could ignore the fight brewing, no way could they slip up the stairs to his loft undetected. He pulled her to a halt before they cleared the tree line and his brothers noticed him. He wasn't sure what to say and only shook his head, but she understood.

"Daddy wants me home for Sunday supper anyway," she said. "Unless you need backup?"

"Better if you go on. I'm sorry. Not the way I wanted the day to end, believe me."

"Me either, but I understand." She kissed his cheek and squeezed his hand before letting go and putting space between them on their approach to the barn. She gave a little wave and disappeared around the side.

Ford and Mack were squared off. Jackson was off to the side like a referee. Only when Wyatt heard Sutton's car start, did he step closer, the hairs on the back of his neck standing on end.

As kids, the brothers were competitive and obstinate and could fight like feral cats, even Wyatt and Jackson on occasion, but Mack and Ford had nurtured and tended their animosity toward each other into adulthood. One part personality driven and one part sibling rivalry, it had festered into something darkly dangerous.

"What's going on?" Wyatt asked, treading softly with his voice, afraid of setting Mack and Ford off like a trip wire.

"Mack's an asshole," Ford said.

"Better that than being a traitor," Mack shot back.

Mack was the biggest of all of them and quick to anger under the best of circumstances. Ford was a talented manipulator, which is probably what made him an excellent salesman, and could stretch Mack's patience reed thin in a matter of minutes. Without their father around to diffuse the situation, Wyatt feared a trip to either the hospital or police station—hell, maybe both—was on the horizon.

Sutton's declaration from the night before popped into his head. Was he more like their pop than he thought? Jackson had taken up his usual stance on the edge of the action, observing and never stepping into the fray. Without either of the aunts there to take them to task, Wyatt was the only one who stood a chance at brokering a peace.

He inserted himself, forcing Ford and Mack out of reach of each other. "What's the problem?"

Without taking his eyes off Ford, Mack said, "Ford seems to think I've sent you into Cottonbloom, Mississippi, to stage a takeover of his territory."

"I told you this morning that Mack has nothing to do with it." Wyatt turned to Ford.

Ford pivoted around. "It was all your idea?"

"First off, I was up there because Sutton invited me."

"Her father's been talking up the garage. What's he getting in exchange?" Ford asked. "Or maybe I should ask what are you giving to Sutton in exchange?"

A hint of salaciousness undercut the question and put Wyatt on the defensive. "You'd best stop right there, brother."

"You always did love your projects. You're taking advantage of her after Tarwater dumped her."

"That's bullshit. She dumped him after she caught him with—" He bit his tongue until he could taste blood. Ford had goaded him into saying too much.

"So it's true. Tarwater was cheating on her." Ford mulled the words as if determining their value to him. He turned his pointed gaze back on Wyatt. "Are you two dating or what?"

"We're hanging out."

"And is the Judge talking up the garage because you're hanging out?"

"I don't know." His eyebrow twitched and he pressed his thumb along the bone, hoping Ford hadn't noticed.

"Goddamn, you *are* whoring yourself out for business. She must be desperate. How much longer can you milk the situation? I'm sure you're itching to move on."

Before he could consider his action, he had Ford's starched dress shirt in his fist and Ford's body up against the wall, his forearm pressed against his throat. "If I hear you talking about Sutton like that, I'll rip your innards out through your throat. You got me?"

A smile hovered at Ford's mouth. Wyatt had given up too much information. Mack patted Wyatt's shoulder, and he stepped back.

Ford rubbed his neck. "I guess after Tarwater she was looking for a different experience, but she'll get tired of dirty picnics in the woods and this place and you." He gestured around the barn, ending with Wyatt.

His words jerked Wyatt back like a punch. Too much truth resided in the insult.

"You're not planning to go to the gala, are you? You'll only mess up my plans and make the garage look like some hick operation."

"Too bad. I'm going."

"I would advise against it. No telling what might happen if you show up."

"Are you threatening me?"

"I'm protecting our business." Ford smoothed a hand down the front of his linen shirt, but the wrinkled imprint of Wyatt's fist remained.

Mack's forced nonchalance did a poor job covering the tension hunching his shoulders and drawing his hands into fists. "Only one problem with that logic, bro. I've had more calls booking estimates in the last week than in the last year from your efforts."

"What are you talking about? The Judge can't be that influential."

"Seems like our boy Wyatt is doing fine without the Judge's seal of approval. A Ms. Eckert called and raved about Wyatt. She wants us to restore her late husband's 1959 Cadillac and take it to auction. Apparently, there's a widow's walk of classic cars collecting dust, and Effie down at the Quilting Bee has passed our info along to several of her friends."

"That dried up old prune had a '59 Caddy sitting in her garage?" Ford tacked on a four-letter word.

Wyatt refrained from giving Mack a high five, but couldn't stop himself from taunting Ford. "You'd have been better off spending your time down at the Quilting Bee instead of the golf course."

Ford didn't answer, but his expression said bridges were

ourning to ash. He left without another word. The slam of he heavy back door to the garage reverberated.

Jackson broke the silence. "So that's what you've been up to. Cozying up to the ladies at the Quilting Bee."

Wyatt went to the fridge, grabbed three beers, and handed them out. The cold beer extinguished a good portion of his anger, leaving only dread in the pit of his stomach. "Crossing paths with Ms. Eckert was total chance. The Quilting Bee was actually Sutton's idea. I'm not a user or a faker like Ford."

Mack uncapped his beer and pointed it at Wyatt. "You don't have to fake it. You've got something none of us have, including Ford."

Mack didn't hand out compliments often or easily. Perfection in the garage was expected, therefore not to be cheered.

"What's that?" Wyatt asked.

"Likeability. Real charm. You exude trustworthiness." Mack killed half his beer in one go and wiped his mouth before saying, "Probably why women have always thrown themselves at your feet."

"I don't think Wyatt cares about how many women his honeyed tongue attracts anymore." Jackson took a measured sip. "You've gotten attached to Sutton Mize."

Twin powers had screwed him once more. Wyatt's response was a shrug and retreat for another beer. He leaned against the jamb of the wide-open double barn doors and slipped to sit on his heels, his arms resting on his knees and his hands dangling.

Jackson mirrored his position at the other door, while Mack lay back on the couch, a beer cradled in his elbow. A few minutes passed in silence until Mack snuffled a snore from the couch.

"Thanks for giving us privacy last night. I should have warned you," Wyatt said.

Jackson chuckled. "I had a foot inside before I realized what was up. Your bedroom door was wide open. Looked like you were having fun. What are you going to do about her?"

"She made it clear from the outset she's not interested in anything long-term or serious."

"But you are." It was a statement that Wyatt didn't bother denying. "Change her mind, then."

"I'm trying." Wyatt traced a series of interlocking circles in the dirt. "I'm worried I care way more than she does."

"You might not have the upper hand, but I wouldn't be too sure she doesn't care."

"Sure, she likes me, but she can live without me. In a few years, I'll be a fond memory and that's it."

"Can you live without her?"

Wyatt was thankful Jackson wasn't teasing him or making light of the situation. "She just got out of a serious relationship. She's not ready."

"Then wait until she is."

Jackson made it sound easy, and maybe it was that easy. Except waiting her out would be agonizing. Wyatt wanted all of her and wanted it yesterday.

"You'll figure it out." Jackson pushed up and went to stand over Mack, and said softly, "I'm worried about him. He's working himself to exhaustion."

"I know."

In sleep, Mack's sharp edges smoothed, and he looked years younger. Wyatt was reminded of the hours in the tree and looking down into Mack's face. Even then, he'd been more mature and serious than any of them. As if wisdom had imprinted on him in the womb.

"If we could diffuse the Ford situation, it would help," Jackson said. "My guess is he's using that threat as leverage for something else. Not even Ford would sell his share out of the family."

The surety reflected in Jackson's tone should have set Wyatt at ease, yet it did nothing to diminish the premonition something bad was lurking to bite them on the collective ass. Not worse than getting his heart ripped out by Sutton, but pretty bad.

"I'm not so sure about that," Wyatt said.

They left Mack to nap and wandered into the garage. Jackson stuffed his hands in his pockets and kicked at some tools left on the floor. His restlessness registered as unusual and expectant. Wyatt had been so caught up in his own problems, he almost missed it.

Wyatt propped his arm up on the hood of the car sitting over the pit. "You want to tell me what's bothering you?"

"What? Nothing."

Twin powers went two ways, and Wyatt knew his brother was lying. "Bullshit. Tell me."

"Do you know how annoying that is?" Jackson sent him a side-eye.

"As a matter·of fact, yes."

"You noticed anything strange going on with Willa?" Jackson kept his gaze down, his feet shuffling various bolts and washers and a screwdriver from side-to-side as if looking for something of vast importance.

"I'm gonna be honest. She's never qualified for normal, even for around here."

Willa Brown was as secretive and closed-off as Jackson. Maybe that's why they made such a good team. Wyatt made it his mission to get her to smile or laugh every day. He had a feeling she hadn't had a chance to do enough of that over her life. But that was only a guess, because she'd rarely volunteered information about herself.

"Ever since Pop died, she's been acting weird."

"Maybe she misses the old man. They were pretty close."

"Yeah, maybe, but things have gotten worse the last few

weeks." Jackson usually kept worry of this magnitude contained to his cars.

"She's like you—an observer. I wouldn't be surprised if she's picked up on the tension. I'm going to throw out a crazy idea here, but stay with me . . . why don't you ask her what's going on?"

"We talk about cars, not personal stuff."

"You've been working side-by-side for two years. Asking her if everything is okay at home wouldn't be out of left field. Does she have a boyfriend?"

"No." Jackson jerked as if a fire ant had bit him in the unmentionables, the single word reverberating against the concrete before he added in a softer tone. "Actually I'm not sure."

"This thing with Ford has us all skittish. That's probably all it is," Wyatt said with more confidence than he actually felt.

Jackson made a noncommittal noise, kicked the bolts like he would a rock down the road, and headed to the door. "I'm going to hit the shower."

If Sutton was right and Wyatt was the glue of the Abbot family, he was thinking he might be defective.

Chapter Eighteen

The week passed as if she'd stepped onto a carnival ride. Her days were busy leading up to the gala, selling dresses to ladies that had waited until the last minute or were looking for something different. She sold the gown Maggie had put in the window on the first day and another she had slipped onto a rack. Any residual gossip about her and Andrew or her and Wyatt didn't seem to be hurting business. In fact, the season was shaping up to be one of their best yet.

Wyatt had been busy as well. Ms. Eckert had brought her car to the garage, and Wyatt had taken on the project. His excitement over having something new was both contagious and concerning. It only made her question where she stood in terms of her personal restoration.

Their work schedules hadn't kept them from having fun. Sutton couldn't remember a time she'd been happier, but it was a bittersweet feeling, like savoring the summer's last harvest of blackberries. Three more days until the gala. The countdown was like the Doomsday Clock.

Determined not to worry about next week or even the next morning, she had planned a surprise that would also check off one of her fantasies. She cuddled next to him on the couch, overlooking the woods. Nerves sizzled in her stomach like frayed wires.

Was she actually going to do this? She glanced over at him under her lashes and found him staring at her, the overtones darkly sexual.

She leaned over and kissed him. As always her body turned to taffy, sweet and malleable. Before he could take control of the situation, she put her plan into action, straddling him. The fact any of his brothers might walk in only amped up her arousal.

The old her would be embarrassed and hesitant over what she was about to do. The new her was armed with research and the desire to experience everything, yet the old her was still there, her body trembling.

She fisted her hands in his T-shirt and circled her hips against his erection. Her only regret was her choice of shorts over wearing a skirt. Too many layers were between them. Even so, he was hard against her.

He dropped his head back and coasted his hands up her outer thighs, his fingertips slipping under the hem of her short-shorts. It would be easy enough to allow his hand to turn her into a writhing, begging shambles until she shattered. He enjoyed her like that, but she hoped he'd find her surprise even more to his liking.

Biting her bottom lip, she slid off his lap to kneel in front of him. Placing her hands on his knees, she pushed them apart to scoot in between. The hands that reached for his belt shook, but she couldn't separate excitement from nerves from anticipation. It was even better than a carnival ride.

He grabbed her shoulders, his thumbs digging at her collarbone. "What are you doing?" Surprise and shock colored his voice.

The bite of his hands heightened her awareness of his

strength. Considering their positions, she thought it was obvious. So obvious she didn't have to utter the words aloud. Looking up at him through her lashes, she said, "I'm . . . you know."

His look was so befuddled, she almost smiled. His lack of confidence in the situation grew hers.

"A blow job. I'm giving you a blow job." The declaration came out far easier than she'd expected. Husky laughter welled out of her. She was acting on her urges, taking charge, and it felt awesome.

"Yeah, I got that. But why?"

How selfish had she been with him? Taking, taking, taking, and never giving him the kind of pleasure he'd freely offered her for the first time in her life. Her emotions were on a zip line, and tears sped to her eyes even as she kept a smile in place.

"Because I want to make you feel good."

His grip eased, and he raised a hand to caress her cheek. She nuzzled into his touch and lay a kiss on his palm. The erotic moment took on a touch of sweetness even as she turned her attention back to his belt.

After fumbling his buckle and button open, she paused with her hand on his zipper. His body was saying "hell, yeah," but his eyes still betrayed an uncharacteristic uncertainty.

"Are you okay with this?" she asked.

"If you're okay, I'm light-years beyond okay. This is a dream come true, actually. Like literally, I've dreamed about this many, many times. I can't believe it's actually happening. I never thought you'd—" He clamped his mouth shut.

Far from being offended, she smiled. "You're right. I never would have. In fact, I should warn you that I never have. How pathetic is that?"

"Not pathetic."

She chuffed and looked to the ground so she wouldn't see the pity in his eyes. He had probably been on the receiving end of dozens—hundreds?—of blow jobs. How was she supposed to measure up?

"I'm a beginner, but I watched some how-to videos." A simple internet search had yielded a varied and very educational list of videos, and she'd watched several from start to the grand finish. If anyone in her immediate family checked her internet history, her embarrassment would probably cause her to spontaneously combust, taking out a mile radius, which would thankfully include her hard drive.

"How-to . . . ? You mean pornos?" His voice raised in tone and volume with his amusement.

Instead of wanting to crawl into a hole, she laughed along with him. Wyatt made her feel playful and empowered, even given her amateur status. "The ladies made it look fun."

With all his uncertainty erased, he sank farther into the couch, lacing his hands behind his head and widening his stance. "Who am I to deny a lady her fun?"

She eased the tab of his zipper south, the parting of the teeth revealing a vee of black underwear. Scraping her fingernails down the length of him, she marveled at the fully visible outline and wondered why she hadn't done this ages ago. But the thought of doing something so intimate with anyone other than Wyatt stirred a squirmy feeling in her stomach.

She gripped the waistband of his underwear and pulled them down. He shifted his hips until jeans and underwear were bunched mid-thigh. Her breathing quickened at the sight. As if faced with an all-you-can-eat buffet after a week of fasting, her mouth watered, and her body reacted in kind. She shifted her knees together, trying to ease the ache between her legs. Later, she would ask him to take care of her, but for now it was all about him.

Forgetting about the videos and her game plan, she acted on instinct, circling her hand around the base and lifting the tip to her lips. A lick across the top had him abandoning his casual stance, her hands catching in her hair. One twirl of her tongue around the flanged head had him whispering, "Jesus Christ."

She blew across the area she'd just licked. "I want to hear you say my name like that."

His chuckle was strained and hoarse. She loved she could have an effect on him before she even got down to business. Opening her mouth, she took him in as far as she was able, starting a rhythm that mimicked sex.

She was wrong, this act wasn't only about his pleasure. She was deriving more satisfaction than she'd imagined possible from making him call out her name and tug at her hair. It went beyond the physical and onto some other plane.

She had no idea how much time passed, but the movement of his hips grew jerkier and she glanced up at him, the sight making her stop. His eyes were closed and his lips parted, a sheen of sweat on his forehead. The tendons of his neck stood out and his biceps bulged. He was a man on the edge.

She'd done that to him. Driven him as wild as he made her feel, and now she wanted to push him over. He opened his eyes, his heavy gaze indiscernibly potent and sexy. Without looking away, she took two more strokes with her mouth. With a yell that bordered on primal, he pushed her away by the shoulder, his body curling forward as he grabbed himself.

After his orgasm, he collapsed back onto the couch and pulled her up with him, his eyes closed and his pants open.

She smiled and snuggled into his side, laying kisses along his jaw. "I would have finished you if you'd let me."

He opened one eye. "Well, then. Something to look forward to for next time. Give me five minutes, and I'll reciprocate. Promise."

"It's okay if you're too tired."

He lifted his head to look at her through barely slit-open eyes then dropped his head back down with a sigh. "I do feel like Superman faced with a huge-ass piece of kryptonite."

"I'm your kryptonite?" She smiled into his shoulder.

"I'm afraid so." The seriousness of his tone had her raising up on her elbow to see his face, but in spite of the good-natured, seemingly simple front he put on, Wyatt Abbott was complicated and confusing and fascinating.

His ringtone sounded, and he fumbled in his pants pocket for his phone, adjusting his underwear and jeans in the process. With his eyes still half-closed, he glanced at the screen before answering.

"Hello, sweets."

The endearment coiled a black, ugly feeling in her chest, and she pushed away from him, curling her hands over her knees. Was it an ex-girlfriend? Or maybe it was the girl that would eventually take her place.

"Of course I can." Wyatt stood, tucked the phone between his ear and shoulder, and did up his pants. "I'll be there in five."

After he'd disconnected, he turned and threw his hands up. "My aunts Hazel and Hyacinth are stranded with a flat."

"That was your aunt." Relief tinged with shame flooded her. Why had she let something so minor send her so far down a dark path? All her sexual confidence and bravado was a thinly spackled façade. She hadn't really changed.

"It's going to be hot and buggy and dirty." He held out a hand and smiled. "You wanna come?"

She slipped her hand in his, her heart skipping ahead. "How could I possibly say no?"

He laughed and lead the way to the Hornet. "On the upside, you'll get to formally meet my aunts."

"You're super close with them, aren't you?" Both her parents were only children, leaving her and Maggie with no extended family.

He pulled out onto the parish road with a spin of tires. "After my mom took off, they attempted to mother us. Neither one of them had the instinct, so we ran wild, but they made sure we had clothes for school and groceries and never let us part ways without a hug. Things worked out pretty good by my reckoning."

"You turned out better than good." Sutton patted his knee but kept her hand there, inching it up his thigh.

He covered it with his own. "No time for more fun."

A car was on the side of the road in a graveled area and two ladies turned to watch them pull in behind. She slipped out of the car and hung back. The setting sun sent every shade of orange across the sky.

"Hello, aunties." Wyatt put an arm around each lady and pulled them in for a hug.

"Sorry if we took you away from your ladyfriend." The smaller of the two ladies smiled, not unkindly but with a shrewdness that set Sutton on edge.

Unlike the casual tracksuit of her taller sister, she might have been on her way to or from church. Black, low-heeled shoes matched a patent-leather pocketbook that was a fashion requirement of ladies of a certain age.

"Sutton, this is Aunt Hazel," Wyatt pointed to the shorter sister, "and that one is Aunt Hyacinth. Now what seems to be the problem?"

"I hit something," Hyacinth said.

"I didn't see any bodies—animal or human—so I'm assuming something inanimate?"

"Har-har. Yes but I don't know what. We were tooling along singing along to some John Denver—" Hyacinth turned abruptly to Sutton. "Do you like John Denver, honey?"

The question drew a surprised laugh from her. "Yeah, sure. 'Rocky Mountain High,' right?"

"Exactly. Speaking of, what do you think about medicinal marijuana for my arthritis, Wyatt?"

"Whatever floats your boat, Aunt Hy." Wyatt's voice was full of easy-going humor.

"Whatever I hit clanked against the underside and next thing I knew the tire just plumb gave out. Come look." Wyatt joined Hyacinth on the other side of the car and squatted, only the top of his head visible.

Sutton's job was to make conversation and put people at ease, but something about the way Hazel looked her over made her think of job interviews and interrogations.

"It's nice to meet you finally. Wyatt's told me so much about you and your sister," Sutton said.

"Has he now?" Her tone was speculative, and Sutton tensed, anticipating more questions. Instead, Hazel said, "I never married."

After a beat of silence, Sutton found her footing again. "Wyatt told me about the family curse."

"Curse." Hazel made a scoffing noise. "Hogwash. I didn't get married because I didn't want some man bossing me around. Our father was bad enough."

Not knowing what else to say, she murmured an apology.

"Wyatt and Jackson have got it in their fool heads that they're destined to never marry or have a family either. Like that sort of thing is predetermined at birth. Silliness."

Wyatt had joked about the curse. Did he really believe it? Any woman would be lucky to have Wyatt. "It is rather silly."

"Don't tell the others but Wyatt's my favorite. I never wanted children—taking care of my younger siblings for too many years soured me—but when his mama left, Hyacinth and I answered the call and never regretted it."

"He told me how you made sure he had school clothes and such."

"That was the easy part." The patent-leather purse creaked as she adjusted her hold. "Wyatt's more like Hyacinth. Open, affectionate. The other boys always acted like a hug was a stealthy method of passing on communicable diseases, but Wyatt always gave as good as he got."

"He's special, isn't he?" Sutton asked, her gaze on the man in question. He had popped his aunts' trunk and was pulling out the jack and spare tire.

"I'm terribly biased, but yes, he is." Without turning to look at Sutton, she continued. "And don't believe all that talk about how many girls he's dated, because never, not once has he brought a young lady to meet us."

"You've never met any of his girlfriends?"

"Not a single one. Until now."

Sutton wasn't sure what to make of that. She wasn't technically Wyatt's girlfriend, even though they'd had sex. Amazing, glorious, life-altering sex didn't necessarily mean anything. Yet, between the sex, they'd laughed and talked. A lot and about everything.

"Jackson tells me Wyatt is your date to the Cottonbloom gala this weekend?"

Dread traipsed around her heart like a crazy bearded man holding a placard with THE END IS NIGH stamped across it.

"That's the plan." She tried to swallow down the sudden onslaught of emotion that turned her eyes watery. Getting serious with Wyatt wasn't an option. Yet neither was walking away. Her mental vertigo returned with a vengeance.

Wyatt released the hydraulic jack and checked the lug nuts one more time. Wiping his hands on the back of his jeans, he joined Sutton and Aunt Hazel. "The donut will get you home and to the shop in the morning. Don't drive it anywhere else."

Something about Sutton's stance and expression had him trying to catch his Aunt Hazel's eye.

"We can always count on you, son." Hazel leaned in to give him a half hug.

Hyacinth gave him a little wave of thanks before slipping behind the wheel. Hazel turned to Sutton and patted her hand. "It was lovely to meet you. I hope we see lots more of each other."

Sutton murmured a polite answer with a tight smile. Once they were cocooned back in his car, he propped one arm across the steering wheel and one along the back of her seat, facing her. "What did Aunt Hazel say to you?"

"Nothing. I mean, we made small talk, is all." She stared out the front window.

His long silence did nothing to make her give up more info. "You sure? Because you seem upset."

"Why would you think that?"

He huffed, started the car, and got them back on the road. "When you're embarrassed or turned on, you flush pink from your chest all the way to your cheeks. When you're angry, you get this cute little crinkle right between your eyes. And, when you're upset, your mouth gets tight and if you do smile, it never gets to your eyes."

When she didn't respond, he glanced from the road to her. She looked stunned, and maybe slightly pleased. Or pissed. He couldn't tell in the darkened interior. When she grabbed his hand in hers, he concluded it was the former.

"I'm dirty." He tugged at his hand, but she kept hold and laid a kiss on the back.

"I don't care," she whispered.

Everything in his chest tightened with the realization he had totally and irrevocably fallen for her. He loved the fact she'd researched pornos for him and brought him a casserole when he'd been grieving and held his hand even though he was filthy. He loved her too-nice beigeness but also the rainbow of colors she'd revealed in his bed. He loved her dedication to the boutique and the fact she was finally letting the dream she'd nurtured for so long bloom.

She didn't feel the same way about him, but maybe someday she would. He would wait a lifetime to find out. The silence that built on the drive back to the shop carried with it expectation. He parked around the side of the garage and made straight for the barn, her hand in his, grease be damned.

As soon as they were up the stairs and in the loft, he kissed her, running his hands down her back to knead her bottom. She wrapped her arms around his shoulders and squirmed closer. He lifted her, and she wrapped her legs around his hips, still kissing him.

He shuffled forward until his knees hit the mattress, both of them falling, him on top of her. Their clothes came off with record speed. Desperation jerked his movements, and she seemed equally as frantic.

For him, though, it wasn't about achieving sexual gratification, it was about possession and surrender. He hooked his hands under her knees and drew her legs apart. She was his definition of heaven, spread out, her hair painting his bedspread, and the telltale flush across her chest. All for him. Only for him.

His thrust was firm and deep, and her response was to arch her back and tempt him with her breasts. He'd taken notes about what she liked, and her breasts were beautifully sensitive to his touch. He dropped her knees to caress over them and pinch her nipples. He left a dark mark of grease along her side. His other hand left another smudge on the white skin of her breast.

The sight fired a primal satisfaction in his chest, and he slid out of her and back in with enough force to move her up the bed. He needed to leave his mark on her, no matter how temporary.

Up until this point, he'd handled her gently, knowing he needed to coax out her obvious passion. But tonight proved she had learned to embrace her desires. He'd never experienced a more erotic blow job in his life. The picture she'd made looking up at him through her lashes, cheeks flushed and hollowed out would be forever locked away in his memories.

"You feel so good." Her breathless encouragement was all he needed to let loose on her.

With his control slipping, he felt her tightening around him, only dimly registering her throaty groans through the rushing in his ears. Tingles shot all the way to his toes, and they curled. An honest-to-God toe-curling orgasm. He collapsed on top of her, both of them damp and breathing hard.

I love you. The words wound around and around his heart and felt like they were cutting off his circulation.

"What? What did you say?" She pushed at his shoulders.

Even though his body begged to stay put, his mind was in full panic mode, and he eased out of her. Had he actually said it out loud? "Nothing. Forget it."

She grabbed the sheet and covered herself, pushing back into the pillows. Her eyes were wide, her mouth open, her hands fisted at the top of the sheet. He imagined her reaction was on par with him having revealed a virulent STD.

"But you said—"

"I said, I love U2. Bono. The Edge. Classic stuff. Pop used to play it when we were kids." He avoided her eyes.

"Wyatt. You couldn't have meant that you actually . . . you know." She deftly skipped over his lame excuse to the heart of the matter.

What choice did he have except to own his stupid honesty? Considering they were at his place, he couldn't exactly make a run for it. He leaned against the headboard and tried unsuccessfully to squash the defensiveness that rose. "What if I did? Is it so horrible a thought? Trust me, I didn't mean for it to happen."

As if the bed had caught fire, she leapt up and grabbed her clothes. She was already moving toward the stairs as she pulled on her shorts, stumbling and nearly toppling over.

The irony of the situation wasn't lost on him, and if he'd been watching it unfold on TV, he would have laughed. How many times had he made a hasty exit when things got too serious or real?

"Sutton." The desperate commanding tenor of his voice made her freeze. He waited until she looked over her shoulder at him. "Don't go."

"I'm not ready . . . I can't . . ."

He took it as a victory she hadn't moved and pulled the sheet around his torso, approaching her slowly, afraid she'd spook like a wild animal avoiding a trap. "I don't expect anything from you."

She looked toward the stairs and escape. "I'm really confused."

"You can't deny there's something between us besides a good time. Don't you feel it too?"

"I do, but—" She turned to face him and for a moment, he thought he'd won. She held a hand up to ward him off and shuffled backward. A retreat. "I can't think right now."

"Babe, please." He hated the pathetic, pleading note in his voice almost as much as he hated the emptiness growing around his heart. It was eerily reminiscent of the days after his father's death. He hadn't realized how fully she'd filled that space until now.

She ran down the stairs barefoot, her shoes dangling from one hand. He followed as fast as his impromptu toga would allow, but he only caught a glimpse of her taillights as she sped away.

Defeat was bitter. Was this a battle he'd lost or the war?

Chapter Nineteen

On the evening of the gala, Wyatt sprawled on the couch and stared out at the trees. Too early yet for the leaves to put on their show. He thought about getting a beer, but the energy it would take to walk the ten feet to the fridge wasn't worth it.

He'd slept like crap the past two nights since his monumental screwup with Sutton. She had returned his text and asked for time to figure things out. He understood, but feared the more time they spent apart, the easier it would be for her to tag whatever they'd shared as an experience and move on.

Mack came through the back of the garage, dressed for a date with the body bag. Wyatt had spent the day avoiding his family, so it was no surprise when Mack joined him on the couch.

"You look like shit." It was good to be confronted with Mack's unvarnished, undiplomatic assessment.

"Thanks."

"Thought tonight was the big night. Did you let Ford scare you away?" Mack adjusted his gloves as if just the mention of Ford made him want to punch something.

His brothers were the most self-contained men Wyatt knew. Would Mack understand Wyatt's predicament? "In a total cliché move, I accidently told Sutton Mize that I loved her right after we had sex."

"Whoa." Mack was silent for a long moment. "But you meant it? Do you love her?"

Wyatt had been prepared for laughter or teasing, not the gentle understanding in his brother's voice. It spiraled him back to his childhood, when his big brother could fix anything. "Yeah. I meant it."

"What did she say?"

"Said she needed time. That she wasn't ready to get serious. I knew going into this I would never be more than her rebound."

"I'm not an expert—in fact, I've screwed up more relationships than I care to admit—but if you feel like that about her, you shouldn't be sitting here with me."

"But she wants time to think." Why did Sutton make him feel so uncertain?

"I'd be careful that she doesn't think herself out of being with you."

His brother's words shot a pulse of adrenaline through his body, making his toes tap. "What would you suggest?"

"Crash the gala, plead your case, and if she blows you off again, then it's her loss."

Wyatt doubted he would be so mellow about a final rejection, but Mack was right. He had to try. "I don't have a tuxedo."

Mack cracked a smile. "I'm not your damn fairy godmother. Wear the suit you bought for Pop's funeral. She won't care."

She might not, but everyone else would. Good thing he didn't give a crap what everyone else thought. He stood up, but before he could take a step toward the stairs, Mack grabbed his wrist and gave a squeeze. "Remember that there's more to life than this garage."

The words were as surprising as they were unexpected. Mack was more complicated than his single-minded focus would lead everyone to believe.

Wyatt nodded and retreated to clean up and change clothes. Straightening his gray-striped tie, he gave himself a pep talk in the mirror. Whatever happened, Mack and Jackson and even Aunt Hyacinth and Aunt Hazel would be there to help pick up the pieces, because that's what people who loved you did.

The drive over the bridge and the river signaled a marked increase in his nerves and his hand slipped on the gear shift the closer he got to the country club. He drove to the front and idled at a valet parking sign. Allowing a total stranger to drive his car didn't seem like a good omen.

A lanky man wearing a red-and-white striped vest that put a barber-shop quartet in mind approached, his mouth agape. The closer he got the younger he appeared, constellations of acne on his cheeks. "This is a seriously cool car, dude."

Wyatt muttered a few choice words under his breath before handing the keys over with a strained smile. "Sixty-three thousand, two hundred, and eight."

At the boy's befuddlement, Wyatt said, "That's how many miles are on the odometer. Don't park it too close to another car."

"Yes, sir." The boy slid into the seat and ran both hands over the steering wheel. "I'll take good care of her."

When he heard the feminine pronoun, a measure of tension eased. His car was in decent—if not expert—hands. His issues with Sutton eclipsed any worry about his car as he mounted the stairs to the double doors. Music from a live band and conversation drifted out.

Sentinels in black dresses flanked the door, but when the right one turned, he wondered if luck might be turning in his direction. Ms. Eckert greeted him with a smile and firm handshake.

"This is the young man I was telling you about, Vera."

The other woman smiled, her demeanor resonating with a subtle power. "Nice to meet you, Mr. Abbott."

He recognized the woman Sutton had been discussing flowers with after church. Vera Carson was part of an old Cottonbloom family dating back to before the Civil War. But then again, so was he. He squared his shoulders. "A pleasure to make your acquaintance, ma'am."

"I have a car sitting in my garage. An Oldsmobile. Dottie thinks I should bring it down to your garage." She nodded toward Ms. Eckert, her sharp blue eyes in contrast to her soft, pale cheeks and fluffy white hair. No doubt she was assessing his worth.

"Do you know what year?"

She hummed and looked thoughtful. "1970, I think. My husband bought it right after our fifth wedding anniversary."

"Two or four door?"

"Definitely two. I told him it was impractical, but he was in love."

A feeling like an electric shock ran through him. It might be an Olds 442. The thought of getting his hands on such a car made him light-headed. "I would love to take a look. It might not be worth your money to fix up depending on the make and condition, but you can count on Abbott Brothers Garage and Restoration to give you an honest assessment."

"In that case, I'll call on Monday for an appointment, shall I?" She offered her hand again, this time to presumably seal the deal.

"Are you here for Sutton?" Ms. Eckert asked with a bluntness that was a welcome part of her personality.

"I am. Have you seen her?"

The room was more crowded than he anticipated. A dance floor took up at least a third, with tables covered in items for the silent auction ringing the room.

"On the dance floor last I caught a gander."

Wyatt thanked her and moved along the edges of the crowd, a yawning pit opening in his stomach. She could be dancing with anyone, even her father, but somehow he wasn't surprised to see her swaying in Tarwater's arms. His only consolation was that she wasn't locked close to his body.

Her red dress was off the shoulder with a demure front but scooped back. He could tell by the perfect fit it was one of her designs. Lace-covered and striking, her dress stood out like a flower in full bloom amongst weeds.

Andrew wore his classic tuxedo like a blond James Bond, debonair and charming. Wyatt shifted in his off-the-rack mall suit, smoothing the tie. Andrew and Sutton looked perfectly matched.

He tortured himself until the song was over. Many of the couples pulled apart to clap, including Sutton and Tarwater. As if somehow sensing his intense focus, she glanced over her shoulder and locked gazes with him. His nerve deserted him. He wasn't sure he'd survive if she had gotten back with Tarwater with her scent still lingering in his sheets.

He took a step back and then another one, only turning when he bumped into an older man holding a whiskey. The doors along the back veranda were thrown open to the cooling night, and he slipped into the darkness, planning to circle around front, find his way home, and get drunk.

Sutton pushed through the crowd, smiling and nodding but wanting to scream at everyone to get the hell out of her way. She kept Wyatt's dark head in view as long as she could. He disappeared out the back door and onto the wide veranda overlooking the pool and ninth hole. A few older men chatted and smoked cigars at the stone rail, but there was no sign of Wyatt.

"Where are you?" she muttered. Screw the gala, it would survive without her. She would get her car from the valet and chase him over the river.

"You could have texted me the news." His voice came from the shadows behind her, and she whirled. He had his shoulder propped against a pillar, his hands in his pockets, one foot crossed over the other. His relaxed stance was in juxtaposition to the expression on his face—anger, frustration, and a touch of devastation.

"What news?"

"That you and Tarwater are back on."

She took a step toward him and touched his arm. His biceps felt ready to burst the seams of his jacket. "We're not back on. Not even close."

"Why were you dancing with him then? Aren't you still upset about him cheating on you and what everyone is saying?"

A strange thing had happened over the last few weeks with Wyatt. She'd stopped worrying about what people were whispering behind her back and couldn't remember why she'd been so upset.

"Did you mean it?" she asked softly.

"Mean what?"

"That you love Bono, the Edge, and U2?"

The flash of his smile was like a lightning bug, and she was encouraged enough to give chase. "I was going to call you tomorrow," she said.

"Sure." Obvious disbelief dripped from the word.

"You took me by surprise. I panicked and acted immature and ran. To be honest, I wasn't sure I believed you."

"You think I make a habit of telling women I love them?"

"I don't know. Maybe. You're more experienced than me and after Andrew—"

"Do not compare me to him." He shifted and pointed a finger at her. "I'm nothing like that liar."

"I know you aren't. It's me I don't trust. It's hard to forget and forgive how naïve I was." She took his hand in both of hers and was grateful when he didn't pull away. "I don't know exactly how I feel." He tugged, but she only tightened her hold. "But I do know I've never felt like this before. And I know I don't want things to end. Especially not like this."

"What about Tarwater and Bree and—"

"This has nothing to do with them. Not anymore. Can we forget about what brought us together and see what happens? Please?"

He stared for so long without speaking and with no change in expression, her entire body began trembling. Finally, he cupped her neck, his thumb running along the sensitive skin behind her ear. Soul-deep relief weakened her knees as if he'd given her a reprieve from the hangman's noose.

He pulled in a deep breath, but before he could say anything, he tensed and looked over her shoulder like a hunting dog catching a scent.

"What in tarnation . . ." His whisper had her spinning around to see a manila envelope being passed from Andrew to Ford Abbott.

The two men were inside the pool area with Ella Boudreaux. Striking if not exactly beautiful, she was the kind of woman that drew the eye even though you couldn't decide why. Her hair was dark and her curves dangerous. Restlessness showed itself in her hand movements and the constant shift of her body as if her energy would build to explosive levels if left unchecked.

The divorcée had stirred talk when she'd bought an

expensive house in the best part of Cottonbloom, Mississippi, a year earlier. Word was that her sudden rise in fortunes had been financed by an advantageous settlement from her older ex-husband. Sutton had only met her once and been thoroughly intimidated by her air of sophistication and experience even though she couldn't be much older than Sutton.

Wyatt pulled away and stalked toward the side gate of the pool. She followed, her heels and fitted dress hampering her progress. Ford's laughter echoed, and he matched Ella's level of animation. If Andrew hadn't been with them, she might wonder if the overtones were sexual.

"What's going on?" Wyatt had rounded the corner and was out of sight between two bushes flanking the gate, but his voice projected and echoed off the glassy surface of the blue pool water.

When she caught up with him, he had faced off with his brother. Sutton and Andrew crossed glances, but his gaze skated to the horizon, where there was nothing but the shadowy tree line beyond the green of the golf course. The tension was palpable, and Sutton didn't attempt to diffuse the situation by injecting social niceties.

"None of your business, little brother." While Ford's goal may have been to put Wyatt in his place, his voice reflected a sense of being caught smoking under the bleachers.

"Well now, that's not quite true, Ford." Ella's voice was a combination of a mature confidence mixed with playfulness. Sutton recognized the dress she wore from her trade catalogues. It was from a high end New York designer and cost several thousand dollars. "Your brother should know."

"Know what?" Wyatt's voice remained calm but held a threat.

Ford glanced over his shoulder and caught her eye. "Does Sutton know what kind of games you've been playing?"

"Shut up, Ford."

"So she doesn't realize you're using her for her daddy's connections?" He directed his next comment directly to her. "We discussed it as a family. My brother likes to take on pity projects. He does it with cars and women."

They'd strategized about her. Her head disassociated itself from her body. *Pity project.* She was nothing more than a hunk of rusted metal with four bald tires. Her fears from the past weeks reared up and took on monstrous proportions in her head.

Wyatt turned so he could see her and Ford as if not sure from which corner to expect an attack. "That's not exactly true, Sutton."

His qualifier ripped her heart into a few more pieces. "Don't lie. You see me as some pathetic loser that you can save with your magical penis."

Ella gasped and covered her mouth, watching them like a tennis match.

"You were never a pathetic loser."

"But you did feel sorry for me. Or was it the promise of business for the garage?"

Wyatt held his hands up. "Where we started has no bearing on where we ended up. You said so yourself. You know how I feel about you."

She wanted to believe him. She did. But how could a relationship based on lies grow into one about truth and love? And how could she trust herself to know the difference when she'd been so blind before?

"I can't do this again. Maybe it's best if we make a clean break like we'd planned." She took a step backward, but it was hard. Like her heart was irrevocably tethered to his.

"Sutton, please." The desperation in his voice was more than she could bear, and she ran—again.

Ella's hollers stopped her on the veranda, and she glanced over her shoulder. Wyatt and Ford were fighting, the noise bringing a crowd outside to gawk. Andrew's attempts to break them apart resulted in an elbow to his face. He staggered out of range, both hands cupped over his nose.

Ford took two loping steps toward the gate, but Wyatt brought him down like a lion on a gazelle, and they grappled on the concrete. This wasn't like any boxing match she'd ever seen. There was nothing civilized about what was happening between Ford and Wyatt. She turned to the people pointing and talking in low voices.

"Get down there and break up the fight," she shrieked, grabbing the arm of the man next to her and shoving him forward.

Her command galvanized a half dozen men. Before they made it to the gate, Ford and Wyatt rolled over the edge of the pool and splashed into the deep end, still locked together. The dark blob of their bodies sank under the water, their continuing struggles highlighted by the underwater lights.

She dug her fingernails into the rail, her knees wobbly. Would stubbornness kill them both? The men who'd gone to help stood around the edge of pool, as helpless as the rest of the crowd.

They surfaced two feet apart, treading water and breathing hard. Everyone seemed to breathe in unison and the chatter around her picked up in volume.

A scant five seconds of peace passed. Wyatt launched himself at Ford, their flailing arms splashing and causing waves throughout the entire pool.

"Out of the way, people." A deep voice used to commanding parted the crowd like Moses. The Cottonbloom, Mississippi, Chief of Police Thaddeus Preston, dressed in a dark suit, strode to the pool. A pretty woman with red streaks in her hair was on his heels. The men who hadn't done squat to diffuse the situation stepped aside. "Alright, boys, out of the pool unless you want me to haul you down to the station."

Sutton wasn't sure whether it was the threat or the way the chief's voice reverberated against the concrete that finally ended the fight. Ford and Wyatt separated themselves and swam to the edge, each of them getting in a few more juvenile splashes along the way.

Wyatt hauled himself out and shook his head like a dog. From this distance, she couldn't see how much damage Ford had managed to inflict on Wyatt, but Ford limped over to the chief, his tuxedo ripped at the shoulder and showing a slash of white shirt.

The three of them hashed things out in voices pitched too low to hear, and in the end they disappeared around the side of the main building instead of running the gauntlet of people on the veranda and in the main room.

She was frantic to make sure he was okay both mentally and physically, but that wasn't her place. She pressed her fingertips against her cheekbones to calm her out-of-control emotions. There would be time enough for tears later.

"I heard the Abbott boys got in a tussle." Her father's voice was like a rescue line. Without being able to stop herself, she tossed herself against him and buried her face in his collar. The familiar scent of Old Spice and the tang of a recently smoked cigar clung to him.

"What's this all about? Is Wyatt hurt?" With an awkwardness born of the unusual, he patted her shoulder and led her to a more secluded corner of the veranda. Now that the excitement had died, most people had returned to the main room to pass on what they'd seen.

"I don't know. Not bad enough he couldn't walk out of here."

"What were they fighting about?"

She took a breath, but let it out on a long sigh. What

had the fight been about? Her? Them? The garage? Or maybe all those things had stacked the tower of resentment so high it had finally toppled. The strange dynamics between the brothers made her thankful for her own normally dysfunctional family.

"All I know for sure is that it's over between me and Wyatt."

Her father looked taken aback. "I'm surprised."

"Why? It's not like we got the most auspicious start."

Her father chuckled. "That's true, but I thought you liked him. And I could sure enough tell that he was smitten with you."

"Smitten?"

"Doesn't take his eyes off you when you're together. Even your mother commented on it. She thought he was awfully sweet that Sunday morning she stopped by your place."

Smitten and *sweet* were not words she normally associated with Wyatt. More like sexy and stubborn.

"But you warned me off him. Told me it wouldn't last."

"I maybe stuck my nose where it didn't belong because Andrew was a familiar, easy choice. We know his family and he'd have fit in well." Her father hummed and rubbed his jaw. "Your mother told me to butt out. She thinks you and Wyatt are good together."

Sutton swallowed past a boulder-sized lump of tears. "We *were* good together. At least, I think we were." Any trust she had in her judgement had been blown to smithereens.

"No shame in taking some time for yourself to decide. You've been put through the wringer by men lately." Her father put an arm around her shoulders and squeezed, taking a step toward the door to the ballroom.

She planted her feet and balked. No way could she smile and put on a brave face. She didn't care what everyone would say about her the next morning. Wyatt had given her that at least. Actually, he'd given her more than she could measure.

"I'm going to slip out and head home."

"Do you want me to get your mother?" It wasn't often she heard doubt in her father's voice.

"No." She leaned in to take one more deep galvanizing breath of Old Spice and kissed his cheek. "I'll be fine."

He nodded, his hands tucked into the pockets of his tuxedo pants. "Call us tomorrow morning. Maggie is leaving for Nashville before lunch, but she might stay if you needed her."

Without a doubt, Maggie would cancel her trip if Sutton asked. She couldn't have said the same a month ago. The fiasco with Andrew had brought them closer than they'd ever been. She wouldn't ask Maggie to give up her trip though. A broken heart wasn't a terminal illness.

A broken heart. Sutton clutched her chest. So this is what it felt like. Like any stored happiness was hemorrhaging from the gashes and cuts inflicted by Wyatt . . . and herself. How much of this was her fault?

She forced the facsimile of a smile on her face, hoping the shadows hid her insincerity, and backed away from her father. She retraced Wyatt's retreat around the side of the country club. The blue line of hydrangeas in full bloom stoked frustration. How dare something so beautiful exist in the bleakness?

She waited in the warm night for the young valet to bring her car around. No sign of Ford or Wyatt. Part of her had hoped he'd be there waiting for her to emerge even though she had no idea what to say or do. Her father was right. She would gift herself with a few days to figure out what to do and decide whether her future tangled with Wyatt's.

Chapter Twenty

The next days passed excruciatingly slowly. The happiness she'd always found in making people feel good in clothes ceased to exist, a casualty of her broken heart. The pre-gala fervor had eased, and a lull had settled over the boutique. With Maggie gone, Sutton had to force herself out of bed and to work every morning. Otherwise, she might be tempted to wallow around in misery.

It didn't help that the weather had turned as gray as her mood. A tropical storm had crept in from the gulf and parked itself over the coast, bringing with it sheets of salt-tinged rain. Foot traffic along River Street was reduced to a few brave souls who stood on the bank and watched the river rise.

It had been decades since the river had flooded, but as the days went by with no abatement, apprehension infected both sides of the river. Contingency plans and sandbags were the talk of every coffee group, but the official word was to hold tight. She tried to summon the same worry expressed by her neighbors along River Street, but it wasn't genuine.

All she could think about was Wyatt. Sutton wasn't sure

if the monotony of her days was because of the weather or the numbness around her heart. Sometimes she laid a hand on her chest to make sure it was still beating.

Wyatt had texted and called several times since the gala, but Sutton had ignored him, not sure yet how to reply. She went over every single memory to tease out the truth. After three days fixating on Wyatt, when the bell over the door chimed, she half-expected to have conjured him to her.

Jackson Abbott sidled in the door acting as if one wrong move would set off an explosion of lace and sequins. Not sure if he was here as emissary or enemy, she waited for him to make the first move.

Slicked back, his dark brown hair appeared closer to Wyatt's black. His jeans and white T-shirt showed wet splotches from the rain. He continued his careful trek toward her. His distinctive hazel eyes snared hers when he was six feet away.

She squirmed on the stool and grasped the edge of the glass top cabinet for support. She had to remind herself that Jackson and Wyatt weren't just brothers, but twins. Their coloring and personalities were so starkly different.

"Hi." His opening salvo was so unexpectedly mundane, a cheery-sounding, "Hi," popped out of her in response.

When he didn't offer up anything else, she said, "I'm assuming you aren't here to shop."

"No." The small quirk of his lips reminded her so much of Wyatt, a pang penetrated her numb limbo. "I'm here because of my brother."

"Did he send you?" She tempered the eagerness with worry. She'd woken more than once from a nightmare of Wyatt never surfacing from the pool. "He's okay, right? Nothing broken?"

"A few bruises is all." He scratched at the stubble along

his jaw. "I'm just going to lay it out there. He's a mess. Miserable and moping around the garage."

If Jackson was going to lay it out, then so could she. "Was I a pity project?"

"Of course not. Why would you even think it?"

"Something Wyatt said once. And Ford insinuated as much the night of the gala."

"Are you pissed or embarrassed or whatever that Wyatt started a fight in front of all your friends?"

She threw his message back in a similar tone of outrage. "No. Why would you think that?"

"You haven't returned his calls or texts. And, no offense, but you seem the type to care about what people think."

She opened her mouth to argue, but he was right to some extent. She used to care. "I'm worried Wyatt will move on to the next project. The next woman." She added the last in a whisper.

His eyes softened. He moved to the side of the counter and propped his hip, slouching closer as if sharing secrets. "More than any of us, Wyatt gets attached to things and people. It's his greatest weakness. And strength."

"You think he's attached to me?"

"Something happened a long time ago between him and Ford that might help you understand. Ford took something that Wyatt had dreamed about for years and ruined it."

"The Barracuda."

Jackson cocked his head. "He told you. Interesting. He's had cars come and go since then, but he'll always long for that Barracuda. Same thing with you. He'll always long for you."

Her heart jumped with a shock of hope. "I get your point even though I'm not sure I appreciate being likened to a car."

"You should be flattered. A Barracuda is one fine-ass car." His smile carved dimples into his cheeks and flipped his demeanor from stern to ridiculously attractive. "He would kill me if he knew I was here, by the way."

"But you came anyway." She returned his smile, her first real one in days. It was obvious to her that Wyatt wasn't the only one in possession of a big heart.

"I can't stand to see him like this. It's just plain pitiful. He cares about you. A lot. You'd be doing all us a favor by giving him another shot."

"I'll think about it." She didn't need to think too hard. She'd been teetering on the edge of texting him back, but no need to tell Jackson so he could go back and tell Wyatt.

"That's all I'm asking." Jackson pushed off the counter, and she followed him to the front door.

The river was hidden behind the veil of gray rain. "What are they saying about the river on your side?" she asked.

"It's already jumped the bank downstream in St. Helena Parish. No major flooding yet in Cottonbloom Parish, but a matter of time, I'd say." He looked around her shop. "You got contingency plans?"

"Downtown Cottonbloom hasn't flooded in fifty years or more."

"Seems about due then, by my reckoning." Jackson dipped his head and ducked outside, lost to the rain.

Sutton stayed in the doorway and stared toward the river. Malice seemed to emanate from where the river raged. Grabbing the umbrella she'd left by the door that morning, she scurried toward the Quilting Bee, stepping ankle deep in a puddle along the way. Shaking out her umbrella and her foot, she pushed the door open.

Expecting the store to be as deserted as hers, she was shocked by the scurry of people boxing and carrying items through the back. More than half the shop floor had been cleared out.

Ms. Leora and Ms. Effie directed a crew of mostly men

that included the Fournette brothers and their sister Tally from the Louisiana side of the river.

Sutton approached Ms. Leora. "Have you been told to evacuate?"

"Hello, dear." The older woman patted Sutton's hand. "No official word as of yet, but Vera, Effie, and I have never been ones to wait for a bunch of men to tell us what to do."

"Where are you taking everything?"

"Cade and Sawyer offered to store most of it in their shop, but we decided they're too close to river and are piling everything in poor Vera's house."

"I guess I could move things to my parents' house," she said more to herself than to Ms. Leora. But her parents' house backed up to the river too. One of the best pieces of real estate in the county.

"For goodness' sake, be careful with that vase, Cade, it's hand-blown." Ms. Leora moved faster than her age would suggest, grabbed a delicate looking green-and-blue glass vase from under Cade Fournette's arm, and cradled it like a baby. He rolled his eyes, but an indulgent smile was on his face. He hauled the heavy bin he was holding higher and headed toward the storeroom in the back.

Sutton backed toward the door, a sense of urgency overtaking her. She'd been wandering around in a fog and ignoring the danger because she was too focused on her anemic heart to care. But now that Jackson had revived it, she could see the consequences of her inattention looming. She could lose everything in a few hours if the river escaped the bank.

She ran out of the Quilting Bee, only realizing when she stepped from under the overhang that she'd left her umbrella. Even going back for it seemed a waste of precious time, and she kept running, rain soaking her before she made it to her front door.

For the next hour, she hauled out boxes from the store-room and packed clothes, starting with the most expensive gowns. At first, she took care to fold everything, but with each glance out the window and the rain pouring over the gutters, the sloppier her folding became until she was tossing in clothes a handful at a time.

With eight boxes packed, she looked at the small dent in inventory she'd made. Pulling out her phone, she called her mother but no one answered. Her father was in court, and she left him a message. She hesitated over Andrew's number, but although a tentative peace had been brokered between them, she didn't want to become indebted to him for any reason. Bree wasn't an option either.

She beat tears back. They wouldn't help her get packed and moved any faster. After another hour, she had boxes stacked on top of boxes and another issue presented itself. It was all well and good to get things boxed up, but the flood water wouldn't care. She needed to get the boxes to her house, and she could only take a few at a time.

Her car was parked in the back, and she managed to squeeze in five boxes. By the time she was finished, she was as wet as if she'd stepped into a shower and shivered in the cool AC of her car. She unloaded the boxes in her den and headed back to the shop, driving slow, her windshield wipers whirring frenetically and still not able to keep up.

A quick calculation widened the pit of despair in her stomach. It would take all night to get everything moved. How much time did she have? She parked in front of the shop, closer to the boxes she'd already packed.

With rainwater in her eyes, she opened the door to Abigail's, not to silence but to the chatter of voices and activity. Wiping a hand down her face, she blinked.

It was the Abbotts. Not just Wyatt and his brothers and aunts, but Landrum Abbott plus some others she didn't

even know. They must have arrived soon after she'd le
because more than half the racks were empty and the boxe
she'd already packed were gone.

She caught Jackson's eye, and he elbowed Wyatt, wh
was standing with his back toward her, pointing a man sh
didn't know out the back. Wyatt turned and took two step
toward her before stopping short. He looked worn dow
shadows under his eyes and his stubble classifying mor
like a beard.

All doubts swept away, she closed the distance an
threw her arms around him. "I'm so sorry," she whispere
into his neck.

"You have nothing to be sorry for. I'm the one who'
sorry. I came on too strong. I embarrassed you at the gal
I'm an idiot, and I totally understand if you kick my sorr
butt out of here and never want to see me again." In con
trast to his declaration, his arms tightened around her.

The laugh that bubbled up was driven by relief. "Ho
did you know I needed help?"

"Jackson had to go out for some parts this morning an
told me the river was rising fast. Your shop would be th
first in trouble. The door was unlocked, but your car wa
gone. When I saw how little you'd gotten packed, I calle
for reinforcements. We're storing the boxes at Mack's."

He chucked his head toward his brother, who was tap
ing up a box a few feet away. At the sound of his name
Mack looked up and winked at her.

"You don't mind having boxes everywhere?" Sutto
asked.

"All I need is a path from the front door to my be
Happy to help." He picked up the box and made his wa
toward her storeroom.

"I should have trusted you." She played with the butto
on his shirt, unable to say her piece looking in his eye

"But between my history and what Ford insinuated, I couldn't think straight. I've been miserable without you."

"Damn, I've missed you so bad." Wyatt hauled her into his chest for a hug. "I overreacted. Something about Ford has always chapped my hide. Ever since—"

He cut himself off, but she filled in the blank. "He bought the Barracuda out from under you."

"Exactly. Plus, he planted the worry that the garage—me—wasn't for someone like you."

She shoved his shoulder. "It's what's under the hood that counts."

He laughed. "Since you said it, I'll whole heartedly agree."

Mack stopped beside them on his second trip. "How about you two finish working things out after the threat of requiring passage on Noah's ark recedes."

"Mack's right. Let's get to moving."

They worked for the next hour with little conversation except what to pack where. The overhead bell chimed and Sutton turned. A feminine figure entered and pushed the hood back on her raincoat. Bree.

If she'd left the house with makeup, it had been washed away. Her face was pale and gaunt. An instant shot of sympathy had Sutton closing the distance between them.

"How can I help?" Bree asked.

She didn't hesitate, pulling Bree in for a hug. While she would never go so far as to thank Bree, Sutton would never have found Wyatt without her betrayal with Andrew. Looking back, it was obvious Sutton and Andrew's engagement had been one of convenience, not love. She had been treading water until Bree had cannonballed into her.

A sob vibrated from Bree's chest.

"It's okay." Sutton patted her back. "Everything will be fine."

"Does this mean you forgive me?" Hope lifted some of the strain Bree had carried inside.

"I forgive you." Sutton pushed Bree's shoulder playfully. "I've missed having you around."

"Yeah, well, it seems like you found someone else to fill my spot." Even though she was smiling, a sadness of what had been lost forever shaded Bree's face.

Bree was right. Sutton had filled the void Bree had left. Maggie had become more friend than sister, and Wyatt had become her best friend, confidant, and cheerleader with major benefits. Her life was fuller than it had ever been, but that didn't mean Bree couldn't earn a place in Sutton's new life.

"No one can take away all the nights we lay looking up at the stars and dreaming." Sutton hip-bumped Bree and chucked her head toward the nearest half-packed box. "Did you come to help?"

As they worked together, Sutton filled her in on the designs she'd found the courage to display and sell in the shop, all thanks to Wyatt and Maggie.

A rumbly sound that Sutton first thought was thunder grew louder, drawing her to the window. Through the deluge, she could make out the hulking outline of Army-style trucks. Wyatt came up behind her and lay his hands on her shoulders.

"What's going on?" She turned to see a grin bloom across his face.

"Hot damn. Those are National Guard trucks. Let me get the lowdown." He gave her shoulders a squeeze, threw a poncho over his head, and disappeared into the rain.

Everyone had joined her at the window to watch the dark figures scurry in the rain, muffled shouts barely penetrating the wall of water.

"Sandbagging," Jackson said. "'Bout time, I'd say."

They said bad things happened in threes, but she had

to wonder if the same went for good things. Because a morning that had started in the crapper was now in contention for the best day ever.

Wyatt's dark figure approached at a jog. He dropped the poncho and shook as much water off himself as possible before stepping back inside Abigail's. Rainwater glistened in his hair and beard and spiked his dark lashes.

"Apparently, Regan Fournette went to battle with the governor and got resources allocated to keep downtown Cottonbloom dry. Both sides. That woman can get shit done." Everyone murmured agreements in the same tone of admiration.

"Should we wait and see what happens?" Sutton asked.

Mack crossed his arms over his chest and took a quick visual inventory. "I say we finish the floor, but leave everything we put in the storeroom. That way we minimize your loss if the worst should happen. I feel like we need to scoot over to the Louisiana side and provide muscle in the sandbagging effort."

"But if Sutton loses everything in the back then—"

"Mack is right." Sutton laid a hand on Wyatt's arm. "With the Guard here, you boys could help save more than just my shop. Bree and I can finish the floor, right?"

Bree had her hands planted on her waist. "You know it."

"We'll stay and help too." Hazel wrapped a hand around Sutton's forearm, the softness of the old lady's skin belying the strength underneath.

Wyatt met her gaze and the fight went out of him. He gave a curt nod. As if that was the signal, the men moved in unison to grab rain slickers and ponchos and disappeared one-by-one through the gray curtain.

She stopped Landrum Abbott before he headed out the door. "Thanks for coming. You barely know me, and I'm afraid I didn't make the best impression at the Tavern."

Landrum winked, his laugh as smooth as the whiskey

she overindulged in that night. "You were perfectly charming. Anyway, I know Wyatt's taken with you, and when he calls in a favor, I answer. We'll be seeing a lot more of each other. Maybe even at the next family reunion."

The implications set her heart off in a lope, but it was one of anticipation and hope.

He disappeared, leaving Wyatt lingering at the door. "I should stay."

"Go. Everything was fine the second I walked in and saw you. All this can be replaced." She waved a hand over the almost empty floor. "I've got hold of what's important, and this time, I'm not letting go."

Wyatt bit his bottom lip. "I know I shouldn't say it again, but damn, I love you. Not sure what I would have done if you'd told me you didn't want me here."

She took a step toward him, but he matched her with a step backward. "Wyatt, I—"

"Don't say something you don't mean. I'm good knowing we're not over and done. We can talk later." He too disappeared.

It took the four of them another two hours to clear the floor of her shop. Hazel and Hyacinth piled into their Crown Victoria and headed home to dry out but not before both giving her a hug. Bree followed her to Mack's house, and they unloaded the last of the boxes, stacking them on the last remaining floor space in the modest den.

Bree retreated to the porch swing, pulled out her phone, and scrolled. After a moment's hesitation, Sutton joined her.

"Forecasters are saying that this front should clear by tomorrow, and we'll dry out, but surge flooding will be a risk for a few days yet." Bree turned her phone to display the yellow and green blobs spinning slowly on the map.

"That's good."

They swung in silence except for a rhythmic squawk of

the chains. Mist covered everything and blew over them. She shivered, but stayed on the damp cushion. Bree obviously needed something else from her.

Sutton glanced over at her from the corner of her eyes. "What's going on with you and Andrew?"

"Nothing. He called me after the gala and acted concerned because I was a no-show. I think that's when he truly gave up on you." Bree stared off toward the field of cotton across the road. "I won't be someone's second choice."

"You deserve better."

"That's what I keep telling myself. Maybe I'll eventually believe it." Tears had thickened her voice.

Sutton scooted a little closer so their shoulders touched. "I'll remind you at regular intervals."

The rain seemed to cleanse their troubled friendship. As gray and gloomy as things appeared now, the sun would be back.

Bree heaved a sigh and stood. "You going to wait for Wyatt here?"

"Yep." She had considered heading back down to help the sandbagging efforts but her arms were already sore and noodly from heaving boxes.

Bree took off in a run toward her BMW, and Sutton watched her disappear down the road. She jogged to the barn and took the steps to his loft two at a time. A hot shower restored blood flow. She discarded her wet clothes and slipped on a pair of Wyatt's boxers and a T-shirt with an Abbott Brothers Garage and Restoration emblem over her heart.

She searched his cabinets and put together a meal of canned soup and crackers. After having a bowl herself, she covered the rest, ready to reheat once Wyatt made it home. Three hours later, boots on the stairs had her sitting up and smoothing her hair.

He burst through the door, his gaze sweeping the room until snaring her.

"I hope you don't mind that I'm here." Even though he was the one who'd declared himself—twice—nerves trembled her voice.

"Coming home to you is a dream come true." None of his usual tease lurked in his voice or face.

"Where's Jackson?"

"Crashing at Mack's."

"Are you hungry?"

"Starved." Longing shaded the word, and she thought for a moment he might toss her on the bed and feast on her. Which actually seemed like an excellent plan. Until she noticed a shiver run through his body that was born of a chill.

"First up is a shower. A long hot one. Then food."

He was already halfway to the bathroom when he asked, "And then?"

"Then we can discuss what's next. In bed."

He disappeared, but not before she noted the relief that smoothed the crinkle between his eyes. By the time he emerged with a towel wrapped around his waist, she was ladling out the rest of the soup and trying to avoid first degree burns when her gaze wouldn't unstick from his body.

The towel dropped to the floor, revealing the hard muscles of his butt through the open door of his room. The ladle slipped from her fingers and clanged against the pot. He pulled on a pair of boxer-briefs and looked over his shoulder with a naughty half-smile.

He didn't bother with pants or a shirt. His amble to join her in the kitchen took seconds, but it was enough time to drive her desire past her good intentions of seeing him fed. As soon as he got within striking distance, she wrapped her arms around his neck and brought their bodies together.

Only the thin T-shirt she wore separated his hard chest from her sensitive breasts.

He swooped down to capture her lips in a kiss so full of frantic desperation, she moaned and clutched him closer, wordlessly asking for more. Except she knew how much he liked her asking for what she wanted.

"The soup will keep. Will you take me to bed?"

He acted as needy as she felt, stripping them naked with an expediency that lacked his usual grace. Something that seemed lost forever had been found, and a new appreciation for each nuance bloomed and carved itself in her memories.

The tickling roughness of the hair on his legs to the hard length of him between her legs to the flexing muscles of his biceps as he held himself over her. It had only been a week since they'd been together, but the moment felt pivotal.

The head of his erection pushed at her entrance. "I need you."

"I'm ready." She grasped his buttocks and egged him on.

He buried himself in one thrust, his husky moan one of deep satisfaction. The sex was quick and dirty and hard. The niceties of lovemaking had been supplanted by something more primal.

She reached her climax first, writhing underneath him and biting his shoulder, the intensity overwhelming. He followed soon after, shuddering and collapsing on top of her.

She ran her fingernails down his back, and he reared up as if she'd applied an electric shock. He flopped next to her, still breathing hard. A wellspring of emotion threatened to burst out of her mouth.

She came up on her side and propped herself over him. His eyes were closed, and she wondered for a moment whether he'd fallen asleep. She laid her hand flat over his heart, reassured by the steady rhythm.

One eye opened. "Everything good?" His voice was husky.

"I need to tell you something."

Both eyes were open now and narrowed on her face. "I'm a patient man. You don't need to tell me something because you think I expect it. I only want the truth from you."

How could he see straight to the heart of the matter like that? "Here's the truth. After everything went down with Andrew and Bree, I wondered if there was something wrong with me."

He snaked a hand into her hair and played. "There's not a damn thing wrong with you."

She leaned in to give him a quick kiss. "I appreciate the sentiment, but I should've been more upset. My heart should've been in pieces. It wasn't."

"That's because you never really loved that jackhole." The mix of confidence and doubt in his voice made her want to blurt out what he needed to hear.

"You're right, I didn't. Because after the gala, I understood what a broken heart felt like. I couldn't think about anything or anyone but you. I went over and over everything we'd said and done together. I wasn't sure how or if I could move on with my life without you in it. I realized then how much I loved you."

"Truth?"

"Nothing but."

He pulled her down to him, both arms coming around her in a hold that stole her breath—literally. She laid kisses on any inch of his skin within reach of her lips while whispering the three words over and over.

"Love you too," he whispered back, his mouth at her temple.

The romantic moment was ruined by a loud rumble from Wyatt's stomach. Laughing, Sutton pulled his T-shirt back on and reheated the soup. While he ate, they talked about practical matters—the rain, the river, her boutique.

"You seem awfully calm about the possibility your shop could flood." His bowl was empty, and he was working his way through the entire sleeve of crackers.

"I'm worried sick, but thanks to you and your family, I've done everything I can do. It's a building and some boxes of clothes. I've already saved what's important."

He linked his hands with hers.

"I'm glad the garage isn't in any danger," she added.

His eyes hardened from warm wool to cutting slate. "Maybe not from the river."

"What do you mean?"

He shook his head. "Let's enjoy tonight. Tomorrow we'll be forced to deal with families and floods."

"But we'll do it together, right?" Her bones already knew the answer. In Wyatt, she'd found a champion, protector, lover, and friend.

"Always." He kissed the palm of her hand. "Always and forever."

Epilogue

Wyatt looked up from under the dash of Vera Carson's
Olds 442. Sutton paced in front of the closed bay door and
peeked through the fogged windows every few seconds.
A cold front had moved in, bringing with it a rare chance
of snow. Children on both sides of Cottonbloom were hoping for a Christmas miracle.

He was smack dab in the middle of his Christmas miracle. While he and Sutton weren't officially living together,
they hadn't spent a night apart since the flood. More often
than not, they ended up at her house, giving Jackson the
run of the loft.

She'd told him she'd loved him so long ago that it was
no longer a shock, but still provided a zing to his heart
every time she whispered it in his ear at night after they'd
made love.

He left the tangle of wires and joined her at the door. A
quick check outside revealed a fallow cotton field across
the road and no snow.

"Thought you had to work this afternoon," he said.

"Maggie is covering for me."

He narrowed his eyes on her, surprised she was skipping
out during their busiest time of the year. The sandbagging

effort had minimized damage to both sides of Cotton-bloom during the rains. The boutique had suffered the worst damage due to its proximity to the river. It had required new carpeting and fresh paint, but had been back in business within two weeks. He knew Sutton was hoping to make up lost profits during the holiday season.

"Did you sit in a mess of fire ants?" he asked after watching her stare outside while shifting back and forth on her feet.

"What?" Her confusion faded into a little laugh. "Ants in my pants? Ha, ha."

"Are you this excited about the chance of snow? It'll melt before the sun comes up. Ground's too warm."

"I'm not waiting for it to snow." A secretive smile curled her lips and made her eyes dance. "I'm waiting on your Christmas present."

"Are you trying to intercept and hide it before I catch a glimpse?" He was too nervous about the present he got her to wonder too much about what she got him.

A ring was burning a hole in his pocket. He couldn't decide whether to end his torture early and ask her now or wrap it and put it under the small tree they'd decorated together at her house.

"It's a little too big to fit under the tree, so I might have to give it to you early. Is that okay?"

"Only if I can give you your present early." The mish-mash of nerves and anticipation made him nauseous. Although he was confident about the strength of her feelings, she was supposed to have been getting married to someone else right about now.

But life had a funny way of turning expectations on their head. It was ironic considering how many years he'd been treading water, focused on the garage and nothing else, to have his life change so drastically in such a short amount of time.

One thing was certain, if Wyatt and Sutton ever had kids, they'd have to come up with a different story of how'd they met. He laughed. *Well, son, I met your mother when I pulled another woman's panties from under the seat of her fiancé's car.*

"What's so funny? Did you get me a gag gift?" she asked.

"Hypothetically, would you be mad if I got you a whoopee cushion?"

A metal trailer clacked as it turned into their parking lot. "Oh my goodness, it's here." She grabbed his hand and pulled him through the side door.

The oversized tow truck parked straight on, blocking the view of the flatbed. Shaking his head and wondering what on earth Sutton was up to, Wyatt walked around the cab of the truck. His head grew swimmy, and he touched the fender with a shaky hand to confirm his imagination wasn't playing tricks on him. A 1970 Plymouth Hemi Barracuda.

It was his car. Not the exact car, of course. That one had long ago been crushed into a cube of metal at the salvage yard, but one so similar, Wyatt felt like he'd reverted into his sixteen-year-old self.

"Where? How?" His mouth seemed capable of uttering only monosyllabic questions, even though a million more complicated ones circled his head.

"We found it in Natchez, Tennessee."

"We?"

"I knew the make and model, but finding one that wasn't too expensive, yet wasn't so far gone to make it worthless was hard. I needed help." She pointed toward the doorway of the shop. Jackson stood with his shoulder propped against the jamb, a huge smile on his face.

He wanted to go give his brother a hug and a sloppy kiss. He wanted to give Sutton a hug and a less-sloppy kiss. Hell, he even wanted to give the 'Cuda a hug.

He looked from his brother to Sutton to the car and back

to the woman who knew everything about him and loved him anyway.

"If you don't like it—"

"This is amazing. Far and away the best present ever."

"You don't mind that she's a project car?" Sutton laid her hand next to his on the fender and put some tease into her smile.

"She won't be a project car. She'll be a labor of love, and I'm never letting her go."

Sutton's expression softened. He hoped she understood his clumsy analogy. There was no time to find out. The tow truck driver came around the side with a clipboard of papers for Sutton to sign, breaking their solitude.

Jackson had disappeared. Wyatt would find him later. He didn't have to tell Jackson how much the gesture meant. Not only the car itself, but the fact his brother had accepted Sutton like a sister, watching out for her and offering help.

Weeks after the fact, Wyatt learned the extent of Jackson's meddling. Wyatt couldn't do anything but thank his brother for it. Jackson's interference had brought him and Sutton back together.

The events of the fall had torn at the fabric of his life, leaving gashes he wasn't sure anyone could mend. Ford was MIA, the future of his share of the garage in question, but Christmas was upon them, and the aunts at least held out hope he'd limp back home like the prodigal son. Wyatt wasn't so sure. Mack's stress level was on simmer, and Wyatt dreaded the day Ford walked back into the shop making demands.

Uncertainty hung over the garage, but the bond between him, Jackson, and Mack had only strengthened through the tribulations. Somehow they would survive. Hopefully, mostly intact.

Although Jackson was being tight-lipped, Wyatt had

sensed a dynamic shift between his brother and Willa's working relationship and not for the better. Asking only sent Jackson further into silence. Wyatt would sit back and observe and meddle as needed. That's what brothers did.

And Ford . . . worry warred with fury. Wyatt shook his head. He didn't want to think about Ford right now. Not with a redo of his past being lowered to the ground and his future standing by his side. Once the tow truck drove off, Wyatt walked around the Barracuda, his mind making lists and cataloguing the tasks.

A look under the hood confirmed his assessment. Jackson had done good. Real good. Yes, it needed work, but the engine would only require an overhaul, not a replacement. He couldn't wait to get started. Sunday drives down all of Cottonbloom Parish's back roads would be in the cards by summer.

Sutton had followed him around on his inspection and picked at one of the numerous rusty spots in the paint. That's what turned most people off, but the outside damage was superficial and easily fixable. It was the inside that counted.

He gripped the cold metal of the hood and turned to Sutton. "Do you want your present now?"

She looked around with a small laugh "Sure. Do you have it stashed in the parking lot?"

"I've been walking around with it for two weeks now." He dropped to one knee and took her hand, fishing around in his pocket.

Her smile faded into shock. Color stained her cheeks, her breaths coming in fast white puffs in the cold air. "You're not . . . are you?"

"Will you marry me?" He'd planned to say more, but in that moment, he could barely remember his name. His fingers closed around the ring, and he pulled it out. The cold made him clumsy, and he fumbled the delicate piece of jewelry.

As if in slow motion, he watched it take an unfavorable bounce against the concrete and roll under the car. He dropped her hand and scrambled on all fours. She joined him to peer underneath.

"Gosh, it's halfway under," she said.

He stuck a hand out and cast around, blind but knowing he was going to have to shimmy farther under. He got on his belly, but before he could wedge his shoulders underneath, she was already under.

"It'll be easier for me to reach. You're too big." Her voice echoed off the metal undercarriage. "Got it!"

She reversed her crawl and sat up, holding the ring out on her dirty palm. He picked it up with fingers that were now covered in streaks of oil and grease. "This is not how I pictured my proposal going at all. I'm sorry."

"This is perfect. If you're still going to ask, that is?" She held out her hand and wiggled her fingers.

"Sutton Mize, would you do me honor of becoming my wife, through sickness and health, rain and sun, good cars and bad, and everything in between?"

"Yes, yes, yes!"

He had just enough time to secure the ring on her finger before she launched herself at him. Both on their knees, they embraced fiercely. Her cheek was cold against his, and something wet registered on his face. Was she crying? He pulled back to see huge wet snowflakes drifting around them.

A stillness and serenity washed over the land and affected him as well. The restlessness that had plagued him for the last year had been soothed and transformed after he'd met her. He was exactly where he was supposed to be.

Right here, right now, Wyatt's world was perfect. The

woman he loved had his ring on her finger and dammed if he'd do anything to give her cause to remove it. Her face tilted to the sky, fat snowflakes gathering in her hair and along her lashes. He leaned in to brush his cold lips across hers.

"Should we go share the news with your brothers?" she asked.

"Nah. I have a better idea."

"What's that?"

"I think we should warm up. In bed. Let's head home."

Laughing, she grabbed his hand, the icy sparkle on her finger as pretty and unexpectedly beautiful as the snow falling around them.

A bang shook the wall. No fist had come through the sheetrock, and it hadn't been violent enough to be a body. Probably a chair then. The breakroom sat a dozen feet from where Willa Brown worked. Indistinct male voices came in spurts and sometimes on top of each other. Overall, a typical Abbott family meeting. Good thing no customers were milling around to witness the fireworks.

Willa ducked her head back under the hood of Vera Carson's Oldsmobile Cutlass 442. She wanted to do the car and Abbott Brothers Garage and Restoration proud, but even more, she wanted to do Jackson Abbott proud. While she'd learned the ins-and-outs of car mechanics from her father, she'd gained an appreciation of the classics over the last two years while working with the brothers. Jackson in particular.

Another harder hit to the sheetrock registered but she didn't look up from where she was finger-tightening a bolt. While she had the disadvantage when it came to brute strength, none of the boys could match her dexterity in tight places.

The office door shot open and bounced against the

wall, deepening the impression of the doorknob. Mack Abbott went out the front door and Wyatt out the back.

Jackson stalked out and slammed the door shut, looking like someone had borrowed his '68 Mustang GT and gotten ketchup on the seats. If it were socially acceptable, Willa wouldn't have been surprised to bear witness to Jackson marrying his Mustang.

Although twins, Jackson and Wyatt approached life from opposite directions. Wyatt was the wild charmer while Jackson was quieter and more circumspect. If past behaviors held, Wyatt was headed to the barn out back of the shop to expend his anger on a punching bag hung from the rafters. Jackson would bottle up his aggression and let it explode all over the dirt track. She almost felt sorry for whoever raced him next.

Jackson headed straight for her. More likely his destination was the Cutlass. That knowledge didn't stop her quick intake of breath as he drew close. He stopped next to her with his hands propped on the open hood, breathing like he'd gone for a sprint around the building. His anger vibrated the air around them. He definitely had a Mr. Rochester from *Jane Eyre* vibe going on. Dark, brooding, mysterious.

She was used to the Abbotts. In fact, their idiosyncrasies made her feel right at home. Growing up a tomboy who knew more about cars than most guys did not help her cred with the girls who'd been more concerned with pageants and cheerleading. It had been just her and her dad for so long that being around men felt normal. Melancholy reared up and bit her in the ass. Whenever she thought about her dad and the life she'd left behind—had to leave behind—regrets threatened to swamp her.

She put her father and her past out of her head and focused instead on her favorite subject—Jackson Abbott. If he were a textbook, she would name him *The Anatomy of the Perfect Male,* or if she was in a philosophical mind-set, *Dwelling on Jackson.* Her mind tended to dwell on him in her waking and sleeping hours.

Not that he saw her as anything but an employee. In fact, sometimes she wasn't sure he saw her at all. Like now. Even though they were three feet apart under the same hood, he ignored her. She thought about making a funny face to see how long it took him to notice. He probably wouldn't and her face would freeze that way.

She smothered a laugh and checked him out from the corner of her eyes, one of her favorite pastimes. He wore baggy, gray work coveralls, same as she did, but in deference to the warm snap, he'd peeled off the top and tied the sleeves around his waist. His black T-shirt molded to his thick chest and emphasized his brown hair. His jaw was tight and his biceps flexed as he stared into the engine compartment.

"So how was the family meeting?" she asked in a sing-songy voice.

"Shitty." His voice was more hoarse-sounding than usual which made her wonder if he'd been doing most of the hollering even though that was unlike him. He was more the strong, silent type. Or the closed-off, brooding type.

Her chest tightened. Was the shop in financial trouble? Had the decision to expand into car restoration and the recent upgrades been too much of a strain? Oh God, were they going to fire her?

Where would she go? She didn't want to start over. Not again. Not when she'd finally found somewhere to settle for longer than a few months. Not that the Abbotts really cared about her, but they felt like a real family. They drove each other crazy more often than not, but at least they'd stuck together and had each other's backs.

Unfortunately, she was the odd-woman-out in the equation. She straightened and faced him. "Am I being fired?"

"What?" Finally, he turned his attention to her. "Of course you're not fired. Where would you get that idea?"

She averted her face and pretended to work on something in the depths of the engine block. Her breath shuddered out. She didn't want Jackson to know how important this job was to her. Without it—without the Abbotts—she would be alone again.

"What was all the arguing about then?" she asked.

"It was about Ford. Ford and his need for something big, something quick. Instead of being patient and building our reputation through hard, honest work, he wants fast cash and is threatening to sell out."

"Can't you and Wyatt and Mack pool your money and buy him out? That would solve a lot of problems." Now that her job was safe for at least another day, she could turn her worry outward for Jackson. He was more than mad. The gamut of emotions that flashed through his typical stoicism came too fast for her to interpret, but his voice reflected betrayal.

"We put most of our cash into the shop, and we're still repaying the loan for the addition. The question is, do we overextend ourselves for another loan, find Ford and appeal to whatever family loyalty he has left, or let things play out?"

Three years earlier when the brothers got serious about expanding into car renovations and not just repairs, they had added two more bays and specialized equipment like a metal bending machine and a top of the line welder. Those upgrades had been necessary but expensive.

To counteract the despondency in his voice, she forced a tease into hers. "I'd let things play out. I mean, who the heck would be interested in buying this grease pit anyway?"

While she didn't garner a smile, tension leaked out of him like a drain being opened. The garage was actually the nicest she'd ever worked in. As the unofficial leader, Mack insisted they clean up after themselves. While she wouldn't eat off the floors, she'd certainly slept in dirtier places.

"You've got a point there. Maybe we don't have anything to worry about." The furrows along his forehead belied his words.

"What about Sutton?"

"What about her?"

"Why don't you see if she'll buy Ford's part?"

Sutton Mize was the daughter of a prominent family in Cottonbloom, Mississippi. She and Wyatt had come together over her ex-fiancé's car and had been inseparable ever since. On paper they shouldn't work, but seeing them together made everyone believers. However, there was no arguing the fact, Sutton changed the dynamics of the garage.

Suddenly it wasn't the Three Musketeers—Mack, Wyatt, Jackson—against the world. Willa had always cast herself as d'Artagnan, but with the addition of Sutton, Willa felt demoted and more of an outsider than ever.

"And if she and Wyatt end things? A vengeful ex who's well connected could wreck our reputation. Hell, Ford could wreck our reputation and drive the garage into the ground. Garages make or break on word of mouth, especially in a town like Cottonbloom."

Desperation stalked through her body. The feeling was only too familiar. Heat bloomed and a sickening wave of faintness passed through her, forcing her to unzip the top of her coveralls and flap the front to cool down.

"Hey, are you okay?" Concern for her replaced any angst he'd carried from the meeting.

"I'm fine. Fine." She half sat on the edge of the engine

compartment. The wave of heat and nausea passed. Her skipped breakfast and lunch were coming back to haunt her. All her extra money and then some were going to repairs to her car. Her clutch was nearly shot, the exhaust was leaking, and her tires were bald. Considering where she worked, the irony of her problems wasn't lost on her. Black humor was the only kind she appreciated these days. But it was payday and since she wasn't getting fired, she'd splurge on a decent meal.

"Wasn't expecting a heat wave in November is all." Her voice was embarrassingly shaky.

"It's not like we have a dress code or anything. You can wear old jeans and T-shirts when it gets hot. And you'd be a sight cooler without a hat." Before she could react, he grabbed the bill of her vintage Texaco ball cap and peeled it off.

Her hair sprang around her face. Usually as soon as it hit her neck, she hacked it off. The monthly ritual seemed a penance she needed to pay for her past transgressions. Plus, it was all around easier to handle when it was short. Since the beginning of summer though, she hadn't taken up scissors, and pieces waved around her face like new growth from a tree. A scraggly tree.

She'd given up her old life. Except for a name that she had shared with her grandmother, Wilhelmina, Willa for short. At the time she'd wanted something to hang on to, something to ground her.

But the hat and her given name aside, her hair had had to go. Wavy, thick, and chestnut-colored, her hair had been her vanity and hacking it off had been symbolic. She wanted to leave the selfish, stupid girl she'd been behind. Unfortunately, cutting it hadn't cut out the memories of her dad singing "Brown Eyed Girl" to her at night while stroking her long hair off her forehead. Her life hadn't been all bad—not even close in retrospect—and remembering the good hurt.

She finger combed her hair behind her ears. It was all split ends and tangles and dulled color. She might be a greasy mechanic and his employee, but she was still a female standing in front of an attractive man. She didn't want Jackson seeing her with sweaty, gross hat head.

"Gimme that back." She grabbed the hat and mashed it on her head, tucking the ends of her hair that stuck out underneath as best she could. Her fingertips stopped to trace the unraveling embroidery on the front. The hat had been her father's. The last thing she'd ever stolen. Did he miss her?

Jackson had never looked at her the way he was looking at her right now. Was he suspicious? Curious? Either was bad. That was the nice thing about working with men, especially Jackson. He didn't gossip. He didn't ask questions unrelated to whatever projects were on the shop floor. He didn't care about where she was from or what had brought her to Cottonbloom. She needed it to stay that way.

"You sure you're okay? You're really pale," he said.

"I'm a-okay." She waved him off even though it was a lie. "What's your plan about Ford?"

"We haven't decided." His voice dropped as if talking to himself. "His selfishness may bring us all low."

Did he mean the garage might go under for real? The garage had been started by their father, Hobart Abbott, and had maintained a steady clientele and stellar reputation for more than forty years. Her heart accelerated from zero to one-twenty, bringing with it another wave of knee-weakening nausea. "Surely there's something you can do to stave off a disaster."

He muttered something unintelligible, ran a hand

down his face, and scratched at the dark stubble along his jaw. "We're talking more after work. I'll let you know."

He pivoted away and stalked toward the back door, maybe to join Wyatt in pounding his worries into the punching bag or maybe he was seeking the privacy of the loft above the barn that he shared with Wyatt.

Turning back to the engine, all she could see was her tidy, small world disintegrating. That morning all she'd been focused on was making it to the end of the day when Mack would hand her the cash she'd worked her butt off for and the barbeque plate from Rufus's Meat and Three she planned to devour for dinner.

But wasn't that the way of all natural disasters? Like the tornado last summer that had peeled the roof off her rented trailer and let the rain in to soak her secondhand clothes and furniture. Thank God, she'd been at the shop with Jackson. They'd huddled in the closet full of cleaning supplies until it passed. He'd never made mention of the fact she'd reached for him during the worst of it. He'd let her hold on.

This disaster felt more like an earthquake, shaking the foundations of what she'd built in Cottonbloom. Could she get out before the fissures exposed her secrets?

Jackson exchanged a grunt with Wyatt, who was attempting to put his fist straight through the leather of the punching bag, and took the steps to their loft two at a time. He was glad to have a few minutes of solitude.

His usually orderly thoughts were like a mixed-up Rubik's Cube he couldn't solve. He gave the center support column a slap on his way to the kitchenette. Going against his rigid set of work rules, he grabbed a beer from the fridge, screwed off the top, and killed half before coming up for air. It was Friday, and everything on the shop floor could keep. He'd make up the time tomorrow. Not like he had any other weekend plans.

His thoughts still whirling, he walked to the windows along the back and braced a hand against the sill, taking more measured sips. Wyatt would be at the punching bag for at least another half hour. Jackson prayed Mack hadn't wrapped his truck around a tree somewhere out in the marshes. They all had their ways of coping.

Except for Ford. He was a runner. Even when they were kids, he spent more time avoiding his chores than it would have taken to just shut his mouth and get them done. Jackson had spent their youth trying to reason with him while Wyatt had preferred to try to punch some sense into him. Neither method had worked. Ford went on and did whatever the fuck he wanted to do, acting like because he was older, he was wiser.

Jackson emptied the bottle, tossed it into the recycle bin, and collapsed onto the overstuffed couch, closing his eyes. The image of Willa's pale face and huge brown eyes came into his mind. The mass of hair he'd accidently released had given him his second shock of the day. The messy waves had framed and highlighted how delicately pretty she was with her thin nose, sharp chin, and heart-shaped face.

Of course, he was aware she was female. A girl. A *woman*. But for the last two years—really until the moment he'd pulled her ball cap off to cool her down and keep her from passing out—she'd first and foremost been a mechanic. And, a damn good one. On her best day, she was better than either Mack or Wyatt, and almost as good as him. On her worst and blindfolded, better than Ford.

How old was she? He tried to recall if he'd ever asked. The day she'd come in with the want ad from the paper in her hand, he'd known she wasn't being a hundred percent upfront. The biggest red flag was her insistence on being paid only in cash. His pop had agreed. All of them had assumed she wouldn't last out the trial week anyway.

She'd not only stuck it out, but impressed the hell out of them. Still, when their pop died, Mack had balked on the legalities of continuing to pay her under the table, but Jackson had argued they should keep it up. She'd become invaluable. But there was something more to it than her skill.

A haunted, desperate look in her eyes. As closely as they worked together day in and day out, he'd expected her to eventually crack and tell him the truth. Two years later and that day still hadn't come to pass.

Damn but she was pretty. Her enormous brown eyes and the dark arch of her brows were usually hidden or shadowed by the hat he'd assumed she wore twenty-four-seven. Didn't matter what she looked like, although it'd have been a sight easier if she'd been hiding a few warts or hairy moles under that hat. He was basically her boss, and as such, he stuffed any inappropriate thoughts back into the deep, dark recesses of his soul.

His frustration wasn't really about Willa anyway. He was pissed at Ford and the way he'd betrayed his blood. Even before he'd headed to LSU and gotten his degree, he'd acted too good for the garage. Their pop had been blind to Ford's lack of devotion to cars and the garage, and when he'd died unexpectedly last year, that blindness had incited a power struggle between Mack and Ford for the garage's future.

The *clomp* of boots sounded on the steps. Jackson opened his eyes, but otherwise didn't move. Still wearing his sparring gloves, Wyatt shot him a look, went to the fridge, uncapped two beers, and joined him on the couch. Jackson took the proffered bottle and sipped. Sweat rolled down Wyatt's face, and after pressing the cold bottle against his forehead, he chugged the beer.

They were fraternal twins, unlike in both temperament and looks, yet the ties that bound them were made of bullet-stopping Kevlar.

"I think we should let things play out." Wyatt tossed his empty bottle toward the bin underhanded. It thumped the side, and rolled back and forth on the floor.

"I'm sorry, what?" Jackson had been sure that Wyatt would cast his vote for tracking Ford down and beating some sense into him.

"I know what you're thinking; Sutton has turned me into a wuss."

Jackson couldn't stop a chuckle from rising up and out. "You're definitely easier to get along with since you've been getting some on a regular basis." He sobered quickly. "What if Ford sells to some asshole out of spite?"

"Let me clarify. I don't propose we do nothing. Just not as in your face as I tend to favor. Sutton's already put some feelers for information out. Ford would have to contact a lawyer for the paperwork." Wyatt grimaced and looked toward the window and the woods beyond. "Considering Ford and Tarwater are golfing buddies, he would be the obvious choice."

"You okay with her talking to her ex like that?"

Wyatt and Sutton had met over a thong he discovered under the seat of Andrew Tarwater's Camaro. The Cottonbloom, Mississippi, lawyer had been Sutton's fiancé, and the scrap of lace had belonged to Sutton's best friend. Tarwater had not remained her fiancé for long. What Jackson had assumed was a simple rebound had turned into love, and Wyatt was indeed the definition of whipped.

But as long as Sutton made Wyatt happy, then Jackson would support her—and them—one hundred and ten percent. If she broke his brother's heart though, he would become her worst nightmare.

"I'm not worried about her having second thoughts, if that's what you're getting at. He's a natural liar, so whether he'll even give up the truth is debatable. Plus, he's an ass-hat. If he says something to hurt her feelings, I'm not sure I won't get myself thrown in jail for assault."

"No worries, I'll bail you out." Jackson punched his arm and flashed a smile. "If you promise to clean my bay for the next month."

Their chuffing, slight laughter petered into a comfortable silence.

"It's a long shot, but Ford might actually do us a favor." Wyatt's tone was serious even though the sentiment sounded like a joke.

"Ford wouldn't cross the road to tell us the garage was on fire. He'd stand there and watch it burn. Him doing us a favor is more than a long shot."

"I don't know. He's lost weight and looks stressed. I'm worried about him."

The fact that this assessment was coming from Wyatt held water, considering their naturally adversarial relationship went back as far as Jackson could remember. "You think he's sick or something?"

"I don't know." Wyatt picked at the laces of his gloves, his voice vague but with an undercurrent of concern. "Let's look at the bright side. Whoever is interested in buying his stake might be doing it because they love cars and restorations, and if they're rich, they might give the garage a leg up."

"That sounds like a moon shot."

"Maybe, but think about it. We'll never attract the kind of cars we need to build the restoration business. Not if we limit ourselves to Cottonbloom."

"You've made huge inroads over the river and brought in three cars in two months."

"The widow's walk of cars will dry up soon enough. Without some influence, this garage will stay small potatoes. We'll make a living, sure. But, no matter how hard we bust our humps, we'll never get rich."

"Is that what you want? Money?"

Had Jackson stepped into the *Twilight Zone*? Wyatt was rock-solid dependable. Did his work without complaining. He never seemed to need or want money, unlike Jackson who had his racing to support. Hearing him now rocked the foundation of not only the garage, but their already-skewed family dynamic.

"I want the freedom money can buy. We're twenty-nine. Haven't you ever wanted to take some time off to travel? See something besides the undercarriage of a car? Are you going to live up here forever? Don't you want to settle down with a good woman and have kids?" Wyatt gestured around the loft and its mismatched furniture. The wall-mounted flat screen TV had been their only splurge. "No offense, but I don't want to grow into a grizzled bachelor with you."

The questions whirred through his head like a misfiring engine. He hadn't thought about the future in those terms. He was focused on the day-to-day micro issues that always arose with the cars under his care, not the macro issues of life in general. All he could do was shrug.

"How long has it been since you brought a woman back here?" Wyatt scrubbed the back of his neck, his dark hair in need of a trim and curling at the ends. "If we had more money, we could hire on more help, and you could work on occasionally getting laid."

A resentment that might have been tinged green with jealousy rose. "Just cuz you're whipped and getting some on the regular, doesn't mean everyone wants that. I prefer being alone. Love it, in fact."

An alarm that signaled a lie went off like a distant tornado warning. Truth was, since Wyatt had taken up with Sutton and spent a majority of his nights at her house instead of their loft, the quiet had become more burden than blessing.

"Your life is this damn garage." Wyatt linked his hands behind his head and looked to the beamed ceiling. "Just like it was for Pop," he added softly.

The subtle admonishment drove a steel rod in Jackson's spine and tensed his shoulders. "What the hell does that mean?"

"It means the most meaningful relationship you have is with your car." The hint of a smile played around Wyatt's mouth. "And, maybe Willa."

"Relationship? Willa and I work together. That's it." An echo of his earlier thoughts drove his kneejerk defensiveness. It wasn't a lie, yet it didn't feel a hundred percent truthful either. He hated waffling through the gray area in between. Life was easier in absolutes. Black and white, right and wrong. One thing he could say with no qualms. "She's the best mechanic we've ever had."

"She's a goddamn prodigy, which brings up another point. We pay her next to nothing. As good as she is, she could make more money over the river in Mississippi changing oil at one of those quickie lube places. I don't know why she hasn't already quit."

"She wouldn't quit on me. Us. I mean, us." He clenched his teeth together to corral his runaway tongue. If Wyatt's raised brows were any indication, he'd noticed Jackson's slip.

"I wouldn't be too sure about that. She asked for her pay and took off early. My guess is she has a job inter

iew somewhere else. Might not even be back on Monday
morning."

Jackson shot to his feet. He couldn't lose her.

Wyatt grabbed his forearm. "Hold up, we have bigger
rogs to gig. Mack texted. He'll be back by five and wants
o talk."

Jackson sank back down and wished for another beer
r six, but he needed to keep his wits sharp, especially if
e was going to drive later. Which he was.

"What is Mack thinking?"

"No clue. He doesn't tell me jack these days." Wyatt's
oice reflected a wariness and worry that didn't sit well
vith Jackson. Wyatt was the most emotionally intuitive of
ll of them, even if that made him reckless and prone to
cting impetuously.

Jackson looked out the window. Trees spanned all the
vay to the horizon. Their family had gone through upheav-
ls and hard times in the past. His grandparents had been
orced to give up cotton farming and sell the rich land.
"ough years followed while his father built the garage. With
noney tight, it sat beside their family home out of necessity.
"he location outside of town hurt their business, but except
or Ford, none of them wanted to pick up and move.

Memories of summers long gone echoed through the
voods. Most of the leaves were gone, leaving green pines
nterspersed with bare branches. After their mother ran off
nd left them, the brothers had taken care of each other
vhile their father had toiled away in the garage. Those
lays were harder, but they'd managed to have fun anyway.
"he resiliency of children.

Jackson had known he was destined to work in the ga-
age from the time he could walk. He'd never wanted
nything else. Fixing a car inside and out provided a
imple joy. Yet, darker impulses drove him to the dirt

track in search of an adrenaline rush. He couldn't expla[i]
the wildness that simmered under his general calm. Ho[n]
estly, he did his best not to scrutinize the uncomfortab[le]
complexity of his moods.

Jackson usually confined his worries to his family an[d]
to the garage, but somehow Willa had gotten tangled u[p]
in his life without him noticing. He stood and held out [a]
hand to haul Wyatt off the couch. "Let's get this ov[er]
with. I have something to take care of."